"Savannah, we're going to kiss," Mike said.

"It might as well be now," he added in a whispered Texas drawl. He slipped his arm around her waist and pulled her to him.

Savannah placed her hands on his chest, ready to voice her protest when his lips brushed hers lightly and her heart thudded.

At that moment she wanted his kiss with all her being. She couldn't think about what was best or if she shouldn't or that he really didn't want this either. The stubble on his jaw scraped her skin slightly while his warmth, his strength and his lean, hard body heightened her pleasure.

Finally, as she paused, he released her slightly.

"A kiss isn't a binding commitment," he said. "A long, warm kiss on a cold winter's night even beats hot chocolate."

She suspected he attempted to make light of the moment, but that ~~was~~ ~~kissed away wise d~~

"Savannah, we wo ~~"~~
So said him.

At the Rancher's Request
is part of Sara Orwig's Texas-set series,
Lone Star Legends.

AT THE RANCHER'S REQUEST

BY
SARA ORWIG

Published in Great Britain 2015
by Mills & Boon, an imprint of Harlequin (UK) Limited,
Eton House, 18-24 Paradise Road, Richmond, Surrey, TW9 1SR

© 2015 Sara Orwig

ISBN: 978-0-263-25253-8

51-0315

Harlequin (UK) Limited's policy is to use papers that are natural, renewable and recyclable products and made from wood grown in sustainable forests. The logging and manufacturing processes conform to the legal environmental regulations of the country of origin.

Printed and bound in Spain
by CPI, Barcelona

Sara Orwig lives in Oklahoma. She has a patient husband who will take her on research trips anywhere, from big cities to old forts. She is an avid collector of Western history books. With a master's degree in English, Sara has written historical romance, mainstream fiction and contemporary romance. Books are beloved treasures that take Sara to magical worlds, and she loves both reading and writing them.

To David and my family with love.

Also, with many thanks to
Stacy Boyd and Maureen Walters.

One

Mike Calhoun frowned, glancing briefly at the small mirror that allowed him to see Scotty in the backseat. Assured his almost-three-year-old son was okay, Mike peered ahead as sheets of gray rain swept against his truck. With the truck wipers maxed, he guessed visibility was less than fifty yards. He hadn't passed a car or seen any sign of life for the past half hour. To his relief he spotted a small light shining on a sign and he turned, thankful to have reached the shelter of the only gas station between the closest town and his West Texas ranch.

He slowed to stop beneath the extended roof covering eight pumps. Ed had locked up and gone home and Mike didn't blame him. On a stormy Saturday night in the last week of January, Ed wouldn't have had much business anyway.

"We're stopping, Scotty," he said, turning to his son while he left the motor running and the car lights switched on so they would not be in complete darkness. "If we wait, the rain will let up and driving conditions will be better," he said as he unfastened his son's seat belt.

Solemnly, Scotty looked at him. "Can we cross the bridge?"

Smiling, Mike tousled Scotty's black curls. "My little worrier," Mike said. "I think so, Scotty. If we can't cross the north bridge in the front, I'll drive around to the west. It'll take longer, but we can get home. Don't worry. This downpour will slack off soon. It can't rain this hard all night."

Twin specks of light emerged from the rain and grew bigger as a car approached. "Here comes someone else. It may be someone from our ranch."

When the car pulled into the lane next to Mike, smoke poured from beneath the hood. The driver passed the pumps, stopping beyond them, still sheltered by the roof.

The driver's door opened and someone in a parka stepped out and shook the hood away, revealing a woman with a long blond braid.

"This isn't anyone we know. Scotty, stay in the car while I see if she needs help." Mike lowered the front window so Scotty could hear him easily. He cut the car engine. "The lady has car trouble."

Pocketing his car keys, Mike stepped out and closed his door. "Hi, I'm Mike Calhoun. Can I help you?" he asked, looking at a blonde with big blue eyes.

Frowning slightly, she walked around her car. "Thank you. I'm Savannah Grayson. I do need help. I don't know what's wrong with my car. I was so scared it would break down while I was on the highway. It's been clattering and smoke was coming out from beneath the hood. Thank heavens I saw your car in this station. It was like getting tossed a lifeline in a stormy ocean." She looked past him.

"You have a little boy in your truck. I shouldn't take your time."

Mike looked at Scotty and waved even though only a few yards separated them. Smiling, Scotty waved back. "He'll be fine for a bit."

"I don't know what the trouble is—"

"Whoa," Mike said, seeing a flickering orange flame curl from beneath the hood. He stepped to his truck, retrieved his fire extinguisher and opened the hood of her car. As flames shot out, Savannah gasped. He held up the extinguisher and in seconds white foam doused the fire.

"I'm sorry, but this car isn't going anywhere until a mechanic works on it," Mike said, bending over the smoldering engine. "Are you visiting someone around here?" he asked when he straightened. He was certain she didn't live in the area or he would know her.

"No, I'm just passing through. I'm on my way to California from Arkansas. I don't know anyone here. I guess this place is locked up for the night." She frowned again as she looked at the dark station.

"When the rain lets up, I can drive you back to Verity where there's a good hotel. I'll call Ed who owns this gas station and tell him you're leaving your car here for the weekend. It'll be Monday before anyone can look at your car. In the meantime, I'll take you back to Verity and you can get a hotel room."

"Thank you," she said, giving him another faint smile.

"Let's go sit with my son Scotty until this rain lets up. This is a whopper of a storm. We've had a long dry spell, so now we're getting the rain all at once to make up for it. This is supposed to change to snow later tonight."

As she nodded, Mike opened the truck door.

Sliding into the truck on the passenger side, she turned to smile at Scotty. "Hi."

"Hi," he replied, staring at her.

Mike turned to her. "Savannah, this is Scotty. Scotty, this is Ms. Grayson."

"Hi, Ms. Grayson," he said.

Mike closed her door. He walked around to sit behind the steering wheel while she shed her parka and smoothed the oversize navy sweatshirt she wore. The interior of his truck had cooled with the window lowered, so Mike turned on the engine, the heater and defrost. Lights from the dash gave a soft glow in the car.

"I don't know what I would have done if you hadn't been here," Savannah said. "Probably driven it out into the rain, opened the hood and then ran. I suppose the rain would have put out the fire."

Mike laughed. "Guess it *is* a good thing I was here. Where in Arkansas are you from?" he asked, looking into big eyes that were the deep blue of a summer sky.

"Little Rock," she replied.

The first hailstone caught their attention. In seconds another struck, then hail began hurtling at the car and ground.

"Thank goodness we're sheltered and I'm not still out on the highway," Savannah said.

"Those are big hailstones. I'm glad we're both here." He took a few minutes to call Ed about her car, then pocketed his phone. "All set for Monday morning," he told Savannah. "Why don't you take what you need from your car and then lock it. You can leave the key in the drop box on the station door."

"This is nice of you. I hate for you to have to drive back to Verity."

"I don't mind," he answered. Hailstones fell harder, faster, bouncing when they hit the pavement. Lightning flashed and thunder rumbled.

"Damn. We're having a bad storm. Excuse me a minute. I want to check at the ranch." He called his foreman, explaining he was waiting out the storm at Ed's station. After a lengthy report from Ray on how things were faring, Mike said he'd check back in later.

He slipped his phone into his pocket. "I don't live far from here. We're not going to get back into Verity tonight because the river is flooding and we'd need to cross a bridge to get into town. Also, the temperature is dropping. If it keeps up, this will turn to sleet and roads can get slick in the blink of an eye."

"Seems I've gone from bad to worse," she said, gazing at the rain.

"Savannah, you're welcome to come back to my ranch with me. You can get a character reference from the sheriff of Verity. I have his phone number—he's my relative. Or if you want to check in with someone who's not a relative of mine, I can give you my banker's or lawyer's number. I just don't want you to worry about coming home with us."

She laughed. "Mercy. That's a lot of references."

"I'm calling the sheriff now and you can talk to him."

"Please, you don't need to call. I think your best reference is sitting in the backseat."

Startled, Mike looked up to see a twinkle in her blue eyes. "Scotty?"

She turned to Scotty. "Scotty, can I trust your daddy?"

"Yes, ma'am."

She smiled at Mike, an enticing smile that revealed even white teeth and made the evening seem suddenly better. "I think you've given me enough assurances that I'll be safe to go with you. You don't need to call the sheriff. Do you need to call your wife and tell her you're bringing a guest home?"

Mike felt a clutch to his insides. No one had asked about

Elise in a long time, but it still hurt when he was questioned. "I'm a widower."

"I'm sorry," she said instantly.

"Thanks. I think the hail has let up slightly. Let's get things out of your car and get going while we can. Scotty, just sit tight. I'm going to help Ms. Grayson move some of her bags to our car."

"Yes, sir," Scotty replied.

In minutes they had moved suitcases, a laptop, two backpacks and a box. As soon as she locked her car and dropped the keys in the drop box, they climbed into his truck and he drove back onto the state highway. She glanced back at her car.

"Your car will be okay there."

"I wasn't worried. It's an older car with a burned, damaged engine and I don't think anyone would want it. And thanks so much for your help," she added. "I hope I don't crowd you. I can sleep anywhere—sofa, floor, anything works."

He smiled. "You won't have to sleep on the floor. I have plenty of room."

They became quiet while Mike concentrated on his driving. The rain was still heavy, but not the downpour it had been, which improved visibility.

Almost an hour later as they neared the turn for the front gate, Mike called his foreman again on a hands-free phone in his truck. When he ended the brief call, he glanced in the mirror at his son. Big brown eyes gazed back at him.

"Scotty, we'll need to go around the creek to get home. But don't worry because I promise we'll get home."

Scotty smiled and nodded, and Mike glanced at Savannah. "My foreman drove to the creek that crosses the ranch. We can't get there the usual way from this road. I have to take a longer route."

"Whatever is necessary. Anything beats staying alone in my burned car in the rain all night," she said, smiling. "I'm just thankful to have a roof over my head tonight and be where people are."

The downpour suddenly thickened, sheets of rain sweeping over the vehicle again and then hailstones began bouncing off his truck.

"Dammit," Mike said softly, glancing quickly in the mirror and seeing Scotty's eyes wide and frightened.

"Daddy, I don't like this."

"It'll quit in a minute, Scotty, and with every mile we're getting closer to home."

"Scotty," Savannah said, rummaging in her purse and turning slightly to reach between the seats. "I keep a tiny flashlight in my purse. You take it. And look at this. It's a compass—it shows you which direction you're headed. See this letter. It's a *W. W* means west. We'll be much closer to your home when the needle points to—" She paused.

"N," Mike said.

"N is for north," Scotty replied.

"Very good, Scotty," Savannah said. "How old is he?" she asked Mike.

"Yes. He'll soon turn three and he's with adults all the time. He knows about a compass."

"Scotty, you can watch that compass to see which direction we're going. You have a flashlight so you can see the letters." As the hail increased, she raised her voice. "You'll know when we turn that you're closer to your home. Look here. I have a marble that was in my purse. I'll hide it in one of my hands and you guess which one it's in."

Mike listened to Savannah play with Scotty. She had gotten his mind off the storm and he was looking at her hands, guessing about the marble. Mike wondered if she had younger siblings. He realized he had been gripping the steering wheel tightly and he relaxed. The hail receded, but the rain still came in pounding sheets over his truck, making driving hazardous.

While Scotty played with the flashlight, Savannah turned back around.

"Thanks," Mike said.

"Sure. Kids are fun."

"Do you have siblings?" Mike asked.

"Oh, yes. There are four of us and I'm the youngest. I have four little nieces and nephews, too. I like babies and children."

Mike wanted to ask her more about herself, but he turned his attention back to his driving and they rode in silence while he concentrated on getting home.

It was almost another thirty minutes when Savannah saw a wide gate ahead with a high iron arch over the road and the letters *MC* in the center at the top. Rain still poured and the wipers were a constant swish. At a post near the gate Mike slowed to reach out to punch a code. When the gate swung open, he drove across a cattle guard, a silver grill of flat steel tubing with a slightly rougher surface than the road, and then the gate closed behind him.

"Your son is asleep," Savannah whispered.

"I figured he would be. He's had a busy day in town. And you don't have to whisper, he's out."

"I don't want to wake him."

"It's just as well he's asleep because he's a worrier and we have to cross a swollen creek. At the main entrance to my ranch, there's a bridge, but it's older, already underwater and less reliable. The bridge on this part of the creek is newer, higher and wider so we've always been able to get across."

"You better," she whispered. "You promised him."

When Mike glanced at her, Savannah smiled.

"Kids have great trust," he said with his attention back on the road.

"Not if it isn't earned. You must have always come through for him."

"I hope I always can. He knows there are some things beyond me," Mike said.

"We'll hope crossing this bridge tonight isn't one of them." Savannah was thankful to have found Mike and Scotty. Otherwise, she would have been on a deserted road in the storm for the rest of the night and maybe a lot longer and she wouldn't have known where or when to get help. Thinking about it, she shivered and studied Mike's profile. He had a wide-brimmed black hat squarely on his head. He was in a leather, fleece-lined parka with fur trim and wore jeans and boots. He looked as competent as he was proving to be. His son was an adorable miniature of his dad with black hair and dark brown eyes.

After a time she wondered how big Mike's ranch was because it seemed as if they had been driving a long time since going through the gate.

"There it is," Mike said as if he guessed her thoughts. She peered through the streaming rain and could see what looked like a river. Swollen with surging black water, it was bigger than any creek she had ever seen. Rushing water had spilled out of the banks earlier in the evening. Mike's truck headlights revealed seven men in slickers getting out of two pickups on the other side of the raging creek.

"I'll be damned," he said quietly, frowning as he peered

through his windshield. "I've never seen the creek this high. Not ever."

Chilled again by apprehension, she looked as the rushing water spread out of creek banks and splashed across the bridge that was already underwater.

"The bridge is covered by the creek," she said, her apprehension mounting swiftly. "Can we cross?"

"We're going to," Mike replied, stopping to phone his foreman. "Thanks for coming, Ray. I really appreciate all of you being here." Mike paused to listen. "I think we'll make it, but I'm glad you're here. Thanks." Mike put away his phone and she watched as the men turned lights on the raging creek.

"They came earlier and strung ropes across the creek tied to trees on each side. If we go into the creek, I'll get Scotty. You try to grab one of those ropes or anything else you can grab. Someone will come to help you. I don't think that will happen, but if it does, we'll have backup. If you go in, swim with the current, but try to angle toward the bank."

"I hate to think about someone risking his life to come into the creek to get me. The water looks fierce. I don't think I can swim in that."

"It is fierce," Mike said. "Just go with the current. The guys will get you. We can't go back and we can't stay out here all night. Thank heavens Scotty is asleep. Don't worry until you have to because I expect the bridge to hold," he said in a tone filled with so much confidence, her fear diminished. He lowered all the windows. "Sorry, but just in case we go in and the truck sinks, we can all get out easily. The pickup might just float because the current will carry it along."

"I don't care to think about the possibilities," she said, staring at the creek.

Mike inched slowly across. Holding her breath and clutching the door handle until her knuckles were white, she watched waves splash over the bridge. They reached the other side and she let out her breath.

"You did it!" she exclaimed, looking at Mike who raised all the windows except his own. The men waved and slapped hands in high fives. One tall man in a hooded parka came to the truck.

"Thanks, Ray," Mike said.

"Glad you made it across. We're supposed to get sleet and later snow. I'm glad you're back."

"We're thankful to be here. Ray, this is Ms. Grayson. She had car trouble and we left her car at Ed's. She'll stay here tonight."

"Howdy, Ms. Grayson," he said, bending down to look at her.

"Just call me Savannah, please."

"Savannah, this is Ray Farndale, my foreman."

"Thanks for waiting to help," she said.

"Glad our help wasn't needed. Mike, we'll see you in the morning. We all better head home before it gets worse. If it keeps up, that bridge will be far enough under water no one can cross."

"What about the animals? Do you guys need any help tonight?"

"Thanks, no. You get Scotty and Ms. Grayson out of the storm. We're fine, so far. I'll call if we need you. If the temperature drops the way they say it will, then tomorrow will bring a different set of problems."

"I'll join you in the morning because we'll need every hand." He raised his window as he drove past the other men and waved.

"Scotty slept right through that," she said. "I have to

say, I'm supremely glad the bridge held. You were very calm. You must not rattle easily."

"It wouldn't have helped for me to get worked up." Mike smiled at her. "Let's go home," he said, the words wrapping around her with a reassurance that was comforting.

In minutes the first lights could be seen through the rain-covered windshield. One truck turned off and headed away. "Where is that pickup going?" she asked.

"Ray and a couple of guys are headed out to see about our livestock. The men all have phones and walkie-talkies so they can keep in touch."

"And you like this ranch life?" she asked.

He smiled. "Yes, the good outweighs the bad. Everything has ups and downs. There is something new every day and constant challenges."

"And you like that?" she repeated, shaking her head. "Good thing you can keep calm. I'd hate to be headed out in the blizzard in the dark." She wondered about his rugged life that was so different from everything she knew. She looked into the darkness and shivered, thankful to be in a warm car.

They passed a large hangar. Farther along, Savannah could see lights from houses set back long distances from both sides of the road. Next, outbuildings came into view and then two large barns and corrals. In seconds the road divided, the remaining truck turned and headed away from them.

"The guys are going home or to the bunkhouse. Some of them have houses and families here."

She rode in silence as they passed more outbuildings and an eight-bay garage. Beyond it was a fence and a sprawling three-story ranch house. Mike punched buttons on his phone and lights came on in the house. The drive circled beneath a porte cochere.

"I guess I won't have to sleep on the floor," she said, startled by the size of his home and outbuildings. She turned to him. "All this from raising cows?"

"All this from having ancestors who were the first cattle barons who settled here. Each generation has built on that. We've been fortunate. We still raise cattle."

With a hiss the rain changed to sleet and Mike's smile vanished as he swore quietly. "This we don't need, but I'm thankful it held off until now."

She nodded and looked up. He gazed into her blue eyes and she gazed back. The low dash lights bathed her face in a pink glow, revealing rosy cheeks, big blue eyes and smooth skin. As he looked into her wide eyes, he became aware of her as a woman. A current sparked and he saw her eyelids flutter at the same time he felt electricity ignite between them. Startled, he stared at her while his surprise held him immobile. He hadn't been aware of another woman since losing Elise to cancer almost two years ago, a year after Scotty's birth. Shocked by his reaction, Mike forgot how he was staring at Savannah. He looked away, turning to gaze at the rain.

She glanced over her shoulder. "Lucky boy. He's still asleep."

"I'll carry him in and come back to get your suitcases," Mike said.

"Don't worry about my things tonight. I'll get the bag I need and the rest can wait until tomorrow. You take care of your son."

"His nanny is away right now or she would come help. Her daughter has a new baby and Nell, Mrs. Lewis, has gone to help for a few weeks."

"I'm in no rush," Savannah said, slipping on a backpack and gathering her laptop, purse and a suitcase.

Mike unbuckled Scotty and picked him up, carrying his sleeping son in his arms.

"He's a sound sleeper," she whispered.

Mike smiled. "Thank heaven." He opened the door and held it wide for her. She stepped inside and turned to hold the door out of his way while he carried Scotty inside and switched off an alarm.

"Scotty is growing up in a comfortable, beautiful home," she said as they walked down a wide hall that held green plants, oil paintings of landscapes and Western scenes in ornate frames, Queen Anne chairs and tables along the walls. Doors opened onto rooms they passed, giving her a glimpse of a formal dining room with a massive table that had to seat twenty. She passed a library with ladders and an open beam ceiling.

"Mike, that's an enormous library. Do you read constantly?"

He smiled and nodded. "It's the family library. Many of the books are very old. Scotty has his own bookshelves in his room, so he doesn't try to pull out valuable first editions from the family collection."

"I don't know how Scotty finds his way around this house."

"This house seems large because it's new to you. You'll know your way around in no time."

"Which means you think I'll be snowed in for several days."

"Don't sound so glum. You didn't mention having a deadline and we'll find some way to pass the time."

He smiled at her and she had to laugh. Was he flirting with her? She didn't know him well enough to know. They branched off into the front hall with a sweeping staircase and she went upstairs beside Mike.

"This ranch is my whole life. My brothers have other

interests, but my world is here. My sister is like me and has a ranch close by. I also have a house in Verity that I never use and a condo in Dallas that I'm rarely in. Do you live in town or in the country in Arkansas?"

"Definitely in town," Savannah answered. "I don't know anything about country living much less life on a Texas ranch."

They walked down another wide hall. "My suite of rooms is at the end of this wing. Any of these bedrooms are empty along here. You might as well be closer so you don't feel isolated. Scotty's suite adjoins mine and his nanny has a suite adjoining his on the other side. Here's where you can stay." Mike entered a room and switched on a light. She looked at a sizable sitting room with a large-screen television, a wide glass desk, bookshelves along one wall, chairs and two sofas. The room had appealing turquoise-and-cream decor with a hardwood floor and thick area rugs. "There's a bedroom beyond this room. If you need anything, just let me know. Make yourself comfortable. As soon as I get Scotty in bed I'll come back and we can go have hot chocolate or a drink or whatever you would like."

"That sounds wonderful."

"See you in a few minutes," he said.

She watched him walk out, his son in his arms. He looked like a typical cowboy, his black hat squarely on his head and his jeans hugging his long, slender legs. Boots gave an already tall man additional height. Once again she was thankful he had been at the station when she had turned in.

Glancing around the sitting room, she thought of the rooms they had passed. Mike was not an ordinary cowboy to afford a house such as this. She walked through the sitting room into a bedroom that was warm, pretty and welcoming with antique maple furniture, a four-poster bed, a rocking chair, another large television and a tall cheval glass. Savannah put her bags on her bed and sent a text, including a photo of her temporary room, to her mother to let her know where she was and why.

She freshened up, then changed into jeans, a blue sweater and her knee-high leather boots. Undoing her braid, she brushed her hair, which fell across her shoulders. She thought about the moment beneath the porte cochere before they stepped out of the truck when she had become aware of Mike as a desirable man. When she had looked into his dark eyes, she had been certain from his intense expression he had felt something. She shook her head. Attraction had no place in her life at this time and it had surprised her that she even had such a reaction for a brief moment, although Mike Calhoun was a good-looking man and his calm in the storm gave him added appeal.

No matter how attractive Mike was, after what she had just been through, she knew better than to go from one problem of the heart straight into another one.

Two

Mike stood over Scotty's bed and looked at his son. His insides tightened with pain. He still missed Elise and he missed her for Scotty. She should have been there to comfort Scotty in the car this afternoon, although Savannah had done a great job of taking the boy's mind off the storm. Mike walked through the connecting door to his bedroom, tossing his hat on a desk and raking his fingers through his hair.

Thinking about Savannah, he turned to go see if she needed anything. He headed toward her bedroom when she stepped into the hall and started toward him.

Surprised, he drew a deep breath. A tall, beautiful blonde approached him. She had brushed out her hair and it fell across her shoulders. The oversize sweatshirt had been replaced by a blue sweater that revealed lush curves. Jeans clung to long legs and she still wore her suede knee boots. His heartbeat quickened and again shock stabbed him that he reacted to her—something he now had done twice this night, a startling response he had not felt for several years. His gaze raked over her once again before she was close and then he made an effort to look into her eyes. His heartbeat raced and even though unwanted, his desire was hot and definitely part of his life once again.

"You don't look as if you've had a harrowing drive," he said, smiling at her.

"Thanks to you," she said, smiling in return. Her winning smile caused another response as his insides tightened. She had full pink lips and even white teeth and when she smiled, her eyes twinkled. "How's Scotty?"

"He's in bed asleep now," Mike answered, her warm, enticing smile drawing him. "Did you have enough dinner? I've got steaks, casseroles in the freezer, an array to choose from."

"I did have dinner. But I'd love something warm to drink."

"How about hot chocolate and popcorn? Or if you want something stronger, we have drinks from wine to whiskey."

She laughed as she walked beside him. "I'll take the hot chocolate and popcorn. Right now that sounds just the thing for a cold, winter night."

"I agree," he said as they headed to the kitchen. As he made the hot chocolate and got the popcorn going, he was aware of her moving around him. Her perfume was light, barely noticeable, yet inviting. While he waited for the popcorn, he realized he was staring at her full lips and wondering what it would be like to kiss her. Again, the attraction startled him. It had been a long time since he had wondered any such thing. He didn't welcome those feelings back into his life yet. He didn't need any more complications for either Scotty or himself.

He still lived with a constant, dull pain over Elise. He missed her every waking hour. At least there was no danger of any complications with Savannah because she was leaving for California as soon as Ed repaired her car. By that time the weather shouldn't be a factor, so she would be gone in days. For all he knew, she was married, although she wasn't wearing a wedding ring.

Finally, they moved to the family room that adjoined the kitchen. Mike placed two cups of hot chocolate on a coffee table while she set down a big bowl of popcorn. He picked up the table to move it closer to the hearth.

"Let me get a fire going," Mike said, adding a few logs to the fireplace. In minutes they sat on the floor in front of the blaze with the popcorn and hot chocolate on the nearby table. As Savannah looked around, he glanced at the familiar surroundings. He never gave them any thought: brown leather furniture, a game table and chairs, a large, wall-mounted flat-screen television, thick area rugs and a stone fireplace that dominated one wall. Adjacent was a glass wall with doors that opened onto a covered patio that now had snow blowing over it.

"So tell me about your life. Who are you and what do you like besides ranching?"

"I have a simple life that centers around my son, my family and friends, my ranch, my horses. I like rodeos, flying, skiing, baseball, tennis, apple pie. Some things I've dropped since Scotty's birth. I have a responsibility now, so I'm not as reckless as I was before. No more bull riding when Scotty is so young."

"That's good."

"It's a simple life. What about you, Savannah?" he asked. She sat facing him with her long legs tucked under her. Firelight gave her a rosy glow and once again desire stirred, increasing his awareness of her appeal, bringing the same surprise that she stirred such feelings, surprise now tinged with guilt for feeling that way even though

Elise had been gone almost two years now. Overriding those feelings was the ever-present sorrow over his and Scotty's loss.

"I think my life may be quieter and more simple than yours," she said, flashing another engaging smile. "My world centers around my family and friends. I'm a neonatal nurse and I love babies and children. As I mentioned earlier, I have three siblings and I'm the youngest. I adore my four little nieces and nephews." She thought for a moment. "The only thing we have in common that you listed is tennis. I still play occasionally."

"Is the trip to California a vacation?" he asked, wondering why she left Arkansas.

"Not really. I have an aunt in California and she wanted me to come," Savannah said, watching the fire while Mike watched her. She was a beautiful woman and he wondered what she was running from.

"My aunt said I won't have difficulty getting a job and I'd love to live in California. I love a beach, swimming, warm weather—so I'm going to try it for a while and see how things work out." She turned to face him. "I've never been away from home before except to college and that was still in Arkansas, so I have mixed feelings," she said. "Since we're a close family, this is an experiment in my life."

Mike nodded and kept silent, thinking she shouldn't gamble because she couldn't bluff her way through anything unless she was playing with Scotty. Her voice was filled with reluctance, so whatever she was leaving behind, she wasn't happy about it.

"How old are your siblings and what are their names?" he asked.

Big blue eyes gazed openly at him. "Dan is thirty-two, Phillip is thirty, Kelsey is twenty-eight and I'm twenty-six. They're all married."

"You can always go home if you don't like California."

"That's the plan," she said. "Now tell me about your family."

"We're close, too. I'm the oldest, thirty-five, and then Jake, who married Madison Milan last fall."

"Madison Milan, the artist?"

"So you've heard of her in Arkansas?"

"Sure. Is she from Texas?"

"Yes, from this area. Josh is next in age and then our baby sister, Lindsay, is the youngest. Lindsay is a full-time rancher, the same as I am. I'm the only one of my siblings with a child and I told you that I'm widowed. Elise died of breast cancer when Scotty was almost a year old."

"That's heartbreaking. I'm so sorry," Savannah said.

He glanced at her and nodded. "Most of my family is in this area," he said to change the subject. "Some more than others. Lindsay and I are the ones that are here most all the time."

The hiss of sleet grew loud and Mike glanced toward the glass doors. Outside lights were on and beyond the covered patio, he could see sleet coming down steadily, tree branches and posts beginning to glisten with a coat of sparkling ice.

"We'll be a solid sheet of ice tomorrow. Power lines will go down in this, although some of ours are underground and we have generators. Look at that stuff come down." He stood and walked to the glass doors, standing with his hands on his hips to watch. "It's a good thing you don't have to be in California by a deadline."

"I am so glad that I'm here in your house," she said, coming to stand beside him.

"It's freezing solid as we speak," he remarked. "I have a feeling no one can cross even the west bridge now," Mike said, glancing at her. "Did you have any food or a blanket in your car?"

"Yes. Not for an emergency like this. I just had some leftover candy and some cold drinks from drive-throughs. I did have a blanket in the trunk. I can't stop thinking about how close I came to being out there by myself in the cold and the dark with a car that wouldn't run."

"You're here. Warm and safe."

Standing close beside him, she looked up. Blue depths ensnared him and that sizzling current of awareness shook him again.

Her eyes widened and he inhaled deeply as desire swept him. Her mouth looked soft, tempting. It had been a long time since he had held a woman in his arms, kissed anyone. He leaned closer as he looked at her mouth and thought of his loss. She closed her eyes and tilted her face for only seconds and then she looked into his eyes.

"Savannah," he whispered, frowning.

"Mike," she whispered at the same moment, shaking her head slightly.

Startled, Savannah stepped away. Her heart raced and she was torn between desire and common sense. His dark brown eyes revealed longing. Now that his hat was gone, his black hair was a tangle of curls, locks curling on his forehead. To her surprise, desire drummed steadily, increasing tension while tugging at her senses. Shocked by her reaction to him, she decided it was the nerve-racking night, her car, the storm, relying on a total stranger. She walked away to sit on the floor in front of the fire again.

She glanced up at the mantel at a picture of Mike and a beautiful black-haired woman who must have been Elise. Her pictures were in every room Savannah had been in so far and some rooms held several pictures of her, which Savannah could understand. She would have probably done the same if she had been the one to suffer the loss of a beloved spouse and the parent of a child.

Mike picked up his cup of cocoa and followed, sitting facing her and taking a long drink. As he lowered the mug, his gaze went from the fire to her. "What are you trying to get away from, Savannah?" he asked quietly. "Can I help?"

Surprised again, Savannah focused intently on him. "How did you know?"

He shrugged. "I've seen a lot of people bluff their way through things. You shouldn't even try," he said softly, smiling at her to take the edge off his words.

"You're wondering why I'm going to California," she said.

"You don't need to tell me. In a few days you'll leave Texas and we'll probably never see each other again. I asked simply to see if I could help in any way."

"It's not private, just difficult to talk about. I was engaged," she said, aware of Mike's dark brown eyes focused steadily on her. He saw too much and the attraction that had flared briefly between them had unnerved her. She didn't want to be attracted to anyone right now. "I was engaged and thought I was so deeply in love. We were going to get married in April and I was busy with wedding plans when it all came crashing around me. Although I'm the one who broke off the engagement, he didn't want to get married after all. It hurt and it upset me that I had judged so poorly. Even though I've known him for years, I didn't see this coming. So many mistakes…" Her voice trailed away as she watched the fire.

"Don't beat yourself up. Relationships are complicated. None of us see things coming sometimes that we should."

She smiled, turning to focus on him again. "You're very sweet, Mike. Scotty is lucky to have you for a dad."

"I'm lucky to have him. He's the best thing in my life."

They sat quietly for a few minutes. She watched logs burn, crackle and pop, before turning back to Mike.

"This is going to be a lot longer trip than I expected. Perhaps I should have flown and bought a car in California."

"Ed will probably be able to fix your car to run just fine."

"Are you always so positive?" she asked, amused by his constant optimism and confidence.

"Try to be. It doesn't help to be negative. I want Scotty to have a good attitude about life."

"That's a good goal for a dad," she said.

He smiled and took a sip of his cocoa. "So is California really about putting distance between you and your ex-fiancé?"

She nodded. "Our families are friends and we move in the same circles. I just want to get away for a while. After a time it won't be such a big deal and I'll go back home."

"Sorry. It hurts to have your life blow up in your face and it hurts even more to lose someone you love."

Her heart went out to him. He definitely knew that first-hand from experience. "I thought I was in love. It's been a shock that hurt badly."

"So this just happened?"

"Yes, the first of the year and maybe I should have stayed home and waited to see how I feel six months from now before packing and moving, but I just wanted to get away from him and everyone else."

"I can see that."

She appreciated what an attentive listener Mike was. "I'm angry with him and I don't want to marry him, but it hurts because I was very much in love with him. Or thought I was. It makes me question my own judgment."

"We all make mistakes. That's part of life," Mike said. "I hope it works out for you when you go to California. Your family will miss you, I'll bet."

She nodded. "I sent a text to my mom to let her know where I am tonight. She would have been wild with worry if I'd had to text that I was stuck on the highway in a storm and the car had caught on fire."

He smiled. "That does sound bad. A neonatal nurse. You have to deal with some tough situations."

"Yes, but we have a lot of wonderful moments that make it all worthwhile. I love taking care of the babies and each one that pulls through is a miracle. That's as good as it gets."

"I'm sure it is." They sat in silence a few minutes while she watched the logs burn and thought about babies she had cared for.

"Sure you're not hungry for dinner?" he asked. "I've got all sorts of things in the freezer and fridge, plus I don't mind cooking something."

"Thanks, but I'm really not hungry. I would love a little more hot chocolate, though."

They stood and headed toward the kitchen, the lights flickering out. "We've got generators, but the lights may come back on like they did before," he said, taking her arm.

Instantly, she was aware of the physical contact with him. His warm, steady hand created a tingling current. It was dark and his deep voice, as he spoke about a previous storm that had knocked out power, drew her as much as his touch, her reaction to him again surprising her.

He stopped and from the sound of his voice, she assumed he had turned to face her. "It's as dark as a cave in here. Are you all right, Savannah?" he asked. His voice had changed, gaining a husky note.

She pulled away a bit. "I'm fine," she whispered. "What about Scotty? His monitor won't work if the power is off."

"I'll start the generator and then go check on him, but

it hasn't been a minute since the power went off. Scotty will be fine."

"It's all right if you want to go check on him now," she whispered.

"I don't want to leave you alone in a strange house in a pitch-black moment," he replied, his voice even lower and the husky note more noticeable. "Did I make you uncomfortable by taking your arm?" he asked. "A gentlemanly touch to lead you down the hall shouldn't be a big deal," he whispered.

Logic said he was right, but her reaction didn't follow logic. She was intensely aware of the contact, of his closeness, of the dark that enclosed them and transformed the moment. The restrictions that light brought—reminders they were almost strangers, ordinary caution—were gone in the blanket of darkness and made Mike essential.

"Mike, I don't need another complication in my life."

"You're being sensible," he said after a stretch of silence and she felt as if he had been about to say something else. His words were in agreement, but his husky tone wasn't and he hadn't moved.

"I have to be. I don't need one more tangled crisis tearing my emotions," she whispered as they remained immobile.

Silence stretched. "Come on," he said finally. "We'll get a funny movie or just talk."

His tone of voice sounded normal again and she felt relieved that he let the moment go, a physical contact with him that had shaken her because mutual attraction once again sprung to life between them. He took both mugs and the bowl from her hands as if to prove he wouldn't touch her again. Lights flickered and came on again.

"Timed just right," he said.

"You go check on Scottie and I'll refill our cocoa," she suggested, taking the mugs and bowl back from him.

Mike nodded and she watched him walk away. Tall, with that thick, curly black hair, he held a growing appeal and her awareness of him had heightened, something that continued to amaze her.

As she entered the kitchen she thought about the past minutes with Mike. This was a complication she really didn't want. She didn't want to risk her heart even in a deep friendship. She didn't trust her judgment of men—she had failed completely to see the defects in Kirk's character. The break with home and family had been stressful enough—her future even more uncertain, lonely and difficult. Lost in thoughts, she reheated and stirred the hot chocolate Mike had made earlier.

He came striding into the kitchen and desire stirred again, physical, unwanted, something she intended to quell. It didn't help that Mike looked virile, energetic and filled with life.

"Scotty is blissfully sleeping. He's a sound sleeper which is great."

"That's wonderful." She handed him a mug of cocoa, taking a sip of her own. She turned to walk to a nearby hutch, pointing to a picture of a dark-haired woman holding a baby. "Is this a picture of your wife and Scotty?"

"Yes," Mike said. A muscle worked in his jaw as he gazed at the picture. "That's Elise."

"She was beautiful. I've noticed her other pictures."

"Since Scotty lost her when he was too young to really remember I feel better with her pictures around. She loved him beyond measure."

"I'm sure. A baby is a treasure," she said. "That's nice to have a lot of her pictures around for him. It'll help him.

He really looks like you, but maybe that's because I know you a little and can see a resemblance."

"People say he looks like me. Right now I don't see it so much except for his curly hair and brown eyes."

He led the way back into the family room, to their spot in front of the fire.

"So would you like to tell me how you met Elise?"

"Sure. We were in college and had an elective class in world history together and just gradually did homework together. We both were dating other people. I broke up first and then she did and we got serious fast. As soon as we graduated, we married and moved to the ranch. After a couple of years we had Scotty. She was diagnosed with breast cancer shortly after he was born and she died right after he turned one." Mike stared into the fire, looking as if his thoughts were far away in another time and place. He turned to face her.

"So what's your life been, Miss Neonatal Nurse?"

She smiled at him. "College and work. I started dating Kirk and got engaged to him last spring. We'd planned to marry in July."

"That's a long engagement."

"It was a long engagement, but we didn't talk about the things we should have. Even though I've known him for years, I didn't know about his feelings on a lot of subjects. We never talked about kids."

"You're a neonatal nurse and you didn't talk about kids?"

"No. I didn't talk about the babies I cared for at the hospital because they all had health issues and that's personal and confidential, even when the patient is hours old—not something to share with others. I should have at least found out his feelings about babies and wanting kids. Kids just didn't come up between us until the breakup. I found out he didn't want to have children. At least not for the next fifteen years while he's young and the business is growing."

"Wow. That would be a shock. Seems like he might have mentioned this to you."

She nodded. "Kids are definitely in my future."

"They will be unless you get a new career. Sorry."

"Well, any feelings between us are over, but I'm still eager to leave for a while. If I don't like living in California, I'll go back home."

"You'll miss your family. I would miss mine since we're fairly close. If you're here long enough, you'll probably meet some of my family. We see each other often."

"I don't plan to be here long. Hopefully, my car is fixable." She took a sip of her cocoa. "So tell me about your rodeos. You mentioned them as something you like."

"Have you ever been to one?"

"Yes," she answered. "Arkansas isn't that far from Texas in more ways than one."

Mike leaned back against a chair, pulled off his boots to set them aside and crossed his long legs at his ankles. She sat cross-legged facing him while they went from one subject to another.

"Don't you get lonesome way out here by yourself?" she asked.

He gave her a lopsided grin. "I'm not exactly by myself."

"I know you have Scotty."

"I have a lot of employees, some have been with my family before they came to work for me, so we've known each other for years. Ray's one of them. We have close, good relationships. I see some of them almost daily. I have a cook, a nanny, a housekeeper, my house staff actually. I see my brothers and my sister fairly often. I do okay. Sometimes it's lonesome, but that just goes with losing Elise. When I was single, I used to go out a lot, honky-tonks, friends, stay in Dallas, go out of town. With Scotty, life has changed and I've become a homebody. It'll change again—it always does, but that's it for now."

"I'm glad you're not as alone as I thought. If I hadn't come along, you and Scotty would have been home alone tonight. He goes to bed early, so what do you do with your evenings?"

"Different things. Sometimes I take care of my personal expenses. Each day I'm up before dawn, out on the ranch with the others and work until dusk or later, depending on what we find. I have an accountant for the ranch and business. At night I'm with Scotty until he goes to bed. Then I read and work out—I have a gym here."

"That's impressive," she said.

Finding Mike good company as they talked, she lost track of time. Occasionally, she glanced beyond him and saw big snowflakes swirling around the outside lights. She felt warm, cozy and fortunate to have found Mike. Stretching, she glanced at her watch. "Mike, it's past one and that's late for me."

"Sure," he said, standing and picking up the bowl and mugs.

"Now it's just snow coming down. Our fire has about died," she said, looking at the glowing orange embers.

"Snow on top of ice. Not a good combination. I imagine everything will be closed today and maybe Monday, too. Depends on the temperature. You may have to wait a little longer for your car," he said as they walked out of the room. "You're welcome here as long as you need. There's room and a staff and I don't have any big agenda right now."

"Thank you. I hope I can get on with my drive."

He left the bowl and mugs in the kitchen and they headed down the hall. "If you want anything—that door at the end of the hall is mine. Don't hesitate to come get me," he said as they reached the door to her suite. She turned to face him. He stood only a couple of feet away and his proximity made her breath catch.

"Thanks for everything today. You were the knight to the rescue, burning car and all."

"I'm glad I was. Today's Sunday, so my cook, Millie, who usually watches Scotty when my nanny is away, is off. But because of the earlier sleet and the fresh snow coming down, the guys will need help first thing. We'll have to get feed to the cattle, break ice for the livestock. Thing is, when the sun comes up, so does Scotty."

"If he doesn't mind being with me when he barely knows me, I can take care of Scotty and his breakfast. You go do what you have to do. I get up early and I can fix my own breakfast and his," she said, looking at Mike's dark eyes that were fringed with thick, curly black lashes. "I hope I didn't make you miss your workout tonight," she said.

"No. I worked out yesterday morning and it doesn't hurt if I miss sometimes. There's a track if you run. Just head in the opposite direction—the gym is at the other end of this hall in the opposite wing and downstairs."

"I won't be working out. Maybe later tomorrow, I'll walk around the track—how many times around for a mile?"

"Eight." Taking a step closer, he placed his hand beyond her on the jamb of the door and leaned toward her. "We're together this weekend and then we'll say goodbye and never see each other. Neither of us are at the point of complicating our lives, but I have to admit that I want to kiss you. Believe me, I haven't felt that way about any woman since I lost Elise." He leaned slightly closer and his voice dropped to almost a whisper. "We're not going to fall into complications from one harmless kiss."

"Why do I have the feeling that your kiss, even one, will not be—harmless?" she whispered, finding it difficult to get her breath. In the silence her heart drummed.

For a moment they gazed into each other's eyes and she felt immobilized by his dark gaze.

"Savannah, we're going to kiss. It might as well be now," he whispered, slipping his arm around her waist and drawing her the last few inches to him.

She placed her hands on his chest, ready to voice her protest when his lips brushed hers lightly and her heart thudded.

At that moment she wanted his kiss with all her being. She couldn't think about what was best or if she shouldn't or that he really didn't want this, either. It was impossible to walk away. Closing her eyes, she leaned into him and his arm tightened, his mouth coming down on hers as he kissed her hungrily in a driving force that took her breath.

His kiss drove away worries. Longing transformed the moment and she would never again view Mike in the same disinterested way.

Standing in his embrace, she kissed him back passionately, for the moment wanting his kiss, wanting to feel desired. She sought release from the tensions of the night as much as from the hurts of her past. Hoping to stir Mike out of his daily life of grief even if it happened only for seconds, she lost herself in kissing him. An intense need consumed her to an extent that shocked her.

The stubble on his jaw scraped her skin slightly while his warmth and strength, his lean, hard body heightened her pleasure. She wanted this. His kiss rocked her, stirring dormant responses. Time ceased and she had no idea how long they kissed, but it wasn't long enough.

Finally, as she paused, he released her slightly.

"I guess we sort of lost it there," she whispered. Both

of them were breathing hard while she stepped away from him. "We can get back where we were."

"Savannah," Mike said, in a husky tone of voice and she turned to look at him. He hadn't moved. He had one hand on his hip as he studied her. "We'll never get back where we were."

Startled, she blinked and her heart thumped faster. "We have to," she said. "There's no place in my life for you and there's no place in your life for me."

"A kiss isn't a binding commitment," he said, more as if to remind himself than inform her. "It was only kisses, Savannah. Warm kisses on a cold winter's night—even beats hot chocolate."

She suspected he attempted to make light of the moment, but that was impossible. He had a slight frown and she had complicated her stay at his ranch. They both had kissed away wise decisions.

"Savannah, we won't fall in love—I promise you."

"You can't promise any such thing. No one can," she said, realizing he had his heart locked away from any deep emotional involvement. "We've each had heartbreak and are vulnerable. I don't need to make another emotional mistake on top of the huge one I've already made," she said, feeling she should beware and guard her own heart because Mike was clearly warning her he would not fall in love.

He shook his head. "You won't have even a tiny wrench to your heart because of one meaningless kiss. I'm not ready for anything serious and neither are you. We're strangers who'll be together only a day or two and never see each other again. Chalk it up to a stormy winter night and two vulnerable people. It was just a kiss that helped each of us on a cold winter's night."

Relieved that the moment was getting less intense, she shook her head. "What a line, Mike."

Something flickered in his dark eyes and he shrugged. "Sounded good to me," he said, continuing to make light of the situation.

"Well, maybe it put things in the proper perspective."

"I think you did that," he said.

"Let's forget that kiss. Good night, Mike. See you in the morning and I'll take care of Scotty if you're out," she said, shaking her head.

She stepped into her suite and closed the door, letting out her breath while she thought about his kiss. For just a few minutes Mike had made her forget her engagement, Kirk, everything else. Mike had made light of their kiss, but he had shaken her. His kiss had been sexy, spectacular, totally consuming.

She didn't want any other complication in her life right now. She definitely didn't trust herself to want to get to know any man better at this time. She had made a colossal mistake in judgment with Kirk, a man she had known when they were kids and yet she hadn't really learned what she should have about him. She couldn't know anything about Mike Calhoun, a man she had known hours when she had misjudged a man she had known well for years.

He certainly didn't know the most important thing about her.

Frowning, she thought of what lay ahead. She placed her hand on her stomach and focused on the baby that she carried.

Three

As Mike walked down the hall to his suite, he raked his fingers through his hair. Savannah had defused the moment, eased them both away from memories that hurt and put their kiss in a better perspective. Even though it was meaningless to both of them, he shouldn't have kissed her. Her kiss had stunned him, but it had been a long, long time since he had kissed a woman other than Elise—or wanted to. Nearly two years. It was natural for Savannah's kiss to rock him. Along with their kiss came guilt, a feeling of betrayal of Elise's memory and most of all, horrendous longing for Elise, the love of his life.

He walked into Scotty's room and looked at his sleeping son who was curled on his side with his knees drawn up. Dark curls framed his face. Mike's love for Scotty overwhelmed him. He ran his knuckles lightly along Scotty's cheek, feeling his soft, smooth skin while love for his son held him by Scotty's bed. He wished Elise could be with him to look at Scotty. "Your baby is beautiful," he whispered to the empty room, thinking of her. "Elise," he said, missing her, wishing she could see her son, wanting her with him and wishing he hadn't kissed Savannah, yet their kiss hadn't carried any significance. He loved Elise and Scotty with all his heart and always would. Tears stung Mike's eyes and he blinked them away, drawing a little blanket up over Scotty's shoulder.

"I love you, Scotty," he whispered.

He left the room, leaving the door between their bedrooms open. Ten minutes later Mike returned with a blanket and stretched out on the brown leather sofa to sleep near his son.

He thought again of Savannah. In spite of a twinge of guilt, he'd had fun just being with her tonight—something that hadn't happened in a long, empty time.

Sunshine spilled into the bedroom through sliding glass doors that opened onto a balcony. Savannah stepped out of bed, surprised she had slept until the sun was up. She showered, pulled on jeans and a red shirt, slipping her feet into loafers. She hurried down the hall. Half a dozen mornings lately, she had had morning sickness and she prayed she didn't this morning. At the moment she was hungry, but in minutes she caught the first whiff of coffee and her stomach tightened. Surprised when she heard voices from the kitchen, she debated going to her room and waiting until Mike and Scotty were out of there, but she suspected they would come find her eventually. With a deep breath, she entered the kitchen.

Mike sat at the table across from Scotty, who was in a high chair that was pulled up to the table. Mike came to his feet as soon as he saw her.

"Good morning," he said, smiling at her.

Tingles increased her awareness of him. How handsome he looked in jeans, a navy Western shirt with rolled back sleeves and his cowboy boots. His thick, black curls were as tangled as they had been last night and he looked appealing, handsome.

"Please sit," she said, smiling at him. "Hi, Scotty. How are you on this beautiful morning?"

"I'm hungry," he answered, smiling at her in return and she laughed.

She turned to Mike. "I thought you had some chores this morning and were going to be gone."

"I've already been out. Scotty was still asleep. I'm going back to join them again after breakfast if you meant what you said about watching Scotty."

"Sure I did if that's all right with Scotty."

"Scotty?" Mike prompted. "You'll stay with Miss Savannah, won't you?"

"Yes, sir," Scotty said and smiled at Savannah again.

"That's nice, Scotty. Did you see the snow this morning?"

"Yes, ma'am," he answered politely. "This afternoon Daddy will help me make a snowman if I eat my breakfast."

"A little bribe," Mike said, grinning. "And it'll be after I get some more chores done," he added to Scotty who nodded. Mike turned to Savannah. "What can I fix you? We have bacon, eggs, orange and/or tomato juice, coffee, hot biscuits, dry cereal, blueberries, oranges, dried apricots—"

"Stop," she said, laughing. "You're naming way too many things. I just want cereal and a glass of milk. I can get my breakfast. You stay with Scotty."

Mike reached the cabinets when she did and he retrieved a glass, turning to get the milk and pour it for her. "Tell me when."

"When," she said. "Not too much. Thanks." She was so aware of Mike beside her, of his dark eyes intently on her. The sight of him made her remember last night, standing in his arms while they kissed.

In minutes she had cereal and a glass of milk as she sat beside Scotty and across from Mike.

"Please go on with your regular routine today and don't let me change it," she said.

"Will you help us build a snowman later?" Scotty asked.

"Sure, I will," she said. "A snowman sounds like fun."

Mike had a covered bowl on the table and when he raised the lid, she saw scrambled eggs.

"If those aren't still hot, tell me. I'll scramble some more," he said.

She shook her head. "No, thank you. What I have is plenty." She sipped her milk. "Do you know if it kept snowing into the night?"

"Oh, yes," Mike replied. "The boys keep up with it and Ray said we had a record-setting eight inches."

"Oh, Mike. I'm sorry—I'm sort of the houseguest who came for a night and stayed for a week. Eight inches—I won't be able to get my car out of that and I doubt if the state road will be cleared."

"You're right on all counts. We're glad to have you, so just relax, Savannah. This is a break in routine winter days."

"Thanks," she said, drinking some milk and eating cereal. After a few bites, her stomach lurched and worry gripped her. She didn't want to be sick in front of Mike. She turned to talk to Scotty.

"I have a scarf you can use to put around your snowman's neck," she said, trying to ignore her queasy stomach.

"Savannah, are you all right?" Mike asked, studying her.

Feeling worse by the second, she shook her head. "Where's the nearest bathroom?"

He stood and came around the table swiftly, taking her arm as she stood. "We'll be right back, Scotty," Mike said, leading Savannah away from the table. Mike headed to the hall and opened a bathroom door.

"Thanks." As soon as the door closed, she lost the small breakfast she had eaten. She washed her face and hands with cold water and waited while her stomach settled slightly. When she opened the door, Mike leaned against the wall with his arms folded. Studying her, he straightened.

"Better now?"

"Yes, I am."

"Do you need a doctor?"

"No, I've been to one. Don't worry, this isn't contagious."

"I didn't think it was," he said quietly.

"You better get back to Scotty. He's in a high chair."

"He gets himself into that chair a dozen times a day and he gets himself down. Scotty is a climber so there's no worry. He's an easy kid to have around, and he's an only child and that makes it easier. C'mon. You probably want to sit."

"Yes, I do."

They went to the family area where Scotty sat on the floor playing a game on a laptop.

"Mike, are you sure Scotty isn't a bit older than you told me? He's on a computer."

"He has some games he likes and I've taught him how to pull them up. He catches on fast." He studied her again. "Can I get you anything?"

"No, thanks. I'm feeling better now. I'll get my dishes in a while."

"Forget them. When's your baby due or would you rather not talk about it?"

Startled, she focused on him. "I didn't think my pregnancy showed yet."

"It doesn't. Elise had morning sickness. I recognize the symptoms."

"I'm surprised you were able to tell by just one morning with me. I'm glad I found you yesterday—you were a lifesaver, but being saved by a mind reader is a little disconcerting."

"I'm no mind reader, just observant. I assume your pregnancy is the reason you wanted to get out of Little Rock and go to California."

"You're right. You might not be a mind reader, but you're definitely astute," she said. His calm acceptance of discovering his guest was pregnant put her more at ease. If he had been shocked, worried about a pregnant woman on his hands or worse—acted disgusted the way her ex-fiancé had, she would have been embarrassed and upset. Also, his enthusiasm over his son helped put her at ease because it was obvious he liked kids and was filled with love for his son. She still hurt when she thought of the last conversation with Kirk and how he had stared at her, his gaze raking sharply over her after she had announced her pregnancy.

Get rid of it, Kirk had said. His first words to her had stabbed as if he had plunged a knife into her heart. His words had hurt, but the blunt dismissal had made her protective of her baby from that moment on. She brought her attention back to Mike.

"Your ex-fiancé didn't want babies—what did you tell me—for another fifteen years? Or he really doesn't ever want children?"

"He said he doesn't want children for at least another

fifteen years. I'm twenty-six and I don't want to have my first child when I'm fifteen to twenty years older. I really don't think he ever wants kids, but he wouldn't say that. He didn't want this baby at all. He didn't care what I did as long as I didn't keep the child."

"That's a hell of a thing," Mike said, a note of steel in his voice that made her feel better. "Scotty is my whole world. I love him with every ounce of my being," he said, looking at his son and a tender note coming into his voice that gave a twist to her heart.

"That's wonderful for both of you. And the way I'd hoped it would be."

"Sorry, but it's good you found out now before you said vows. He gave up his baby and let you walk away—that's the mistake of his life."

"He didn't view it that way. When he found out I was pregnant, I think he wanted to be rid of me. He signed over all parental rights, too. He wouldn't have given any financial support anyway, but I didn't want any from him."

"I'd say you're a hell of a lot better off without this jerk."

"I feel as if I am. I don't miss him—or if I do, I just think of the hurtful things he said to me about the baby and that changes any feelings I have for him."

"That's tough. So when's your baby due?"

"I'm into my second month. I've been given an October date. We'll see. What shakes me is my poor judgment about a man I had such a close relationship with and planned to spend my life with. I've known him since we were about eight or nine. I misjudged him in the worst way and that's frightening."

"Looks to me like you've learned from the experience."

"It shakes my faith in myself. I don't trust myself to fall in love again."

"I imagine next time you'll get to know the guy better

in ways you didn't the first time." Mike stood. "Now I'm going to put the dishes into the dishwasher. You sit tight and don't do anything. Then I need to get back to help the guys. When I return, Scotty," he said, looking at his son who waited expectantly, "we'll go build a snowman."

Scotty grinned and returned to his computer game.

"My foreman said he has plenty of help, but I want to make sure. Usually, Nell, our nanny, is here and I work on the ranch with the others. They were still breaking ice and dropping bales of hay for feed when I left this morning. We need to make sure animals don't get cut off and lost from the herd."

"Don't let me interfere. I'm happy to stay with Scotty."

Mike loaded the dishwasher and cleaned up the kitchen, working efficiently. "I'll be back in a few hours. I have my phone and the number is written clearly there on a piece of paper. Scotty knows how to call me, too." He gave his son a kiss on the head, then left.

"Well, aren't you the smart boy, Scotty," she said, glancing at him and receiving another smile. "After you finish your breakfast in the kitchen, we can play a game if you'd like," she told him.

"Yes, ma'am," he replied.

While Scotty was happily drawing, Savannah walked to the mantel to pick up the picture and look closely at Mike with his arm around his late wife as they smiled at each other. Elise had been a beautiful woman. Mike was still deeply in love with her. Last night, their proximity, maybe hurt and loneliness, made them both vulnerable.

She sighed. It wouldn't matter this time because she would soon tell Mike goodbye, but she would have to be cautious in the future. She never wanted to be hurt the way she had been. If she couldn't trust her own judgment about men, then she should stay out of a relationship. How could she have been so blind to Kirk's shortcomings? He had never liked her nieces and nephews, never cared to hear about them or ask about them, yet she hadn't stopped to think about his lack of interest.

Her pregnancy had been a surprise. They had taken precautions, but she had gotten pregnant anyway. She still couldn't bear to think about the night she told Kirk and how hurtful he had been.

With a long sigh, she picked up her phone and took a couple of pictures of Scotty drawing to try to get Kirk out of her thoughts.

Mike arrived home after one, stomping his feet to shake snow off his boots and finally sweeping into the room, bringing cold air with him. He swung Scotty up to hug him.

"Sorry to be gone so long."

"We've been fine and I had a good time with your smart son."

"I'll grab a bite to eat and then take him out to build a snowman. You don't have to go."

"It sounds like fun," she said, glancing outside at the snow-covered ranch.

He headed into the kitchen. "Did you and Scotty have lunch?"

"Yes. I made some macaroni for us both."

Fifteen minutes later, after a quick sandwich, Mike returned to the family room. "So, Scotty," he said, "we can go outside now if you want."

"Yes," Scotty answered, jumping to his feet.

"Get all your snow gear on and whatever we'll need for a snowman. I'll get two lumps of coal for eyes and a carrot nose. How's that? You find an old hat, okay?"

"Yes, sir," he said over his shoulder as he ran out of the room.

"Are you going out with us?" Mike asked. "You don't have to."

"Right now, the cold air sounds refreshing. It'll be fun," she said, standing. "I'm not fragile. My stomach is fragile at breakfast time—that's all."

"Better get bundled up, then. It's cold out there and the wind is blowing."

"Sure," she said and they walked down the hall together and again she was aware of him so close beside her. "I'll see you and Scotty where—back door, outside?"

He nodded. "Scotty is about to pop to get out in the snow. It all looks wonderful to him."

She laughed. "Oh, to be a child again—"

He grinned. "I kinda like some of the things that come with adulthood," he said, a teasing note in his voice that made her think of their kiss and her cheeks grew warm. "I think you do, too, or you wouldn't be blushing now," he added softly, looking at her mouth.

"I'll see you outside," she said, her voice breathless, betraying her feelings.

"Sure," he said, heading for his suite.

Lost in thought about him, she stared at his back. She didn't need another attraction in her life and she was risking one every hour she spent with Mike. His kiss set her on fire and made her forget everything else. He was likeable, fun, discerning, capable—caring—something that wrapped around her heart at this moment in time when she was vulnerable from being hurt. Mike held far too many appealing qualities all contained in over six feet of sexy male with thick black hair and dark brown eyes. Or was she just making another misjudgment based on assumptions and wishful thinking, projections of her hopes?

Whatever the truth, she needed to remember she would tell Mike goodbye within the week, maybe in another day or two at the most. His heart belonged to his first wife and he was far from getting over his loss or ever loving again.

At his door, Mike glanced back and caught her watching him.

Embarrassed, she entered her bedroom and glanced outside at the white world. Beneath all that snow was a thick layer of ice, plus she had a car that wouldn't run and she didn't know when anyone could even get to it to see if it could be fixed or had burned beyond repair.

She rushed to get her boots and pull a red sweater over her shirt. She put her hair in a thick braid and pulled on her coat as she hurried down the hall. She had a stocking cap, gloves, sunglasses. At the last minute she had grabbed a scarf for Scotty's snowman and her phone.

Mike and Scotty waited by the back door. Mike was hunkered down, fastening Scotty's cap beneath his chin. He stood and reached into his pocket to hold out two packets for her. "Hand warmers. Drop them in your gloves and clap your hands when you want to warm them."

She smiled and took them. "Thanks."

In minutes they were busy rolling a big snowball for the snowman. Finally, Mike held Scotty to let him place the lumps of coal for the eyes and a carrot for the nose. Mike had a short length of thick rope he gave Scotty for the mouth which gave the snowman a huge grin.

Mike scooped up one of his old broad-brimmed Western straw hats and Scotty placed it on the snowman. She watched Mike work with Scotty and felt a pang. Too much about Mike and Scotty reminded her of what she had lost, constantly bringing to mind the terrible mistake she had made in falling in love with Kirk. She was thankful she wouldn't be long with Mike and Scotty because she could easily fall in love again and make just as big a mistake as before.

"Here, Scotty, take this scarf and you can put it around his neck," she said, holding out a plaid red-and-blue scarf.

Mike lifted him up so Scotty could get it on the snowman while Savannah walked to the back side to help put the scarf around the snowman. As soon as they finished, she stepped away.

"Let me get a picture of the two of you with the cowboy snowman," Savannah said while she pulled out her phone and snapped pictures of Mike holding Scotty, standing beside the snow cowboy. Then Mike told Scotty to shake the snowman's stick hand and she took another picture. Mike set Scotty on his feet and trudged toward her through the snow. "Now I'll take one of you and Scotty and then we'll do a selfie."

When Mike came over for the selfie, he picked up Scotty and held him in one arm, then handed Savannah the camera and put his other arm around her. "Savannah, you take the picture."

"Everyone give me a big smile," she said, sliding her free arm around Mike's shoulder and taking their picture. "One more," she added and took another.

"Good boy, Scotty," Mike said and kissed him on the cheek. "And good girl, Savannah," he teased, brushing a kiss on her cheek, a playful kiss that should have been nothing, yet her heart skipped a beat.

They looked at their pictures, taking a few more before they put away the phones.

It was almost four when they finally went inside. "I know everyone will welcome a snack," Mike said. "I'll slice some apples."

"I'll slice the apples," Savannah offered, heading into the kitchen and taking three apples from the fruit bowl.

Soon Scotty was munching on slices of apples while he played a game on the laptop. He yawned, scooted off the chair and lay down on the soft rug near the fireplace, falling fast asleep. Mike picked him up to carry him to his room.

Savannah sat near the fire, getting warm and relaxed while she looked at the pictures she had taken outside. When Mike returned he sat close to look at the pictures with her. "Scotty is adorable. I hope my baby is just like him."

"He's a good kid. We have fun and he's my salvation without Elise."

"I can imagine. Your heart still belongs to Elise and your memories. You're definitely unattainable. I will have to be careful not to fall in love even though you and Scotty are so lovable."

"No kidding?" he said, smiling, making light of what had turned into a solemn moment. "That's a first for someone to tell me."

"As I said, although lovable, you're as out of reach as a star. I don't intend to forget. On a lighter note, that was fun today. What a snowman."

He glanced out the wall of glass. "I got a text from Ray. He said another snowstorm is moving in tonight." He stood and put another log on the dying fire.

"Oh no!"

"You're welcome here, Savannah. You don't have to be in California at any set time, do you?"

"Not really. I'll text my aunt and let her know there will be another delay. I talked to her briefly this morning."

"Tell her to stop sending this crummy weather our way," he said, smiling at her. "Want to watch a movie, or maybe just sit, play a game?"

"Just sitting after all that giant snowball rolling is fine with me. If you have things you have to do, go ahead."

"I don't have anything urgent—" he said, interrupted by a commotion at the back door.

"Must be Ray or one of the boys. Just a minute and I'll be back," Mike said, leaving the room.

He was talking to someone, her curiosity rising when she heard a woman's voice. He entered the room with a tall blonde beside him and for an instant, Savannah wondered if he had a woman in his life.

His guest had shed her coat and she wore a thick navy sweater, jeans and boots.

"Savannah, we have company. This is my sister, Lindsay Calhoun. Lindsay, meet Savannah Grayson."

As Savannah greeted his sister, she couldn't see any family resemblance between the blue-eyed blonde and the black-haired Mike with his dark brown eyes.

"Hi. I have a ranch near here and since we're snowed in, I rode over because I thought my brother and Scotty would be bored shut in the house and stuck because of the storm. I knew Mrs. Lewis was still away."

"You should have sent a text and I could have told you—but now you're here and I'm happy for you to meet Savannah. Yesterday Savannah had car trouble, including the car catching on fire, so after dousing the fire, we left it at Ed's station."

"I'm sorry. You did have trouble and this weather doesn't help. I doubt if Ed will open tomorrow."

"So you drove over here—that means the roads are open?" Savannah asked.

Mike and Lindsay both smiled. "No, they're not," Lindsay replied. "I came on horseback. I left home almost two hours ago."

"Oh, my word. Two hours on horseback."

"It's pretty out there and quiet. I figured Mike would be lonesome. Had I known he had company—"

"Did you see the snowman when you came in?"

"Yes, very cute dude. I'm sure Scotty had fun. I want some pop, and do you have some cookies?"

"Sure," Mike said, standing and she motioned to him to sit again.

"I'll find them and then I'll be back. Want anything, Savannah?"

"No, thank you," she said.

In a short time Lindsay was settled in a chair near the fire. She sat with her long legs tucked under her while she talked about their family. "You'll hear if you stick around very long—for over a century our Calhoun family has been feuding with another family, the Milans. Recently our brother Jake married a Milan, which meant a lot of us had to make adjustments. Then only months ago, a Milan married a woman who is a Calhoun descendent, although she didn't grow up in this area."

"Aunt Lindsay—"

Scotty stood in the doorway, his curls a bigger tangle than ever. He held a worn stuffed bear in his arms. A slow grin spread and he ran across the room. Lindsay scooped him up and hugged him while he clung tightly to her in turn.

"Hey, I thought you and your daddy would be so lonesome with all this snow so I rode Sergeant over."

"Did you see the snow cowboy?" Scotty asked.

"I certainly did. It's the happiest snow cowboy I ever did see. I love it."

Lindsay sat with Scotty on her lap for the next half hour before he jumped down and ran to get some of his toys. Lindsay stood. "I'm going to start home, Mike. Ray said to call when I'm ready. He's going to take Sergeant and me as far as the west bridge. Some of the guys shoveled it off today."

"Stay tonight. I've got a casserole in the oven for dinner. There's no need for you to make that long trek twice in a day and you'll be alone when you get home."

"You know I'm used to that and we've got another storm coming. I better be home when it hits. Savannah, it was nice to meet you. I'm glad you found my brother and he could help. You take care of yourself."

"Lindsay, I'm happy to have met you," Savannah said, following them to the door.

Ray drove up, his truck pulling a horse trailer and she could see Lindsay's horse through an opening. Ray lowered his window. "Hi, Savannah, Mike, Scotty."

"Bye, Mike," Lindsay said, giving him a quick hug and then turning to hug Scotty. She climbed into the truck.

"I'll take them home if I can get through," Ray said, closing his window and driving out, turning west.

"He can't even see a road," Savannah said, amazed that Mike's sister would ride over to see him.

"Ray knows the way, plus he can follow her horse tracks now."

"Is she safe when she has to ride her horse?"

"Yes, she is. I imagine if Ray can cross the creek, he'll get her home."

"If he can do that, I can get my car when it's ready."

"Driving back to Ed's or anywhere on the highway is different. Ray's in a truck cutting across country he knows on paths the guys already drove over earlier. He may not be able to cross the bridge anyway. If he can't, she'll ride her horse to the far west side of my property. From there she'll cross the highway and she'll be on her own land. It'll be nearly dark when she gets home, but her dogs will meet her. She'll be okay."

"It's her world and she knows it and she thinks it's beautiful, but it looks desolate and frightening to me," Savannah said. "I'm glad to have met her and heard some of the family tales."

"We've got plenty. Old legends, tales—some have proven to be true this past year." They went inside and Mike tossed another log on the fire. "That casserole should be about ready to take out of the oven. I hope you like baked spaghetti."

"Sounds delicious on a cold snowy night. Let me help."

Within the hour they sat with Scotty to eat baked spaghetti. Mike was efficient and easygoing about getting things done. She helped him clear the dishes after dinner, aware of enjoying his company, realizing she would miss him for a few days when she left. Once in, she hoped to get a job and be busy enough to help heal her hurts and to forget a lot of her past and she expected to forget her time with Mike. She thought about his kiss and wondered how long before she could forget that.

"Daddy, can we watch *Ice Age*?"

"We have a world of ice and snow. Wouldn't you rather watch something with a palm tree and a beach?"

"No, sir."

Mike looked at Savannah and shrugged.

"You asked," she said, smiling at Scotty who stood looking hopefully at Mike.

"Let's see what our company wants to do, okay?"

Scotty turned big brown eyes on her.

"I'd love to watch *Ice Age*, Scotty. It's a fun movie."

"I lose," Mike said, shaking his head and smiling at Scotty.

During the movie, Mike received a text. After checking his phone, he leaned close to Savannah. "That was Lindsay. Ray took her and her horse home and he's back here."

"I'm relieved to know they're both safe," she whispered and Mike smiled at her.

While they watched the movie, Scotty climbed into Mike's lap. Looking at the two of them, sadness stabbed her. She could hear Kirk's harsh words to get rid of their baby when what she wanted was the kind of love and closeness Mike and Scotty had. How could she have misjudged Kirk so badly? Could she trust her judgment in the future? How many times was she going to be plagued by that question? Would she ever again feel sure in her judgment about a relationship?

When she glanced again at Mike, her gaze rested on his mouth while she thought about his kiss and wanted to kiss again. She assumed it was because she was hurt and vulnerable. Or would she have felt that way about it if there were no hurts or problems in her life? At the moment Mike loomed larger-than-life and was so desirable he took her breath.

When the movie finished, Mike announced that it was time to get Scotty ready for bed.

"When you have your pajamas on, call me and I'll come read a story to you," Savannah offered as Mike picked him up and placed him on his shoulders to leave the room.

"Yes, ma'am." Scotty laughed and wound his fingers in Mike's curls.

Thirty minutes later, she sat in a rocker in Scotty's room while he brought her a book. As she picked him up, Mike crossed the room in quick strides.

"You shouldn't be lifting him."

"I'm fine. Mike, pregnant women have been lifting little kids since the beginning of time," she said, settling Scotty in her lap. He had had a bath and wore soft pajamas. He smelled like soap and was small and warm in her arms.

"It's been a fun day, hasn't it?" she asked, giving him a slight hug.

"Yes, ma'am," he answered politely. He opened a book for her to read. As she read, he played with her hair. She was aware of Scotty studying her and she wondered what he was thinking. She was also aware Mike sat quietly in a wing-back chair and watched them as she read. Was he wishing it was Elise instead? She wouldn't blame him. He'd had a happy marriage.

As soon as she finished, Scotty picked up another book. "Will you read this one?"

"Scotty, she read one," Mike said.

"I'll read it," she said. "I'd love to." Scotty smiled at her. As she read, Scotty continued to play with locks of her hair, winding them around his fingers. Once she glanced up as she turned the page and met Mike's steady gaze. He had a solemn expression as he watched her. She looked down to continue her reading. The moment she read *The End* Scotty picked up another book.

"Thank you. Will you please read this one?"

"Scotty," Mike said, standing.

She waved her hand at him. "One more, Mike. These stories are fun," she said, looking at Scotty who smiled at her.

"Scotty, this is the last one," Mike stated firmly. "It's getting late and you've had a long day."

"Yes, sir," he said, happily snuggling in Savannah's arms and looking expectantly at his book as she began to read.

When she finished, his eyes were almost closed, but he looked up at her. "Thank you," he said.

"Tell Miss Savannah good-night," Mike instructed.

"Good night," Scotty said. He wrapped his arms around her neck and hugged her, kissing her cheek.

Startled, she hugged him lightly in return and brushed his cheek with a kiss. "Night, Scotty. Today was lots of fun. It's nice to be here with you and your daddy."

Scotty smiled at her as Mike leaned close, taking Scotty from her, for a brief moment causing her to be intensely aware of Mike, his aftershave, his hand brushing her leg as he picked up his son, his face only inches from her. "I'll put him in bed."

As soon as Mike stepped away, she stood and watched him kiss his son on his forehead. Leaving them, she walked into the playroom adjoining Scotty's bedroom. Scotty was adorable and she had had a wonderful day with father and son. She hurt for Mike and Scotty losing a wife and mother, which made her problems loom a lot smaller. Even though her breakup had hurt badly, she had wanted to break off with Kirk.

She couldn't let herself fall in love with Mike, who was still very much in love with Elise, mourning his loss and wrapped in his own problems. She hoped the coming storm would blow through quickly or pass them by altogether so she could go on her way because Mike's attractiveness grew daily.

She looked around the room that had murals of storybook characters and a decor of bright and cheerful primary colors that she guessed Elise had selected. There was a laptop, electronic games and a huge toy box with a lid that closed everything from sight. Framed pictures of Mike, Elise and Scotty were on shelves while a large oil of Elise holding Scotty hung on one wall. It was a touching, beautiful picture. As she looked at it, she felt certain Mike would never love anyone else or marry again. He kept memories of Elise in every room in the house, talked about her, obviously still loved her to the point he didn't want any other woman in his life. She didn't think he would change and she could understand. Living out on the ranch with just Scotty and people who worked for him probably helped support that love.

Mike came out. "Scotty is already asleep and the monitor is cranked up, so we can go watch a movie or just talk. Or we can play tennis if you want. I have an indoor tennis court."

She smiled. "Maybe I should ask what you don't have."

"I'm very well equipped," he said, giving a double meaning to his words.

"I believe you and we don't need to pursue that one further," she said, laughing.

"It's nice to have you around," he said. "You brighten things up around here."

"Thank you. Since you're stuck with me, I'm glad you feel that way. Let's try the tennis because except for building the snowman, all we've done is sit around."

"Speak for yourself. I've been out on the ranch part of the day and giving Scotty a bath is a chore."

"I know Scotty is company, but don't you get lonesome here all by yourself?"

"No. Ray and the boys are here and I can walk down to the bunkhouse and get in a poker game or on nice evenings when Mrs. Lewis is here, I join them at the corral to ride some of the horses that really aren't broken in yet. We've even got an old bull that they ride sometimes. I've done that and then I'm ready to come up here and have some peace and quiet. I read, work on keeping my records of ranch expenses or I work out. I keep busy."

"I'm surprised local women don't come out to visit."

"They have, but I don't do anything much without Scotty and that seems to discourage the ones who have dropped in on me."

"That surprises me. Scotty is adorable."

"Miss Neonatal Nurse, you said you like children. Not everyone is quite that enthusiastic about a one- or two-year-old."

"I've found that out the hard way when I told Kirk I'm pregnant and his hateful reaction really cut. I never expected him to react that way."

"That is finding out the hard way. Your brothers might be angry with him. If a man did my sister that way—I know how my brothers and I would feel."

"As I told you, my family is centered on children with my four nieces and nephews."

"That's nice. That's why you're good with kids. Scotty likes you."

"I'll bet Scotty likes everybody."

"No, no. I've had some women come by when he was a baby. He didn't take to them and vice versa. Needless to say, those women and I didn't see much of each other. If you want to play tennis, we better change shoes. There's no running around the court in my boots or the shoes you're wearing. I'll go back and change shoes and meet you here in the hall."

She headed into her room to change into a T-shirt, shorts and her tennis shoes, and when she stepped out of her suite, Mike was waiting. She noticed that he glanced from her head to her toes.

"Do you have a monitor on the court?" she asked as they went downstairs.

"Yes, and I can hear Scotty on it easily. Turn right at the corner. This wing of the house has been built onto the back. I've thought about an indoor pool, but I'm waiting until Scotty is older and can swim. That's something I don't want to have to worry about when I'm away from the house."

They walked past open doors and she saw an exercise

room with equipment. They passed a large theater room with a huge screen, big leather recliners and small stands to hold drinks. Mike turned into another spacious room with a tennis court.

"This is a first. My first experience with an indoor tennis court except in a school gym."

He stood close and his dark eyes twinkled. "We could make it another first experience while we're in here," he said in a deeper voice.

"Mike, stop flirting," she said lightly. "I've had enough firsts—first time I've been in Texas. First time I've been in West Texas. First snow cowboy I've helped build. First kiss by a Texas cowboy," she said, knowing she was flirting back with him and she should stop. "First time I've stayed on a ranch. First time I've ever gone home with a Texan. I think that's enough."

"That isn't nearly enough," he said. "I can give you some far more interesting firsts. We'll get back to your list later."

"You just stick to tennis."

They spent the next hour playing tennis and she had the feeling that he was deliberately trying to let her win. She suspected he politely held back. Whether he did or not, she had fun and it felt good to move around and be active.

"Let's go get cold drinks, and we can sit and talk," he suggested when the match was over.

Back in the family room, Mike built a fire and they both kicked off their shoes and sat on the floor. He had turned on music, and it played softly in the background.

Later, when a fast song played, Mike took her drink from her hands and set it on a table beside his, leading her over where carpet didn't cover the hardwood floor. "Let's dance," he said.

Mike was a good dancer, which didn't surprise her, and

she had fun dancing with him. She watched him, moving with him, his dark eyes constantly on her. Even though she barely knew him, she was going to remember him for a long time—no way would she forget him in a few days as she thought she might once she got to California. When the music changed again to a slow number, he caught her hand and began the next dance holding her in his arms.

Her heartbeat quickened and she looked away, scared what his perceptive gaze might see in her eyes. Dancing close in his arms made her think of his kisses and stirred longings better left undisturbed.

As they danced, she looked outside. Lights were on the yard and patio, and she could see snowflakes falling. "Mike, it's snowing."

"I know," he said, turning to look outside while they moved slowly together. "We're getting a lot of snow tonight. I'll need to get out in the morning to help the guys again. The animals need attention in this kind of weather even more than usual. I can call Millie and Baxter about dropping Scotty off at their house to watch him or—"

"Leave him with me. It didn't seem to startle him to get up and find you gone."

"No, it won't. That's the usual way when Mrs. Lewis is here with him. He's accustomed to being with his nanny."

"In the morning, go see about your animals and whatever else you have to do."

"Thanks. The best thing about more snow is, you'll be here longer with us. Scotty and I will both like that."

She smiled. "Thank you. That's polite, but I didn't mean to move in."

"You can move in with me any old time," he said in a husky voice that stirred tingles.

"What's the old saying, 'Fish and houseguests get old after three days.'"

"Doesn't apply in the case of a beautiful, fun blonde."

"Thanks for making me feel wanted because you're stuck with me."

"You're wanted, Savannah," he said in a deeper tone that changed the moment for her.

She drew a deep breath as he stopped dancing, and she looked up into his brown eyes filled with unmistakable desire. Mike's dark gaze melted away logic and resistance. What she wanted most was for Mike to kiss her. Longing for his kiss dominated her feelings while the wisdom to keep her distance vanished. Responding to him would bring trouble into her life, but at the moment she didn't care.

Four

Mike's temperature jumped as desire shook him. His gaze went over her silky skin, her rosy cheeks and full lips that at moments were temptation. His love was for Elise and he wanted to resist Savannah, for his sake and for hers. He wasn't in love with her and wouldn't be, so he should squelch the lusty feelings she evoked. Any lovemaking would be temporary, unfair to her because she was vulnerable now and could get hurt emotionally.

In spite of knowing who filled his heart, he wanted to wrap his arms around Savannah and kiss her. Her blond hair fell across her shoulders and he imagined winding his fingers in it. Far more, he longed to feel her softness against him while he kissed her again. As he gazed into her big blue eyes, she inhaled deeply, her lips parting.

Knowing she felt something sent his temperature soaring. She responded to the slightest look. Unable to resist, he slid his arm around her waist. "Savannah," he whispered.

Even though his conscience screamed to resist, he drew her into his embrace. He'd told her that kisses were meaningless, insignificant, a delightful way to spend a cold winter's night together. While tinged with guilt, he still felt that way. He wasn't into commitment or any serious involvement and he had made that clear, but this was the first time since his loss that he had wanted a woman, wanted to hold her and kiss her and have her return his kisses. Savannah was bringing him back to life, back into the world, something he didn't know would ever happen again and tonight he was caught in the attraction.

Whatever they found together, it would be as fleeting for her as for him. They had disconnected lives and would go their separate ways, so there was little risk now of having the heart involved for either one of them. She didn't want to be attracted to him, yet she was, but it had to be as purely physical as what he felt. Looking into her wide blue eyes, his heartbeat drummed as he drew her to him while his arm tightened around her waist.

"I can't stop wanting you," he admitted, fighting a steady inner battle. "In some ways I'm glad you're here in my house, in my arms," he whispered. He leaned closer to cover her mouth with his in a kiss that set his heart pounding.

He felt locked into blue depths, drawn to her, wanting her softness. Her lips were warm, incredibly soft, yet a hot brand searing him, intensifying the attraction they each felt.

He wanted her more than ever—a response that startled him. Wrapping her arms around his neck, she held him tightly, pressing against him. Her kisses heightened his longing and increased his excitement. He leaned over her, kissing her passionately while he yielded to desire.

Continuing to kiss her, he picked her up and carried her

to the sofa to sit with her on his lap. After a few minutes
she leaned away from him. "Mike, I can't. I don't want any
kind of attraction to draw me into another mistake. I'm
not ready for an affair or another complication in my life.
I've made one huge mistake in judgment. I don't want to
make another now. I already hurt. This I don't need," she
whispered, the words spilling out as if she were arguing
with herself. "My emotions will get caught up and I'm not
ready at all. You're not, either. This is lust totally—lust and
maybe a little loneliness, just physical needs."

"You're right, but it's nice to feel alive again for even a
few minutes. You need me, Savannah, as much as I need
you. We'll help heal each other's wounds in a physical way.
We may not be able to reach deeper, but this is a consolation, a temporary bonding. The void in my life is monu-
mental and at this moment, you fill part of it," he replied.

"I can't deal with more hurtful complications. I can't
bond with anyone else now. I really can't get involved. I
just can't do it," she whispered. "My body is changing and
my life is changing. I have too much to deal with. You're
thinking a few kisses, but sometimes they can turn into
something more. I don't need another emotional upheaval."

She slid off his lap and walked away from him. With
a pounding pulse, Mike watched her as she pulled herself back together. Knowing he should do the same, he
stretched and stood, walking to the window, giving her
space and letting things cool between them.

He ached with wanting her—part was pure lust, just
being so long without a woman's love, part was wanting
Savannah. She had brought joy and warmth into his life.
He didn't want to do anything to hurt her, which meant
he needed to back off and leave her alone, for himself as
well as for her.

When she left, he would tell her goodbye and not expect to see her again. If she was one of those who could easily fall in love, then it was best for both of them to keep their distance.

After a time she came to stand beside him. "The snow is beautiful, but it's going to cause a lot of delays. I know that firsthand."

"You don't have to be in California at any certain time and we're enjoying having you. Even if we don't kiss, in some ways you're bringing me to life, Savannah," he said, turning to her.

"Please don't tell me things like that. My emotions get all tangled up in what I do, and I can't view an affair as purely physical," she added as he placed his hands on her shoulders. "My ex-fiancé was hateful, mean. You're a warm, kind, appealing, sexy man, so your friendliness can capture my love easily. I don't have defenses right now. I've been hurt, and someone nice seems like Mr. Super Wonderful. I don't want to fall in love and you don't want that, either."

"You don't have to explain why you feel the way you do. We've agreed that neither of us needs another tangle in our lives. There's no affair and we've barely kissed," he said, thinking the word *barely* didn't apply to her kisses. He draped his arm across her shoulders and hugged her gently, then stepped away. "Want to just sit in front of the fire and talk?" he asked, not trusting himself to go back to dancing with her.

"Sure," she said, flashing him a smile that made him want to pull her into his arms and kiss her again. He had done what she wanted and sounded casual about it, but it wasn't working out casually for his libido. He wanted to kiss her, to make love to her and to hold her the rest of the night. His gaze ran over her features, her thickly lashed big eyes and rosy lips. Her blond hair was silky and just looking at her took his breath and made him want to reach for her again.

"Mike?" she asked, tilting her head to gaze at him intently.

"Sorry, lost in my thoughts," he said. His voice was husky and desire threatened his self-control and intentions. But in minutes he had better control, focusing on listening to her talk about growing up in Hot Springs.

While they sat and talked, she tried to keep their conversation impersonal and avoid flirting. Mike seemed relaxed, yet she was aware of his dark gaze on her constantly. Sometimes he would flirt, but they both kept it light.

"Mike, you said Scotty's birthday is coming up."

"It's Friday. He's too little for a kid party, and we don't move in kid circles like someone who lives in town, so the celebration will be family only. You'll meet his aunts and uncles. Elise's parents live in Boston so they won't be here for the party, but they'll put in a Skype call to Scotty."

"His birthday is days away—I don't think I'll be here that long."

He smiled at her. "In a hurry to go?"

"No, I didn't mean that," she said, feeling her face flush.

"I know you didn't. Besides the problem of the snow and ice, the temperatures are supposed to stay below freezing for the next four days and there may be more snow this week. Your car caught on fire—no telling what has to be done to fix it. You might even be here past Scotty's birthday. If it turns out that you need to stay for a few more days anyway, I hope you'll stay for his birthday, too. He likes you or he never would have kissed you."

"That makes me happy."

"It made me happy," he admitted, thinking about watching her with Scotty. But was that entirely true? He had mixed feelings. As she'd read to Scotty, Mike had one of those gut-wrenching moments when he missed Elise. Elise should be rocking Scotty and holding him, and it hurt badly to see another woman with his son. By the next book Savannah had read, though, he had a grip on his emotions and a fleeting thought came that Scotty liked Savannah. She was winning his son's friendship, which was nice.

They were quiet with the only sound the fire crackling as logs burned. Finally, Mike turned to her again. "Savannah, this is changing the subject, but don't you want your mother around and your family near when you have your baby? You won't have a husband, and in California, you have only your aunt."

Savannah studied him so long that he tilted his head. "What?" he asked. "What haven't you told me?"

"Oh, gee. I feel as if you can just read my thoughts. The truth is that the only other person in my family who knows that I'm pregnant is my mother. I haven't told you about my brothers—they're very protective of their families and their little sisters. They can get physical. Frankly, I was afraid they would beat up my former fiancé."

"There's a law against that."

"Might be, but they all know each other really well. If they did, I'm not sure he'd sue. He might do something through business that would hurt them—that would be more his style. I just wanted some time to pass so they're calmer when they find out about my baby. Besides that, they are just old-fashioned enough to demand that he 'do right by me.' Even if Kirk did want to 'do the right thing,' I wouldn't marry him and I wouldn't want them pressuring me to accept. They're really old-fashioned. They're worse than my dad who will be bad enough when he finds out. I may go home after a couple of months in California because I'd rather be surrounded by family."

"Are your brothers going to show up on my doorstep?"

"No," she said, smiling at him. "I promise you that you're quite safe. Until yesterday you were no part of my life, and for them, you don't exist. Besides, when they hear about you, they'll be grateful to you for the help you gave me. If they ever did show up, it would just be to thank you."

"Does your ex-fiancé know he might have to face their ire?"

"I imagine he has a good idea. He knows them."

"Then he won't be caught off guard and taken by surprise?"

"No, he won't. I hadn't thought about that. He'll probably take some precautions, like leaving town for a while. Right now, my brothers don't know anything. They think I broke off the engagement because I just got cold feet about getting married. They probably expect me to get over it and come right back to him."

"Won't they be angry whenever they learn the truth?"

"Mom and I don't think so. She thinks they'll be accustomed to me not being engaged to him. At first they won't know it's his baby."

"Pity whoever they think the father is."

"I'll see to it that I don't put someone else at risk. Also, by the time the baby comes, I think everyone will love him or her so much, they'll forget the other. My whole family is very close and they will welcome and love this baby and help me take care of it. My family is sort of goofy about babies—they adore them."

"That's good."

"Now we were talking about another little kid who will have a birthday soon. Where can I go to get Scotty a present? I may not have a car for the next week and there aren't any department stores out here on this ranch."

"Do I detect a bit of dislike for my ranch?"

"Moments like this, a ranch isn't the most practical place to be."

"You don't need to get Scotty anything. If you're here, he'll be delighted."

"If I'm here for his party, I want to get him a gift. He'll be easy to choose for and it'll be fun for me. Between now and then, will you go to Verity?"

"Probably. Our weather can swing from one extreme to another in the blink of an eye. You may be surprised, although I'd guess Little Rock weather can do about the same. I think we can get to Verity and you can find a present for Scotty there. Don't get him any big deal because he has a lot of toys."

She nodded. "Do you have any special paper plates and napkins and centerpiece for a party?"

"No, but Elise had some cowboy decorations—Scotty loves the cowboy stuff. Winnie the Pooh characters, too. I don't remember what we have, but they're in a couple of boxes in the attic."

"Tomorrow let's get them and see if there are things to use this year. I'd guess he'll have fun putting up birthday decorations—unless it will make you sad to put them up."

"No. If it gives Scotty pleasure, then it will be fun. He keeps me cheered. I can't be sad all the time with him around."

"I'm sure you can't," she said, slipping on her shoes. "Mike, it's past my bedtime. I should turn in."

"Sure," he said, smiling at her. He stood, stepping into his shoes, and draped an arm casually across her shoulders as they walked toward the stairs. "I'll never feel the same about rainstorms or snowstorms because they will remind me of when you came to visit. I'm glad Scotty and I were at Ed's station."

"You think *you're* glad—I don't know what I would have done."

"You'd have managed some way. This time of year if you travel by car, you should toss in some candy bars, some bottles of fruit juice, a blanket—emergency stuff if you get stranded. Heading west through the wide open spaces of Texas, New Mexico and Arizona, you can get caught in some big storms like this one. I'll load your car before you leave here."

"Thanks, Mike," she answered without thought. Most of her attention was on Mike being so close, his arm keeping her against his side. She had stopped their loving earlier, but it hadn't stopped her desire. She wanted him, longed for his kisses, wanted to be in his arms and make love. She tried to get her thoughts elsewhere, to do what would cause her the least grief when she had to tell him goodbye soon.

Tonight when she had held Scotty and read to him, it had been the first time it dawned on her that it would be difficult for her when she left Scotty as well as Mike.

Scotty was lovable and she was going to miss him. It had never occurred to her that a little almost-three-year-old might wrap around her heartstrings and make her want to stay. Father and son—she didn't want to get hurt by both of them. Each day spent with Mike and Scotty bound her closer to them.

At the door to her room, Mike stopped. As he turned to face her, he kept his arm around her which pulled her closer to him. "It's been a great day, Savannah."

"It has for me. You and Scotty are good company. Mike, he's so good. Does he ever give you trouble?"

"Oh, sure. He's a normal kid, but he's an only child and when it's a one-on-one with me, he's usually happy, cooperative, just plain fun to have around."

"That makes life nice."

"It helps. I couldn't deal with a bratty kid."

She smiled. "Yes, you could. I doubt if you would let that go on very long." Silence descended as she gazed into Mike's dark brown eyes. Her heart drummed. She wanted to kiss him more than anything. Soon she would be so alone. Just kisses—what could it hurt?

"Thanks again, Mike," she whispered, starting to step away, feeling warmth, friendship, excitement, all of it going out of her life. She turned back to look into his dark eyes. Slipping her arm around his neck, she kissed him full on the mouth.

The moment her lips touched his, his arm circled her waist and he pulled her tightly against him, wrapping both arms around her. He leaned over her, kissing her passionately.

She should have just said good-night and gone into her suite and closed the door and left him alone. He had been doing what she had asked—cool the relations between them and avoid anything that would lead to an affair. And then she had turned around and been the one who stirred them up again.

Thought fled as his kiss set her ablaze. Desire rocked her and she clung to him while he kissed her as if he would never get to kiss again.

She didn't know how much time passed, but finally she stepped away and gasped for breath.

"Why are you so appealing?" she asked.

"Savannah," he said, his voice thick and deep as he reached for her.

She sidestepped his grasp. "I shouldn't have started something. Good night, Mike. It was a wonderful day," she said breathlessly and rushed into her suite, closing the door to lean against it.

She shouldn't have kissed him. Desire had overthrown

wisdom. She moved around the room getting ready for bed, finally crawling beneath the sheets in the dark and longing to be in Mike's arms and sharing his kisses. She shouldn't have kissed him for either of their best interests. She had to move on even if she had to junk her car and buy another one. Her trunk was packed, filled with her things. She could ship them and fly to California and get a car out there. Mike could help her get her things shipped. Temptation was growing every hour she was with Mike, growing for both of them and becoming a good way for each of them to get hurt more.

Reminding herself this was best, she finally fell asleep to dream about Mike and being in his arms.

On Monday morning Mike left early with others who worked on the ranch, all of them on horseback. The gray day enveloped them with swirling snow and howling wind. Mike pulled up the fur collar of his heaviest parka, trying to block the wind. They passed a pickup where ranch hands were loading bales of hay. Mike and the men with him rode to the hangar where workers had cleared snow from a helipad and now loaded hay bales into the chopper.

"I'll go in the chopper," Mike said to Ray. "We'll look for any cattle cut off by the storm and we can drop the hay where it's needed. I'll keep in touch with you about where we are."

"We've got to get food to them and break the ice so they'll have water. This has been a helluva storm. The trucks can carry a lot of hay." Ray looked up. "I hope this snow ends soon. Be careful, Mike. This is bad weather to fly."

"We'll be careful, but we need to see about the livestock. I'll keep in touch in case you find any that have gotten where they can't get feed or water," Mike said, speaking louder over the wind howling around them. As Ray and the others left, Mike helped load two more bales into the helicopter and shortly they took off. Because of the wind and the cold, he kept his focus on ranching, on searching for cattle below, except he longed to be done and get back to the house where Savannah and Scotty waited and everything was warm.

Savannah dressed in a heavy blue sweater, jeans and her suede knee-length boots. Before she reached the kitchen she could smell the aroma of hot coffee and freshly baked bread. She took a deep breath, hoping she wouldn't be sick again.

Mike had already gone, but he had left coffee and warm bread that he must have made in a bread machine. She got a small glass of milk and sat to wait for Scotty to waken.

She spent the morning playing with Scotty, missing Mike and wondering when he would be back. After she fed Scotty lunch and ate a little herself, she lay down with Scotty, reading to him before he fell asleep for his afternoon nap.

She was on her way to the kitchen when she heard a truck. She looked out the back window and saw Mike park a pickup and get out, heading toward the back door. His broad-brimmed black hat was squarely on his head and he crossed the ground in long strides. Dark glasses hid his eyes. Her pulse quickened and she went to the back to greet him. He swept inside, bringing cold air with him as he shed his coat and hat, hanging them on a coat tree.

"The snow finally stopped falling, but it's damn cold out there. Was Scotty a good kid?" Mike asked, removing his sunglasses and pulling leather gloves from his hip pocket and placing them on a shelf by the door. Dark stubble covered his jaw. His cheeks were red from the cold. He looked gorgeous and she wanted him to cross the small space between them, and hug and kiss her, but that wasn't going to happen and she shouldn't want it to.

"He was wonderful, adorable. Of course he was good. I had fun with him."

"I needed to be out there this morning more than usual."

"Don't change your routine because of me. I'm fine here with Scotty." She glanced away for a moment. "I called the gas station where I left my car and no one answered, so I guess it's still closed."

"In this weather, I know it is. So are the roads. I'm going to shower and I'll be back soon."

When he reappeared in his bulky black sweater, jeans and boots, looking dynamic and bright-eyed as if he hadn't been out in the cold working for hours, his appeal heightened. Scotty was with him, holding a box of Lego blocks. He sat on the floor to build with them.

"Scotty, this is February and your birthday is coming up. Why don't we get out the birthday decorations and put them up?" Mike asked.

"Decorations—like Christmas?"

"That's right, except not as many as Christmas. Some balloons and characters you like. We'll have your aunts and uncles over and have a birthday cake."

"Yes," Scotty answered, standing to jump up and down. "A party—a party," he chanted, hopping in a circle.

"Cool it, Scotty. Also, we'll talk about what kind of cake you would like to have."

"Chocolate, hooray," he said, his brown eyes sparkling with such eagerness that she had to laugh.

"Want to go with us?" Mike asked and she nodded.

They went to the walk-in attic that had finished storage rooms with shelves. Mike led the way to boxes labeled Birthday Decorations.

For a moment Mike looked grim and a muscle worked in his jaw. She guessed he was remembering Elise and the two of them either getting the decorations out or putting them away, and Savannah hurt for him and wished she could say or do something to ease his pain, but she knew she couldn't.

"Mike, if you don't want to do this, we can get new decorations in town," she said.

"I'm okay. I'm just remembering the last time this stuff was touched was when Elise and I put it away."

"Sorry," Savannah said and turned, suspecting Mike might want to be alone.

Quietly, Mike carried boxes out of the attic and set them down to wipe away the dust. Then he brought them downstairs to the family room where everyone would gather for a party.

Opening a big box, he lifted out Happy Birthday banners. Mike brought in a ladder and climbed up to hang the banners where Savannah decided they should go.

Soon they had streamers and banners up. Savannah looked in the boxes and saw packages of paper plates and cups that had never been opened, but they would have been more appropriate when Scotty was two. "Mike, let's get Scotty some new plates with characters he likes."

"Sure," he said. "Just make a list of what you want when we go to town."

She watched Mike hold Scotty up so he could place a cardboard birthday cake on the mantel. Father and son looked happy and she had another twist to her heart. She was sorry for their loss, sad over her own, yet Mike was a good dad for Scotty and she hoped Mike would someday marry again.

In another box she found a stuffed bear holding a wrapped present. The bear was worn but still charming, so she looked around to let Scotty select a place to place it.

Mike took the bear from her hands. "Leave that in the box. It's old. It was Elise's when she was a child."

"Scotty might like it someday especially for that reason," she said gently. "If he grows up with it and learns his mother loved the bear as a little girl, it might be very special to him."

Mike inhaled deeply. "You're right," he said in a tight voice.

She saw Mike was hurting and instantly decided the bear wasn't that important. "Mike, let's put the bear back in the box. I intruded on your life with Scotty. I'll leave in a day or two and you'll have to look at the bear indefinitely. If it causes you to hurt, let's pack it away this year. One year won't matter. Scotty won't even remember."

"I think you're right about Scotty enjoying the bear now, and later appreciating and loving it because his mother did."

"Let it go," she whispered. "You don't need to hurt needlessly."

Mike gave her an intense look. She couldn't guess his feelings, but suddenly he hugged her. She held him tightly, suspecting he was having an emotional moment. She felt a tug on her leg and looked down to see Scotty, gazing up and trying to hug them, wanting to be part of the hug.

"C'mon, Scotty, we'll all hug," she whispered and turned slightly.

Mike looked at his son and picked him up, holding Scotty as he hugged Savannah. "We'll have a group hug," Mike said hoarsely. She felt Scotty's thin arm around her neck and he leaned against her as she held them tightly, wishing she could help erase Mike's hurt but knowing that couldn't happen, and having a brief fling with him wouldn't really help him and could hurt her even more. For the rest of his life there would be times he would hurt over Elise.

"Okay, folks, let's look at our work," Mike finally said, and she assumed he had his emotions under control. The hug broke up and she moved away from Mike, looking around at all the birthday decorations.

By the time they finished setting up and putting the boxes away, the sun was out in late afternoon. Scotty asked to go outside in the snow. They bundled up and in the next hour had another snowman and this time a snow dog beside it.

"Let's walk down to look at Rocky Creek across the front of the ranch. You'll be surprised how much the creek has gone down," Mike said.

Scotty ran ahead, jumping and then running in circles. As their steps crunched in the pristine snow, Scotty bent over something ahead. When they caught up with him, Mike stopped beside him and she saw the animal tracks in the snow.

"What are these?" Scotty asked.

Mike looked at paw prints. "Coyotes probably. We have plenty."

Scotty tried to hop on the prints and fell, laughing and rolling in the snow as Mike and Savannah walked past him.

"It's hard to dislike this snow and the icy cold when Scotty is having such a wonderful time," Savannah said.

"He's having the time of his life, just rolling around in freezing snow. Every day is something exciting for him. Right now, every day is something exciting for me," Mike added and she turned to look at him.

His brown eyes were warm, filled with desire. "It's

good to have you here," he said. "I want a date tonight. Hot chocolate, a dance, maybe a kiss."

"Mike, slow down," she said, laughing, trying to ignore her racing heartbeat or how badly she wanted to just answer yes and accept his offer. "Maybe you need to roll around in the snow and cool down, too." Her smile vanished. "Being here has been good for me. I'll always remember this time," she said, wondering how badly she would miss him when she left.

"We've had a fun time, which has been a huge surprise. I'll wonder whether you had a boy or girl and whether you stayed in California or went back home to Arkansas. I'd think you'd be happier in Arkansas, but that's just because I love home and family and wouldn't want to pack up and leave mine."

"That's probably what I'll do."

"If you drive back through here, call me," he said. "We can have lunch or something."

"Sure," she said, knowing she wouldn't. Once she left, she doubted if Mike would really care. As soon as some of the snow melted, Ed could probably get to his station and fix her car. She needed to wait now for Scotty's birthday party. After that, she would be gone.

How hard was it going to be to tell Mike and Scotty goodbye? If she stayed much longer, could she avoid making love with Mike, who had no place in his life for love and marriage?

Each time she thought how appealing Mike was, worry nagged at her that maybe she was misjudging another man as much as she had Kirk. How could she possibly really know about Mike in such a short time?

Five

"Mike, look at the creek," she said.

Ahead, a black ribbon of water gushed between snowy banks. The splashing stream looked ominous, even in the bright sunny day.

"Scotty, come here," Mike instructed and picked up his son to swing him onto his shoulders. "I don't want you to fall into the creek. That water is icy."

Scotty plunked Mike's wide-brimmed hat on his own head and wound his small fingers in Mike's curly hair. The pom-pom of Scotty's stocking cap kept Mike's hat from falling over Scotty's face, and she had to get a picture of the two of them. Wind caught locks of Mike's raven hair, blowing curls while Scotty smiled at her.

They slowed as they walked closer to the roaring creek. "Next summer when there is only a trickle of water running through the center of the dry creek bed, it will be difficult to believe that this is what it was like in winter," Mike said.

When the creek had swept over the bridge, debris had caught in the rails and long yellowed weeds had wrapped around the supports beneath the bridge. The bank was muddy where water had been higher and gone down slightly during late afternoon.

Savannah shivered. "Thank heavens the other bridge held when you drove across. If we would have to go into one of these creeks... I don't know if I could get out of the car. That looks threatening even now."

"We would have gotten out of the car and the guys would have fished us out, but I'm glad we didn't go in."

She could hear the force in Mike's voice and wondered if he got his way in most everything in his life. It was obvious from several instances that he was filled with self-confidence and accustomed to getting what he wanted.

Elise's loss had been the one thing that he hadn't been able to control. When Scotty started asking him questions about his mother, to have to try to explain to his young son would have been another heartbreak to a man who was filled with confidence, achievement and success. She could imagine Mike would never want to make himself vulnerable to such an emotional upheaval a second time. Pity any woman who ever fell in love with him and hoped to change him.

"I'm having this bridge rebuilt," Mike said. "I won't ever run that kind of risk again if I can avoid it. I should have replaced this bridge before now, but it's easy to get complacent and put off a job when the creek is almost a hundred percent dry some years. Sometimes in July, you can't fill a teacup out of the water in this creek."

She took a picture of the creek and then walked along the bank to see if she could get another picture of the bridge. In the sunlight something glittered in the mud along the bank and she ran her toe across it. Something

shiny and gold was half-buried in the mud where the creek
had been higher and now had receded. Curious, she picked
up a stick and scraped mud away.

"What did you find?" Mike asked, walking toward her,
holding Scotty's ankles lightly while the boy rode on his
shoulders.

"I found a ring."

Mike knelt to pick up some small rocks, then held out
his hand for Scotty. "Here, you can throw these into the
creek, but make sure they go into the creek. Do not hit me
or Miss Savannah with a rock."

"Thank you," Scotty said politely and took a rock to
toss it into the creek.

While Scotty tossed rocks, she knelt, holding the ring in
the rushing, muddy water to wash the mud away. "Look,
Mike," she said, standing. "What a pretty ring."

Mike moved closer to look at the gold ring sparkling in
the sunlight in the palm of her hand. The gold was inlaid
with chips of turquoise.

"That doesn't look like brass. I think you found a gold
ring."

She turned it over in her palm. The largest bit of turquoise was heart shaped.

"Someone lost this pretty ring."

"I'll be damned," he said. "Someone did lose it, but according to one of those old legends that has been passed
from generation to generation, there's a story about a
golden ring tossed into the creek." He turned the ring in her
palm. It left a smudge of mud, but the gold shone brightly.

"I'm amazed," Mike said, turning it again in her palm.
"Except this was probably lost pretty recently."

"Are you going to tell me the legend or not?" she asked,
laughing at him.

"There's an old Texas myth about a Kiowa maiden

whose true love made a ring for her. When the warrior was killed in battle, she didn't want to live. According to the myth, she tossed the ring into the creek, saying the finder would also find true love."

"It sounds like a myth, but that makes the ring fun to find," Savannah said.

"According to the legend, after tossing away her beloved ring, she was supposed to have walked off a cliff to her death."

"That's a sad ending," Savannah said, turning the ring in her hand again, watching it catch the sunlight that highlighted the gold.

"Well, it's a myth, I'm sure. There are no cliffs anywhere around here. Of course, that's never mattered in the legend surviving generation after generation."

"I want to think of the story of the ring as a legend come true. If it's true love for me, he has to be a nice family guy."

"Just ask up front. No one would hide their feelings on that subject," Mike said, and she laughed. "I figured the ring was as imaginary as the legend," he continued. "But this ring is very real." He smiled. "It has to be an interesting coincidence."

"Maybe," she said, "but I hope someday I'll find true love and I hope you do again, Mike." She looked into his eyes and momentarily was caught and held in a look she couldn't fathom as he gazed back at her.

"I hope we both do, too," he said in a husky voice. He ran his finger along her cheek. "You deserve better than you've gotten."

"Thanks. You and Scotty definitely do. You have each other and I'll have my baby. Those are the biggest blessings, Mike. Scotty, look what I found in the muddy creek bank." She held up the ring to show to Scotty.

He took it from her hand to slip it onto his small finger.

"Careful, Scotty," Mike said. "Afraid that's way too big for you, kiddo." Mike held out his hand and Scotty let it slide off his finger into it.

Mike reached for Savannah's right hand and slipped the ring on a finger.

"Perfect fit," he said, smiling at her as she laughed and wriggled her fingers.

"Actually, when it's washed, I think it will be very pretty."

"You found it so now it's yours. No telling how long it's been buried in the mud."

"This should be yours—it's on your ranch."

He shook his head. "You found it, so you keep it. And I hope you do find true love," he said, his voice changing to a deeper tone. As she looked up at him, she felt a squeeze to her heart. Mike leaned forward to kiss her briefly. When he stepped away, she smiled at him, glancing at Scotty to see him smiling.

"I'll have to tell my family," Mike said. "We've had a couple of other legends proven to be true, so maybe this will join those. Those were a little more possible than this one and based on family history, but this ring reminds me of the other legends of hidden treasures, a deed and a letter."

"Well, I expect my true love to appear soon," she said, laughing and wriggling her fingers as she looked at the ring. "There's nothing in that legend about being able to know it really is your true love, is there?" she asked, thinking it might be more important to be a better judge of character and no ring from a creek or an old legend would give her that.

"Savannah, with your looks, I would bet on you finding true love," Mike said as Scotty lobbed another small rock into the creek. "And everybody makes mistakes. It doesn't mean you'll keep making them."

"Thank you," she said, suddenly glad for the snowstorm that left her stranded to have a wonderful time with Mike and Scotty.

"Well, if this sun stays out and it doesn't start snowing again, the bridges will be passable. When we get back, I'll text Ed and see if he will open the gas station tomorrow. My guess is that he will."

Dread nipped at her, making her want to see time stop for just a short while. She loved being with Mike and Scotty, and it was going to be lonely without them and much harder to leave than it had been to tell Kirk goodbye after the hateful things he had said.

"Let's head home, Scotty," Mike said. As soon as they were a short distance from the creek, Mike swung Scotty to stand him on his own feet. Scotty ran ahead.

"I'm ready for a warm house and a hot dinner by a blazing fireplace," Mike said, draping his arm across her shoulders.

"Mike, I hope you marry again someday and have more children. You're a wonderful dad."

"Wow. Is this a proposal?" he asked, grinning. "Just kidding. Thank you," he said, before she could answer and tightened his arm across her shoulders to give her a slight squeeze.

"If I propose, you'll know it," she teased.

"Aw, shucks, lady. I thought we'd found a way to entertain ourselves tonight after Scotty goes to bed."

"Maybe you should run some more with Scotty and work off that energy you have."

"Later, I'll show you a much better way to get rid of some of this energy."

"Forget that one," she said, laughing at him, having fun

flirting with him and thinking every hour spent with Mike and Scotty bound her heart to them a little more. "Mike, you two are fun. I'll just never forget these few days and I'm glad to stay for his birthday. I'll think about what we can do for him that would be fun."

"Just keep it simple. He's only turning three. Right now it doesn't take much to make him happy."

"I guess not," she replied, laughing and looking at Scotty kicking snow into the air as he walked along. He fell and jumped up instantly to continue kicking more snow.

"Makes me wonder if my life was ever that simple," Mike said, watching his son. "I always had siblings complicating my life. Sometimes I'm sorry Scotty doesn't have a sibling, but he's happy."

"You'll marry again, Mike," she said. "He'll have a sibling."

"You think?" Mike said, focusing on her.

"Of course you will. You're young, good-looking, likeable, wealthy—"

"Damn, I didn't know I was such a paragon. I think we'll get back to this conversation after Scotty is down for the night."

"I think we won't. Enough said. You can forget what I said and it's changing as we speak. Besides, I've got lousy judgment in men."

He turned to her. "Don't carry that with you, Savannah," he said, suddenly sounding earnest. "You made a mistake. You probably learned from it and you'll also probably never make one like it again. You're an intelligent woman—trust yourself."

She looked up at him, for a moment feeling a twist to her heart. "It's not that easy anymore. I'm going to need some time."

They were silent the rest of the way to his house. After

shedding all the outer clothing, Mike went to the kitchen to start dinner while Savannah headed to her suite to wash her hands and wash the ring again.

When she returned to the kitchen, she smiled at Scotty in his high chair and held out the ring for Mike. "Look how beautiful it is, very simple, very pretty. It has a date engraved on it," she said, handing him the ring.

Mike looked at the date and his head jerked up as he met her gaze. "It's from 1861—I can't believe it's really that old."

She shrugged. "That's the date."

He handed back the ring and she slipped it on. "Enjoy it. After dinner I'll call Lindsay and tell her about the ring. She'll be shocked you ever found any such thing."

"Miss Savannah, will you play with me?" Scotty asked.

"I'd love to, but I'm going to help your daddy fix dinner—"

"Go play," Mike told Savannah. "I'm just heating up another chicken and noodle casserole."

Scotty grinned as she scooped him out of his high chair. She set him down and he ran to get a game.

After dinner they played more games with Scotty until Mike told him it was time for bed and they all headed upstairs. Once Scotty was tucked in bed, Savannah sat down to read to Scotty again. After two books, she kissed Scotty and left so that Mike could read one last story before good-night kisses.

When Mike returned they sat on the family room floor near the roaring fire and she listened while he called Lindsay to tell her about the gold ring.

As they talked, he paused and turned to Savannah. "Lindsay wants you to take a picture of it and text it to her."

"Sure," Savannah said, grabbing her phone. In minutes Savannah looked up. "Tell Lindsay she should have a picture now."

She heard Lindsay yell loudly enough to carry clearly over his phone, and Mike laughed. "Hey, my ear. Yes, it's real and we're not playing a joke. She found it embedded in the muddy bank of the creek where the water had risen and then receded."

After a few more minutes he told his sister goodbye. "I'm going to let her tell my brothers or I'll be on the phone all night, although they won't have as many questions about it as Lindsay. Since no money was involved, they'll shrug it off as sheer coincidence and forget it."

"I have part of a legend now," she said, looking at the gold. "I fully expect to find my true love someday," she said and laughed. "Today has been fun."

"I think so and you're way too pretty to not find your true love," he replied.

"Thank you," she said as they smiled at each other.

Mike glanced around at the room, full of decorations for Scotty's party. "This room looks great for a birthday party. Thanks for your help. I wouldn't have done this alone because I wouldn't have known where to start. Scotty loves it and is excited about his birthday. It's nice, Savannah."

"I'm glad. I've been looking on my laptop for chocolate-cake recipes."

"Wait a minute." Mike left and she heard pots and pans and got up to see what he was doing. She found him in the pantry. He had three cookbooks and what looked like a scrapbook.

"I thought you might want to look at some of these. These are Elise's recipe books."

"Perfect," she said, carrying the books back to the family room. She placed them on a game table and sat down with one and flipped through it.

"While you do that, I'm going to check on Ray and the livestock and see if they're home now or still out. I left them early today."

"That's because I'm here and interfering with you."

He stood near her with his phone in hand. He looked at her and put the phone in his pocket, then touched her chin lightly. Tilting her face up, he looked into her eyes.

"You have never interfered in any way whatsoever," he said, looking intently at her. His gaze lowered to her mouth and she couldn't get her breath.

"That's good," she whispered, barely able to get out the words.

He leaned down, his lips brushing hers lightly and her heart slammed against her ribs. His mouth opened hers as he kissed her.

While they kissed, his hands slipped beneath her arms and he pulled her up into his embrace.

Desire ignited, heating her, causing her to cling to him tightly and kiss him in return. His warm body was hard against her, his kiss breathtaking. She wanted him more than ever and realized the risks to her heart climbed with each second they kissed.

At the moment, she was willing to risk her heart. She wanted Mike to kiss her as much as she wanted to hold and kiss him. He was too many wonderful things rolled into six feet of sexy male and her desire had built steadily every minute they had been together.

Would she look back with regret that she had not risked more of herself and her heart? Maybe this time was a once in a lifetime event. She stopped thinking and kissed him fervently. He yanked his sweater off, dropping it and reaching to pull her sweater over her head to toss it away and she gazed into his dark eyes that held fires in their depths. She ran her hands lightly across his chest that was muscled, solid, tapering to a narrow waist and a flat, muscled stomach. He was hard, handsome, too appealing, and she inhaled deeply, looking up to meet his hungry gaze.

The desire in his expression shook her as he unfastened her bra and it fell away. He cupped her breasts, caressing her, holding her, leaning down to kiss each breast.

Moaning softly with pleasure, she clutched his muscled shoulder and ran her other hand through his hair.

"Mike, please," she whispered, wanting his kisses, wanting his loving. In moments of passion she couldn't guard her heart.

His hands were at her waist and in seconds her jeans fell around her ankles. His hands followed them, caressing her, sliding lower over her, between her thighs, stroking her while he kissed her.

She moved beneath his touch, desire engulfing her. She still wore boots and her jeans wrapped around her legs. "Mike, wait," she whispered, trying to gather her wits and do what was practical.

"Wait," she whispered again. As she tried to get her breath and talk, she tugged up her jeans, aware of Mike's steady gaze. As if to emphasize what she said, his cell phone played a tune. Mike ignored it, still studying her, looking at her as if memorizing how she looked.

"Savannah," he whispered, reaching for her.

She shook her head. "Get your phone, Mike, or I will. We'll wait for a time with fewer interruptions and when I can think things through. I'll be here all week."

He still stared at her with a hungry look that made it difficult to stick by what she said to him. She grabbed up her bra and sweater and turned away, walking away from him before they were back in each other's arms.

What she had said to him had been sensible, what she should have done. It was not what she wanted. She wanted

Mike's loving. If she gave herself to him, how much would she give her heart to him at the same time?

As he answered his phone, his voice was husky and quiet. He watched her with that solemn, hungry look that made her heartbeat speed. He was still aroused, ready to love, obviously wanting her.

From the first moment Mike had come into her life, he had changed it and taken away a lot of her hurt. She wanted him. Was it just one more big mistake she was about to make in her life?

As she stood looking into his dark eyes, she felt drawn to him. His desire was palpable, tugging at her. She tingled from his every touch while her lips still could feel the pressure of his.

With ragged breathing, she took a step toward him, realized she was going right back to him when she shouldn't. She turned, forcing herself to move, every inch of her wanting to return to his arms, but this wasn't the time. She needed to think because if and when she did yield to loving, it was going to cause her a lot of turmoil.

She went upstairs to her suite, closing the door and trying to get a sensible perspective, hoping to cool so she could go back into a room with him without walking straight into his arms.

How hard would it be to drive memories of him out of her life? To tell Mike and Scotty goodbye? Scotty had become a factor in the equation because he had stolen her heart away, too. Could she view them as simply two wonderful beings that she had had the good fortune to meet, get to know and then tell them goodbye forever?

Common sense said it would be a lot easier if she and Mike did not make love.

She took a deep breath. Could she resist if he kissed her again? Did she want to resist? Making love with Mike at this time in her life might help heal some of her heartache over her broken engagement. Each time she thought that, she also thought how much more difficult it would be to tell Mike goodbye. The question constantly nagged her now—was this more poor judgment about a man? She couldn't really know Mike well in the time they had been together.

She needed to resist him for some strong reasons, for his sake and for her own. If only she could hold to what she knew was best for both of them. Otherwise, she would just be compounding the hurt they each already suffered.

Six

On Tuesday morning, Mike and Ray each wielded chain saws, cutting fallen tree limbs, while three more men carried the logs to the back of a pickup. Mike paused to gaze at a smashed barbed wire fence while two men worked to erect a new section of fence where the tree limbs had fallen. He looked up at the tall oak that stood over the fence.

Ray straightened. "A couple more big limbs and we'll be through."

"I'm still surprised the limbs broke. This tree has been here since I bought the place and I don't recall this happening before," Mike said, looking up at a tall oak with thick branches.

"We had a lot of ice and a lot of wind. Bad combination," Ray remarked before bending to continue sawing a downed branch. "Those limbs fell squarely on that part of the fence and took the gate down with it. Ice made it all heavy."

Mike returned to work, glad to have a chain saw for the job and that they didn't have cattle in this section when the fence went down.

"So far, the main bridge and this are the worst damages we have?" he asked.

Ray nodded. "Since you're replacing the main bridge across the creek, we put up barricades and a sign in case any stranger tried to cross. Not likely we'll have anyone."

"No, but I'm glad for the barricades."

"Some lines were down, but they're getting fixed today. We've got hay out and ice chopped for the livestock and the men are still checking on them."

"All right. Let's get this done," Mike said, resuming sawing up another fallen limb. He focused on what he was doing and when he had the logs cut, he moved on to another limb to cut more while a man began stacking logs to carry a pile to the truck.

Mike worked until midafternoon, then climbed into the pickup. He and the men had driven out here before dawn and he was ready to get back home to Scotty and Savannah.

He wanted her in his bed and he thought it was only a matter of time. He felt she was just a breath away from seduction. She made it obvious that desire consumed her at moments, too. At the same time, guilt fell over him because he didn't want to add to her pain. For that matter, he didn't want to add to his own. He couldn't love her the way she deserved with a whole heart, the way he had fallen in love with Elise. It would be a temporary fling, something that would make him happy briefly, but could hurt Savannah in far too many ways.

He sighed and shook his head. He needed to leave her alone, let her go on with her life and heal in her own time and way without adding more hurt.

She had driven out of the storm into his life and changed so much about his daily existence. He liked having her around and so did Scotty.

Was he ready to get out now? To start seeing more friends and socializing more? Or was it just that he liked Savannah staying in his house and with him constantly?

He suspected the latter because he didn't feel ready for any serious relationship or even any light entanglement. He knew full well that Savannah didn't want one, either, and that made a huge difference in being with her. He could fully relax because she didn't want commitment. They weren't going to fall in love with each other. She understood his loss and he understood all that had happened to her.

She shouldn't blame herself for misjudging the guy she had planned to marry, but Mike didn't blame her for worrying about her brothers. If someone got his sister pregnant and then told her he didn't want the baby, Mike would have a difficult time ignoring the whole thing. What a jerk Savannah had fallen in love with and she didn't need any further complications in her life.

For different reasons they each didn't want commitment, involvement, a lasting relationship. But the warmth, the reaffirmation of loving, the fun and release, the excitement—he thought she wanted that as much as he did. If he had tried, he thought last night he could have overcome her reluctance, but he had done the right thing in leaving her alone.

She had driven some of his grief away. He hoped she would find real happiness and someone to love her, a dad for her baby. He recalled watching her read to Scotty as Scotty had turned locks of her hair in his tiny fingers. That had stirred mixed feelings in him—she would make a good mother for Scotty was one thought. Another was a deep ache that it wasn't Elise. At moments life seemed tough, but that was just part of living. Mike wished Savannah would be here longer and not going so far away.

The idea of a marriage of convenience occurred to him, but he rejected it for a lot of reasons. It wouldn't be fair to her. She deserved so much more. They would both be tied into a relationship and Mike wasn't ready for that. He didn't want any marriage of convenience and she probably wouldn't, either.

Feeling eagerness to be home grow, Mike pulled beneath the roof over the drive by the side door, locked up and went inside. He heard Savannah's laughter and followed the sound, stepping into the family room. She sat on the floor with Scotty with a board game between them. Scotty lay on his stomach with his feet in the air while he studied the board. When she looked up, her big blue eyes focused on him and excitement bubbled in Mike.

Scotty jumped up and ran to him. "Daddy!" he exclaimed. Mike caught him to swing him up and hug him. Scotty hugged Mike, his small arms wrapping around Mike's neck. "We're playing a game."

"It's fun. Come play with us," Savannah said.

"You finish this game and then I'll play," Mike said, setting Scotty on his feet. Scotty ran back to plop down cross-legged and look at the board again.

Mike sat on the floor beside them. "You're nice to come home to," he said and she looked up.

"You're a family man to the core, Mike. That's nice of you to say."

"I meant it," he said, wondering whether she thought he was just trying to make her feel good.

"Thank you kindly. I'll remember you telling me long after I'm gone," she said. "We're in a big game."

"I'm sure. Scotty is a little competitive."

"I wonder where in the world he gets that," she said and Mike grinned.

"When you're ready, you can take my place so you can play with Scotty."

"Finish your game. I'll play the next one," Mike said, his cell jingling. He pulled it out of a pocket and glanced at the screen. "Ed. This will be about your car." Mike answered and was silent while he listened.

"Okay, Ed. Whatever you need to do. Russ is going to call me?" He was quiet a moment, then said, "Sure. Thanks so much." As soon as Mike told Ed goodbye and put his phone away, he turned to her.

"Your car was badly damaged. It's beyond Ed's equipment and expertise, so he had it towed to Verity to a dealer there. Russ will call me after he's looked at the car and figures out what you'll need, but it may be Wednesday before he can get to it because of this storm. He's backed up with customers with car problems. Sorry, this may take longer and it may be more expensive."

"I'm just thankful to be where I can get help. I still can't bear to think how close I came to getting caught out in that storm with no help."

"Just forget it. Don't think about what didn't happen," he said.

"It may be more worthwhile for me to buy another car. I didn't pay attention—is Verity a good place to get a car or should I go back to Fort Worth or Dallas?"

"It depends on what you want," he said. "There is a good dealership in Verity. But Ed will see to it that the mechanic calls you with a report and estimate before he does any work to the car."

"Oh, good. Did anyone say anything about the roads today?"

"I'm guessing by now we can get through, but I don't

know the official answer. If we don't get more snow, what we have will melt and be gone, particularly on the roads. It'll refreeze at night, but by tomorrow afternoon, the roads should be clear enough to travel. If we can, do you want to go to town tomorrow afternoon?"

"That's fine with me."

"And that is more than fine with me," he said. "I'll go see what I can rustle up for dinner tonight. We have a freezer full. You and Scotty just keep playing."

Mike left, finding a pot roast with vegetables that he placed in the oven. He also found a pie that he'd serve for dessert. Over a counter dividing the kitchen from the family room, he could see Savannah and Scotty. Savannah was laughing, Scotty looked happy and again, Mike was glad Savannah was with them.

Mike set the table and poured ice water into tumblers, then turned and found Savannah standing a few feet away, watching him. "You're doing a fine job."

"I've learned how. If we don't get more snow, Millie will be here tomorrow and the food will improve."

"It doesn't need to improve. It's delicious and I'm impressed with your culinary skills."

"I'd rather you'd be impressed with some other skills I have," he said quietly, stepping close to her. "I'll show you later."

She smiled at him and fanned herself. "I can't wait," she said in a sultry voice. She glanced into the other room at Scotty. "You better get in there," she said in a practical tone. "It's your turn to play now, so don't disappoint him."

"I'll go play. We have another twenty minutes to wait while everything heats up. I'll put rolls in during the last ten minutes."

"I can do that. Where are they?"

"In a bag in the freezer right at the front. Just holler if you can't find them."

"Daddy, it's your turn."

"I'm coming, Scotty," he said. "Thanks for playing with him."

"I had fun," she said. "You better get in there. He's coming to get you."

"Here I am and I'll race you back there," Mike said. Scotty hurried to the board and threw himself down to laugh.

"I beat you, Daddy."

"So you did." Mike sat on the floor, aware Savannah came to sit near them and watch. He thought about being in the kitchen with her. Whenever he flirted with her, she would flirt in return and then end it, or if they kissed, her responses were brief. Was she scared to let go and trust herself with having fun flirting and kissing? He had always trusted his judgment and he had a feeling this misjudgment of her ex-fiancé had shaken her badly. He looked at her as she sat watching Scotty, but as if she felt his gaze on her, she turned to look at him. For a moment the air between them seemed to sizzle. He saw her draw a deep breath and thought she felt it, too.

He wanted to kiss her. Whether wisdom or folly, he definitely wanted to hold and kiss her.

After a time, she went to the kitchen and he could hear her putting the rolls in the oven.

Mike let Scotty win, aware his son was getting better at the game. "So how many times have you won today, Scotty?"

"I won this morning, this afternoon and I won once with Miss Savannah and I won now."

"So that's how many times?" Mike asked. Scotty counted on his fingers and then held up four fingers.

"I have won four times."

"Very good," Mike said. "That's right, Scotty. Let's go wash our hands because I'm guessing it's almost time to eat." He stood and they headed to a bathroom.

All through dinner Mike was aware of Savannah. He was eager to be alone with her, yet wanted his time with Scotty. He got Scotty ready for bed and then let him pick out three books for Savannah to read to him.

Mike turned down his bed and listened to her read a familiar Dr. Seuss story that Scotty loved. Mike sat near them, looking at Savannah in the rocking chair, Scotty on her lap as she read to him. He toyed with a long lock of her hair, turning it in his fingers while he looked at the page as she read.

When she reached the end of the page, Scotty turned the page for her.

"Thank you, Scotty," she said and continued to read.

By the third book, Scotty's eyes were beginning to close. Mike watched Scotty fight going to sleep. Even so, before she reached the last page, Scotty fell asleep.

"I can put him in bed," she said, starting to gather up Scotty. Mike stepped to her quickly to take Scotty.

"Oh, no, you don't," he said softly. "Don't pick him up. Asleep, he's a dead weight and much heavier. Let me carry him always."

"You're babying me."

"And you should let me," he said, leaning down and looking into her wide blue eyes.

"Is the story over?" Scotty asked, his eyes fluttering open.

"Yes, Scotty," Savannah said. "You fell asleep on the last page."

Scotty smiled at her. "Kiss me good-night, Miss Savannah."

She leaned forward to kiss his cheek. Scotty wrapped thin arms around her neck and kissed her cheek. "Night, Miss Savannah. I love you."

As her eyes widened, she brushed curls off his forehead. "I love you, too, Scotty," she said softly. As if punched in the chest, Mike ached. There was still a void in Scotty's life that he couldn't totally fill and it hurt each time he was reminded.

"Good night, Scotty," she said as Mike took him from her arms and placed him in bed, tucking him in.

"Night, Scotty. It's been a fun day," Mike said, sitting on the side of the bed and holding Scotty's hand. "Let's say bedtime prayers. You say them tonight."

He listened to Scotty's childish voice in the prayer that he himself had said as a small boy. "Night, Daddy," Scotty said, putting his arms around Mike's neck to hug him and kiss his cheek. "Daddy, tell me one quick story."

Mike held Scotty's hand and spoke softly, telling the story of three billy goats. He was only halfway through when Scotty was breathing deeply and evenly, his lashes dark above his cheeks as he slept. Mike brushed another kiss on his cheek, pulled the covers up and tiptoed out, checking the monitor and switching off the light, leaving night-lights burning.

He went downstairs and found Savannah standing at the glass wall, gazing out at the snow-covered yard where yard lights cast long shadows on the glistening snow.

"Scotty loves you, Savannah," Mike said as pain again squeezed his heart.

"He's precious, Mike. You're so fortunate to have him."

"I think so, too. You're good with him and I'll bet you're very good at the job you do."

"I hope so. I like it and the challenges, the precious little babies."

"Since you won't have even worked a year when you have your baby, can you get off for maternity leave?"

"Different systems have different policies and rules, but Mom said to just quit and come home if I want and let them handle the bills the first year so I can stay home. I'll take them up on their offer if Dad is agreeable and I imagine he will be. When I go back to work, I think Mom will watch my baby during the hours I work."

Mike nodded, thinking about what she said. There was only the light from the fire and one small lamp on in the room and he had soft music in the background. The dim light highlighted her prominent cheekbones, showed her wide blue eyes and gave a rosy cast to her cheeks. Her blond hair fell over her shoulders and she looked gorgeous.

Desire stole his thoughts and held him focused on her. Forgetting their conversation, he wanted her softness pressed against him. He longed to feel her warmth, smell her enticing perfume, see her lips part for his kiss. Just thinking about kissing her made him want to more than ever.

Was he vulnerable just because he hadn't made love in a long time? Or was it Savannah who sent his pulse flying and was pure temptation, stirring desire with just a glance? He couldn't answer his own questions. All he knew was he wanted her when he shouldn't. And he should exercise self-control and leave her alone.

Savannah turned to walk away. The way Mike looked at her stirred longing. Did she want to risk trusting her judgment about him? There was no way to keep from being shaken by her blindness with Kirk. Before she had been incredibly blind, seeing only what she wanted to see. Mike had urged her to trust herself, but that was easy advice from him because he radiated self-confidence.

In some ways she felt as if she had known him a long time. Could she make love and then tell him goodbye and never look back?

"You look deep in thought," he said, sitting close. "What's on your mind?"

"I'm thinking what I want to do between now and the time I leave here," she said, looking into brown eyes that could captivate and hold her. Her heart drummed and she wanted to be in his arms.

Mike pulled off his boots and set them beside his chair. He stood and left, changing the music to ballads and coming back to stop in front of her.

"Take off your boots and dance with me," he said. "Give me your foot," he instructed and she raised her foot for Mike to tug off her boot. He did the next one and then held out his hand to take hers.

They walked off the rug to where the hardwood floor was bare and there was room to dance. Mike switched off the lamp, leaving only the light from the fire and light from outdoors that spilled through the glass walls. Outside, everything was blanketed with snow while overhead the sky was a solid black.

Mike drew her into his arms to dance. His gaze was on her and her heart drummed. As she looked into Mike's eyes, she thought about kisses. Her heart beat faster and her gaze lowered to his lips.

"Savannah," he whispered while he wrapped his arms around her to kiss her. In seconds, he picked her up to carry her to the sofa where he sat with her on his lap.

At that moment she felt as if she never wanted to leave his embrace. Mike had grown important to her, which scared her because soon she would have to leave, but tonight she was in his arms, holding him and returning his kisses and she no longer wanted to think about tomorrow.

As he tightened his arms, he leaned over her, kissing her passionately. While one arm banded her waist to hold her close, his other hand caressed her nape lightly, making feathery strokes that built the blaze she felt.

"Mike," she whispered while she showered kisses on his face, feeling the faint stubble, still detecting his after-shave, wanting to make him feel what she felt, want what she wanted, while at the same time caution urged her to stop. She slipped her hand down to unfasten buttons and then tugged his shirt free and tossed it aside.

The excitement of just touching him shook her. As lightly as possible, she ran her hands over his strong chest that was sculpted, solid muscle. As she spread her palm against his chest, she felt his heart beating. Was the beat faster because of her hands on him? Her fingers drifted lower to unbuckle his belt and pull it free. She heard the clatter when she dropped it out of the way.

"Mike, tonight I need you," she whispered. She opened her eyes to look into his as he raised his head a fraction.

Winding his fingers in her hair, he continued to gaze into her eyes.

"I want you, Savannah. Desire has not been part of my life for a long, long time, but suddenly I'm fully alive again. I want you and you can't imagine how much. At the same time, I don't want to hurt you. I can't give you any kind of commitment."

She looked into his brown eyes. His honest and up-front words hurt in a way, yet she understood because she wasn't looking for commitment, either.

At the same time, she knew her own feelings and views and she couldn't take intimacy lightly. It would be binding to her heart—she just didn't know to what extent.

As they gazed into each other's eyes, desire heightened,

filling her, making her want his vitality, his loving, his kisses. If she wanted to stop, now was the time.

She couldn't be in the same room with him without a tingling awareness of him tugging at her. Longing for him had built steadily from that first encounter, growing with each hour together. She wanted to kiss, to touch and to hold him—for just a little while to forget all the problems she and Mike faced. She understood the physical hunger he felt. Passion was a confirmation of part of the best of life, the hope and exuberance, the energy and rapture.

Aware of his need and understanding what tonight meant to each of them, she thought about the risks to her heart. At the moment, she needed him totally and she was willing to accept the risks. His mouth covered hers and her thoughts fled again, driven away. His breath was hot, damp and sensual on her sensitive skin.

He drew off her sweater and her bra, tossing them aside. He cupped her breasts in his callous hands, caressing her with his thumbs, showering kisses on her while her hands roamed over his shoulders and back.

Pleasure streaked from her head to her toes as she gave herself to loving, her hands moving lightly over him, her lips following. Showering kisses across his chest, she slipped off his lap to stand and tug on him so he came to his feet. He framed her face with his hands, his dark gaze enveloping her.

"I don't want to hurt you," he said in a deep, hoarse tone. "I want you to be sure about what you want to do." She shook with longing. Mike was special. Would she fall in love if they made love tonight? Could she take physical intimacy as lightly as he would? He swung her up into his arms.

"Let's find a bedroom," he said, carrying her across the hall to a guest suite. As he walked along, he kissed her.

Savannah had her arm around his neck and she clung to him. He set her on her feet beside a bed and wrapped her in his embrace as he continued kissing her possessively.

She lost all sense of time. They had been together seconds; they had been together for a long time. She felt his fingers at her waist and then her jeans fell around her ankles and she stepped out of them.

She heard his deep intake of breath. His hands were on her hips as he looked at her. He peeled away her lacy bikini and tossed it away. Mike leaned away slightly to look at her in a slow, lingering perusal that made her blush and tremble beneath his touch and gaze.

"Oh, Mike," she whispered as he showered kisses on her throat, moving lower. Her hands fluttered over him. "This is so foolish and so wonderful," she whispered without thinking. "I want to make love all night."

He kissed her passionately, leaning over her so she was pressed against him. One arm held her close while his other hand roamed down her back and over her bottom, caressing and stroking her, building more fires, making her gasp with pleasure and thrust against him.

She kissed him back, wanting to melt him, to drive all the hurts away for a few hours and to take all of Mike's attention for tonight.

He picked her up and laid her down on the bed, his hands and mouth erasing all rational thought, making her want him desperately.

She was astounded by his boundless energy, his control as he continued to kiss and caress her even when she was more than eager and ready for him.

She showered kisses on him, caressing him, rubbing against him, using her hands and mouth to drive him over the edge and make him lose the iron will that held him in check.

Finally, he moved between her legs and entered her, slowly filling her. As she arched to meet him, his dark gaze was as binding as their physical union.

"Mike," she whispered, pulling him to her, moving with him and crying out because she wanted him, all of him. He kissed her, his control still holding while she clung to his damp shoulders and held him tightly until finally he let go to pump hard and fast, building her need.

"Mike!" she cried his name again as she sought release until her own control shattered. Satisfaction burst over her and ecstasy enveloped her. She felt Mike's shuddering climax, his wild thrusts heightening her pleasure. Her heart pounded and her pulse roared in her ears, while she gasped for breath.

Gradually, they slowed, still moving together, hearts beating in unison. She held him tightly, wanting to make the moment last as long as possible, wishing she could make the night last for hours and hours.

At this moment she was in paradise with him. Loving made her world marvelous. Another fantasy, but briefly she basked in it and relished what she had found with him.

When she showered kisses on his jaw and cheek, he turned his head to kiss her on her mouth. It was a kiss of happiness, a kiss that made her feel cherished and she clung to him tightly. He raised his head to smile at her and then kissed her again.

He rolled on his side, keeping her with him, their legs entwined. She still held him tightly and they were silent. She didn't want to talk, to say anything to destroy the moment that bound her to Mike in a union that made everything seem right.

For a while they stayed enveloped in the cocoon of silence, hearts beating together while they held each other close.

"Saturday night when you rescued me, I thought that

other than being home in Arkansas, I was in the best place in the whole world that I could have been for that night, but this is better."

"Damn straight it's better," he whispered, stroking her long hair away from her cheek. "I want you right here the rest of the night."

"We don't have to worry about that now," she answered, trailing her fingers over his chest as she snuggled against him.

"You take my breath," he said, kissing her lightly.

"I hope so," she said, smiling at him. "I want to dazzle you, make you forget everything else and I want you to do that to me—as you did tonight. All the problems, the hurts, everything for a few moments are forgotten and cease to exist. I know they'll come back, but, hey, for right now, they're banished from my life and that's fantastic."

He smiled at her. "Living in fantasy?"

"A sexual fantasy—that's not so bad."

"No. How about heading up to my bathroom, soaking in a hot tub and then seeing if you like my bed?"

Relaxed, she was in a state of euphoria, happy in his arms, barely thinking about what she said to him. For this night, everything was right and she wanted to enjoy the moment fully. Tomorrow would come all too soon.

"Good idea, Mike. In a little while. For now, let's stay the way we are."

"Whatever pleases you pleases me just fine," he replied, still toying with her hair.

They stayed locked in each other's embrace for the next half hour and then she slipped out of bed, tugging the sheet around her.

"I'll get my clothes and head upstairs."

"I can carry you."

"So you have that much energy left. I'll have to do better next time to really wear you out," she teased.

"Just give it a try," he countered, pulling on his jeans. "I welcome that challenge."

"I'll bet you do," she replied, laughing as they left the room to gather her clothes.

As they headed upstairs, Savannah said, "I've never seen your bedroom or bathroom."

"I'll give you the grand tour."

They entered the sitting room of the master suite, a glass wall on one side offering a panoramic view of the front of the ranch. Bookshelves lined another wall and the room held a huge television, a large wooden desk, leather chairs and two sofas. She went with him into a bedroom with a king-size bed that had a high antique headboard. A box filled with Scotty's toys was in the corner. Nearby, a door opened into a closet that was large enough to have held her bedroom. His bedroom had a glass wall that overlooked the east side of the ranch and opened out onto a wide balcony filled with wrought-iron furniture. Mike pressed a button and shutters slid down to block the transparency of the glass wall.

"That's better. I'd prefer some privacy here. I have plans," she said and he smiled.

"We'll see if they match my plans." Mike picked her up and carried her into a bath that was even bigger than she had guessed it would be. It had potted palms, mirrors, a large shower and a sunken tub. Mike set her on her feet and turned on faucets.

She spent the next half hour in the tub with him, listening to him talk about growing up in Texas, telling him about her life in Arkansas.

They made love again several times before dawn and as the room grew a degree lighter, Mike fell asleep in her arms.

She held him, lightly combing his black curls off his forehead. Had she filled her life this night with a temporary joy that would help her get over the pain of her broken engagement? Or was she falling in love with Mike and increasing her loss a hundred times over?

Seven

Savannah stirred and Mike's arm tightened around her. She smiled at him. "I'm really getting up and out of this bed. I want to go to my own room."

"Stay in here with me," he whispered.

"Sorry. We can discuss that later. Right now, I'm headed to my room and I'll see you when you get back from work this afternoon."

"Rats. This isn't what I'd planned," he teased.

"Look the other way," she said, stepping out of bed and yanking up her clothes.

"Not for anything will I look the other way," he replied.

Hiding her grin, she hurried out of the room without looking back. She yanked on her jeans and sweater in the sitting room before grabbing the rest of her things and rushing down the hall to her room.

Almost an hour later after she had showered and dressed for the day, she went downstairs. When she entered the kitchen Mike stood near the sink talking to a short, gray-haired woman with an apron over black slacks and a white blouse. She couldn't take her eyes off Mike, though. Dressed in a long-sleeved navy denim shirt, jeans and boots, he looked gorgeous.

Scotty sat at the table with a bowl of oatmeal in front of him. "Good morning," she said, giving him a light hug.

"Savannah, meet Millie Anders who cooks for me. Millie, this is Savannah Grayson."

"So glad to meet you," Millie said. "What can I get you for breakfast? We have bagels, orange juice—"

"Thank you," Savannah said. "I'll help myself and just get a bagel and maybe a little glass of milk."

Millie smiled and said she was heading to the market and would be back in a couple of hours.

As Savannah toasted a bagel and selected a strawberry jam, Mike's cell phone rang and he answered to talk a moment. She wasn't paying attention until she heard her name. "Yes, Savannah found a gold ring in the creek. This is the year for the legends. It's gold. I'm still at the house. I told Ray I'd be late this morning."

He paused to listen before he continued, "We'll stop in Poindexter's and let them look at it, but I'm sure it's gold and it's been in the creek." Mike listened a moment. "Sure. I'll get back with you later. Okay." He put away his phone and smiled. "That was my brother, Jake. Lindsay has sent a text to each one of them with the picture of the ring you found. They will want to talk to you and see the ring. It's interesting to have part of a legend turn out to be real. When you do find your true love, you'll have to get in touch with me so I'll know that the old legend is based in fact."

She laughed and turned the gold ring on her finger. "I

don't need to find true love, but I love the ring and the legend is fun to me."

"Even though my brother Josh is out of town, he'll still call about the ring. I'll give him an hour or two."

She sat down at the table with her bagel and a glass of milk. "As long as I'm here, they can all look at the ring."

"They will in due time. You'll get a lot of attention."

"I hope the birthday boy gets the attention and I imagine he will since he's the only one in that generation in your family. That makes him special to everyone."

"Does it ever—just wait until you see them with him. He's a good kid or he would be spoiled rotten by the attention he gets from them."

"Scotty isn't spoiled. He's a sweetie."

"I think so." Mike glanced around and then leaned closer to her. "So is someone else," he said, looking intently at her mouth and making her think of his kisses.

"Maybe you better sit up straight again and let me eat my breakfast." As he moved away, she took a dainty bite of bagel, relieved that it didn't seem to upset her stomach.

Mike's cell rang again and he walked away from the table as he took the call. In a short time he returned to sit again.

"That was Russ about your car. They're backed up because of the storm and wrecks. It may be several more days before he can even look at it. I told him okay because that's the best place to take it unless you have it towed to Dallas."

"As long as you don't mind a houseguest," she said.

He smiled. "I'll show you later how I feel about that," he said softly.

"Is that a promise?" she asked, flirting with him, teasing and having fun, yet at the same time, too, aware that another night of lovemaking could make her unable to say goodbye. Making love, getting to know Mike intimately was a huge risk to her heart.

"Definitely. If we were alone, I'd show you now."

"We're not alone, so you sit back." She ate about one-fourth of the bagel and had enough, but no morning sickness had hit yet and it was a relief. "I think I'm doing better with a bagel. I'm almost scared to say that."

Mike smiled. "Good. We have a freezer that has a shelf filled with bagels. Now I know what to do with them."

"More than a week of bagels? I don't think so," she replied.

"Maybe more than a week," Mike said cheerfully. "Your car may take time. I'll check with Ray about the highway. We still may be able to get into town and run errands."

"Maybe there will be some snowmen in yards in town, Scotty," she said.

"Can I see them?"

"Now you've started something," Mike said with a smile. "Sure, Scotty. We'll drive around to see the snowmen."

"It'll give him something to look forward to," she said.

"And what are you giving me to look forward to?" Mike asked.

"Maybe I'll think of something by nightfall," she said, flirting with him.

"Now, that gets more interesting. And I'll give you something to look forward to after we finish breakfast before we go."

"Daddy, I'm through."

"You're excused, then. Tell Miss Savannah *excuse me please*," he said.

Scotty looked at her and smiled. "'Cuse me, please."

"You are excused, Scotty," she said, smiling back at

him. He climbed down quickly and ran to toys he had spread on the family room floor.

"He's already learned from his daddy how to get his way—a big smile."

"I wasn't aware that's all it took. I'll have to try that soon."

"I've finished my breakfast and I suppose you finished long ago."

"Indeed, I did," Mike said. She carried her dishes to the sink to rinse them and place them in the dishwasher while Mike brought Scotty's.

As they started up the stairs, Mike took her arm. "I'll step into your room and show you something else that I'm looking forward to."

"I can well imagine," she replied drily. "Scotty is up, running around, so don't embarrass me."

"Wouldn't dream of it," Mike said. In her room, he followed her inside, closed the door and wrapped his arms around her waist. "I couldn't wait until we could be alone."

As his mouth covered hers, his arms tightened around her and he pulled her close. For one moment she stood still and then she slipped her arms around his neck, leaning into him, kissing him in return.

He shifted and his hand slipped beneath her sweater, fondling her breast, sending streaks of fire from his touch. She wanted him, aching for him as if it had been weeks since they made love instead of hours.

"Savannah, I don't want to wait. There's a lock on the door to my room—"

"No. We wait. Too much is going on and we're going to town." She kissed him again and the conversation ended. He caressed her breast, making her gasp with pleasure. His hand tugged up her skirt to slide beneath it and caress her thigh, touching her intimately.

"Mike," she whispered. "Wait—"

"I can't wait. Savannah, you can't imagine how much I want you," he said gruffly between kisses.

"Mike," she whispered, holding him tightly and kissing him, knowing they had to stop, yet wanting his hands and mouth on her while she reminded herself that with Mike this was lust and nothing deeper. Nothing long-lasting. Even though they made love, she should keep her heart locked away. But she knew she was probably already falling in love with him. How deep would her regrets run over Mike?

Finally, she leaned away to look at him. "We should get ready and go to town."

He stared at her, desire reflected in his dark eyes. "I want you," he said in a husky voice. "I want my hands and my mouth all over you. Today will be torment because I want to make love to you and I'll have to keep my hands to myself. I want to spend days with you. Lindsay wants to have Scotty stay over soon anyway. They get along great and he likes having a sleepover at Aunt Lindsay's. Savannah, before you know it, you'll go. Stay awhile. I mean longer than just until Scotty's birthday. You don't have to be in California right away."

"I didn't think there was a risk, but now we've been intimate and if I stay, Mike, that will compound what we feel. It'll be a lot bigger deal. I have to think about your question. I'm not ready for commitment and you're not, either."

"No, I'm not. I don't want commitment. Just more days together so we can make love and maybe heal a little from the wounds. I wish you'd move into my room."

"I can't move in with you. Continuing to make love will cause new wounds."

"I don't want that to happen," he whispered, pulling her into his arms to kiss her hungrily, a demanding kiss that demolished her argument and made her want to say yes to anything he asked. He raised his head to look at her. She opened her eyes and gazed into his, feeling as if he could see every thought and fear she had.

"You've had too much heartbreak just recently to turn around and get your life ensnared in a way that might hurt you all over again. I don't want to cause that to happen," he said.

"Sometimes we don't do the smart thing, Mike. You can't guarantee the outcome."

"All right," he said, suddenly reaching for her again to draw her to him and kiss her one more time.

Her heart pounded. Even just kisses tied her more firmly to Mike. He was slowly dazzling her, becoming close friends with her, helping her. She wasn't going to be able to walk away as indifferently as she could have before they made love. Not that she'd been indifferent to him then, anyway.

"Let's get ready to go to Verity and run our errands," she said.

He looked at her so long she would have thought he hadn't heard her, but Mike could hear fine and he hadn't moved.

"All right, Savannah. Get ready and we'll drive to Verity. But tonight will come and you'll be in my arms and we'll talk about how long you can stay."

"I'll think about it, Mike," she replied. Her voice came out a whisper and she could barely get her breath as she thought about making love again. She turned to open her door for him to leave.

After he walked past her, she closed the door. She felt weak in the knees, as if she had had a major battle, but the major battle was with herself. She wanted to say yes, to toss aside caution and stay longer with him. What kind of risk would that be to her heart?

Mike wanted Savannah now. It was as if all the pent-up emotions that he had bottled up and held in during the past years now were spilling out. He felt alive again, even experiencing joy, hope, things he hadn't felt since losing Elise.

He wanted to be with Savannah. He wanted her in his arms. He wanted to dance with her, to play games with her, to eat with her and most of all—he wanted to make love with her all through the night, every night for at least another few weeks. What could that hurt? It could even help *heal* their hurts—hers and his.

He thought about her kisses just now and then about making love in the early hours of the morning. He groaned and went to his room, closing the door. Savannah might have to stay far longer than she expected because of her car. If her car was fixed soon, he wasn't ready for her to leave for California.

He went to get his billfold and what he needed to take to town, trying to think about the day ahead and the errands he should run while in Verity. He made a mental note to let his family know about the time of the birthday party for Scotty.

He wanted Savannah in his bed every night for the rest of this week and the next, and longer if he could talk her into it. He couldn't wait for evening to come. She was wrong if she thought either of them would fall in love and get hurt because that wasn't going to happen. She wasn't ready for love and neither was he.

Again, a twinge of guilt plagued him because he couldn't love her the way she should be loved—she deserved a man's whole heart. Was he going to cause her deep pain on top of what she had already been through?

He didn't want that to happen. The concerns about her welfare cooled his desire. He needed to think through his actions with her because he didn't want to add to her problems. Swearing softly to himself, he picked up his phone to call Ray. As he had guessed, the roads were beginning to be passable.

Within the hour, Mike, Savannah and Scotty were on the road to Verity. Snow still covered the road, but was melted in spots where there were tracks from vehicles. His truck had new tires with thick treads and he had sandbags in the back for added weight.

"We'll go by the oldest and best jewelry store in Verity and let the owner look at the ring you found. Now, if we do that, you run a chance that someone has notified the store of losing the ring."

"I'll be happy to get it back to the rightful owner. It was just fun to find it and hear about the legend, but I don't mind giving it back."

"If you're sure. We'll split up and you get what you want for Scotty's party. Then if you'll take him with you, I'll get what I want."

"Sure," she said, glancing over her shoulder at Scotty who played with toys in his car seat.

As they drove into town, streets had been scraped and sidewalks cleared. Piles of snow stood on corners, a cover of brown dirt over the mounds of snow. Dripping icicles hung from lampposts and rooftops. After they parked, Mike took Scotty's hand and directed her across the street. She hurried into a bookstore and made purchases. Next she went to a general store and got more decorations, birthday cards and wrapping paper.

On her way to meet Mike, she saw him and Scotty coming down the street. Mike was taller than most people. With packages in one arm, he held Scotty's hand. His broad-brimmed black hat was squarely on his head and Scotty's was the same. Father and son had on fleece-lined suede and leather jackets and wore Western boots. Just looking at Mike, her heartbeat quickened while longing to be with him filled her.

She dreaded the goodbye, but as soon as she was out of Texas she expected to look forward to California and adjusting to life there, for a little while, at least. Memories faded with time and her memories of Mike would be like others.

Right now, though, she wished she could walk up and hug both Mike and Scotty. At this moment they meant more to her than she would have dreamed possible. Mike had given her a haven. He was sexy, exciting, fun, solid and secure. Scotty was adorable and would wrap around anyone's heart.

"Give me your packages," Mike said, taking them from her. "We'll put them in the truck and go to the jewelry store. There's no need to see about your car yet because Russ hasn't had a chance to look at it."

As soon as they had the packages in the truck, they went to Poindexter's jewelry store. Everyone in the store greeted Mike and said hello to Scotty, talking about how much he had grown until she wondered whether Mike ever brought Scotty into town.

"Is Chuck here?" Mike asked someone who left to return a minute later with a tall, white-haired man who greeted Mike and then shook hands with Scotty. "Scotty, you are getting all grown up. How old are you?"

"Almost three," Scotty said, holding up three fingers.

"Almost three. You're a very big boy."

"Chuck, this is Savannah Grayson. Savannah, meet Chuck Poindexter. We want you to look at a ring."

Savannah slipped the ring off her finger to hand it to the jeweler.

"She found the ring along the Rocky Creek bed after the storm. Have you ever had anyone report losing a gold ring? And is it really gold?"

Chuck placed the ring on a black background beneath a light. "We haven't ever had anyone come in and ask about a lost gold ring. We've had people ask about diamonds that have fallen out of settings on rings, but never a gold ring in all my years here. Pretty ring. It has a date inscribed."

She leaned forward as Mike did. "The inscription is tiny."

Chuck slipped on glasses and looked at it. "The correct date is 1861. This is an old ring."

"That's incredibly old for this area," Mike said.

"No telling where that ring was lost originally. It could have been carried by birds or people—who knows. I'd say you found yourself a ring, Savannah."

"One of us. The ring was in Mike's creek."

Mike and Chuck both smiled. "Thanks, Chuck. I just wanted to check because if someone had been in recently missing a ring, then we'd get this back to them."

"Not at all. Congratulations on an interesting find. I'd guess," he said, turning the ring in his hand and looking at it, "this ring could have been brought from the East by someone. Or it could have been fashioned by one of the Native Americans who roamed through Texas. Who knows? Actually, we never will know. Just enjoy your ring."

They thanked him and left the shop, Scotty in Mike's arms and the ring back on Savannah's finger.

"Want to go get some ice cream?"

Scotty began to clap his hands and Savannah laughed. "Who could refuse now?" she asked, looking at Scotty.

They had ice cream and walked back to the pickup to

drive home. As on the drive to Verity, she was aware Mike drove far more slowly than the first time she had ridden with him and he watched the snow-packed road carefully.

"From the way you're driving, it must be slick."

"It's okay, but there's ice under this snow and we've hit some slick spots."

"Then you're doing well because I didn't realize that it was that slick."

"Good. The bad news is—another snowstorm is on the way. You picked a dilly of a winter to drive west."

"I didn't even think about the weather because we'd had warm days before I left. I was worrying about other things."

He glanced at her and nodded, understanding what she meant. "Which brings up another subject. A contractor is coming out tomorrow to look at the bridge that I am going to have rebuilt. I want a bridge strong enough to withstand even more rain than we had. With all the people working here, I don't want a bridge collapsing with anyone."

"No. I'll have to admit that was scary and someone should be able to build a bridge to withstand whatever kind of weather we have unless it's a tornado or earthquake."

"I'll be gone all morning about the bridge. I'll take Scotty with me and bring him to my—"

"I would love to have Scotty stay at the ranch with me." She glanced back and saw that the little boy had fallen asleep. "It's going to be dreadful for me when I finally have to leave him."

"And leaving me will be easy and won't matter?" Mike teased. She turned to look into his brown eyes and the world momentarily ceased to exist for her as she was aware only of him.

"No, you'll be hard to leave, too," she said quietly. He

had been teasing, but she saw something flicker in the depths of his eyes and his expression became somber.

"Don't go, then. Wait a few more weeks," he said as his attention went back to the road.

"A few more weeks won't make saying goodbye any easier. Actually, I think it works the other way around. The more I'm around the two of you, the more I want to be with you. Neither one of us is ready for another upheaval in our lives. We're both having enough of one without compounding it, so I should go after Scotty's party and after I have a car. If Russ can fix it and it isn't too expensive."

"You'll know soon enough. All right. Also, Scotty stays with you tomorrow. If you change your mind, just let me know. My sister is always happy to have Scotty over."

After dinner that night they watched a movie with Scotty and then Savannah read to him before Mike tucked him into bed.

As Mike joined her in the family room and closed the door behind him, he said, "Scotty's asleep and we're very much alone now."

"So come sit and we'll relax and talk and enjoy the evening."

"Oh, yes, I intend to enjoy the evening and the rest of the night, and all my plans involve you every single second of the time."

She laughed as he crossed the room and picked her up. He sat, holding her on his lap and wrapping his arm around her waist as he kissed her.

Forgetting everything else, she focused on Mike, kissing him and holding him tightly with one hand while she ran her other hand over him. Even though she hadn't admitted it to him, she felt as if she couldn't get enough of their making love either.

As she held and kissed him, her heartbeat raced. Desire was a raging blaze that made her want him beyond any need for loving she had ever experienced before.

"Mike, I want to love and kiss you all night and I want you to do the same," she whispered.

"I'm going to try." His voice was a hoarse whisper as he tightened his arm around her waist. "We'll love until the sun comes up."

Was loving him a bigger mistake than her engagement had been? She had entered into an intimate relationship with a man who would never be committed to anything long-term. If that was another mistake in judgment, it was already done and she would have to pay the price to her heart.

Eight

On Thursday afternoon Mike came in the back door. He had been out on the ranch since before dawn and Scotty ran to greet him. Savannah followed until she heard Mike's cell ring. When she heard him answer, she turned around and went back to sit at the game table where she had been helping Scotty put together a puzzle.

She could hear Mike talking but paid no attention until he came in from the other room.

"Hello," she said, smiling when Mike came in the family room. "I started to come greet you, but I heard you get a call."

He held up his phone. He had shed his hat and coat, but his face was still red from being out in the cold all day. "It's Russ about your car. To fix it, he'll have to order parts and it will take a few days. He can give you all the details if you want to speak to him directly. I told him time didn't matter. The big deal is—Russ said it will probably cost about two thousand."

"Oh, my. Mike, I know very little about cars. I usually get my brother's advice. If you don't know cars, does anyone who works for you?"

"I know a little and I'll talk to Ray and a couple of dealers. It's still cheaper to fix the car than to even buy a used one, let alone a new car. You said it's only three years old."

She thought about it for a moment. "I think I'd rather get it fixed than go through the hassle of getting another car. I need a car—I can't stay months with you."

"Yes, you can," he said, smiling at her.

"No, I can't. You see what you can find out, but I'm leaning with fixing it. I'll call Russ if you'll give me the number. I can talk to him about it and if I feel I need to call my brother, then I will."

Mike jotted the number and handed it to her. "Savannah, there's no hurry. You can stay here as long as you want. He has to order parts."

"I'll call him," she said, getting her cell phone and stepping into the hallway.

After her call, she returned to the family room. Scotty sat drawing a picture and coloring it while Mike stood by the fire and turned to face her.

"I told Russ to fix the car. He said it probably won't be ready until the middle of next week."

"That's far too soon," Mike said, sounding as if he meant what he said, which surprised her.

"Well, you have a houseguest a little while longer. Millie passed me in the hall and I let her know."

"Millie cooks enough for me to have a flock of houseguests all the time, so she'll be pleased. Whatever she's cooking now, I can't wait. She ran me out of the kitchen before I could look."

Scotty looked up from his drawing. "Miss Savannah, will you be here for my birthday party?"

"Definitely, Scotty. My car won't be ready until next week. Your party is tomorrow."

He smiled and went back to his coloring.

By party time Friday night Scotty could not be still. He hopped and jumped and kept asking Mike the time.

"I think he's going to fall apart before a single relative gets here," Mike said.

"No, I won't fall apart," Scotty said and she laughed. "There's the doorbell."

Scotty disappeared out of the room and she shook her head. "He's so excited."

"This was a good idea you had, Savannah. He's a happy kid. It'll be a fun birthday." The warmth in Mike's eyes made her heart skip a beat. Mike's appeal was growing daily and even though he wanted her to stay, she felt more strongly that as soon as her car was fixed, she should move on.

Mike crossed the room to hug her.

"Mike, Millie and her husband are in the kitchen, Scotty is running around, company is coming and I'll be a wrinkled mess."

"I don't care who sees me hug you and it makes Scotty happy for us to hug. He likes you, Savannah. I don't think fuzzy sweaters wrinkle."

Smiling, she stepped away from him while happiness enveloped her.

Mike's brother Jake, a tall black-haired man, and his wife, Madison, a beautiful brunette wearing a navy sweater, slacks and knee-high boots, arrived and Mike made the introductions.

"Hey, here's the birthday boy," Jake said, picking up Scotty and giving him a hug.

"Hi, Scotty," Madison said. "Happy birthday." She

handed him a big wrapped present which Mike took and put on a nearby game table.

"We've heard a lot about you, Savannah," Jake said. "Very good things. I'll be the one to ask—are you going to show us the legendary gold ring?"

Savannah laughed as she held up her hand.

"See, I told you so," Mike said. "They'll all want to see it." He glanced toward the door. "Here comes Lindsay."

"Hi, Jake, Madison, Savannah," Lindsay said. Looking warm in a brown sweater, jeans and brown fur-lined boots, she bent down to hug Scotty. When he put his arms around her neck to hug her back, she picked him up, carrying him with her. "Here's our big boy. How old will you be, Scotty?" Lindsay asked.

He held up three fingers. "Three years old," he answered. "I'm big."

"Yes, you are big," she replied. "I saw your snow cowboy, your snowman and your snow dog. If we'd had more snow, you would have had a whole town of people and animals."

Scotty smiled at her. "Daddy said they'll melt this week."

"That's what sunshine does, but then warm weather will come and you'll have fun outside in the sunshine."

He nodded and wiggled, so she set him on his feet and he ran off. She turned to Savannah. "Let me see this fabled ring," she said and Savannah held out her hand again.

"It's really pretty," Lindsay said. "How odd for you to find that in the creek bank."

"Actually, it's just fun to hear that I might have a tiny part of a legend. It has a date inscribed," she said, pulling the ring off her finger. "It says 1861."

They all bent over the ring again. Lindsay took it to look closely and then hand it to Madison who studied it and passed it on to Jake who examined it and handed it back to Savannah.

"I'm sorry you had so much damage to your car, but I'm glad you're here," Jake said.

"Here are Destiny and Wyatt Milan," Lindsay said. Savannah turned to see a tall man with the bluest eyes she had ever seen. At his side was a stunning redhead who bore no resemblance to anyone in the room, but who looked familiar.

"I've seen her somewhere."

Lindsay smiled. "Yes, you have. She is a television personality and has had a bestselling book. Right now she has a new show about little-known places in history. She is a Calhoun. She and Wyatt haven't been married long, so I don't know how much longer she'll do the show. She married Verity's sheriff. So now we have two Calhouns married to Milans. My grandparents couldn't deal with that but they're deceased, so they don't have to."

"So the feud is real and still ongoing?"

"Definitely," Lindsay said.

"It is with Lindsay and Tony Milan," Mike remarked and Lindsay shrugged.

"I didn't start it," she said.

As Wyatt and Destiny approached they greeted everyone. "Destiny, Wyatt, this is Savannah who is staying at the ranch while she gets her car fixed. Savannah, meet our newest Calhoun cousin, Destiny, who we met not too long ago, and her newlywed husband, Wyatt Milan. Here's another Calhoun and a Milan who get along," Mike said.

"Destiny, I've seen you on television and it's exciting to meet you," Savannah said.

"Thank you. I hear you are now involved in one of the local legends—let's see the famous ring you found in the creek with *1861* inscribed on it. I heard that Chuck Poin-dexter thinks it's authentic."

As she held out her hand, Wyatt glanced at it and Des-tiny bent over it. "It's beautiful," Destiny said. "This is fascinating. Mike said Chuck told you that no one has ever said they've lost a gold ring in all the years he's been in business."

"That made me feel better about keeping it because I would give it back instantly if we found the owner."

"You're the owner now, I'd say."

"Wyatt," Mike said, "Baxter is passing out drinks, but he's also getting the door, so let's go to the bar and I'll get you a drink and you can bring one to Destiny."

"I'll wait for Baxter," she said, smiling and looking again at the ring.

"Destiny, stop trying to figure a way to get this legend into your show," Wyatt remarked with a smile. "C'mon, Mike. I'll take you up on your offer."

In minutes Savannah heard a commotion and glanced around to see a tall, brown-eyed man with straight brown hair come into the room. He carried Scotty and both were laughing while Scotty held a wrapped birthday gift in his arms. Mike took the gift as Scotty got down and ran to play.

"Savannah, meet the last Calhoun to arrive tonight— my brother Josh Calhoun. Josh, this is Savannah Grayson, Mike's houseguest," Destiny said.

"Whom your brother rescued," Savannah said smil-ing at Josh. "I'm glad to meet you, Josh. It's nice to get to meet Mike's family."

"We're all around this area except our folks who retired to California. I'm glad you were stuck out in this storm. Glad to meet you." He turned to Destiny. "It's good to see you, Destiny. I think you're transforming Wyatt into such a talkative guy I don't recognize him."

She laughed. "It probably won't last, so be patient."

"May I see the legendary ring?" he asked Savannah and she held out her hand. "All of us have to see this ring. With all the junk and stuff that has been washed up by the creeks around here, no one has ever found a beautiful ring until you, Savannah." He held her hand, studying the ring. "There are lots of legends, so some of them are bound to be based on truth while others are purely myth, but also may have been based on some kernel of truth."

"Good theory," Lindsay said. "We can hope that Savannah finds true love now, but I told her a good horse might be more worthwhile."

Destiny laughed. "I hope it's true love and if that happens, let me know. Wyatt's right—I'm trying to think how I can get this into my book or my show."

As the women talked, Savannah glanced across the room to see Mike watching her. Surprised, she gazed back at him a moment before trying to focus on the conversation around her and forget Mike, something she couldn't do totally.

When dinner was announced, they went through a buffet line and then sat at the big table in the informal dining room with Scotty in his high chair that was pulled up to the head of the table beside Mike. She sat to Mike's right with Lindsay beside her. While they ate, she enjoyed the Calhoun family who seemed close, and from the conversations she heard, they saw each other often.

Even though Wyatt was a Milan, he seemed accepted by the Calhouns and close to some of them. It was even more so with Madison, except Lindsay kept most of her conversation with the Calhouns or she talked to Savannah a lot of the time during dinner.

When dinner was over, Baxter and Millie carried in a birthday cake with three burning candles and placed it in front of Scotty. Everyone sang "Happy Birthday" to Scotty, who wriggled with eagerness and gazed intently at the cake.

"Make a wish, Scotty, and blow out the candles," Mike said.

"I wish…"

"Don't tell," Mike said. "Just wish," he added.

Scotty nodded and moved his lips and then blew. His cheeks puffed out and his aunts and uncles cheered him on until the third candle flickered out and everyone applauded.

Millie came into the room and picked up the cake. "I'll slice the cake in the kitchen and we'll serve," she said and left after taking orders for ice cream with cake.

Savannah didn't have much appetite and she was aware of Mike seated so close beside her. It was fun to see Mike enjoying his family and Scotty having a wonderful birthday celebration as the center of attention.

After dessert they gathered around and Scotty opened each present, thanking the givers and running to give each one a hug and a kiss.

As he opened the package with the books Savannah had bought for him, he smiled and ran to hug her. As she leaned down to hug him in return, he kissed her cheek.

"Thank you for my books," he said. When he leaned away, his brown eyes sparkled. "Will you read one to me tonight?"

"Yes," she replied, laughing. "Happy birthday, Scotty."

"Thank you!" he flung as he ran back to open the next present.

Laughing, she looked up to meet Mike's gaze. As his dark eyes rested on her, she tingled and remembered that next week she intended to leave for California, even though Mike urged her to stay longer. The approaching departure hurt because she would miss Mike. When she looked at Scotty, more pain stabbed her. She would miss Scotty, too. Father and son filled a big void in her life.

As soon as she drove away and focused on California, she would try to forget Texas. That's what she'd have to do. Her gaze went back to Mike to meet his again. This time she remembered moments from last night. With an effort she turned her head so she had to look elsewhere and for the next half hour, she tried to avoid glancing his way.

When Scotty finished opening his presents, people stood to refresh drinks, look at the presents or just move around to talk to others.

Wyatt and Jake helped Scotty put together two model helicopters that could be flown by remote controls. He had two choppers and sat on the floor with his uncles with helicopter pieces spread in front of them as they put them together.

Destiny and Madison sat talking and Lindsay was beside Savannah, turning to her. "You should stay another week, Savannah. We'll get some spring weather before you know it and things will pretty up. Too bad you won't be here when the bluebonnets bloom. They're beautiful. Stay next week and I'll have you over and show you some of my prize horses."

"Thank you, Lindsay. I don't know much about horses. Whether I stay or go depends on my car. As soon as it's ready, I'll be on my way. Besides, Mike has had enough of me."

"I don't think he has," Lindsay said. "That's why I asked you to stay. He seems happier than he has been since losing Elise. He hasn't had a party for Scotty before. Scotty is so excited and he likes you, too."

Savannah smiled at Lindsay. "Don't worry about your brother. He's a fun, good-looking guy and he'll get back to really living, and Scotty is a happy little kid. They'll both do all right and all of you are a support for them. They don't need me and Mike isn't ready for a relationship and I'm not, either."

Lindsay laughed. "I'm that obvious? I worry about my big brother."

"You and your siblings are a nice family and that's good that you're concerned about each other. I'm close with my family."

Lindsay tilted her head. "I'd think if you're close, you wouldn't leave for California. That's far from Arkansas."

"Guess what?" Mike said, suddenly appearing behind them and taking Savannah's arm. "Scotty wants you to see what he just built. C'mon, Lindsay, you, too. Scotty is pleased with his efforts. His uncles have been helping him, but as far as he's concerned, he has done this single-handedly, so you'll both have to ooh and aah. And then he wants us all to play a new game with him. Let's go look at his remote-control choppers."

"He is way too young to manage those. Won't he just step on them?" Savannah asked.

"We hope not. He's sort of good with the remote-control toys and there is no stopping his uncles from giving them to him."

As they walked away, Mike moved closer to Savannah. "I thought maybe I needed to rescue you from my sister. She had an earnest look on her face and I know Lindsay. She has probably decided you're good for Scotty and maybe for me, too, and was trying to prevail on you to stay longer, which I am all for, but I don't want it to be because Lindsay pestered and pressured you into it. Lindsay worries about me, which I appreciate, but if I interfered in her life, I probably would regret it very quickly. Fortunately, she likes Mrs. Lewis and she likes Millie and both of them are around for Scotty, so most of the time Lindsay feels that he has two women who are good influences in his life. She tries to be, but she's busy. She runs that big ranch and even though she has a good foreman, she's active."

"It's nice that she worries about you, and she isn't going to pressure me."

"Good. Scotty is in the playroom. Follow the sound. Everyone else is in there."

"Scotty acts way older than he is. He's an angel and he's very smart. If you ever have just an ordinary kid, you're going to be wild and not know what to do," she said, staring at him and thinking about her own siblings and her nieces and nephews.

He chuckled. "Maybe any more kids I have will be just as good and smart and capable and lovable as Scotty. After all, they will have me for their dad."

She laughed at his joke. "You laugh now, but you wait. Some little boy or girl is going to stand you on your head."

"I think it will be a big girl with big blue eyes. A blonde. And she has already turned me into a drooling wreck who can't think about anything else."

"A 'drooling wreck'? I'm not sure I want to get into bed with a drooling wreck," she said, smiling at him.

"You make me wish they would all go home now."

"Do I really? Whatever would you want to do?" she asked in great innocence, and then shook her head. "I'm teasing. I don't really want to hear."

"Oh, I'm going to answer that one—later on tonight," he said, his dark eyes filled with desire as he looked intently at her.

They entered the downstairs playroom where the relatives were gathered in a semicircle around Scotty and his new helicopters. Wyatt had the controls of one and Scotty had the controls of the other with Jake's help as they flew the choppers around the room.

"Keep your eyes on the choppers and duck if they come your way," Mike whispered. "As you pointed out, Scotty is way too young for this and they'll crash somewhere in a few minutes."

"Stop worrying. He does have fun and so do his uncles. Just look."

She watched Wyatt and Jake work the remote controls. Jake was hunkered down behind Scotty. Jake's long arms reached around Scotty to grab the controls if it looked as if disaster was about to happen.

"This is how my brothers are with their kids. Sometimes you wonder who these toys are really for," said Savannah.

Mike grinned and crossed his arms, standing to watch the fun.

She looked at Scotty's happy smile and wished his mother was here with him and with Mike, yet Scotty's laughter had to ease Mike's pain. Thinking of her own situation, she realized for the past few days she hadn't hurt as badly or thought about Kirk. She glanced again at Mike. Maybe Mike was helping her to get over her heartache. Or was she exchanging one hurt for another when she had to say goodbye?

Lindsay yelled and Jake took the controls, but it was too late as a chopper crashed into the stone fireplace and everyone broke up while Jake and Wyatt tried to fix the smashed helicopter.

"Scotty will expect them to put it back together and sometimes they manage to do so. I'll go help."

She watched him walk away, tingling, thinking about later tonight. Just the sight of him had gotten to be enough to make her breathless. Each day he became more exciting to her and more important. She hoped he wasn't becoming essential.

"So will you stay another week?"

Startled, Savannah glanced around to see Lindsay beside her.

"You're good for my brother and for Scotty," Lindsay said. "And I apologize if I'm interfering, but I thought maybe you'd be uncertain about how much he would welcome you staying."

"Thank you. You're not interfering. He's already asked me to stay longer. When my car is ready, I should go to California. I have an aunt who is expecting me. Lindsay, did Mike tell you that I just broke an engagement? Or that I'm pregnant?"

"Oh?" Lindsay's eyes widened and surprise filled her expression. Her face flushed. "Savannah, I'm sorry. I didn't know. I apologize. I just figured you were going to California to be a little more independent and on your own than staying at home in Arkansas."

When Savannah nodded, Lindsay continued. "I'm sorry, I didn't know you had someone in your life. I apologize for inviting you to stay when I really didn't know your circumstances. I was thinking of Mike."

"Don't apologize. There are just complications. Lindsay—"

"Forget it. I'm sorry. Both of you have enough troubles in your lives. You don't need to take on each other's problems, too. Let's go look at Scotty's birthday presents. He'll be more than happy to show them to us, I know."

Savannah didn't pursue the subject because she could see the regret, embarrassment and surprise in Lindsay's expression and in her apology. For the rest of the evening Lindsay spent her time with the others and Savannah sus-

pected Lindsay no longer wanted her to stay and compli-
cate Mike's life further.

When they finally were all gone, Mike locked up. "I
think Scotty may be asleep before I can carry him upstairs."

Mike carried Scotty and Savannah went along in case
Scotty wanted a story, but by the time they reached the
stairs, Scotty was asleep. "I'll put him in bed and just
take off his boots and jeans and let him sleep in the rest
of his clothes."

Savannah stayed to pick up and switch off lights downstairs. When he reappeared, he crossed the room to drape
his arm across her shoulders.

"Since he's so young, he probably won't remember the
party, but I'm glad he had a good time."

"I had a good time tonight," he said. "The best part was
knowing you would be here when the party was over."
Switching off lights, Mike turned on night-lights. "The
monitors are on. Let's go to my sitting room. It's comfortable and I can build a fire."

"Sure," she said. "That's fine."

Upstairs, she watched him get the fire going. "Mike,
your sister is a beautiful woman. Why hasn't Lindsay married?"

He glanced over his shoulder and then returned his attention to the fire. "Lindsay scares the hell out of men.
Either that or they are more interested in her knowledge
about a ranch and horses than they are in her. Some years
she's in a charity auction," he said, standing as the logs
began to blaze. He walked back to Savannah. "Guys from
out of town bid on her, thinking the pretty blonde is something she's not, and Lindsay won't put up with any non-
sense or passes if she doesn't like the guy. Then if a local
bids and wins her, he does it to talk about his horses. She's

damn good with animals. I hope she didn't wear you down tonight about me."

"Actually, I told her that I'm pregnant and I just broke my engagement. I don't think your sister wants me anywhere near you."

He grinned. "We won't worry about Lindsay. Her intentions are good and usually she doesn't meddle badly." Motioning to a wet bar in a corner of the spacious room, Mike asked, "Want something to drink?"

"Sure. Have milk in that bar of yours?"

"Actually, I do. I have milk and chocolate milk."

"Plain milk," she said, walking across the room to join him and pour a glass.

Opening a cold beer, he turned to hold it up. "Here's to a big thank-you for the party tonight."

"I'll drink to that," she said, touching his bottle lightly with her glass of milk and taking a sip. Mike set down his bottle and took her milk from her hand to set it on the counter beside his beer.

Her pulse drummed and she gazed up at him. The hungry look in his eyes made her tingle and feel wanted. She could not recall ever seeing so much desire in any man's expression as she did now with Mike.

"Come here, Savannah," he whispered, drawing her to him. His arm slipped around her waist and he drew her tightly against him as he leaned down to cover her mouth with his.

Wrapping her arms around him, she kissed him passionately, letting her feelings for him pour into her kiss. While the temperature in the room climbed, her heart pounded. She pressed against him, wanting his kisses and loving.

Still kissing her, Mike picked her up, carrying her to his bedroom and closing the door, standing her on her feet while he kissed her and held her tightly in his arms.

* * *

They loved through the night. Afterward, Mike held her close against him, finally dozing. When Savannah pulled away, he drew her back to him.

"Leaving me?"

"It's dawn out—the waking hour. It's Saturday morning so soon the house will be busy because Millie will be in. Scotty will get up. You'll go to work. It's time for the world to get going so that means I should go to my room."

"We're isolated up here and Scotty will run down to the kitchen because he loves to eat breakfast and he likes Millie."

"So he never gets up and comes in here?"

"Yes, he does, but he's barely three years old and he won't think a thing of finding you in my bed."

"Ha. Like this? I think not," she said and Mike couldn't hold back a grin. As she started to move away, he tightened his arm around her to hold her and rolled over to kiss her, relishing her soft warmth beneath him and wanting to love her before he was gone for the day.

It was another hour before she left, shutting the door quietly. With his thoughts on her, he shaved, showered and dressed, pulling on his jeans, boots and a red-and-blue sweater.

Tonight he was taking Savannah out to dinner while Scotty stayed with Lindsay. He couldn't wait to have an evening with her, just the two of them, and then come home and make love the rest of the night and part of the day tomorrow.

Russ had called yesterday and said she could pick up her car on Monday afternoon, only a couple of days away. As soon as she had her car, she would be gone. Mike had never talked her into staying beyond Scotty's party. Pain tugged on his heart. Another goodbye in his life, but this would be quick and soon forgotten. Not likely. He was certain he wouldn't forget Savannah for a long time. In case he wanted to see her again, he would get her cell number and her parents' names, although he didn't think he would likely ever see her after she left Texas.

He was going to miss her dreadfully at first. He expected that to pass swiftly because he was accustomed to living on the ranch with Scotty and with the people who worked for him.

Savannah had temporarily filled a huge void in his life and in Scotty's life, but they would go back to the way they were, maybe a little more healed from their loss.

He picked up Elise's picture. It would always hurt, but not like it had that first year. He didn't want to think about that time or when Scotty had hurt and hadn't even known why because he was just a baby.

How Scotty had gone through that loss and come out with such a sunny disposition, Mike didn't know. He had expected Scotty to have all sorts of problems, to cry easily and cling to him. Instead, he had a happy, cheerful, self-reliant for his age, little three-year-old who brought joy into Mike's life. Maybe it was part of Elise shining through her son.

He set down Elise's picture and thought of Savannah. She had been wonderful, exciting, sexy, fun, and a temptation that he hadn't been able to resist. At the same time, she had been so good with Scotty, something he would never forget. He was certain Scotty would adjust to saying goodbye just as he adjusted to everything else that had happened in his young life.

Mike combed his hair, gave up controlling the curls and went downstairs.

He wanted to stay all day with Savannah, but with the storms they still needed all hands at work on the ranch.

Millie was cooking for the coming week and bustling all over the kitchen. Nadine had come to clean and Baxter was helping Millie in the kitchen.

Savannah wanted to go into town to get something to wear because she hadn't expected to go out any time in the foreseeable future and one bag of her things was still locked up and in the trunk of her car, so he agreed to take her into town later this afternoon.

That night, by the time six rolled around, Mike felt as if it had been days since the hour he left his room that morning. Now he was in the downstairs family room, gazing out the window and waiting for Savannah. Scotty was already at Lindsay's house so he and Savannah were the only ones home now and he was tempted to skip their plans and stay at home and make love all through the night.

He heard her heels on the marble floor in the hallway and looked up. She swept into the room and he couldn't get his breath. Unable to avoid staring, he stood immobile. His gaze roamed over her as if he had never seen a woman before. Her red dress clung to her figure and ended with a flare just above her knees. Her blond hair was pinned up slightly on either side of her head by sparkling pins and then it fell in a blond cascade over her shoulders.

Her wide, thickly-lashed blue eyes were as beautiful as her full red lips. His gaze ran swiftly down her figure. He crossed the room to her to stop only a foot away.

"You're gorgeous," he said, his voice gravelly and barely audible.

"Thank you. You look handsome yourself," she said, her eyes twinkling as she smiled at him. "I suspect you've had women running after you since you were five years old."

Realizing what she said to him, he smiled. "I don't think so unless they were chasing me down for something ornery my brothers and I had done. We could just stay home tonight. We have this whole place to ourselves."

"I've been looking forward to this all day. I have on my good dress and have worked on my hair, and now you want to cancel?"

"When you put it that way, I suppose we'll go. At least I get to look at you all evening. We're flying to Dallas."

"I can't wait," she said.

He took her arm, wanting to kiss her senseless and peel her out of that sexy dress. Inhaling deeply and trying to get his thoughts elsewhere, Mike led her outside where a limo waited and a chauffeur sat reading.

"Glad to meet you, Ms. Grayson," he said, opening the limo door and stepping back.

In minutes they were headed to the airport and Mike wondered how soon he could talk her into coming home.

Mike's handsome looks in his charcoal suit and black boots made her heart race. She could hardly eat and wanted to dance with him, to be alone with him, to kiss him—to spend the entire weekend with him. Excitement bubbled in her as she faced him across a table with candlelight, music from a band in another room carrying into the alcove Mike had reserved at a Dallas country club for them. The look in his eyes, holding promises of passion and desire, kept her pulse pounding.

Moving the candle out of the way, Mike reached across the table to take her hand. He touched the gold ring lightly. The gold shimmered in the candlelight. "The ring looks pretty on you. I'm glad you found it and I hope you find true love and make the old legend come true."

I have found true love, was the first thought that popped into her head as she looked into Mike's dark eyes. She was in love with Mike. Was it infatuation? Lust? Or was it really love? A rebound from Kirk? Mike had become special and she wanted to be with him constantly. She admired him, trusted him, thought he was a great dad to his son— she was in love, something she had known she was risking.

"Let's dance, Savannah," he said, looking at her mouth and making her think of his kisses.

"Yes," she whispered.

She loved dancing with him whether the music was a fast beat or a slow ballad. Soon, after three lively dances, Mike shed his jacket and they danced to the fast music and pounding drums that ramped up the sensuality of the evening and being with him.

Later, when she stepped into his arms to slow dance, she wanted to kiss him.

"Mike, you rescued me from the storm and you've rescued me from my broken heart. Tonight has been sexy, fun, thrilling, and has made me forget the hurt and pain for now."

"Good." He drew her closer and they danced in silence a few more minutes until she leaned away to look up at him.

"It's a long flight back to the ranch, isn't it?" It actually was a short flight, but she wanted to be in his arms in his bed with him now.

Something flickered in the depths of his brown eyes. "Are you ready to go home?" he asked. His voice was husky, deeper than most of the time.

"Yes," she whispered. "Oh, yes, let's go home, Mike."

He took her hand and they left. As soon as they were in the hall he retrieved his cell phone to call his chauffeur and then his pilot.

In less than an hour they were airborne, heading back to the ranch. As he looked out the window of the plane, she looked at his profile and his dark curls. There was no doubt in her mind—Savannah had fallen in love.

Nine

Sunshine spilled into the room when she stirred and Mike's arm tightened around her. She turned to slide her fingers across his chest and kiss his shoulder lightly. Was she going from one disaster at home to an even bigger loss and upheaval in Texas?

She had too many questions and no answers for them. One thing she did know—Mike would not marry again any time soon. She had helped bring him out of his grief, but he wasn't ready for commitment. Mike was deep in lust and open to companionship and was coming to life again, but he wasn't thinking about love or commitment.

Mike's world revolved around Scotty and his ranch. She was merely a fun interlude, excitement, hot sex, nothing more. She had no illusions about his heart.

Even so, Mike had helped her get over the pain of her breakup. It wouldn't hurt if she stayed a few more days and then left for California. Either way, it would be hard to leave. How could a little three-year-old boy she had known only a short time so ensnare her heart? She loved Scotty and she was going to miss him terribly. She was ready for him to come back from Lindsay's. She hoped her baby was as adorable and cheerful as Scotty.

She turned to look at Mike. Running her finger along his jaw, she felt the faint stubble as she leaned over him to shower light kisses on his chest.

His arm tightened around her again and he pulled her to him. When she looked into his eyes, she felt hot and tingly all over as he wound his fingers in her hair and kissed her.

It was hours later when they ate breakfast. She had only a couple of bites of bagel and couldn't take another bite. "Mike, how soon will Lindsay bring Scotty back? I miss him."

"You'd rather play with a little kid than with me?" he asked, looking amused.

"He's just so cute."

"And I'm not?" he said, teasing her.

She slid onto his lap and wrapped her arms around his neck. "You, darlin', are just the most handsome, sexiest man I have ever known in my entire life and you just make my heart go wild. Of course, you're cute," she said.

He laughed and pulled her close to kiss her and in seconds their teasing play was forgotten as she clung to him tightly while she returned his kisses.

That afternoon Savannah was in bed again with Mike. His arm wrapped around her and held her close against his bare side. His cell phone rang and he stretched out a long arm to pick it up.

She listened as Mike told Lindsay that Scotty could stay another night if he wanted. Mike talked to Scotty then for ten minutes, listening to the boy tell him what he had been doing. Finally, Mike turned to look at her. "Yes, you can talk to Miss Savannah."

Surprised, she sat up, pulling the sheet beneath her chin while Mike handed her his cell and she heard Scotty's childish voice as he began to tell her what he had been doing with his Aunt Lindsay.

As they talked, Mike sat up and lifted her hair off her neck. She felt his warm breath on her nape when he trailed light kisses over her. He began to kiss and caress her and she turned her back to him, swinging her legs over the side of the bed.

While she continued to try to talk to Scotty, Mike showered kisses on her, caressing her, distracting her. She stood up and stepped away, turning to glare at Mike who smiled and caught the bottom of the sheet she held in front of her. He tugged lightly, rolling the sheet into a ball. She pulled harder to hang on to the sheet which covered her. With a yank she got it away from Mike and walked away to talk to Scotty while she heard Mike laugh.

When she finally told Scotty goodbye, she gave the phone to Mike. He told Scotty goodbye and then Lindsay.

As soon as he turned off his phone and set it on the table, Savannah pounced on him. "You're really a nuisance sometimes."

"You loved the attention," he said, laughing. "Scotty is staying with her tonight and he'll be home tomorrow afternoon."

"I'll miss him."

"I'll try to keep you too busy to think about it," Mike said, pulling her down and moving over her to kiss her.

The next morning she stepped out of bed, wrapping the sheet around her while he pulled a light blanket over himself.

"I'm going to shower and get dressed. Millie and maybe Baxter will be downstairs. I'll get ready for Lindsay and Scotty," she said.

"They won't be here for hours, but Millie is probably downstairs now. All right, I'll shower with you—"

"No, you won't, or we won't get ready now."

He slipped his arm around her waist. "Stay this week, Savannah. We can have fun. You don't have to go. Stay just a little longer."

She looked into his dark eyes and in that moment felt she never wanted to leave. A few more days with Mike and Scotty couldn't hurt. "All right, until Thursday. I'll check the weather and see if that will work."

"Good," he replied, smiling at her. "See you downstairs."

Gathering her clothes, she left to go to her suite to shower and dress. All the time she thought about staying longer, she questioned her feelings for Mike. Was she really in love with him, or had he simply been a relief from the emotional upheaval she had just gone through at home?

Whatever she felt, she had to move on soon. Mike had not asked her for any kind of commitment beyond a few more days with them. When the time came for her to go, she expected him to kiss her, wish her well and say goodbye forever.

Just the thought of telling him goodbye hurt. Hopefully, when she got away from him, out of Texas, she would get over the strong feelings she had right now when she was with him, but she suspected it was not going to happen.

She looked at the ring on her finger. That ring would forever remind her of Mike and Scotty.

It was late in the day when Lindsay brought Scotty home. He ran to Mike who swept him up to hug and kiss him. "Look what Aunt Lindsay helped me make," he said, and tossed a paper airplane that soared and then crashed into a potted plant.

"Aunt Lindsay should have told you to be careful where you fly those," Mike said, and Lindsay smiled and shrugged.

"As if you didn't lob those and worse all over the house when you were much older than Scotty."

"And good morning to you, too," he said to his sister. Scotty held out his arms and looked at Savannah. Smiling, Mike carried him closer and Scotty leaned out to wrap his arms around her neck.

She took him, but Mike wouldn't let go of him. "He's too heavy. You've hugged Miss Savannah, Scotty. C'mon." Mike pulled him away.

"Mike, I'm sure I can carry him. I'm not fragile."

"He's heavy. End of argument." He set Scotty on his feet. "Come in, Lindsay."

"Thanks, but I need to get back. And thanks for letting him visit. He's always fun to have. Good to see you, Savannah. Bye, Scotty."

Scotty ran to her to hug her when she leaned down. Lindsay hugged him and then straightened as he scampered away. "He is one busy kid," she said. "See you, Mike. Bye, Savannah."

Lindsay left and Mike stepped outside to walk to her car with her. Savannah closed the door behind him, suspecting the two of them would talk a few more minutes.

She went to find Scotty and play with him. She had only a short time left with the adorable little boy.

On Wednesday afternoon Mike worked on information to give his accountant. While Scotty napped, Savannah got out her bag and backpack and carry-on to pack. She had her car and it ran fine, so there was no reason for her to stay other than Mike and Scotty wanted her there and she wanted to be with them.

It was time to go and she tried to not even think about how much she would miss them when she left tomorrow.

She was halfway through filling her suitcase. She came out of her closet with some folded sweaters and walked toward the bed where she had the open suitcase and backpack.

Startling her, Scotty stood at the foot of the bed. His sleep-filled eyes looked at her suitcase, and then at her, and back to the suitcase.

"What are you doing, Miss Savannah?" he asked. His green corduroy shirt was rumpled, his hair in a tangle, and he held his brown bear tightly in his arms.

"I'm packing, Scotty," she said firmly while she placed sweaters in her suitcase. "It's time I go on to California as I had planned. I'll go tomorrow morning." When he didn't reply, she glanced at him. His mouth turned down and tears filled his eyes. Her heart hurt as if she had just been struck.

"Scotty, I can't stay here forever. You and your daddy have your lives. I have to go to California."

"You don't like us?" he whispered, his lower lip quivering.

"Of course I like you." She walked to the rocker. "Scotty, come here."

Giving her a sorrowful look, he crossed the room. She picked him up to put him in her lap, and he wrapped his arm around her waist, turning his face against her as he cried. "I don't want you to go. I love you."

Her heart turned over and she couldn't speak for a moment as she fought her own emotions and tried to hold back tears.

"Scotty, I have to go. When I first came, you knew that someday I would leave."

He sobbed, clinging to her. "Please don't leave us," he cried.

"What the hell—" she heard and looked up to see Mike in the doorway. He crossed the room. "Scotty." His forceful voice didn't stop his son as Scotty continued to sob.

"Mike, he's just hurt because I'm leaving. I'm touched and I don't mind holding him."

"Scotty, come here," Mike said, his voice becoming gentle, picking him up. "I'll talk to him."

"I don't mind holding him a while. I understand if he cries and wants to be in here with me."

"He can come back," Mike said, a muscle working in his jaw as if he hurt for his son. He stopped to look at the bags on her bed. "Don't carry any of that down. I will." He left the room and she hurt for all of them. She didn't want to leave, either, and she was sure Mike would hurt even more because Scotty was unhappy. Probably the sooner she left, the better. Once she was gone, Scotty would go on to other things and be his usual happy self.

Mike picked Scotty up and carried him to his room to sit in a big rocking chair. He held Scotty tightly and rocked.

"Scotty, Miss Savannah has to go. You knew that someday she would go. She's just here because she had car trouble in the storm."

"I want her to stay with us. I love her."

Mike's insides twisted and he hurt. He held his son close. He didn't want Scotty to suffer, but he wasn't ready for a commitment and Savannah wasn't, either. If he asked her to stay or even to marry for convenience, she wouldn't do it. She was battling the pain from her broken engagement and from discovering she was pregnant and that her fiancé didn't want their child.

Mike didn't want to see her go, either. They weren't ready for commitment, but he wished with all his heart she was only going to Dallas where he could keep seeing her.

"I want her to stay, Daddy."

Mike's insides ached again as if he had been stabbed through the heart. "I know, Scotty. It's nice having her here. We can talk on the phone to her. Maybe she'll come back and see us."

"No, she won't," he bawled. "Please make her stay."

"I can't do that. She has her life just as we have ours. If she asked us to go to California with her, we would have to say no. Our home is here and our lives are here."

"She doesn't love us?"

"Scotty, I'm sure she likes us, but she has her own life and she has to go. Someone is waiting for her in California."

"He doesn't love her as much as I do."

"It's her aunt and yes, she does love her."

"Don't you love her?"

"Scotty, I like Miss Savannah, but I still have to let her go. And sometimes you let someone go because you love them, when you know that they really need to go."

"I don't want her to leave us." Scotty cried, burying his face against Mike's chest. Mike stroked his son's head and back.

"Scotty, I love you more than anything else or anyone else in this whole world. You have all my love. That should count for something."

Scotty looked up at him. "She is going no matter what we do?"

"That's right."

He started crying again. Mike held him and rocked and gradually Scotty stopped crying. "I want to go see her."

"Can you see her without crying? And without pestering her to stay?"

Scotty wiped his eyes and nodded. "Yes, sir."

"Okay. We'll do something fun later. Okay?"

Scotty nodded and then he jumped down and walked off. Mike watched him go. He would miss her and he hated seeing Scotty hurt. The sooner she was on the road, the better off they would be.

Savannah finished packing, certain if she tried to carry things downstairs, Mike would be unhappy. She sent a text to her mother, another to a friend. As she closed her phone, Scotty came into the room. He looked solemn and still carried his bear tightly in his arms when he crossed the room to her. She placed him in her lap, and he lay back against her.

"How would you like chocolate cookies?"

"I'd like it better if you stayed here."

"Well, I have to go to California. But before I go, I can bake some cookies and you can help. How would that be?"

He sat up to look at her. "I get to help?"

"If you want to."

He nodded. "I want to. Will Ms. Millie say okay?"

"Yes, she will. She'll be happy to see you learn how to bake cookies."

Scotty smiled at her. "When?"

"When do you want to? How about now?"

"Yes, ma'am," he said, hopping down, and then placed his bear in an empty chair.

Savannah took his hand and they walked to the kitchen where Millie was making casseroles to put in the freezer for the weekend.

"Millie, when will be a good time for us to bake some chocolate-chip cookies?" Savannah asked. She held Scotty's hand and glanced at him to see him waiting for Millie's answer.

"Whenever you'd like because you won't be in my way and we have four ovens in this kitchen."

"Good. We can get started," Savannah said. "First thing, Scotty, is to wash your hands."

"Yes, ma'am," he said and ran off. She smiled, glad he had temporarily stopped thinking about her leaving. Hopefully, that would be the last until she drove away. Mike would deal with him and probably had already figured some way to cheer him or to get Lindsay to come over.

Savannah gathered all the ingredients, utensils and bowls, and Scotty came back and helped grease the cookie sheet and make the dough. He was eager to do anything Savannah would show him how to do.

She watched as he stood on a chair and stirred the mixture while she held the big bowl. When she heard boots approach, she watched Scotty because she didn't want him to step off the chair and fall.

When Mike entered the room, she glanced at him. For seconds she couldn't get her breath. She wanted him to step close and put his arms around her. Looking handsome in spite of a slight frown, Mike was in his heavy fleece-lined jacket and had on his hat. "What's going on? I thought Scotty might want to play in the snow."

"Yes, I do," Scotty said, without looking up. "When I get through."

Mike smiled. Scotty's tongue stuck out the corner of his mouth and he carefully tried to stir the way Savannah had showed him.

"Very good, Scotty," she said, watching him, but aware

of Mike's arm around her shoulders pulling her against his side.

"Looks like all is okay here."

"Very okay for now," she said. She frowned and gasped.

"What's wrong?"

"I don't know—just a cramp. I haven't had anything like that before and hope I don't again," she said. She was aware of Mike's steady gaze on her. "I'm okay, Mike."

"Tell me if that happens again."

"Sure," she said. "Other than the morning sickness, I've been fine."

"I think I might as well put away my hat and coat."

"No," Scotty said, turning. Mike grabbed him before he fell off the chair.

"Watch what you're doing. We'll go out when you're through here."

Scotty smiled and went back to stirring. Mike looked at her. "Why don't you go sit and I'll help him finish making the cookies."

"Go put up your hat and coat and then—"

She stopped as another painful cramp tightened low inside her.

"You go sit."

She started to protest, but decided Mike was right and left to go to a comfortable chair in the adjoining family area.

"That is a great job, Scotty," Mike praised his son and then watched while Scotty rinsed his hands.

Mike read the recipe. "Looks as if we add chocolate chips now. I'll open the package and you can pour them into the bowl and we'll stir them into the mix." They worked together quietly until Mike put the first batch into the oven.

As he set a timer, he glanced at Scotty. "Now we wait for those to bake. Be quiet in case Miss Savannah is asleep."

Scotty jumped down and ran out of the kitchen to his toys on the other side of the family room. She heard Mike's boots on the hardwood and then he stood in front of her. "Any more cramps?"

"Yes."

"I'll call the doc who delivered Scotty. Okay?"

"Mike, I should wait a little while. This may be a very temporary thing."

"And it might not be so temporary and we would have lost important time. Let's let a doc decide. I'll call him."

She listened to him make the call, feeling foolish that he was overreacting, but then her muscles cramped again.

"He said he would meet us at the ER. I'm calling an ambulance—"

"Mike, it may just be a stomachache."

"It's too low for that. I saw you put your hand on your stomach."

She squeezed her eyes shut for a moment. "I hate this and I'm scared. I don't want to lose this baby."

"Don't worry. You'll be in good hands," he said getting out his cell phone to send a text to Lindsay. Next he called Scotty over. "Scotty, you're going to Aunt Lindsay's house for a little while. Get your jacket. I need to take Miss Savannah to town." With a grin Scotty ran out of the room.

Scotty reappeared and had on his coat and cap. "I'm almost ready."

"Good for you," Mike said, tying Scotty's cap and fastening his jacket. Savannah's fists clenched as she had another small cramp. Fear chilled her and she hated disrupting Mike's life even further. His calm manner helped because she couldn't have dealt with a man who would have gone to pieces.

When Mike's cell rang, he turned to walk away, speaking softly, and Savannah assumed he didn't want to alarm Scotty. It seemed a long time that he was gone, but she could see a clock and it was only about ten minutes later when he returned to cross the room to her.

"I've got my truck and the motor's running so it will be warm. Ray's coming to take Scotty to Lindsay's house. I'll get your coat. We'll meet the ambulance and that will shave a little time off getting you to the hospital."

Mike helped her into her coat and then picked her up. After a knock at the back door Ray entered. "Anybody still home?"

They met him in the hall. "Here we are," Mike answered. "Thanks, Ray, for getting Scotty to Lindsay. She's expecting you."

"Glad to. Come on, Scotty, we'll open the door for your dad and then come back to get your things and lock up the house."

In a minute she was on the backseat of Mike's biggest truck. She had her feet up on the seat and a blanket over her. Looking worried, Scotty threw her a kiss. She smiled and threw him an imaginary kiss in return.

Mike swung Scotty up in his arms. "Don't worry. I'll call you, and Miss Savannah will be fine. Okay?"

"Okay," Scotty said, hugging his dad's neck. Mike drove away, seeing Ray racing Scotty and letting Scotty win as they ran back to the house.

"Mike, I'm sorry. I don't know what's the matter."

"Don't worry needlessly. The doctor who'll be meeting us has an excellent reputation and the hospital is top-notch with a great staff."

"I guess I won't be leaving after all when I thought I would."

"You sure as hell won't," he said emphatically.

She was silent, worried, wanting to text her mother about what was happening, but resisting until she knew more because she didn't want to worry anyone at home needlessly.

It seemed a long time had passed since they left, but she suspected it actually wasn't. She heard a siren and Mike slowed. In minutes they moved her to the ambulance. Mike brushed a kiss on her cheek. "I'll be right behind you."

She squeezed his hand and they put her in the ambulance, then Mike turned away to get back into his truck.

She met a gray-haired doctor at the hospital, gave her medical information and history, and the rest of the evening became a blur. They gave her a shot, attached an IV and soon she dozed easily, to waken and then drift back asleep. Aware of nurses, the doctor, of an ultrasound, she slept easily when she could.

Later, they moved her from a gurney to a bed. Several times she stirred to see Mike leaning back in a chair with his feet propped up, his hat and coat tossed on another chair.

"Mike, you need to go home to Scotty—" Her words were slow and she struggled to stay awake. "I can't stay awake. Did the doctor say the baby is okay, or did I dream it?"

"Dr. Nash said the baby is fine. He said your cramping stopped before you reached the hospital, so they couldn't find any cause or anything wrong. Just to be safe, Dr. Nash wants you to take it easy. Don't worry about anything. I'm fine. Scotty is with Lindsay and very happy. They said for you to just rest."

"That's easy," she said, closing her eyes and thinking a short nap was welcome. "I don't hurt any longer. I haven't since shortly after I got into the ambulance."

"Everyone takes that as a good sign," he said and pulled his chair close to the bed. "If you want anything, tell me."

"I might not leave for California tomorrow."

He smiled. "You might not leave here for the ranch tomorrow. Scotty and I will be happy to have you stay longer so don't even think about it."

She smiled and closed her eyes, feeling Mike's hand close over hers. "Suppose I want a hamburger?" she asked sleepily.

"Sorry. That you'll have to take up with Dr. Nash."

"I'm kidding. I just wanted to see what you'd say," she said and he shook his head.

He smiled. "You must be feeling better."

"Mike, can't you get a cot? Find some place to sleep, or go home and come back tomorrow."

"I'm fine. I can sleep in a chair. I've done it plenty of times. I can sleep on the floor if I have to. Don't worry."

"I've been trouble to you since the first minute we were together."

"I don't view it that way and you're worth any trouble you've caused."

Smiling, she closed her eyes, finding it difficult to stay awake.

Mike sat watching her, thinking about how scared he had been getting her to the ambulance and then to the hospital. He had felt chilled to the bone and a choking terror froze him for a brief time until he got a grip on his emotions and began to think rationally.

Mike hoped she had told her mother about being in the hospital. He didn't know how to call her family except taking her phone and finding their number on it.

He thought how scared he had been before they got to the hospital. The cold fear that had racked him also shocked him. Was he just upset for her, or did he care more than he realized for her? How important had she become to him?

The question nagged and was one he couldn't answer. He should be able to answer about his own feelings, but he couldn't. And Scotty had torn him up today. He hated to see Scotty hurting, but he expected Scotty to get over telling Savannah goodbye about an hour after she drove away.

Now she would be with them longer. He had to admit that he was glad. Part of it was because he would worry about her, but part was simply because he and Scotty wanted her to be there.

How deep did his feelings run for her? He hadn't thought they were deep until this happened, but he had been terrified for her. He needed to be certain how he felt before he told her goodbye and she drove out of his life forever.

He held her hand, rubbing it lightly while she slept. He brushed a light kiss over the back of her hand, another across her knuckles. Was he in love with Savannah?

The idea shocked him because he had been so certain he wasn't, so sure he wouldn't fall in love at this point in his life, but they had spent hours in intimacy and every minute that ticked past with her was better and more binding than the ones before.

He tried to keep Scotty's unhappiness from influencing him because Scotty was a baby and Savannah had been good to him and filled a void in his life.

In truth, she had filled emptiness in his own life.

No matter how he questioned his feelings and motives, he came up with the same answer—he was in love with her. When had that happened? He wasn't ready for love or its complications and it would be incredibly complicated with Savannah.

He had thought Wyatt Milan had been crazy to fall in love with Destiny Calhoun, a dynamic woman who would set any man's world spinning in a new direction. Wyatt's life had been turned upside down, yet here he was, Mike thought, doing the same thing himself.

He looked at Savannah and felt a rush of love. He didn't want her to leave them any more than Scotty did. He hadn't even recognized that he was falling in love with her.

When *had* he fallen in love with her? Had it been that first night they were together? Or each time, with their love just gradually building?

He leaned closer. "Savannah," he whispered, the barest of sounds. "I love you."

He kissed her fingers lightly and touched the golden ring. He spread her fingers in his hand to look at the ring—true love. How would he know if that's what he felt?

He had never questioned his feelings with Elise. They had been wildly in love, younger, sure of what they felt. Now, he was hurt, vulnerable because of losing Elise, vulnerable because of Scotty. Was he making a huge mistake? Was his judgment about love as off this time as Savannah's had been in her first engagement? He didn't think so.

When had Savannah become important to him? Enough that he wanted to wrap his arms around her and hold her safe.

He needed to step back and take a long look at what he wanted before he made the mistake of his life. If he loved her, he shouldn't let her go. If he didn't love her, he should make sure they didn't marry for the wrong reasons. Was he rushing into something he would regret?

Ten

It was Friday afternoon before she was dismissed to go to his home. Mike had driven her to the airport where they took his jet to the ranch. She was settled in a tilted-back recliner in the family room with her feet up and a blanket over her.

"Mike, I can sit up."

"You heard Dr. Nash prescribe bed rest for the next few days. You can be up some, but you're to relax, take it easy and not do anything strenuous. You're to stay with us and not drive to California this month for certain. And we'll love having you," Mike said. "Scotty is going to be deliriously happy."

"I know Scotty will be happy, but this wasn't in your plans when you took me home in the rain."

"Don't even say things like that with what's already between us," he said. His dark eyes were filled with warmth and she smiled at him as he reached to take her hand.

"Thanks, Mike, for wanting me to stay. This will all make it much more difficult when I do go. I'm rethinking California. I may just call my folks and fly home. Mom will come and fly home with me and then they will all take care of me. My brothers will behave if they're scared of upsetting me and making me sick."

"That's one bright thing from this," Mike remarked. "From what Dr. Nash said, you shouldn't travel at all for a while. I can talk to your mom if you want. I was with you through all this and I haven't been given any medication to make my thinking fuzzy," Mike said.

She shook her head. She reached over to take his hand again. "Mike, thank you for taking care of me. You've come to the rescue twice now."

He hugged her lightly. Looking into her blue eyes, he held her. "No loving for a while until they see how you are, but I can kiss you. I'm sure kisses are good."

She wound her arms around his neck. "Kisses are spectacular," she whispered. "The most highly therapeutic thing you can do," she added.

He kissed her, holding her tightly in his embrace.

Mike finally moved away. "I may have to walk around and cool down."

"I feel normal and I haven't had any cramps or anything."

"Well, they couldn't find anything wrong. Dr. Nash is just being cautious. I'm glad you feel all right."

"I was so scared I'd lose my baby."

"You didn't and you're doing well. Don't think about what could have happened. Everything is fine now and you'll be better off not going to California."

"Tomorrow is Valentine's Day—ask Lindsay to come over and let's have some little something for Scotty. I have a present from the hospital gift shop for him and I know you do, too."

"How about you just taking it easy like Doc said to do," Mike said, sitting by her again.

"Stop worrying about me. I'll be careful. It won't be any big deal and he'll like having Lindsay here for a while."

Mike pulled her close to kiss her again and then he left the room to call Lindsay. He returned about twenty minutes later. "Lindsay is bringing Scotty home. She offered to keep him another night, so if you'd rather she did, tell me and I'll call her right back. It'll be quieter without him."

"Don't be ridiculous. I'll be happy to see him."

"Okay, they'll be here before you know it, so I get just a few more kisses while we're alone."

She smiled at him and held out her arms.

When Lindsay opened the back door, Scotty dashed into the house. Mike caught him up, swinging him in a circle and making Scotty giggle. "Look what we made, Daddy," Scotty said and turned as Lindsay came into the room. She had shed her coat and shook her long pigtail behind her head as she smoothed her deep green sweater over her jeans.

"What did you make?" Mike asked.

"See for yourself. Here they are," Lindsay said, handing Mike a box. He opened it to find all kinds of valentines made by Scotty with stick figure drawings.

Scotty came to look, selected a big red valentine and ran off.

"He's gone to give that to Savannah. How is she?"

"Doc Nash said they couldn't find anything wrong. He said bed rest, no traveling to California this month, just take it easy. She's been doing fine since she got to the hospital."

"Mike, take care of yourself," Lindsay whispered, stepping close to him.

Surprised, he looked at her.

"We've been through this already, but I have to say it again. Savannah is nice, but she has concerns and I'm looking out for my brother. You don't need more problems."

"Your intentions are good, Lindsay, but let go the anxiety over me. Worry about your horses and dogs. I'm fine. Savannah isn't a burden and she's working her problems out."

"Mike, you don't need more problems in your life."

"We've gone full circle with this conversation. I'm fine. Get rid of your concerns. I'm a big boy now. You're a nice sister, but this isn't necessary," he said, patting her shoulder. Lindsay frowned as she stared at him. "You let me take care of me. I promise you, I'm happy."

She studied him intently. "Well, I'll admit you look happy. I just want to see you stay that way."

"I'll be even happier if we can wind up this conversation soon. You've been responsible for that big ranch of yours so long, you're turning into a mama bear about everyone around you."

"Okay, big brother. You're on your own as of now. I'll go say hello to Savannah."

Shaking his head and smiling, Mike watched her walk away with the box of valentines. His baby sister was growing up, but the constant responsibilities she shouldered were changing her. Mike walked into the family room beside Lindsay. Scotty sat against Savannah, who had her arm around him as she looked at all the valentines he had made.

"Hi, Lindsay. Scotty gave me a pretty valentine."

"He's getting better at drawing and pasting. We had a good time making valentines. I'm glad you're doing well and sorry you had trouble."

"Thank you. They couldn't find anything wrong. Hopefully, that won't happen again, but I'm here for a while longer."

Lindsay smiled and squeezed her hand, then played with Scotty the next hour before standing and telling them goodbye. Mike walked out with her. As he watched her drive away, he smiled again, thinking about her worries. When had Lindsay started hovering over him and worrying about him?

Was he complicating his life with his love for Savannah as Lindsay feared? He shook his head. He may have already complicated the hell out of it.

Lindsay's pickup disappeared around a curve so he went inside, locked up and walked back toward the family room, thinking about his feelings for Savannah.

That night after dinner when he was ready to take Scotty to bed, Savannah hugged Scotty's neck. "Scotty, thanks for showing me your valentines, which are beautiful."

He grinned and hugged her. "Will you read me a story?"

"Scotty," Mike cautioned. "She's supposed to be quiet and still. And say thank you when someone tells you that you have made beautiful valentines."

"I'll stay right here to read to you," Savannah told Scotty. "You get ready for bed and then bring a book."

"Thank you," Scotty flung over his shoulder as he raced from the room while Mike shook his head at her.

"I think the thank-you was because I told him to say that. If you had kept quiet about reading, you could have taken a night off."

"Do you know how much I love to read to him?"

"That's what you're going to get to do." Mike helped Scotty get ready for bed and pick out two books for Savannah. As they went back to the family room, Scotty took a book and ran ahead. By the time Mike entered the room, Savannah had Scotty in the chair beside her while she read to him. After she read both books, Mike stood.

"C'mon, Scotty. You've had a long day and Miss Savannah has had a long day. It's bedtime."

Scotty kissed her cheek. "Good night, Miss Savannah. I love you."

"I love you, too, Scotty. Good night," she said quietly, giving him a hug.

He jumped down to go with Mike, who paused at the doorway. "I'll be back shortly."

"Take your time," she replied, smiling and picking up her phone to call her family.

It was almost an hour before Mike returned. "He's finally asleep. Occasionally, it takes him a while to unwind." Mike crossed the room and put his hands on the arms of her chair and leaned down. "I don't want you walking up stairs on your own, so you'll either sleep downstairs tonight or I get to carry you upstairs. I'd prefer you'd be upstairs."

"If that's what you want," she said.

"Let's go now," he said, picking her up. She felt soft, warm in his arms and he wanted to kiss her.

"Take me to my room. I can get around and I'll be fine by myself while I get ready for bed."

Upstairs, he set her down near her bed. "I'll sleep on your sofa in the sitting room so I can hear you if you need something."

"Mike, I'll be fine or they wouldn't have sent me home."

"I'll sleep on the sofa in your suite," he repeated and she shook her head.

"All right, but you don't need to. Suppose Scotty looks for you."

"He rarely wakes up during the night. When I put him

to bed tonight, I told him that's where I would be," Mike said. He gazed at her. "You look pretty, Savannah, even after being in the hospital."

"You're ridiculous, but that's nice to hear because I don't feel pretty."

He wrapped his arms around her. "Tell me—do you really feel all right?"

"Yes, I do. I don't have a lot of energy, but I feel well."

"Good," he said. "Maybe you were just meant to stay here. I'm glad you're here and we both know exactly how Scotty feels about you."

"I'm glad to be here, Mike."

He wanted to hold her and love her, but that was out. He'd like to have her in his bed where he could hold her all night long. He slipped his hand behind her head to kiss her and felt her arms around his waist as she stepped close.

She shifted and he released her.

"I'll be back in about twenty minutes," he said as he turned to go.

Later, as he walked down the hall he saw Savannah's bedroom door was open and the light on, so he walked to the door and knocked lightly. She lowered an iPad to look at him. "I thought maybe you decided to sleep in your own bed."

"No. I'll be on the sofa so just call if you need any-thing—or want me to move in here," he said, smiling at her.

"I'd love for you to move in here if you'll get up and go in the morning before Scotty wakes up."

"I'd like to take you up on that, but Doc said no. I might disturb you and keep you from getting a peaceful night's sleep just by turning over or breathing loudly. You'll sleep better by yourself."

"That's what you think," she said, laughing.

"Savannah, one more remark like that and I'm going to ignore Doc's orders for what's best for you."

She waved her hand at him and scooted down in bed and he ached to join her and hold her in his arms and kiss her.

"Good night, Savannah," he said, walking away without looking back, trying to exercise willpower.

The next morning, after assuring Mike she would be fine on her own for a few hours and would likely nap, Mike had gone to Verity for errands and to take Scotty to get a haircut. Lindsay was coming for Valentine's Day and then taking Scotty home with her for that night. Mike had said it would give Savannah more peace and quiet, but she didn't need any more than she had and she loved having Scotty around. Millie fixed Scotty's meals and Mike helped him dress and undress—all she had to do was play with him and he was a little charmer.

She spent the time deciding what she would wear for Valentine's Day. She felt better and had more energy and was ready to go back to the doctor for the follow-up appointment. She hoped he told her to resume life as normal except for the long car trips and excessive activities.

On late Saturday afternoon when she dressed for the evening, she tingled with anticipation of spending the holiday with Mike and making a small party out of it for Scotty.

They had Millie's special baked spaghetti, a favorite of Scotty's, and a heart-shaped chocolate cake with pink icing.

Savannah dressed in a red sweater and matching slacks. The sweater covered her waist and she left the top buttons of her slacks unfastened, realizing this would be the last time she would wear them for a while. She turned to study herself in the mirror. Her waist had definitely thickened.

Taking the stairs slowly, she went down to find Mike by himself in the front room. "Is the party in here? The decorations are in the family room."

"Wow," he said, turning to look at her from her head to her toes. She tingled and forgot her question. He wore a blue long-sleeved dress shirt with an open collar, Western cut slacks and his black boots, and she wanted to walk into his embrace and kiss him.

Instead, she stood still and enjoyed watching him walk toward her, her heart beating faster the closer he came. "You look gorgeous," he said in a husky voice.

"Mike," she whispered, barely able to get her breath.

When he slipped his arms around her, she stepped close against him and turned her face up for his kiss. His arms tightened around her as he kissed her passionately.

When they finally moved apart, she gasped for breath. "I can't wait for the doctor to tell me I can resume normal activities. There's a particular activity I miss," she whispered and his gaze became more intense as he focused on her mouth.

"Savannah, I can't wait for us to be alone."

"I think we are right now," she said, kissing him and ending the conversation.

She walked beside him into the hall as Scotty came running from the kitchen.

"Aunt Lindsay is here," Scotty said. "She said to tell you."

"Thank you," Mike said. "Run and tell her we're coming."

Scotty was gone, dashing down the hall and disappearing through the open door into the family room.

There were presents on the table for Scotty in the informal dining area with the table set with a red tablecloth, a centerpiece of red, white and pink mixed flowers and hearts that Mike had given to her in the hospital and then brought home for her.

Millie and Baxter served the spaghetti and later the valentine cake Millie had baked and ice cream.

Finally, after dinner they gathered in the family room and Scotty passed out valentines while Mike piled Scotty's presents by a chair.

With Savannah's help Scotty had made little valentines for each of them and one for her he had made by himself. She looked at the poorly cut red valentine with a stick figure that had wobbly legs and arms and a large head with big dots for eyes. The printed letters ran together and the *e* had been left off "I love you," but Savannah knew she would keep the valentine and treasure it always.

Through dinner and afterward, whenever she looked at Mike, there was a sparkle in his dark eyes she had never seen before, a warmth when he looked at her that made her want to be alone with him.

Scotty was excited over an electronic game from Mike, more books from her and a magic kit from Lindsay. He immediately put on the hat from the magic kit and wanted Lindsay to show him how to do some of the tricks.

When it was time for Lindsay to take Scotty home with her, they said their goodbyes and Savannah waited in the family room, while Mike walked out to Lindsay's pickup with them.

He came back in, crossing the room to take her hand. "Come sit with me—either on the sofa or in front of the fire on the floor. Which will be the most comfortable for you?"

"Probably the sofa at this point in my life," she said. He took her hand to gently pull her to her feet. As soon as she stood, Mike stepped close and wrapped his arms around her. "Lindsay will call when they get home, so we'll get an interruption shortly. Let's go up to my room. I'll build a fire there."

"Tonight was fun, Mike. I'll treasure my valentine that Scotty made for me."

He smiled. "You and Scotty have bonded from the first."

She felt a pang in her heart at the thought of leaving the little boy soon, but she said, "Scotty probably bonds with everyone he meets."

They went to Mike's room and she watched as he got a fire blazing and closed the screen. His phone rang and he talked briefly to Lindsay and then placed his phone on a table and took Savannah's hand to draw her to her feet and wrap his arms around her.

"At last. I've waited for this moment far too long," he whispered. She started to answer, but he covered her mouth and kissed her.

Savannah's heart thudded and she tightened her arms around him, clinging to him and kissing him as if she had waited too long also.

As she had always done with Mike, she shut out all thoughts of the past or future and kissed him passionately, knowing that she loved him. Even if she had to tell him goodbye forever at the end of the month, she had already fallen in love with him and that couldn't change.

Mike paused to lean back and look at her. "Savannah, you did what I didn't think anyone could ever do again."

"What's that, Mike?" she asked, thinking more about kissing him than what he was saying.

"You caused me to fall in love with you. I love you," he said.

Stunned, she looked up at him and saw the love in his brown eyes. She couldn't get her breath and sparks danced in her middle. "Mike, are you sure?" she asked. Without waiting for his answer, she hugged him. "I love you. I love you and I didn't think you would ever love again."

He tilted her face up. "Savannah, will you marry me?"

She blinked in surprise, never expecting to hear a proposal from him or even a declaration of love. "Marry?"

"Will you marry me?" he repeated.

"Mike, you want me and my baby? This won't be your baby."

"If you marry me, it'll be my baby. I will adopt him or her and it will be my baby and I'll love this baby and so will Scotty. We have room in our hearts for more babies. You haven't answered my question."

She studied him, her heart pounding so hard she felt certain he could hear it. "You're sure?"

"I'm very sure about what I want. Will you marry me?"

Joy and amazement filled her while tears of happiness spilled on her cheeks. "Oh, Mike," she answered. "I love you, Mike." She kissed him hard and then pulled away. "Have you asked Scotty?"

"You've got to be kidding," Mike said, drawing her back into his arms and kissing away her reply. She held him tightly, joy dancing in her. "He'll be thrilled."

Pausing, he reached into his pocket to pull out a box. "This is for you."

He placed the small velvet box in her hand. She opened it to look at a dazzling ring with a huge sparkling emerald-cut diamond, surrounded by smaller diamonds. "Mike, this is the most beautiful ring. I love it and thank you. Put it on my finger."

He took her hand in his, as he looked at her.

"Will you marry me?"

"Yes, oh, yes! I love you with all my heart and this time, Mike, I'm not making a mistake and I can trust my judgment."

"You don't know that for sure, but I'm going to try to prove you right. I love you. I can't tell you what joy you've already brought in my life and helped me out of my grief. Elise would have wanted me to marry again, just as I would have wanted her to if it had been the other way around. Life was meant to be lived, not shut away from the world. I love you." He slipped the ring on her finger and drew her to him to kiss her, holding her so tightly, she could barely breathe. She didn't know how long they kissed before he raised his head. "I think we should call Lindsay and Scotty and tell them. Then we can tell the others."

She felt like laughing and dancing and spinning around for joy. "Yes, let's tell them. Lindsay may not get Scotty to bed tonight, but I want to tell them and call my family who will think I've lost it. They don't know you."

"Are the brothers going to be coming after me with fire?"

"No. Not when they see how happy I am and if they notice my pregnancy they may think this is your baby. Did you think of that? I'll tell them if they ask, but they may just assume." She looked at her ring again. "Mike, this is beautiful. I didn't have any idea—you've never told me you love me."

"I guess I hadn't faced my feelings until you were sick. That scared me badly. When I was so worried, so scared for you, I realized that my feelings ran deep," he said, tightening his arm around her. "Savannah, let's wait until morning to call our families and tell them. Lindsay will bring Scotty back in the morning and I want to tell him next. Is that all right with you?"

"I think that's the best thing to do because right now I have you all to myself," she said, kissing him. When she paused, she looked into his dark eyes. "I hope we have so much joy and a wonderful life together and fill our lives with babies."

"Oh, my. Miss Neonatal Nurse. Do you have a number in mind?"

Feeling giddy and bubbling with happiness, she laughed again. "No. Just maybe three or four or five." Suddenly, she sobered and placed her hand on his arm. "Mike, what if I can't carry this baby or have any more?"

"I love you, Savannah. I'm not marrying for babies. I'm marrying because I'm in love with you. Whatever happens we'll work it out together."

"Thank you," she whispered.

He kissed her and raised his head. "On that subject— we'll have two children right after we marry. I can take care of us—can you give up your career while the children are home and growing up? I haven't asked if you'll live out on my ranch. I haven't asked you a lot of things and I think that was the mistake you made with your ex-fiancé, but here, I've done the same thing with you."

"You asked the important questions. Yes, I can give up my career for babies. Yes, I can live on your ranch if you and the babies are here. I just want to be with you, Mike. I love you with all my heart."

She slept little that night, waking up pressed against Mike who had his arm around her. She smiled in the darkness and felt as if she should glow with the happiness that filled her. She was going to marry Mike—how long would she be in shock because of his proposal? She had never dreamed he had fallen in love, never expected a proposal. Joy bubbled inside and she smiled, turning to hold Mike close in her arms. He loved her and she loved him and this time she was certain.

Lindsay and Scotty didn't arrive until after lunch. Mike hugged Scotty and set him on his feet, then turned to Lindsay while Scotty ran to greet Savannah.

"Lindsay, I proposed to Savannah and she accepted."

Lindsay took a deep breath. "You're sure?"

"Very," he replied.

Lindsay smiled and hugged him. "Congratulations! If you're happy, then I'm happy. Mike, if you're happy, then it's wonderful."

"You're the first person we've told. I'd like to talk to Scotty alone for a minute."

"Sure. He's going to be so wound up the rest of the day. Let me take him home for one more night."

"I might take you up on your offer."

"Let's go find Scotty." They both walked to the family room where Scotty was holding a white scarf and waving his magician's wand for Savannah.

"I'm going to interrupt the magician's act. Scotty, I'd like to talk to you a moment."

"Yes, sir," he said, setting aside the scarf and wand to leave with Mike. As they left the room, Lindsay crossed to Savannah and held out her hand. "Savannah, welcome to the Calhoun family," she said.

Savannah stood to hug Lindsay lightly. "Thank you. I hope all of you are happy with what Mike is doing."

"How could we not be? He really does look happier than he has since Elise's diagnosis. His happiness is all we really care about."

"Me, too. He has a wonderful family and it was nice to meet all of you."

"Well, now you'll be part of the family. And you'll know some of the Milans, too, because of Jake marrying Madison, plus Wyatt and Destiny. Scotty is going to be overjoyed. He likes you and that's the real test."

"I already love him. You can understand that because you're with him so much."

"I've worried about my brother, but now I can stop worrying. You'll be good for him."

"Mike will be good for me. All of you will be. This is so like a dream. I hope Scotty is happy. That's essential."

"You'll know when they come back and join us."

Mike sat in a chair in his study and put Scotty on his lap. "I want to tell you something. I hope it makes you very happy," Mike said, feeling certain of the reaction he would get. "Scotty, tonight I gave Savannah a diamond ring and I asked her to marry me and she said yes. We are going to get married. She will be my wife and your second mother. Your mother will always be the woman who gave birth to you and loved you with all her being. But now you'll have another mother who will live with us and be a huge part of our lives."

"Miss Savannah's not going to leave us?" he asked, his eyes wide.

"No, she's not," Mike said.

"Yay!" Scotty cried and jumped down. "Can I go see her?"

"Yes. I take this as an answer from you that you are happy that she will be your second mother."

"Yes, sir." His smile vanished and he leaned against Mike's knee. "Daddy, can I call her Mom? Mama wouldn't mind, would she?"

Mike ached for Scotty's loss and his need for a mother who loved him. "No, your mama wouldn't mind if you call Miss Savannah Mom. You ask Miss Savannah if you can call her that. I imagine she will like it."

"Miss Savannah isn't going to leave us," Scotty repeated and tossed his magician's hat into the air. Mike caught it before it could fly across the room and hit something.

"Let's go see her and you can give her a hug so she'll

know you're happy that she's going to marry me and live with us for the rest of our lives."

Scotty grinned at him and hopped up and down as they headed back to join Lindsay and Savannah.

Mike smiled and let out his breath. This was the reaction he expected, but he was relieved that Scotty approved and liked his decision. Mike felt like jumping up and down with joy also. Lindsay had taken it so well, too, and seemed to realize he was truly happy.

They walked into the family room and Scotty raced to Savannah. "You're going to stay and never leave us," he cried, throwing his arms around her neck as she laughed and hugged him.

Mike caught up to him. "Take it easy, Scotty."

Scotty wriggled and beamed at her. "You'll be my second mother."

"Yes, I will, and I'm so happy about it, Scotty. We don't have to say goodbye."

Lindsay looked at Mike. "Congratulations. You have Scotty's full approval, which I knew you would."

Mike smiled at Savannah.

"Now, when's a wedding?" Lindsay asked.

Savannah and Mike looked at each other and laughed. "We haven't even talked about a wedding," Savannah said.

"We wanted to see you and Scotty before we did anything else," Mike said. "We'll tell the others and Savannah's family now."

"When will you see my magic tricks?" Scotty asked and the adults laughed.

"Soon, Scotty. We have some calls to make."

Lindsay stepped closer. "Mike, if you'd like, let's watch the magic act—it's short, and I'll take Scotty home with me for the afternoon or tonight if he wants to stay over. That way you can make your calls undisturbed."

He glanced at Scotty, who was gazing up at him. "Want to do that, Scotty? We'll see your magic act and then you go back to Aunt Lindsay's for a while."

"Yes," he replied, smiling at Lindsay.

"Okay, Scotty, we're ready to see some magic," Mike said, sitting close to Savannah and taking her hand in his.

Eleven

On the first Saturday of March after a small church ceremony in Dallas with only family and very close friends, a reception was held at a country club. As Savannah danced with Mike, she smiled. "I don't think I've ever met so many relatives in one family in my life."

"I was just thinking the same thing," he said, glancing over her head and seeing one of her brothers gazing back at him. "Your brothers are watching me like two hawks over a rabbit."

She laughed. "Don't worry. They'll love you and they already love Scotty. He's playing with my nieces and nephews and they are all having fun. He's the youngest, so they think he is adorable, which he is."

Mike looked down at her. "Are you okay? If you're tired, let's stop dancing."

"Dr. Nash said I can lead a normal life as long as I don't do anything too strenuous and I don't call this slow dance where we're barely moving strenuous."

"Save a little strength for later. And speaking of later. I've told my family farewell and we've told some of your family goodbye. The nanny is here and will go to Lindsay's ranch to take care of Scotty. I say why don't we slip out now? We just have to tell Scotty goodbye."

"Sounds like the best plan."

"I'll call Nell and have her and Scotty meet us outside. She'll manage that without drawing any attention."

Savannah's eagerness grew as Mike danced them toward the door, where Lindsay, Wyatt and Destiny were standing.

"Trying to make a quick exit?" Lindsay asked and laughed.

"Yes, we are," Mike replied. "Don't you interfere."

"Don't worry, she won't," Wyatt said. "I've been there and done that and I know you want to get in the limo and go."

"I suppose a farewell hug is out," Lindsay said.

"If I give you a hug," Mike said, "everyone in this room will know we're leaving. How about a hello hug when I return?"

"Deal," she said, laughing and stepping back. "Nell and I will take good care of Scotty."

"Thanks, Lindsay," Mike said.

They turned and left, hurrying around a corner of the building to the waiting limo where Nell stood by Scotty, who was in a tuxedo and black Western boots. He knelt to poke an anthill with a stick.

"Hey, buddy," Mike said, picking him up. "Tell us goodbye."

Scotty hugged his dad and kissed his cheek. Mike hugged him and turned to let Savannah hug him and kiss him. Mike set him down, turning to Nell. "Thanks for taking care of him."

"His aunt Lindsay and I will take very good care of him."

"I'm sure you will. We'll see you next week," Mike said, letting Savannah get into the limo and then climbing in behind her.

In minutes they were on the way to the airport and the private jet owned by Mike and his siblings.

Later that day, they walked out of the villa Mike owned on a Caribbean island.

"Mike, it is beautiful here," Savannah said, happiness making her giddy and feeling like she floated a few feet above the ground.

"You're what dazzles me," he said, wrapping his arms around her. "Now that it's over, did you mind a small— relatively so—wedding with relatives and only close friends?"

"It was perfect and plenty big."

"We can have a bigger reception at a later time if you want."

"No. We've said our vows. We're married. I'm your wife and I don't need to do any of that over again on a bigger scale. Mike, I'm so happy. I hope you always are."

He tightened his arms around her and kissed her. Savannah clung to him, kissing him in return, happiness filling her. She opened her eyes to glance at her hand on his shoulder and her golden heart ring. Leaning back, she waved her hand in front of him.

"Well, you made the old legend about the ring found in the creek come true. You are my true love, Mike, now and forever."

Smiling, he leaned closer to kiss her again.

* * * * *

"No, Sam. You don't get to stand there and pretend to know me."

"I do know you, Lacy," he argued, coming around the desk. "We were married."

"*Were* being the operative word," she reminded him. "You don't know me anymore. I've changed."

"I can see that. But the basics are the same. You still smell like lilacs. You still wear your hair in that thick braid I used to love to undo and spill across your shoulders..."

Lacy's stomach did a fast, jittery spin and her heartbeat leaped into a gallop. How was it fair that he could still make her body come alive with a few soft words and a heated look? Why hadn't the need for him drowned in the sea of hurt and anger that had enveloped her when he'd left?

AFTER HOURS
WITH HER EX

BY
MAUREEN CHILD

Published in Great Britain 2015
by Mills & Boon, an imprint of Harlequin (UK) Limited,
Eton House, 18-24 Paradise Road, Richmond, Surrey, TW9 1SR

© 2015 Maureen Child

ISBN: 978-0-263-25253-8

51-0315

Harlequin (UK) Limited's policy is to use papers that are natural, renewable and recyclable products and made from wood grown in sustainable forests. The logging and manufacturing processes conform to the legal environmental regulations of the country of origin.

Printed and bound in Spain
by CPI, Barcelona

Maureen Child writes for the Mills & Boon® Desire™ line and can't imagine a better job. A seven-time finalist for the prestigious Romance Writers of America RITA® Award, Maureen is the author of more than one hundred romance novels. Her books regularly appear on bestseller lists and have won several awards, including a Prism Award, a National Readers' Choice Award, a Colorado Romance Writers Award of Excellence and a Golden Quill Award.

One of her books, *The Soul Collector,* was made into a CBS TV movie starring Melissa Gilbert, Bruce Greenwood and Ossie Davis. If you look closely, in the last five minutes of the movie you'll spot Maureen, who was an extra in the last scene.

Maureen believes that laughter goes hand in hand with love, so her stories are always filled with humor. The many letters she receives assure her that her readers love to laugh as much as she does. Maureen Child is a native Californian but has recently moved to the mountains of Utah.

To La Ferrovia in Ogden, Utah
Thanks for the best calzones ever

One

"You actually *can* go home again," Sam Wyatt murmured as he stared at the main lodge of his family's resort. "The question is, will anyone be happy to see you."

But then, why should they be? He'd left Snow Vista, Utah, two years before, when his twin brother had died. And in walking away, he'd left his family to pick up the pieces strewn in the wake of Jack's death.

Guilt had forced Sam to leave. Had kept him away. And now, a different kind of guilt had brought him home again. Maybe it was time, he told himself. Time to face the ghosts that haunted this mountain.

The lodge looked the same. Rough-hewn logs, gray, weathered shingles and a wide front porch studded with Adirondack chairs fitted with jewel-toned cushions. The building itself was three stories; the Wyatt family had added that third level as family quarters just a few years ago. Guest rooms crowded the bottom two floors and there were a few cabins on the property as well, offering privacy along with a view that simply couldn't be beat.

Mostly, though, the tourists who came to ski at Snow Vista stayed in hotels a mile or so down the mountain. The Wyatt resort couldn't hold them all. A few years ago, Sam and his twin, Jack, had laid out plans for expanding the lodge, adding cabins and building the Wyatt holdings into the go-to place in the Utah mountains. Sam's parents, Bob and Connie, had been eager to expand, but from the looks of it, any idea of expansion had stopped when Sam left the mountain. But then, a lot of things had stopped, hadn't they?

His grip tightened on his duffel bag, and briefly Sam wished to hell he could as easily get ahold of the thoughts racing maniacally through his mind. Coming home wouldn't be easy. But the decision was made. Time to face the past.

"Sam!"

The voice calling his name was familiar. His sister, Kristi, headed right for him, walking in long brisk strides. She wore an electric blue parka and ski pants tucked into black boots trimmed with black fur at the tops. Her big blue eyes were flashing—and not in welcome. But hell, he told himself, he hadn't been expecting a parade, had he?

"Hi, Kristi."

"Hi?" She walked right up to him, tilted her head back and met his gaze with narrowed eyes. "That's the best you've got? 'Hi, Kristi'? After two years?"

He met her anger with cool acceptance. Sam had known what he would face when he came home and there was no time like the present to jump in and get some of it over with. "What would you like me to say?"

She snorted. "It's a little late to be asking me what

I want, isn't it? If you cared, you would have asked before you left in the first place."

Hard to argue that point. And his sister's expression told him it would be pointless to try even if he could. Remembering the way Kristi had once looked up to him and Jack, Sam realized it wasn't easy to accept that her hero worship phase was over. Of course, he'd pushed that phase over a cliff himself.

But this wasn't why he'd come home. He wasn't going to rehash old decisions. He'd done what he had to do back then, just as he was doing today.

"Back then, I would have told you not to go," Kristi was saying and as she stared up at him, Sam saw a film of tears cover her eyes. She blinked quickly, though, as if determined to keep those tears at bay—for which he was grateful. "You left us. Just walked away. Like none of us mattered to you anymore…"

He blew out a breath, dropped his duffel bag and shoved both hands through his hair. "Of course you mattered. All of you did. *Do*."

"Easy to say, isn't it, Sam?"

Would it do any good to explain that he had thought about calling home all the time?

No, he told himself. Because he hadn't called. Hadn't been in touch at all—except for a couple of postcards letting them know where he happened to be at the time—until his mother had found a way to track him down in Switzerland last week.

He still wasn't sure how she'd found him. But Connie Wyatt was a force to be reckoned with when she had a goal in mind. Probably, she had called every hotel in the city until she'd tracked him down.

"Look, I'm not getting into this with you. Not right

now anyway. Not until I've seen Dad." He paused, then asked, "How is he?"

A flicker of fear darted across her eyes, then was swept away in a fresh surge of anger. "Alive. And the doctor says he's going to be fine. It's just sad that all it took to get you to come home was Dad having a heart attack."

This was going great.

Then it seemed her fury drained away as her voice dropped and her gaze shifted from him to the mountain. "It was scary. Mom was a rock, like always, but it was scary. Hearing that it was a warning made it a little better but now it feels like…"

Her words trailed off, but Sam could have finished that sentence for her. A warning simply meant that the family was now watching Bob as if he were a live grenade, waiting to see if he'd explode. Probably driving his father nuts.

"Anyway," she said, her voice snapping back to knifelike sharpness. "If you're expecting a big welcome, you're in for a disappointment. We're too busy to care."

"That's fine by me," he said, though damned if it didn't bother him to have his little sister be so dismissive. "I'm not here looking for forgiveness."

"Why are you here, then?"

He looked into his sister's eyes. "Because this is where I'm needed."

"You were needed two years ago, too," she said, and he heard the hurt in her voice this time.

"Kristi…"

She shook her head, plastered a hard smile on her face and said, "I've got a lesson in a few minutes. I'll talk to you later. If you're still here."

With that, she turned and left, headed for one of the

bunny runs where inexperienced skiers got their first introduction to the sport. Kristi had been one of the instructors here since she was fourteen. All of the Wyatt kids had grown up on skis, and teaching newbies had been part of the family business.

When she disappeared into the crowd, Sam turned for the main lodge. Well, he'd known when he decided to come home that it wasn't going to be easy. But then, nothing in the past two years had been easy, had it?

Head down, strides long, he walked toward home a lot slower than he had left it.

The lodge was as he remembered it.

When he left, the renovations had been almost finished, and now the place looked as though the changes had settled in and claimed their place. The front windows were wider; there were dozens of leather club chairs gathered in conversational groups and huddled in front of the stone hearth where a fire burned brightly.

It might be cold outside, with the wind and snow, but here in the lodge, there was warmth and welcome. He wondered if any of that would extend to him.

He waved to Patrick Hennessey, manning the reception desk, then skirted past the stairs and around the corner to the private elevator to the third floor. Sam took a breath, flipped open the numerical code box and punched in the four numbers he knew so well, half expecting the family to have changed the code after he left. They hadn't, though, and the door shushed open for him to step inside.

They'd installed the elevator a few years ago when they added the third story. This way, none of their guests accidentally gained access to the family's space and the Wyatt's kept their privacy. The short ride ended, the door swished open and Sam was suddenly standing in the family room.

He had time for one brief glance around the familiar surroundings. Framed family photos hung on the cream-colored walls alongside professional shots of the mountain in winter and springtime. Gleaming tables held handcrafted lamps and the low wood table set between twin burgundy leather sofas displayed a selection of magazines and books. Windows framed a wide view of the resort and a river-stone hearth on one wall boasted a fire that crackled and leaped with heat and light.

But it was the two people in the room who caught and held his attention. His mother was curled up in her favorite, floral upholstered chair, an open book on her lap. And his father, Sam saw with a sigh of relief, was sitting in his oversize leather club chair, his booted feet resting on a matching hassock. The flat-screen TV hanging over the fireplace was turned to an old Western movie.

On the long flight from Switzerland and during the time spent traveling from the airport to the lodge, all Sam had been able to think about was his father having a heart attack. Sure, he'd been told that Bob Wyatt was all right and had been released from the hospital. But he hadn't really allowed himself to believe it until now.

Seeing the big man where he belonged, looking as rugged and larger than life as usual, eased that last, cold knot in the pit of Sam's stomach.

"Sam!" Connie Wyatt tossed her book onto a side table, jumped to her feet and raced across the room to him. She threaded her arms around him and held on tightly, as if preventing him from vanishing again. "Sam, you're here." She tipped her head back to smile up at him. "It's so good to see you."

He smiled back at her and realized how much he'd missed her and the rest of the family. For two years, Sam had been a gypsy, traveling from one country to another, chasing the next experience. He'd lived out of the duffel bag he still held tightly and hadn't looked any further ahead than the next airport or train connection.

He'd done some skiing of course. Sam didn't compete professionally anymore, but he couldn't go too long without hitting the slopes. Skiing was in his blood, even when he spent most of his time building his business. Designing ski runs at some of the top resort destinations in the world. The skiwear company he and Jack had begun was thriving as well, and between those two businesses, he'd managed to keep busy enough to not do much thinking.

Now he was here, meeting his father's studying gaze over the top of his mother's head. It was both surreal and right.

With a deliberate move, he dropped the duffel bag, then wrapped both arms around his much-shorter mother and gave her a hard hug. "Hi, Mom."

She pushed back, gave his chest a playful slap and shook her head. "I can't believe you're really here. You must be hungry. I'll go fix you something—"

"You don't have to do that," he said, knowing nothing could stop her. Connie Wyatt treated all difficult situations as a reason to feed people.

"Won't be a minute," she said, then shot her husband a quick glance. "I'll bring us all some coffee, too. You stay in that chair, mister."

Bob Wyatt waved one hand at his wife, but kept his gaze fixed on his son. As Connie rushed out of the room and headed for the family kitchen, Sam walked over to his father and took a seat on the footstool in front of him. "Dad. You look good."

Scowling, the older man brushed his gray-streaked hair back from his forehead and narrowed the green eyes he'd bequeathed to his sons. "I'm fine. Doctor says it wasn't anything. Just too much stress."

Stress. Because he'd lost one son, had another disappear on him and was forced to do most of the running of the family resort himself. Guilt Sam didn't want to acknowledge pinged him again as he realized that leaving the way he did had left everyone scrambling.

Frowning more deeply, his father looked over to the doorway where his wife had disappeared. "Your mother's bound and determined to make me an invalid, though."

"You scared her," Sam said. "Hell, you scared me."

His father watched him for several long minutes before saying, "Well now, you did some scaring of your own a couple years ago. Taking off, not letting us know where you were or how you were…"

Sam took a breath and blew it out. And there was the guilt again, settling back onto his shoulders like an unwelcome guest. It had been with him so long now, Sam thought he would probably never get rid of it entirely.

"Couple of postcards just weren't enough, son."

"I couldn't call," Sam said, and knew it sounded cowardly. "Couldn't hear your voices. Couldn't—hell, Dad. I was a damn mess."

"You weren't the only one hurting, Sam."

"I know that," he said, and felt a flicker of shame. "I do. But losing Jack…" Sam scowled at the memory as if that action alone could push it so far out of sight he'd never have to look at it again.

"He was your twin," Bob mused. "But he was our child. Just as you and Kristi are."

There it was. Sam had to accept that he'd caused his parents more pain at a time when they had already had more than enough loss to deal with. But back then, there had seemed to Sam to be only one answer.

"I had to go."

One short sentence that encapsulated the myriad emotions that had driven him from his home, his family.

"I know that." His father's gaze was steady and there was understanding there as well as sorrow. "Doesn't mean I have to like it, but I understand. Still, you're back now. For how long?"

He'd been expecting that question. The problem was, he didn't have an answer for it yet. Sam ducked his head briefly, then looked at his father again. "I don't know."

"Well," the older man said sadly, "that's honest at least."

"I can tell you," Sam assured him, "that this time I'll let you know before I leave. I can promise not to disappear again."

Nodding, his father said, "Then I guess that'll have to do. For now." He paused and asked, "Have you seen... anyone else yet?"

"No. Just Kristi." Sam stiffened. There were still minefields to step through. Hard feelings and pain to be faced. There was no way out but through.

As hard as it was to face his family, he'd chosen to see them first, because what was still to come would be far more difficult.

"Well then," his father spoke up, "you should know that—"

The elevator swished open. Sam turned to face whoever was arriving and instantly went still as stone. He

hardly heard his father complete the sentence that had
been interrupted.

"—Lacy's on her way over here."

Lacy Sills.

She stood just inside the room, clutching at a basket
of muffins that filled the room with a tantalizing scent.
Sam's heart gave one hard lurch in his chest. She looked
good. Too damn good.

She stood five foot eight and her long blond hair
hung in a single thick braid over her left shoulder. Her
navy blue coat was unbuttoned to reveal a heavy, fish-
erman's knit, forest-green sweater over her black jeans.
Her boots were black, too, and came to her knees. Her
features were the same: a generous mouth; a straight,
small nose; and blue eyes the color of deep summer. She
didn't smile. Didn't speak. And didn't have to.

In a split second, blood rushed from his head to his
lap and just like that, he was hard as a rock. Lacy had
always had that effect on him.

That's why he'd married her.

Lacy couldn't move. Couldn't seem to draw a breath
past the tight knot of emotion lodged in her throat. Her
heartbeat was too fast and she felt a head rush, as if
she'd had one too many glasses of wine.

She should have called first. Should have made sure
the Wyatts were alone here at the lodge. But then, her
mind argued, why should she? It wasn't as if she'd expected to see Sam sitting there opposite his father. And
now that she had, she was determined to hide her reaction to him. After all, she wasn't the one who'd walked
out on her family. Her *life*. She'd done nothing to be
ashamed of.

Except of course, for missing him. Her insides were

jumping, her pulse raced and an all too familiar swirl of desire spun in the pit of her stomach. How was it possible that she could still feel so much for a man who had tossed her aside without a second thought?

When Sam left, she had gone through so many different stages of grief, she had thought she'd never come out the other side of it all. But she had. Finally.

How was it fair that he was here again when she was just getting her life back?

"Hello, Lacy."

His voice was the deep rumble of an avalanche forming and she knew that, to her, it held the same threat of destruction. He was watching her out of grass-green eyes she had once gotten lost in. And he looked so darn good. Why did he have to look so good? By all rights, he should be covered in boils and blisters as punishment for what he'd done.

Silence stretched out until it became a presence in the room. She had to speak. She couldn't just stand there. Couldn't let him know what it cost her to meet his gaze.

"Hello, Sam," she finally managed to say. "It's been a while."

Two years. Two years of no word except for a few lousy postcards sent to his parents. He'd never contacted Lacy. Never let her know he was sorry. That he missed her. That he wished he hadn't gone. Nothing. She'd spent countless nights worrying about whether he was alive or dead. Wondering why she should care either way. Wondering when the pain of betrayal and abandonment would stop.

"Lacy." Bob Wyatt spoke up and held out one hand toward her. In welcome? Or in the hope that she wouldn't bolt?

Lacy's spine went poker straight. She wouldn't run.

This mountain was her home. She wouldn't be chased away by the very man who had run from everything he'd loved.

"Did you bake me something?" Bob asked. "Smells good enough to eat."

Grateful for the older man's attempt to help her through this oh-so-weird situation, Lacy gave him a smile as she took a deep, steadying breath. In the past two years, she had spent a lot of nights figuring out how she would handle herself when she first saw Sam again. Now it was time to put all of those mental exercises into practice.

She would be cool, calm. She would never let on that simply looking at him made everything inside her weep for what they'd lost. And blast it, she would never let him know just how badly he'd broken her heart.

Forcing a smile she didn't quite feel, she headed across the room, looking only at Bob, her father-in-law. That's how she thought of him still, despite the divorce that Sam had demanded. Bob and Connie Wyatt had been family to Lacy since she was a girl, and she wasn't about to let that end just because their son was a low-down miserable excuse for a man.

"I did bake, just for you," she said, setting the basket in Bob's lap and bending down to plant a quick kiss on the older man's forehead. "Your favorite, cranberry-orange."

Bob took a whiff, sighed and gave her a grin. "Girl, you are a wonder in the kitchen."

"And *you* are a sucker for sugar," she teased.

"Guilty as charged." He glanced from her to Sam. "Why don't you sit down, visit for a while? Connie went off to get some snacks. Join us."

They used to all gather together in this room and

there was laughter and talking and a bond she had thought was stronger than anything. Those times were gone, though. Besides, with Sam sitting there watching her, Lacy's stomach twisted, making even the thought of food a hideous one to contemplate. Now, a gigantic glass of wine, on the other hand, was a distinct possibility.

"No, but thanks. I've got to get out to the bunny run. I've got lessons stacked up for the next couple of hours."

"If you're sure…" Bob's tone told her he knew exactly why she was leaving and the compassion in his eyes let her know he understood.

Oh, if he started being sympathetic, this could get ugly fast and she wasn't about to let a single tear drop anywhere in the vicinity of Sam Wyatt. She'd already done enough crying over him to last a lifetime. Blast if she'd put on a personal show for him!

"I'm sure," she said quickly. "But I'll come back tomorrow to check on you."

"That'd be good," Bob told her and gave her hand a pat.

Lacy didn't even look at Sam as she turned for the elevator. Frankly, she wasn't sure what she might do or say if she met those green eyes again. Better to just go about her life—teaching little kids and their scared mamas to ski. Then she'd go home, have that massive glass of wine, watch some silly chick flick and cry to release all of the tears now clogging her throat. Right now, though, all she wanted was to get out of there as quickly as she could.

But she should have known her tactic wouldn't work.

"Lacy, wait."

Sam was right behind her—she heard his footsteps on the wood floor—but she didn't stop. Didn't dare. She made it to the elevator and stabbed at the button.

But even as the door slid open, Sam's hand fell onto her shoulder.

That one touch sent heat slicing through her and she hissed in a breath in an attempt to keep that heat from spreading. Deliberately, she dipped down, escaping his touch, then stepped into the elevator.

Sam slapped one hand onto the elevator door to keep it open as he leaned toward her. "Damn it, Lacy, we have to talk."

"Why?" she countered. "Because you say so? No, Sam. We have nothing to talk about."

"I'm—"

Her head snapped up and she glared at him. "And so help me, if you say 'I'm sorry,' I will find a way to make sure you are."

"You're not making this easy," he remarked.

"Oh, you mean like you did, two years ago?" Despite her fury, she kept her voice a low hiss. She didn't want to upset Bob.

God, she hadn't wanted to get into this at all. She never wanted to talk about the day Sam had handed her divorce papers and then left the mountain—and *her*—behind.

Deliberately keeping her gaze fixed to his, she punched the button for the lobby. "I have to work. Let go of the door."

"You're going to have to talk to me at some point."

She reached up, pulled his fingers off the cold steel and as the door closed quietly, she assured him, "No, Sam. I really don't."

Two

Thank God, Lacy thought, for the class of toddlers she was teaching. It kept her so busy she didn't have time to think about Sam. Or about what it might mean having him back home.

But because her mind was occupied didn't mean that her body hadn't gone into a sort of sense memory celebration. Even her skin seemed to recall what it felt like when Sam touched her. And every square inch of her buzzed with anticipation.

"Are you sure it's safe to teach her how to ski so soon?" A woman with worried brown eyes looked from Lacy to her three-year-old daughter, struggling to stay upright on a pair of tiny skis.

"Absolutely," Lacy answered, pushing thoughts of Sam to the back of her mind, where she hoped they would stay. If her body was looking forward to being with Sam again, it would just have to deal with disappointment. "My father started me off at two. When you begin this young, there's no fear. Only a sense of adventure."

The woman laughed a little. "That I understand." Her gaze lifted to the top of the lift at the mountain's summit. "I've got plenty of fear, but my husband loves skiing so…"

Lacy smiled as she watched her assistant help a little boy up from where he'd toppled over into the soft, powdery snow. "You'll love it. I promise."

"Hope so," she said wistfully. "Right now, Mike's up there somewhere—" she pointed at the top of the mountain "—with his brother. He's going to watch Kaylee while I have my lesson this afternoon."

"Kristi Wyatt's teaching your class," Lacy told her. "And she's wonderful. You'll enjoy it. Really."

The woman's gaze swung back to her. "The Wyatt family. My husband used to come here on ski trips just to watch the Wyatt brothers ski."

Lacy's smile felt a little stiff, but she gave herself points for keeping it in place. "A lot of people did."

"It was just tragic what happened to Jack Wyatt."

The woman wasn't the first person to bring up the past, and no doubt she wouldn't be the last, either. Even two years after Jack's death, his fans still came to Snow Vista in a sort of pilgrimage. He hadn't been forgotten. Neither had Sam. In the skiing world, the Wyatt twins had been, and always would be, rock stars.

The woman's eyes were kind, sympathetic and yet, curious. Of course she was. Everyone remembered Jack Wyatt, champion skier, and everyone knew how Jack's story had ended.

What they didn't know was what that pain had done to the family left behind. Two years ago, it had been all

Lacy could think about. She'd driven herself half-crazy asking herself the kind of what-if questions that had no answers, only possibilities. And those possibilities had haunted her. Had kept her awake at night, alone in her bed. She'd wondered and cried and wondered again until her emotions were wrung out and she was left with only a sad reality staring her in the face.

Jack had died, but it was the people he'd left behind who had suffered.

"Yes," Lacy agreed, feeling her oh-so-tight smile slipping away. "It was." And tragic that the ripple effect of what happened to Jack had slammed its way through the Wyatt family like an avalanche, wiping out everything in its path.

While the kids practiced and Lacy's assistant supervised, the woman continued in a hushed voice. "My husband keeps up with everything even mildly related to the skiing world. He said that Jack's twin, Sam, left Snow Vista after his brother's death."

God, how could Lacy get out of this conversation?

"Yes, he did."

"Apparently, he left competitive skiing and he's some kind of amazing ski resort designer now and he's got a line of ski equipment and he's apparently spent the last couple of years dating royalty in Europe."

Lacy's heart gave one vicious tug and she took a deep breath, hoping to keep all the emotions churning inside her locked away. It wasn't easy. After all, though Sam hadn't contacted the family except for the occasional postcard, he was a high-profile athlete with a tragic past who got more than his share of media attention.

So it hadn't been difficult to keep up with what he'd been doing the past couple of years. Lacy knew all about his businesses and how he'd put his name on ev-

erything from goggles to ski poles. He was rich, famous and gorgeous. Of course the media was all over
him. So naturally, Lacy had been treated to paparazzi
photos of Sam escorting beautiful women to glamor-
ous events—and yes, he had been photographed with
a dark-haired, skinny countess who looked as though
she hadn't had a regular meal in ten years.

But it didn't matter what he did, because Sam was
Lacy's *ex*-husband. So they could both date whomever
they wanted to. Not that she had dated much—or any
for that matter. But she could if she wanted to and that's
what mattered.

"Do you actually know the Wyatts?" the woman
asked, then stopped and caught herself. "Silly question. Of course you do. You work for them."

True. And up until two years ago, Lacy had been one
of them. But that was another life and this was the one
she had to focus on.

"Yes, I do," Lacy said, forcing another smile she
didn't feel. "And speaking of work, I should really get
to today's lessons."

Then she walked to join her assistant Andi and the
group of kids who demanded nothing but her time.

Sam waited for hours.

He kept an eye on Lacy's classes and marveled that
she could be so patient—not just with the kids but with
the hovering parents who seemed to have an opinion
on everything that happened. She hadn't changed, he
thought with some small satisfaction. She was still patient, reasonable. But then, Lacy had always been the
calm one. The cool head that invariably had smoothed
over any trouble that rose up between Sam and Jack.

He and his twin had argued over everything, and

damned if Sam didn't still miss it. A twinge pulled at his heart and he ignored it as he had for the past two years. Memories clamored in the back of his mind and he ignored them, as well. He'd spent too much time burying all reminders of the pain that had chased him away from his home.

Muttering under his breath, he shoved one hand through his hair and focused on the woman he hadn't been able to forget. She hadn't changed, he thought again and found that intriguing as well as comforting. The stir of need and desire inside him thickened into a hot flow like lava through his veins.

That hadn't changed, either.

"Okay, that's it for today," Lacy was saying and the sound of her voice rippled along his spine like a touch.

Sam shook his head to clear it of any thoughts that would get in the way of the conversation he was about to have and then he waited.

"Parents," Lacy called out with a smile, "thanks for trusting us with your children. And if you want to sign up for another lesson, just see my assistant Andi and she'll take care of it."

Andi was new, Sam thought, barely glancing at the young woman with the bright red hair and a face full of freckles. His concentration was fixed on Lacy. As if she felt his focused stare, she lifted her head and met his gaze over the heads of the kids gathered around her.

She tore her gaze from his, smiled and laughed with the kids, and then slowly made her way to him. He watched every step. Her long legs looked great in black jeans and the heavy sweater she wore clung to a figure he remembered all too well.

Despite the snow covering the ground and the surrounding pines, the sun shone brilliantly out of a bright blue sky, making the air warm in spite of the snow. Lacy flipped her long blond braid over her shoulder to lie down the center of her back and never slowed her steps until she was right in front of him.

"Sam."

"Lacy, we need to talk."

"I already told you we have nothing to say to each other."

She tried to brush past him, but he caught her arm in a firm grip and kept her at his side. Her gaze snapped to his hand and made her meaning clear. He didn't care. If anything, he tightened his hold on her.

"Time to clear the air," he said softly, mindful of the fact that there was a huge crowd ebbing and flowing around them.

"That's funny coming from you," she countered. "I don't remember you wanting to talk two years ago. All I remember is seeing you walk away. Oh, yeah. And I remember divorce papers arriving two weeks later. You didn't want to talk then. Why all of a sudden are you feeling chatty?"

He stared at her, a little stunned at her response. Not that it wasn't justified; it was only that the Lacy he remembered never would have said any of it. She was always so controlled. So…soft.

"You've changed some," he mused.

"If you mean I speak for myself now, then yes. I have changed. Enough that I don't want to go back to who I was then—easily breakable."

He clenched his jaw at the accusation that *he* had been the one to break her. Sam could admit that he'd handled everything badly two years ago, but if she

was so damaged, how was she standing there glaring at him?

"Looks to me like you recovered nicely," he pointed
out.

"No thanks to you." She glanced around, as if to
make sure no one could overhear them.

"You're right about that," he acknowledged. "But we
still have to talk."

Staring into his eyes now, she said, "Because you say
so? Sorry, Sam. Not how it works. You can't disappear
for two years, then drop back in and expect me to roll
over and do whatever it is you want."

Her voice was cool, and her eyes were anything but.
He could see sparks of indignation in those blue depths
that surprised him. The new attitude also came with a
temper. But then, she had every right to be furious. She
was still going to listen to him.

"Lacy," he ground out, "I'm here now. We'll have to
see each other every day."

"Not if I can help it," she countered, and the flash in
her eyes went bright.

Around them, the day went on. Couples walked hand
in hand. Parents herded children and squeals of excitement sliced through the air. Up on the mountain, skiers in a rainbow of brightly colored parkas raced down
the slopes.

Here, though, Sam was facing a challenge of a different kind. She'd been in his thoughts and dreams for
two years. Soft, sweet, trusting. Yet this new side of
Lacy appealed to him, too. He liked the fire sparking
in her eyes, even if it was threatening to engulf him.

When she tugged to get free of his grip, he let her
go, but his fingertips burned as if he'd been holding on
to a live electrical wire. "Lacy, you work for me—"

"I work for your father," she corrected.

"You work for the Wyatts," he reminded her. "I'm a Wyatt."

Her head snapped up and those furious blue eyes narrowed to slits. "And you're the one Wyatt I want nothing to do with."

"Lacy?"

Kristi's voice came from right behind him and Sam bit back an oath. His sister had lousy timing was his first thought, then he realized that she was interrupting on purpose. As if riding to Lacy's rescue.

"Hi, Kristi." Lacy gave her a smile and blatantly ignored Sam's presence. "You need something?"

"Actually, yeah." Kristi gave her brother one long, hard look, then turned back to Lacy. "If you're not busy, I'd like to go over some of the plans for next weekend's End of Season ski party."

"I'm not busy at all." Lacy gave Sam a meaningful look. "We were done here, right?"

If he said no, he'd have two angry women to face. If he said yes, Lacy would believe that he was willing to step away from the confrontation they needed to have— which he wasn't. Yeah, two years ago he'd walked away. But he was back now and they were both going to have to find a way to deal with it.

For however long he was here.

"For now," he finally said, and saw the shimmer of relief in Lacy's eyes. It would be short-lived, though, because the two of them weren't finished.

After Lacy and Kristi left, Sam wandered the resort, familiarizing himself with it all. He could have drawn the place from memory—from the bunny runs to the slalom courses to the small snack shops. And yet, after being gone for two years, Sam was looking at the place through new eyes.

He'd been making some changes to the resort, beginning the expansion he'd once dreamed of, when Jack died. Then, like a light switch flipping off, his dreams for the place had winked out of existence. Sam frowned and stared up at the top of the mountain. There were other resorts in Utah. Big ones, small ones, each of them drawing away a slice of tourism skiing that Snow Vista should be able to claim.

While he looked around, his mind worked. They needed more cabins for guests. Maybe another inn, separate from the hotel. A restaurant at the summit. Something that offered more substantial fare than hot dogs and popcorn. And for serious skiers, they needed to open a run on the backside of the mountain where the slope was sheer and there were enough trees and jumps to make for a dangerous—and exciting—run.

God knew he had more than enough money to invest in Snow Vista. All it would take was his father's approval, and why the hell wouldn't he go for it? With work and some inventive publicity, Sam could turn Snow Vista into the premier ski resort in the country.

But to make all of these changes would mean that he'd have to stay. To dig his heels in and reclaim the life that he'd once walked away from. And he wasn't sure he wanted to do that. Or that he could. He wasn't the same man who had left here two years ago. He'd changed as much as Lacy had. Maybe more.

Staying here would mean accepting everything he'd once run from. It would mean living with Jack's ghost. Seeing him on every ski run. Hearing his laugh on the wind.

Sam's gaze fixed on a lone skier making his way

down the mountain. Snow flared up from the sides of his skis and as he bent low to pick up speed, Sam could almost feel the guy's exhilaration. Sam had grown up on that mountain and just seeing it again was easing all of the rough edges on his soul that he'd been carrying around for two years. It wouldn't be easy, but he belonged here. A part of him always would.

And just like that, he knew that he would stay. At least as long as it took to make all of the changes he'd once dreamed of making to his family's resort.

The first step on that journey was laying it out for his father.

"And you want to oversee all of this yourself?"

"Yeah," Sam said, leaning back in one of the leather chairs in the family great room. "I do. We can make Snow Vista the place everyone wants to come."

"You've only been back a couple hours." Bob's eyes narrowed on his son. "You're not taking much more time over this decision than you did with the one to leave."

Sam shifted in his chair. He'd made his choice. He just needed to convince his father that it was the right one.

"You sure you want to do this?"

The decision had come easily. Quickly, even though he'd barely arrived. Maybe he should take some time. Settle in. Determine if this was what he really wanted to do. But even as he considered it, he dismissed it.

Looking at his father, Sam realized that his first concern—the worry that had brought him home—had been eased. His dad was in no danger. His health wasn't deteriorating. But still, the old man would have to rest up, take it easy, which meant that Sam was needed here. At least for the time being.

And if he didn't involve himself in the family resort, what the hell would he do with himself while he was here? He scrubbed one hand across the back of his neck. If he got right to work he could have most of the changes made and completed within a few months. By then, his dad should be up and feeling himself again and Sam could... "Yeah, Dad. I'm sure I want to do it. If I get started right away, most of it can be finished within a few months."

"I remember you and Jack sitting up half the night with drawings and notebooks, planning out what you were going to do to the place." His father sighed heavily and Sam could feel his pain. But then his father nodded, tapped the fingers of his right hand against his knee. "You'll supervise it all? Take charge?"

"I will." Heat swarmed through the room, rushing from the hearth where a fire burned with licks and hisses of flames.

"So this means you're staying?" His father's gaze was wise and steady and somehow way too perceptive.

"I'll stay. Until I've got everything done anyway." That was all he could promise. All he could swear to.

"Could take months."

"To finish everything? I figure at least six," Sam agreed.

His father shifted his gaze to stare out the window at the sprawling view of the Salt Lake Valley. "I shouldn't let you put your money on the line," he finally said quietly. "You've got your own life now."

"I'm still a Wyatt," Sam said easily.

Bob slowly turned his head to look at his son. "Glad to hear you remember that."

Guilt poked at Sam again and he didn't care for it. Hell, until two years ago, guilt had never been a part of his life, but since then, it had been his constant companion. "I remember."

"Took you long enough," his father said softly. "We missed you here."

"I know, Dad." He leaned forward, braced his elbows on his knees and let his hands hang in front of him. "But I had to go. Had to get away from—"

"Us."

Sam's head snapped up and his gaze fixed on his father's face, wreathed in sorrow. "No, Dad. I wasn't trying to get away from the family. I was trying to lose myself."

"Not real smart," the older man mused, "since you took you with you when you left."

"Yeah," Sam muttered, jumping to his feet and pacing. His father's point made perfect sense when said out loud like that. But two years ago, Sam hadn't been willing or able to listen to anyone. He hadn't wanted advice. Or sympathy. He'd only wanted space. Between himself and everything that reminded him he was alive and his twin was dead.

He stalked back and forth across the wide floor until he finally came to a stop in front of the man sitting quietly, watching him. "At the time, it seemed like the only thing to do. After Jack…" He shook his head and bit back words that were useless.

Didn't matter now why he'd done what he had. Hearing him say that he regretted his choices wouldn't change the fact that he had walked out on the people who loved him. Needed him. But they, none of them, could understand what it had meant when his twin— the other half of himself—had died.

His dad nodded glumly. "Losing Jack took a huge chunk out of this family. Tore us all to pieces, you more than the rest of us, I'm guessing. But putting all that aside, I need to know, Sam. If you start something here, I need to know you'll stay to see it through."

"I give you my word, Dad. I'll stay till it's done."

"That's good enough for me," his father said, and pushed out of his chair. Standing, he offered his hand to Sam and when they shook on it, Bob Wyatt smiled and said, "You'll have to work with our resort manager to get this up and running."

Sam nodded. Their resort manager had been with the Wyatts for twenty years. "Dave Mendez. I'll see him tomorrow."

"Guess you haven't heard yet. Dave retired last year."

"What?" Surprised, Sam asked, "Well who replaced him?"

His father gave him a wide grin. "Lacy Sills."

First thing the next morning, Lacy was sipping a latte as she opened the door to her office. She nearly choked on the swallow of hot milk and espresso. Gasping for air, she slapped one hand on her chest and glared at the man sitting behind *her* desk.

"What're you doing here?"

Sam took his time looking up from the sheaf of papers in front of him. "I'm going over the reports for the hotel, the cabins and the snack bar. Haven't gotten to the ski runs yet, but I will."

"Why?" She managed one word, her fingers tightening on the paper cup in her hand.

God, it was a wonder she could think, let alone talk. Her head was fuzzed out and her brain hadn't quite clicked into top gear. It was all Kristi's fault, Lacy told herself. Sam's sister had come over to Lacy's cabin the night before, carrying two bottles of wine and a huge platter of brownies.

At the time it had seemed like a great idea. Getting a little drunk with her oldest friend. Talking trash about the man who was such a central part in both of their lives.

Sam.

It always came down to Sam, she thought and wished to heaven she had a clear enough head to be on top of this situation. But, she thought sadly, even without a hangover, she wouldn't be at her best facing the man who had shattered her heart.

It was still hard for her to believe that he'd come back. Even harder to know what to do about it. The safest thing, she knew, would be to keep her distance. To avoid him as much as possible and to remind herself often that no doubt he'd be leaving again. He had left, he said at the time, because he hadn't been able to face living with the memories of Jack.

Nothing had changed.

Which meant that Sam wouldn't stay.

And Lacy would do whatever she had to, to keep from being broken again.

"When I left," Sam said quietly, "we had just started making changes around here."

"Yes, I remember." She edged farther into the office, but the room on the first floor of the Wyatt lodge was a small one and every step she took brought her closer to *him*. "We finished the reno to the lodge, but once that was done, we put off most of the rest. Your folks just weren't…" Her voice trailed off.

The Wyatts hadn't been in the mood to change anything after Jack's death changed *everything*.

"Well, while I'm here, we're going to tackle the rest of the plans."

While he was here.

That was plain enough, Lacy thought. He was making himself perfectly clear. "You talked to your dad about this?"

"Yeah." Sam folded his hands atop his flat abdomen and watched her. "He's good with it so we're going to get moving as quickly as possible."

"On what exactly?"

"For starters," he said, sitting forward again and picking up a single piece of paper, "we're going to expand the snack bar at the top of the lift. I want a real restaurant up there. Something that will draw people in, make them linger for a while."

"A restaurant." She thought of the spot he meant and had to admit it was a good idea. Hot dogs and popcorn only appealed to so many people. "That's a big start."

"No point in staying small, is there?"

"I suppose not," she said, leaning back against the wall, clutching her latte cup hard enough she was surprised she hadn't crushed it in her fist. "What else?"

"We'll be building more cabins," he told her. "People like the privacy of their own space."

"They do."

"Glad you agree," he said with a sharp nod.

"Is there more?" she asked.

"Plenty," he said and waved one hand at the chair in front of the desk. "Sit down and we'll talk about it."

A spurt of anger shot through her. He had commandeered her office and her desk and now she was being relegated to the visitor's chair. A subtle move for power?

Shaking her head, she dropped into the seat and

looked at the man sitting opposite her. He was watching her as if he knew exactly what she was thinking.

"We're going to be working together on this, Lacy," he said quietly. "I hope that's not going to be a problem."

"I can do my job, Sam," she assured him.

"So can I, Lacy," he said. "The question is, can we do the job together?"

Three

It went wrong right from the jump. For the next hour, they butted heads continuously until Lacy had a headache the size of Idaho.

"You closed the intermediate run on the east side of the mountain," he said, glancing up from the reports. "I want that opened up again."

"We can't open it until next season," Lacy said, pausing for a sip of the latte that had gone cold over the past hour.

He dropped a pen onto the desk top. "And why's that?"

She met his almost-accusatory stare with cool indifference. "We had a storm come through late December. Tore down a few pines and dropped a foot and a half of snow." She crossed her legs and held her latte between her palms. "The pines are blocking the run and we can't get a crew in there to clear it out because the snow in the pass is too deep."

He frowned. "You waited too long to send in a crew."

At the insinuation of incompetence in his voice, she stood up and stared down at him. "I waited until the storm passed," she argued. "Once we got a look at the damage and I factored in the risks to the guys of clearing it, I closed that run."

Leaning back in his chair, he met her gaze. "So you ran the rest of the season on half power."

"We did fine," she said tightly. "Check the numbers."

"I have." Almost lazily, he stood so that he loomed over her, forcing her to lift her gaze. "You didn't do badly…"

"Thanks so much." Sarcasm dripped from every word.

"It would have been a better season with that run open."

"Well yeah," she said, setting her latte cup onto *her* desk. "But we don't always get what we want, do we?"

His eyes narrowed and she gave herself a mental pat on the back for that well-aimed barb. Before Sam had walked out on her and everyone else, she couldn't remember a time when she'd lost her temper. Now that he was back, though, the anger she used to keep tamped down kept bubbling up.

"Leaving that alone for the moment," he said, "the revenue from the snack bar isn't as high as it used to be."

She shrugged. This was not news to her. "Not that many people are interested in hot dogs, really. Most people go for a real lunch in town."

"Which is why building a restaurant at the summit is important," he said.

She hated that he was right. "I agree."

A half smile curved his mouth briefly and her stomach gave a quick twist in response. It was involuntary, she consoled herself. Sam smiled; she quivered. Didn't mean she had to let him know.

"If we can agree on one thing, there may be more."

"Don't count on it," she warned.

He tipped his head to one side and stared at her. "I don't remember you being so stubborn. Or having a temper."

"I learned how to stand up for myself while you were gone, Sam," she told him, lifting her chin to emphasize her feelings on this. "I won't smile and nod just because Sam Wyatt says something. When I disagree, you'll know it."

Nodding, he said, "I think I like the new Lacy as much as I did the old one. You're a strong woman. Always have been, whether you ever chose to show it or not."

"No," Lacy said softly. "You don't get to do that, Sam. You don't get to stand there and pretend to know me."

"I do know you, Lacy," he argued, coming around the desk. "We were married."

"*Were* being the operative word in that sentence," she reminded him, and took two steps back. "You don't know me anymore. I've changed."

"I can see that. But the basics are the same," he said, closing the distance between them again. "You still smell like lilacs. You still wear your hair in that thick braid I used to love to undo and spill across your shoulders…"

Lacy's stomach did a fast, jittery spin and her heartbeat leaped into a gallop. How was it fair that he could still make her body come alive with a few soft words and a heated look? Why hadn't the need for him drowned in the sea of hurt and anger that had enveloped her when he left?

"Stop it."

"Why?" He shook his head and kept coming, one long, slow step after another. "You're still beautiful. And I like the way temper makes your eyes flash."

The office just wasn't big enough for this, Lacy told herself, and crowded around behind the desk, trying to keep the solid piece of furniture between them. She didn't trust herself around him. Never had been able to. From the time she was a girl, she had wanted Sam and that feeling had never left her. Not even when he'd broken her heart by abandoning her.

"You don't have the right to talk to me like that now. You left, Sam. And I moved on."

Liar, her mind screamed. She hadn't moved on. How could she? Sam Wyatt was the love of her life. He was the only man she had ever wanted. The only one she still wanted, damn it. But he wasn't going to know that.

Because she had trusted him. More than anyone in her life, she had trusted him and he'd left her without a backward glance. The pain of that hadn't faded.

He narrowed his gaze on her. "There's someone else?"

She laughed, but the sharp edge of it scraped her throat. "Why do you sound so surprised? You've been gone two years, Sam. Did you think I'd enter a convent or something? That I'd throw myself on our torn-up marriage certificate and vow to never love another man?"

His jaw tightened, the muscle there twitching as he ground his teeth together. "Who is he?"

She sucked in a gulp of air. "None of your business."

"I hate that. But yeah, it's not," he agreed, moving

closer. So close that Lacy couldn't draw a breath without taking the scent of him—his shampoo, the barest hint of a foresty cologne—deep into her lungs. He looked the same. He felt the same. But *nothing* was the same.

Lacy felt the swirl of need she always associated with Sam. No other man affected her as he did. No other man had ever tempted her into believing in forever. And look how that had turned out.

"Sam." The window was at her back, the glass cold through her sweater and still doing nothing to chill the heat that pulsed inside her.

"Who is he, Lacy?" He reached up and fingered the end of her braid. "Do I know him?"

"No," she muttered, looking for a way out and not finding one. She could slip to the side, but he'd only move with her. Too close. She took another breath. "Why does it matter, Sam? Why would you care?"

"Like I said, we were married once," he said as if he had to remind her.

"We're not now," she told him flatly.

"No," he said, then lifted his fingers to tip up her chin, drawing her gaze to meet his. "Your eyes are still so damn blue."

His whisper shivered inside her. His touch sent bolts of heat jolting through her and Lacy took another breath to steady herself and instead was swamped by his scent, filling her, fogging her mind, awakening memories she'd worked so hard to bury.

"Do you taste the same?" he wondered softly, and lowered his head to hers.

She should stop him, she knew, and yet, she didn't. Couldn't. His mouth came down on hers and everything fell away but for what he could make her feel. Lacy's heart pounded like a drum. Her body ached; her mind swirled with the pleasure, the passion that she'd only ever found with Sam.

It was reaction, she told herself. That was all. It was the ache of her bones, the pain in her heart, finally being assuaged by the man who had caused it all in the first place.

He pulled her in tightly to him and for a brief, amazing moment, she allowed herself to feel the joy in being pressed against his hard, muscled chest again. To experience his arms wrap around her, enfolding her. To part her lips for his tongue and know the wild rush of sensation sweeping through her.

It was all there. Two years and all it took was a single kiss to remind her of everything they'd once shared, they'd once known. Her body leaned into him even as her mind was screaming at her to stop. She burned and in the flames, felt the heat sear every nerve ending. That was finally enough, after what felt like a small eternity, to make her listen to that small, rational internal voice.

Pulling away from him, Lacy shook her head and said, "No. No more. I won't do it."

"We just did."

Her head snapped up, furious with him, but more so with herself. How could she be so stupid? He'd *abandoned* her and he's back on the mountain for a single day and she's kissing him? God, it was humiliating. "That was a mistake."

"Not from where I'm standing," Sam said, but she was pleased to see he looked as shaken as she felt.

Small consolation, but she'd take it. The office suddenly seemed claustrophobic. She had to get out. Get into the open where she could think again, where she could force herself to remember all of the pain she'd been through because of him.

"You can't touch me again, Sam," Lacy said, and it cost her, because her body was still buzzing as if she'd brushed up against a live wire. "I won't let you."

Frowning, he asked, "Loyal to the new guy, huh?"

"No," she told him flatly, "this is about me. And about protecting myself."

"From *me*?" He actually looked astonished. "You really think you need protection from me?"

Could he really not understand this? "You once asked me to trust you. To believe that you loved me and you'd never leave."

His features went taut, his eyes shuttered. She *felt* him closing himself down, but she couldn't stop now.

"But you lied. You *did* leave."

His eyes flashed once—with hurt or shame, she didn't know, couldn't tell. "You think I planned to leave, Lacy? You think it was something I wanted?"

"How would I know?" she countered, anger and hurt clawing at her insides. "You didn't talk to me, Sam. You shut me out. And then you walked away. You hurt me once, Sam. I won't let you do it again. So you really need to back off."

"I'm here now, Lacy. And there's no way I'm backing off. This is still my home."

"But *I'm* not yours," she told him, accepting the pain of those words. "Not anymore."

He took a breath, blew it out and scrubbed one hand across the back of his neck. The familiarity of that gesture tugged at her.

"I thought of you," he admitted, fixing his gaze to hers as his voice dropped to a low throb that seemed to rumble along her spine. "I missed you."

Equal parts pleasure and pain tore at her heart. The taste of him was still on her mouth, flavoring every breath. Her senses were so full she felt as if she might explode. So she held tight to the pain and let the pleasure slide away. "It's your own fault you missed me, Sam. You're the one who left."

"I did what I had to do at the time."

"And screw anyone else," she added for him.

Pushing one hand through his hair, he finally took a step back, giving Lacy the breathing room she so badly needed. "That's what it looked like, I guess."

"That's what it was, Sam," she told him, and took the opportunity to slip out and move around until the desk once again stood between them like a solid barrier. "You left us all. Me. Your parents. Your sister. You walked away from your home and left the rest of us to pick up the pieces."

"I couldn't do it." He whirled around to face her, green eyes flashing like a forest burning. "You need to hear me say it? That I couldn't take it? That Jack died and I lost it? Fine. There." He slapped both hands onto the desk and glared at her. "That make it better for you? Easier?"

Overwhelmed with fury, Lacy thought she actually *saw* red. So many emotions surged inside her, she could hardly separate them. Lacy felt the crash and slam of the feelings she'd tried to bury two years ago as they rushed to the surface, demanding to be acknowledged.

"Better? Really?" Her voice was hard, but low. She wouldn't shout. Wouldn't give him the satisfaction of knowing just how deeply his words had cut her. "You think it can get better? My *husband* left me with all the casualness of tossing out an old shirt."

"I didn't—"

"Don't even try to argue," she interrupted him before he could.

"I won't." He fisted his hands on the desktop, then carefully, deliberately, released them again. "I can't explain it to myself, so how could I explain it to you or anyone else? Yeah, I left and maybe that was wrong."

"Maybe?"

"But I'm back now."

Lacy shook her head and swallowed the rest of her temper. Clashing with him was no way to prove to Sam that she was over him. She would *not* get pulled into a Wyatt family drama. She wasn't one of them anymore. Sam returning had nothing to do with her. In spite of the heat inside her, the yearning gnawing at her, she knew she had to protect herself.

"You didn't come back for me, Sam. So let's not pretend different, okay?"

"What if I had?" he whispered, gaze locked with hers.

"It wouldn't matter," she told him, and hoped to heaven he believed her. "What we had is done and gone."

He studied her for a long minute. Seconds ticked past, counting off with every heartbeat. Tension coiled and bristled in the air between them.

"I think," he said at last, "we just proved that what we had isn't completely gone."

"That doesn't count."

Surprised, he snorted, and laughter glinted in his eyes for a split second. "Oh, it counts. But we'll let it go for now."

She released a breath she hadn't realized she was holding. Ridiculous to feel both relieved and irritated all at once. How easily he turned what he was feeling on and off. How easily he had walked away from his life. From her.

"Back to business, then," he said, voice cool, dispassionate, as if that soul-shaking kiss hadn't happened. "Yesterday, you and Kristi were talking about the End of Season party."

"Yes. The plans are finalized."

Fine. Business she could do. She had been running the Wyatt resort for the past year and she'd done a damn good job. Let him go over the records and he would see for himself that she hadn't curled up and died just because he left. Lacy had a life she loved, a job she was good at. She was *happy*, damn it.

Coming around the desk, she ignored him and hit a few keys on the computer to pull up the file. "You can see for yourself, everything's in motion and right on schedule."

She moved out of the way as he stepped in to glance at the monitor. Scrolling down, he gave the figures there a quick look, then shifted his gaze to hers. "Looks fine. But end of season's usually not until March. Why are we closing the slopes early?"

Lacy was on familiar ground here and she relaxed a little as she explained, "There hasn't been any significant snowfall since early January. Weather's been cold enough to keep the snowpack in good shape, but we're getting icy now. Our guests expect the best powder in the world—"

"Yeah," he said wryly, "I know."

Of course he knew. He had, just like Lacy, grown up skiing the very slopes they were discussing now. He'd built a life, a profession, a reputation on skiing.

"Right. Then you should appreciate why we're doing the official closing early." Lacy walked around the desk until it stood between them again. She sighed and said, "Numbers have been falling off lately. People know there's no fresh snow, so they're not in a rush to come up the mountain.

"Throwing the End of Season party early will bring them up here. The hotel's already booked and we just have two of the cabins left empty…"

"One," he said, interrupting the flow of words while he continued to scan the plans for the party.

"One what?"

"One cabin's empty." He shrugged. "I moved my stuff into Cabin 6."

A sinking sensation opened up in the pit of her stomach. Cabin 6 was close to her house. Way too close. And he knew that. So had he chosen that cabin purposely? "I thought you'd be staying in the family quarters at the lodge."

He shook his head. "No. The cabin will suit me. I need the space."

"Fine," she said shortly, determined not to let it matter where he stayed. "Anyway, locals will still come ski whether we're 'officially' closed or not. We'll keep the lifts running and if we get more snow, then others will come, too. But holding the party early gives us publicity that could keep tourists coming in until the snow melts."

"It's a good idea."

He said it grudgingly and Lacy scowled at him. "You sound surprised."

"I'm not," he said, then dropped into the desk chair. "You know this place as well as I do. You were a good choice to run the resort. Why would I be surprised that you're good at your job?"

Was there a compliment in there?

"I want to go over the rest of the records, then, since you're the manager now, I'll want to talk tomorrow about the plans for the resort."

"Fine," she said, headed for the door. "I'll see you here tomorrow, then."

"That'll work."

She opened the door and stopped when he spoke again.

"And Lacy..."

She looked over her shoulder at him. His eyes met hers. "We're not done. We'll *never* be done."

There was nothing she could say to that, so she left, closing the door softly behind her.

That kiss stayed with him for hours.

For two years, he'd lived without her. It hadn't been easy, especially at first. But the grief and rage and guilt had colored everything then and he'd buried her memory in the swamp of other emotions. He'd convinced himself she was fine because the reality was too brutal. She'd come to haunt him at night of course. His sleep was crowded with her image, with her scent, with her taste.

And now he'd had a taste of her again and his system was on fire.

Need crouched inside him, clawing at his guts, tearing at what was left of his heart. He'd loved her back then. But love hadn't been enough to survive his own pain. Now there was desire, rich and thick and tormenting him in ways he hadn't felt since the last time he'd seen Lacy Sills.

She'd said she had a new man. Who the hell was touching her? Who heard her whisper of breath when she climaxed? Who felt her small, strong hands sliding up and down his skin? It was making Sam crazy just thinking about it. And yet, he couldn't seem to stop, either.

Yeah, none of it was rational. He didn't care.

When he'd headed home, his only thought had been for his father. Worry had driven every action. He hadn't stopped to think what it would be like to be near Lacy again. To face her and what he'd done by leaving. His heart told him he was a bastard, but his brain kept reminding him that he'd had to leave. That he might have made even more of a mess of things if he'd stayed.

Now he was here, for at least a few months. How was he going to make it without touching her? Answer— he wouldn't. The truth was, he was *going* to touch her. As soon and as often as possible. Her response to his kiss told him that whether she wanted to admit it or not, she wanted him, too. So to hell with the new guy, whoever he was.

Sam turned in the chair and looked out at the night. The lights glittering in the Salt Lake Valley below smudged the horizon with a glow that dimmed the stars. His gaze shifted, sweeping across the resort, where lights were golden, tossing puddled yellow illumination on the snow. It was pristine, beautiful, and he'd missed the place.

Acknowledging it was hard, but Sam knew that coming back here eased something inside him that had been drawn tight as a bowstring for two years. Coming home hadn't been easy. He'd spent the past two years trying to convince himself that he'd never come back. Now that he was here, though, there were ghosts to face, the past to confront and, mostly, there was the need to make a kind of peace with Lacy.

But then, he thought as he stood and walked out of the office, maybe it wasn't peace he was after with her.

For the next few days, Lacy avoided him at every turn and Sam let her get away with it. There was time to settle what was between them. He didn't have to rush, and besides, if he made her that nervous, drawing out the tension would only make her more on edge.

And that could only work to his benefit. Lacy cool and calm wasn't what he wanted. The temper she'd developed intrigued him and made him think of how passionate she had always been in bed. Together, they had been combustible. He wanted that back.

He glanced at her and almost smiled at the deliberate distance she kept. As if it would help. As if it could cool the fires burning between them. The day was cold and clear and the snow-covered ground at the summit crunched underfoot as they walked toward the site for the restaurant he was planning.

Tearing his gaze from Lacy momentarily, Sam studied the snack shop that had been there since before he was born. Small and filled with tradition, it had outlived its purpose. These days, most people wanted healthy food, not hot dogs smothered in mustard and chili.

"What're you thinking?" Lacy looked up at him, clearly still irritated that he'd dragged her away from the inn to come up here and look around.

He glanced at her. "That I want a chili dog."

For a split second, the ice in her eyes drained away. "You always did love Mike's chili."

"I've been all over the world and never found anything like it."

"Not surprising," Lacy answered. "I think he puts rocket fuel in that stuff."

Sam grinned and she gave him a smile in return that surprised and pleased him. A cold wind rushed across the mountaintop and lifted her blond braid off her shoulder. Her cheeks were pink, her blue eyes glittering and she looked so good it was all he could do not to grab her. But even as he thought it, her smile faded.

"I think we'll keep the snack shack for old time's sake," he said, forcing himself to look away from her and back out over the grounds where he would build the new restaurant. "But the new place, I'd like it to go over there," he pointed, "so the pines can ring the back of it. We'll have a deck out there, too, a garden area, and the trees will provide some shade, as well."

She looked where he pointed and nodded. "It's a good spot. But a wood deck requires a lot of upkeep. What about flagstone?"

Sam thought about it. "Good idea. Easier to clean, too. I called Dennis Barclay's construction company last night and he's going to come up tomorrow, make some measurements, draw up some plans so we can go to the city and line up the permits."

"Dennis does good work." She made a note on her iPad. "Franklin stone could lay the gravel paths and the flagstone. They've got a yard in Ogden with samples."

"Good idea. We can check that out once we get the permits and an architect's drawing on the restaurant."

"Right." Her voice was cool, clipped. "We used Nancy Frampton's firm for the addition to the inn."

"I remember." He nodded. "She's good. Okay, I'll call and talk to her tomorrow. Tell her what we want up here."

She made another note and he almost chuckled. She was so damn determined to keep him at arm's length. To pretend that what they'd shared in the office last night hadn't really happened. And he was willing to let that pretense go on. For a while.

"As long as you're making notes, write down that we want to get some ideas for where to build an addition to the inn. I want it close enough to the main lodge that it's still a part of us. But separate, too. Maybe joined by a covered walkway so even during storms, people can go back and forth."

"That'd work." She stopped, paused and said, "You know, a year ago, we put in a restaurant-grade stove, oven and fridge in the main lodge kitchen. We're equipped to provide more than breakfast and lunch now."

He turned his head and looked at her. "Then why aren't you?"

"We need a new chef." Lacy sighed and pulled her sunglasses off the top of her head to rest on the bridge of her nose. "Maria's ready to retire but she won't go until she's sure we'll survive without her."

Sam smiled, thinking of the woman who'd been at the lodge since he was a boy. Maria was a part of Sam's childhood, as much a fixture on the mountain as the Wyatt lodge itself. "Then she'll never leave."

Lacy smiled, too, and he wondered if she realized it. "Probably not. But if we want to serve a wider menu to more people, we need another chef to take some of the work off her shoulders. Maria doesn't really want to retire anyway, but she can't handle a larger load, no matter what she says. Another chef would make all the difference."

"Make a note," he said.

"Already done."

"Okay then." Sam took her elbow and turned her toward the snack bar. "Come on. We've got to go down and finalize the party setup. But first—chili dogs. On me."

"No thanks. I'm not hungry."

"As I remember it, you're always hungry, Lacy," he said, practically dragging her to the snack bar.

"Oh, for—" She broke off, gave in and started walking with him. "Things change, you know."

She was right. A lot had changed. But that buzz of something hot and electric that hummed between them was still there. Stronger than ever. Two years away hadn't eased what he felt for her. And since that kiss, he knew she felt the same.

"Mike's chili hasn't changed. And that's all I'm thinking about right now."

Of course, he was also planning ahead. So no onions.

Four

"Dad's really glad Sam's home." Kristi drained the last of her wine, then reached out and snagged the bottle off the coffee table for a refill.

"I know," Lacy said, sipping hers more slowly. She remembered the too-much-wine-and-brownies fest she and Kristi had had just a few days ago, and Lacy could live without another morning-after headache. "Your mom's happy, too."

Kristi sighed and snuggled deeper into the faded, overstuffed chair opposite Lacy. "I know. She hasn't stopped baking. Pies, cakes, the cookies I brought over to share. It's nuts, really. I don't think the oven's cooled off once since Sam arrived. Between Mom's sugar overload and Maria making all of Sam's favorites for dinner…I think I've gained five pounds."

While her best friend talked, Lacy stared at the fire in the brick hearth. Outside, the night was cold and still, moonlight glittering on snow. Inside, there was warmth from the fire and from the deep threads of friendship.

It felt good to sit here relaxing—or as much as she could relax when the conversation was about Sam. But at least he wasn't *here*. He wasn't walking through the resort with her, hunched over her desk going over plans, smelling so good she wanted to crawl onto his lap, tuck her head against his chest and just breathe him in.

Oh, God.

It had been days now and her very righteous anger kept sliding away to dissolve in a puddle of want and need. She didn't *want* to want Sam, but it seemed there was no choice. And damn it, Lacy told herself, she should know better.

What they had together hadn't been enough to keep him with her two years ago. It wouldn't be enough now. Wanting him was something she couldn't help. That didn't mean that she would surrender to what she felt for him again, though.

"They're all so happy he's back," Kristi was saying. "It's like they've forgotten all about how he left."

"I can understand that," Lacy told her, pausing for another sip of wine to ease the dryness in her suddenly tight throat. It was different for his family, of course. Having Sam back meant filling holes in their lives that had stood empty for too long. There was no second-guessing what they felt at his return. They weren't focused on their pain now, but on the alleviation of it.

Taking a breath, Lacy gave her friend a smile she really didn't feel. "Your parents missed him horribly. They're just grateful to have him home."

"Yeah, I get it." Kristi frowned into her straw-colored wine. "But how do they just ignore how he left? What he did to all of us by leaving *when* he did?"

"I don't know." Lacy reached out to snag a chocolate chip cookie off the plate on the table. Taking a bite, she chewed thoughtfully while Kristi continued to rant about her older brother, then she said, "I think for your mom and dad, it's more about getting their son back than it is punishing him for leaving."

"He hurt us all."

"Yeah. He did." Lacy knew how the other woman felt. *She* couldn't get past how Sam had left, either. Having him here now was so hard. Every time she saw him. Every time he stepped close to her, her heartbeat staggered and the bottom dropped out of her stomach.

Plus, there was the whole kiss thing, too. She hadn't been able to forget it. Hadn't been able to stop thinking about it. Had spent the past several days on red alert, waiting for him to try it again so she could shut him down flat.

And he hadn't tried.

Damn it.

"I used to think," Kristi said softly, "that everything would be better if Sam just came home." She paused for a sip of wine. "Now he has and it's not better. It's just… I don't know."

"He's your brother, Kristi," Lacy said, propping her feet on the coffee table and crossing them at the ankles. "You're still mad at him, but you love him and you know you're glad he's back."

"Do you?"

"Do I what?"

"Still love him."

Lacy's heart gave a hard thump. "That's not the point."

"It's completely pointy."

"Funny." Lacy took a long drink of her wine and

when she'd swallowed, said, "But this isn't about me. Or what I feel."

"So," Kristi mused, a half smile on her face, "that's a yes."

"No, it's not." Because her heart hammered every time he was near didn't necessarily mean *love*. Desire would always be there and that she could accept. Love was something else again and, "Even if it was, it wouldn't matter."

"You're still mad, too."

Lacy sighed. "Yeah. I am."

"He's worked really hard on the End of Season party," Kristi grudgingly admitted. "Sam even called one of his old friends. Tom Summer? He has a band that's really popular now and Sam talked Tom into bringing the band in for the party. Live music's going to be way better than the stereo we had arranged."

"Yes, it will." Irritating to admit that Sam had so easily arranged for a good band when everyone Lacy had spoken to about playing at the party had already been booked. He had friends everywhere and they were all as pleased to have him back as his family was. Here at Snow Vista, it was a regular *Celebration of Sam*. And Lacy was the only one not playing along. Well, okay, there was Kristi, as well. But she would eventually join the parade—Sam was her brother and that connection would win in the end.

When that happened, Lacy would be off by herself. Standing on the sidelines. Alone.

"It's like he's stepped right back into his life without a miss." Kristi shook her head again. "He steers away from most of the skiers—I think that's because everyone wants to ask him about Jack and he doesn't want to talk about him. I can't blame Sam for that." Her index finger ringed the rim of her wineglass. "None of us do."

"True." Lacy herself had seen Sam keep away from strangers, from the tourists who flocked to ski at Snow Vista. Just as she had watched him visit all of the runs on the mountain but the one that Jack had favored. She knew that memories were choking him just as her own had for two years.

Even this cabin—where she had grown up—wasn't a sanctuary anymore. Instead of memories of days spent with her father, the images in her mind were all of her and Sam, starting their life together. Lacy glanced around the familiar room, seeing the faded but comfortable furniture, the brightly colored throw rugs, the photos and framed prints hanging on the wall.

When she and Sam had married, they'd moved into her place—the plan had been to stay there and add on to the simple cabin until they had their dream house. The cabin was in a perfect spot—great views, close to the lodge and the ski runs—plus it was hers, free and clear, left to her after her father's death. Of course, those building plans were gathering dust in a closet and the rooms for the children they'd planned to have had never been built.

But staying here in this cabin had been a sort of exquisite torture. She'd heard Sam's voice, felt his presence, long after he left. Even her bed felt too big without him sharing it with her. Sam had torn up the foundation of her life and left her sitting in the rubble.

"Sam's even talking to Dad about building a summer luge ride. One like Park City has, to give tourists something to do up here in summer." Frowning, she took a sip of wine and grumbled, "I hate that it's a good idea."

"I know what you mean," Lacy admitted, chewing

on another cookie. "I want him to be out of step, you know? To stumble a little when he takes charge after two years gone. And yet, he's doing it all and he's getting a lot done. He's already had a contractor up at the summit to see about building the new restaurant and he's hired Nancy Frampton to draw up plans." She took a huge bite of the cookie and ground her teeth together. "He's gotten more done in the last few days than we have in two years."

"Irritating as hell, isn't it?" Kristi muttered.

"Really is."

"I don't know if I want him here or not. I mean, I'm glad for Mom and Dad—they missed him so much. But seeing him every day…" She stopped, her eyes widened and she groaned out loud. "God, I'm spewing all over the place and this has got to be so much worse on you." Instantly, Kristi looked contrite, embarrassed. "How are you handling it?"

"I'm fine." Lacy figured if she said those two words often enough, they might actually click in and she'd *be* fine.

At the moment, though, not so much. Her gaze shifted to the closest window. Through it, she had a view of the snow-covered forest, a wide sweep of sky, and there, she thought, through the trees, a glimpse of Cabin 6.

Most of the time she could pretend he wasn't there, but at night, when he had the lights on, he was impossible to ignore. As she watched, she saw his shadow pass a window and her heartbeat fluttered. Having him that close was a new kind of torture, she told herself.

For two years, she hadn't known where he was or what he was doing, except for the occasional updates from his parents or snippets in the media. Being apart from him tore at her—at least in the first few months. Now he was here, and still out of reach—not that she wanted to reach out and touch him. But having him close by and yet separate was harder than she'd imagined it could be.

When he first told her he'd be staying in the cabin closest to her home, Lacy had worried that he'd be coming over. But not once had Sam walked to her door. And she didn't know if that made her feel better or worse. The only thing she was sure of was that her nerves were stretched taut and sooner or later, they were going to snap.

"You're not fine." Kristi's voice was soft and filled with understanding.

Lacy might have argued that point, but Kristi was her best friend. They'd seen each other through high school, college courses, mean girls and heartbreak. What would be the point of trying to hold out now?

"Okay, no, I'm not." Nodding, Lacy held her wineglass a little tighter and drew a long, deep breath. "But I can be. It's just going to take some time."

"I hate that you're getting all twisted up by him again."

"Thanks," Lacy said, forcing a smile. "Me, too."

"The problem is, we're letting him get to us," Kristi said, grabbing another cookie and taking a bite. "That gives him all the power. What we have to do is take it back."

"You've been reading self-help books again." Lacy shook her head.

A quick grin flashed over Kristi's face. "Guilty. But you know, some of what they say makes sense. He can only bug us if we allow it. So we just have to stop allowing it."

"What a great idea," Lacy said, laughing, and God it felt good to laugh. "Got any ideas on how?"

Kristi shrugged. "Haven't gotten to that chapter yet."

"How does Tony maintain sanity around you?"

Tony DeLeon was smart, gorgeous and hopelessly in love with Kristi. For the past year or so, they'd been inseparable and Lacy really tried to be happy for her friend and not envious.

"He loves me." Kristi sighed dreamily. "Who would have guessed that I'd fall for an accountant?"

"Good thing you did—he's done a great job handling the inn's books."

"Yeah, he's pretty amazing," Kristi mused. "And so not the issue here. The problem is Sam."

Lacy's problem had always been Sam. She'd known from the time she was fifteen that he was the one she wanted. Oh, Jack was what the newspapers had always called "the fun twin" and she supposed that was true. Sam was quieter. More intense. Jack had been larger than life. His laugh was loud and booming; his love for life had been huge.

And when he died, he'd taken pieces of everyone who loved him with him. The largest piece had come from Sam. Those had been dark, terrible days. Lacy had helplessly watched Sam sink into a pit of misery and grief. Even lying beside him in their bed here at the cabin, she'd felt him slipping away from her.

He'd gotten lost, somehow, in the pain and he hadn't been able to find his way out.

But knowing that didn't make what had happened between them any easier to bear.

"Kristi," she said, "he's your brother. You can't stay mad at him forever."

Unexpectedly Kristi's eyes filled with tears, but she

blinked them back. "We *all* lost Jack and Sam didn't seem to understand that. He hurt me. Hurt all of us. Are we just supposed to forgive and forget?"

"I don't know," Lacy said, though she knew that she would never forget that she'd been left behind. Shut out. Made to feel that she didn't matter. She'd lived through that as a child and she'd trusted Sam when he promised he would never leave her—then he did, and that pain would never completely disappear.

"I don't think I can," Kristi admitted. She set her wineglass on the table and stood up. Then she walked to a window and stared out at the lamplight streaming from Sam's cabin. "I want to," she said, sending a short glance over her shoulder at Lacy. "I really do. And Tony keeps telling me that I'm only hurting myself by hanging on to all of this anger…"

Smiling, Lacy asked, "Gave him one of your books to read, did you?"

A soft, sad chuckle shot from Kristi's throat. "Yeah, guess I'm going to have to stop that." She turned her back on the window and shrugged. "It shouldn't be this hard."

No, it shouldn't.

"You'll just have to keep trying," Lacy told her.

"What about you?" her friend asked quietly. "Are you going to try?"

"My situation's different, Kristi. He's your family." Lacy stood up and cleared the coffee table of the cookies and wine. It had been a long day and clearly this girlfest was winding down into a pit of melancholy. She'd rather take a hot bath and go to bed. Straightening, she looked at the woman watching her. "He was my family, now he's not. So it doesn't really matter what I think of him."

Kristi gave her a sad smile. "Of course it matters. *You* matter, Lacy. I don't want him to hurt you again."

Winking, Lacy deliberately brought up Kristi's self-help advice. "He can only hurt me if I *allow* it. And trust me, I won't."

The party was a huge success. It was still early in the evening and Snow Vista was packed with locals and tourists who were enjoying the clear, cold weather and the hum of energy. The crowds were thick; music pumped into the air with a pounding beat that seemed to reverberate up from the ground. All around Sam, people were talking, laughing, dancing. The party was a success. So why the hell was he so on edge?

Then he realized why.

It had been two years since he'd been in a crowd this size. He'd avoided mobs of people like the plague. It was always Jack who'd enjoyed the adoring masses. Sam's twin had fed off the admiration and applause. He'd loved being the center of attention, always making his ski runs faster, his jumps higher, his freestyle twists riskier.

All to push the edges of an envelope that never had a chance to hold him. Jack was the adventurer, Sam thought, a half smile curving his mouth as he remembered. Even as kids, Jack would go off the beaten path, skiing between trees, jumping over rocks, and once he'd even gone over a cliff edge and landed himself in a thigh-high cast for eight weeks.

Basically, Jack had loved the rush of speed. If he hadn't, maybe he wouldn't have died in a fiery car wreck. So useless. Such a waste. And so like Jack to drive himself to his own limits and beyond. He hadn't considered risks. Hadn't worried about consequences.

It was almost as if he'd come into his life hungry for every experience he could find. There was a time Sam had admired—envied—Jack's ability to cruise through the world getting exactly what he wanted out of it.

Jack had loved the publicity, the reporters, seeing himself on the glossy pages of magazines. Adulation had been his drug of choice.

"Hell," Sam muttered, "this party would have been a showcase for Jack. He'd have been right in the center of it all, holding court, laughing." Shoving his hands into his jeans pockets, Sam glanced at the black sky overhead. "Damned if I don't miss you."

"Mr. Wyatt!"

Sam's head swiveled and he spotted a slim blonde woman with short hair clutching a microphone, headed right at him. Worse, there was a cameraman hot on her heels.

A reporter.

Everything in him tightened, like fists ready for battle. There was a time when Sam had handled the media like a pro. When he was skiing, competing, he was used to being in front of a camera and answering what always seemed like moronic questions. But then Jack died and the questions had changed and ever since, Sam had dodged as many reporters as he could.

That wasn't an option tonight, though, and he knew it. The End of Season party was big news around here, and as Lacy had pointed out, the more publicity they got, the better it was for Snow Vista's bottom line.

So he gritted his teeth, planted his feet wide apart in a fighting stance and waited.

"Mr. Wyatt," the woman said again as she got closer. She gave him a fabulous smile, then turned and looked at her cameraman. "Scott, just set up right here. We'll get the party in the background for atmosphere."

She hadn't even asked if he'd speak to her. Just assumed he would. The reporter was probably used to most people wanting to do anything to get on camera for a few minutes.

When the light flashed on, Sam squinted briefly, then looked to the woman. Around him, the curious began to gather, with the occasional teenager making faces and waving to the camera.

"I'm Megan Short reporting for Channel Five," the woman said, her smile fake, her voice sharp and clipped. "I'd like to talk to you about this event, if you've got a few minutes."

"Sure," he said with what he hoped was more enthusiasm than he felt.

"Great." She turned, faced the camera and, when the guy behind the lens gave her a signal, she started right in. "This is Megan Short and I'm reporting from Snow Vista resort where the annual End of Season party is under way."

Sam forced himself to relax, taking a deep breath. While he half listened to the reporter, he let his gaze slide over the raucous crowd. More gathered behind him, jostling to get on camera, but most were too busy partying to pay attention. The music still pounded, people were laughing, kids were ice-skating on the pond. The air was cold and the sky was clear. A perfect night really—but for the reporter.

"In recent years, the party at Snow Vista just hasn't been the same, some residents have claimed," Megan was saying as she turned from the camera to look up at Sam. "But tonight, it looks like everything is as it should be. And I think that's due to the return of local champion Sam Wyatt." She turned, gave him another fatuous smile and continued, "What's it like for you, Sam, to be back here where you and your twin, Jack, once ruled the slopes?"

He sucked in a gulp of frosty air and pushed it forcefully into his lungs. *Of course she would bring up Jack. Tragedy made for great TV, after all.*

"It's good to be home." He hoped she let it go at that, but he knew she wouldn't.

"Your brother's tragic death two years ago left the entire state reeling," she was saying, with a thread of insincere sympathy coloring the words. "We were all invested in the success of the Wyatt twins. How does it feel, Sam, to be here without Jack?"

Under the building rage ran a slender thread of helpless frustration. Why did reporters always ask *how does it feel*? Could they really not guess? Or did they not care that they were digging into open wounds and dumping handfuls of salt into them? He had a feeling it was a little of both along with the hope of getting an emotional reaction out of their victims—and if there were tears, that was a bonus.

Well she wouldn't get what she wanted from him. He had plenty of experience dealing with those who sought to pry into feelings best left alone. His features shuttered as he locked away emotions and buried them deep.

"Jack loved the End of Season party," he said, keeping his voice even and steady, though the effort cost him. "So it's good to be here, watching locals and visitors alike enjoy the festivities."

"I'm sure, but—"

He cut her off and pretended not to see the flash of anger in her eyes. "Tom Summer's band is great. If you'll swing your camera around, you'll see we've got the kiddie pond open for ice-skating and there are more than two dozen food booths set up offering everything from pizza to Korean barbecue to funnel cakes." He smiled into the camera and ignored the sputtering reporter beside him.

"Yes," she said, determined to steer him back on the course she'd chosen. "And yet, how much more special would it be for you to be here tonight if your twin hadn't died so tragically? Is that loss still resonating within the Wyatt family?"

He'd tried, Sam assured himself. He'd put on a good face, pushed the resort and made an effort to ignore the woman's painful digging. But there was only so much a man could take. Damned if he'd let this woman feed off his family's pain. He sent her a steely-eyed glare that had her backing up one small step. But the determination in her eyes didn't dim.

"No comment," he said tightly even though he realized that a statement as simple as that one to a reporter was like waving a red flag at a bull.

"The loss of a twin has to be difficult to deal with—"

"Difficult?" Such a small, weak word to describe what Jack's loss had done to him. To the family. "I think this interview is finished."

She was relentless. Obviously, she'd set a goal for herself and had no intention of walking away until she'd succeeded in her mission.

"I can't imagine what it must have been like for you," she was saying, moving in closer so that she and Sam shared the same camera frame. "Competing with your twin, then becoming a bone-marrow donor during his battle with leukemia…"

Sam kept breathing—that was all he could do. If he spoke now, it wouldn't be pretty. It all rushed back at

him. The stunning news that Jack had cancer. The treat-
ments. Watching his strong, fit brother weaken under
the stress of the chemo. And finally, Sam, donating his
bone marrow in a last-ditch attempt to save the other
half of himself.

The transplant worked. And over the span of several
weeks, Jack's strength returned. His powerful will and
resolve to reclaim his life drove him to recover, become
the man he used to be.

Just in time to die.

"…helping him win that battle," the reporter was saying, "defeat cancer only to die in an horrific car accident
on his way to the airport to compete in the international
ski trials." She pushed the microphone up higher. "Tell
us," she urged, "in your own words, what it cost you
and your family to survive such a personal tragedy."

His brain was buzzing. His heartbeat thundered in
his own ears. His mouth was dry and once again, he
clenched his hands into useless fists. Sam gritted his
teeth because he knew, if he opened his mouth to speak,
he was going to blast the woman for her feigned sympathy in the name of ratings.

"Megan Short!" Lacy stepped up beside Sam, smiled
at the reporter and said, "This is great! I'm Lacy Sills,
manager of the resort. We're so happy to have Channel Five at Snow Vista. I hope everyone in your audi-
ence will come on up to join the party! We've got free
food, a skating rink for the kids, dancing to a live band
and the best desserts in Utah. The evening's young so
come up and join us!"

Undeterred, Megan shifted her attention to Lacy.
"Thank you, Lacy, for that invitation. Maybe you could
answer my question, though. Our viewers watched Sam
and Jack Wyatt over the years, as the twins scooped up

pretty much every available prize and award available
for skiing. Now, since you were once married to Sam,
maybe you could share with our viewers just how hard it
is for you to deal not only with the ghost of Jack Wyatt,
but with your own ex-husband."

For a split second, Sam had been torn when Lacy
hurried up. Glad to see her, but irritated that she'd obviously believed he needed rescuing. What was most
surprising, though, was that she would come to his aid
in the first place. He'd been home nearly a week and
she'd done everything she could to avoid him. Now she
rushed in? Why?

He looked at her, wearing a navy blue sweater, jeans
and boots, her thick blond braid hanging over one shoulder. No one else would have noticed, but Sam could see
what it cost Lacy to stand there and smile at the woman
taunting her.

Lacy's chin lifted, her eyes flashed and Sam felt a
swell of pride. When she met the reporter's gaze, he
remembered all of the times over the years when Lacy
had stood her ground in spite of everything. Damn, she
was something to see. Admiration and desire twisted
together inside him.

"I really can't talk about Jack Wyatt other than to
say we all miss him. Always will." Face frozen into a
tight smile, Lacy added, "Thanks so much for coming to the resort tonight and I hope all of your viewers
will come up the mountain to enjoy the End of Season
party! Now, if you'll excuse us, Sam and I have a few
things to take care of…"

Not waiting for an assent, Lacy threaded her arm
through Sam's and tugged. He took the escape she offered. Leading her away from the crowds, Sam stalked
around the peripheries of the noisy mob until they were

far enough away from everyone that he felt he could draw an easy breath again. They stood in the shadows behind the main lodge. Here, the music was distanced and so were the shouts and conversations and laughter.

If Lacy hadn't shown up when she did, Sam thought he might have told that reporter exactly what he thought of her. And that wouldn't have been good for him or the resort. "Thanks," he said when he could unclench his teeth enough for words to sneak past.

"No problem," she assured him, and leaned against the building. "I've been dealing with Megan Short for the last two years. She's relentless."

"Like a damn shark," he muttered, shoving one hand through his hair, furious that he'd allowed the woman to get to him.

"Please," Lacy said on a snort of laughter. "She makes sharks look like fluffy kittens. Everyone she interviews on camera either ends up crying or screaming at her or threatening her."

"You handled her."

She shrugged.

"What I'm wondering is why," he said. "You could have left me swinging in the wind and didn't. So… why?"

Lacy pushed away from the wall. "I saw the look on your face. Another minute or two alone with her and you'd have ruined all the good publicity we're getting."

"That's it? For the good of the resort?"

She tipped her head back to look up at him. "Why else, Sam?"

"That's what I want to know." His gaze moved over her, sweeping up and down before settling finally on her eyes. "See, I think there's more to it than that. I think you still feel something."

She snorted. "I feel plenty. Just not for you."

A grin curved his mouth as Sam watched her fiddle with the end of her braid. She'd always done that when she was skirting the truth. "You're playing with your hair and we both know what that means."

Instantly, she stopped, tossed her braid behind her back and glared at him. "You know, here in the real world, when someone helps you out, you just say 'thanks.'"

"Already said thanks."

"Right. You did. You're welcome."

She turned to go and he stopped her with one hand on her arm. "We're not done."

Then he kissed her.

Five

Lacy should have pushed him away.

Should have kicked him, stomped on his foot, *something*.

Instead, she kissed him back.

How could she not? Two years of hungering for him made her just crazy enough to want his arms around her again. To feel his mouth on hers. His breath on her cheek.

For a heart-stopping moment, there was just the heat of him, holding her, tasting her. The erotic slide of his tongue against hers sent sparks of awareness dazzling through her body like tiny flames, awakening and dying and starting up again.

She leaned into him, the sound of the party nothing more than a buzz in her ears. How could she hear more, when her own heartbeat was crashing so loudly it drowned out everything else?

The black leather jacket he wore felt cold and slick

beneath her hands as she clung to his shoulders. Reaching up, she threaded her fingers through his hair, holding his mouth to hers, reveling in the sensations rushing inside.

He moved her backward until she was pressed against the back wall of the inn. The thick, cold logs sent chills down her spine even as the heat Sam engendered swamped them both. Years fell back, pain slipped away and all she was left with was the amazing sensations she'd only experienced with Sam. Anger fell beneath layers of passion and she *knew* it would be back, stronger than ever. Anger at him. At herself.

But right at the moment, she didn't care.

It was crazy. A party attended by crowds of people was going on not a hundred yards from them. They were out in the open, where anyone could stumble across them. And yet, all she could think was, *yes. More.*

His hands slid beneath the hem of her sweater to stroke across her abdomen and the chill of his touch warred with the heat—and lost. Lacy pushed herself into him, moving as close as she could and still it wasn't enough to feed the raw need pulsing within.

He tore his mouth from hers and they stared at each other, breaths coming fast and harsh, clouds of vapor pushing into the air between them. His gaze moved over her face. His eyes were shadowed in the dim light and still they seemed to shine a brilliant green.

A moment later, raucous laughter and a girl's flirty squeal shattered the spell holding them in a silent grip. Sam stepped back from her with a muttered curse just as a young couple ran around the side of the inn.

They came to a sliding stop on the snowy path. "Oh hey, man. Sorry. We were just looking…um…"

Clearly the young couple had been looking for the same privacy she and Sam were just enjoying.

Sam stuffed both hands into his jeans pockets. "It's fine. Enjoy the party."

"Yeah," the boy said and shot his girlfriend a quick grin. "We are."

They left as quickly as they'd appeared.

"Well, that was embarrassing." Lacy blew out a long breath, straightened her sweater and stepped back from Sam so she wouldn't be tempted to leap at him again.

"Lousy timing," he mumbled, his gaze locked on her.

"I think it was pretty good timing," she said, though her body disagreed. Another minute or two of Sam's kisses and she might have forgotten everything. Might have just given in to the need still clamoring inside her. Oh, there was no *might* about it, she admitted silently.

She'd wanted to be touched, kissed, loved. She'd wanted Sam as she had always wanted him. Knowing better didn't seem to help. Lacy had nearly drowned in the sea of her own anger and misery when Sam first left. To survive, she'd clawed her way out then closed and locked the door on those feelings, good and bad. She had had to forget—or at least try to forget, just how much she loved Sam.

Life would be a lot easier right now, she thought, if she'd only been able to hold on to that anger. Instead, it was the heat of lost love she felt, not the ice of pain.

"Lacy..."

"Don't," she said, holding up one hand and shaking her head. Talking to him was almost as dangerous to her as kissing him. His voice alone was a kind of music to her, that seemed to seep into her heart and soul whether she wanted it to or not. "Just...don't say anything."

"I want you."

"Damn it," she snapped, walking now, with long strides, moving toward the light and sound of the party, "I asked you not to say anything." Especially *that*.

"Not saying it doesn't change anything." He followed her, his much longer legs outpacing hers easily.

She whipped her head up to look at him. "This was a kiss, Sam. Just a kiss." It had been more and she knew it but damned if she'd admit it to him. Heck, she wasn't entirely comfortable admitting it to herself. "We were both strung a little tight and the tension snapped. That's *all*."

If that were true, she told herself, she'd be feeling a heck of a lot better right now. Instead, she was wound tighter than ever. It was a wonder her body wasn't throwing off sparks with every slam of her heartbeat.

He moved closer and Lacy held her ground. Probably dumb, but she wasn't going to give him the satisfaction of thinking that she couldn't handle being near him. Especially since she couldn't.

"If those kids hadn't come crashing around the corner, we'd still be having at each other."

"Call it fate," she said with a shrug that belied the tension still coursing through her. "Someone somewhere knows that this shouldn't have happened and they were cutting us a break."

"Or trying to kill me," he said, and one corner of his mouth lifted, though there wasn't a sign of humor in his eyes.

"The easy answer is," she pointed out, "keep your lips to yourself."

"I never did 'easy.' You should know that."

"Not fair," she said, shaking her head and giving him a hard look. "You don't get to do the 'remember when' thing with me, Sam." She backed up a step for good measure, but when he followed that move, she didn't bother backing up farther.

"It's our past, Lacy," he reminded her, his voice dropping to a low, sexy rumble.

"*Past* being the operative word." Lacy sighed and told herself to gather up the wispy threads of what had once been her self-control. "There's nothing between us anymore, so you shouldn't have kissed me again."

"Wasn't just me," he reminded her, and a cold wind whipped around the edge of the building and lifted his dark hair. "Won't be just me when it happens next time, either."

The band finished one song and the pause between it and the next hung in the sudden stillness. When the pounding beat of the drums kicked in once more, Lacy forced herself to say, "It won't happen."

"You said that the last time and yet, here we are."

She had said it. At the time, she had meant it, too. Lacy didn't want to get drawn back into the still-smoldering feelings she had for Sam. Didn't want to put herself through another agonizing heartbreak. It was just a damn shame that her body didn't have the same resolve as her mind.

"Why are you kissing me at all, Sam?" She asked the question again because she still didn't have an answer. "Why do you even want to? *You* left *me*, remember? You walked away from us and never gave me another thought. Why pretend now that this is anything more than raging hormones with nowhere else to go?"

He looked at her, but didn't speak. But then, what could he say?

With her words hanging in the cold, clear air, Lacy turned and walked hurriedly back to the safety of the crowd, losing herself in the mob of people.

* * *

By midnight, the party was over. Everyone had gone home or to their hotel rooms and the mountain was quiet again. The Snow Vista crew had taken care of cleanup, so all that was left to clear out in the morning were the booths that would have to be disassembled and stored until the next time they were needed.

The mountain was dark, but for the sprinkling of lamplight shining through windows at the main lodge and surrounding cabins. The sky was black and starlit, leaving a peaceful, serene night.

In contrast, Sam felt like a damned caged tiger. He couldn't settle. Couldn't relax. Just like he couldn't get Lacy out of his mind. She remained there, a shadow on his thoughts, even when he knew he shouldn't be thinking of her at all. Even when he knew it might be easier for all of them if he just did as she asked and left her alone.

But hell. Easier wasn't always what it was cracked up to be. He'd grown up skiing the fastest, most dangerous runs he could find. Memories crowded his mind. But they weren't of skiing. They weren't of him and his twin, Jack, chasing danger all over the mountain. These memories were all Lacy. Her kiss. Her touch. The way she laughed one night when they'd walked through a snowstorm, tipping her head back and letting the fat flakes caress her cheeks. The shine in her hair, the warmth of her skin. All the things that had haunted him for the past two years.

Every moment with her stood out in his mind with glaring clarity and he knew he wouldn't be able to stay away from her.

Leaning against the doorjamb of his cabin, he looked through the woods toward Lacy's place. What had once been *their* place. There were lights in the windows and smoke curling lazily from the chimney.

His guts fisted. This was the hardest part of being home. Facing his family had been tough but being close to Lacy and not *with* her was torture. Leaving her had torn him up, coming home was harder still. A couple of kisses had only fed the banked fires inside him, and yet, all he wanted was another one.

"No," he muttered, one hand tightening on the wood door frame. "You want more than that. Much more."

He thought back over the past several days and realized that beneath the lust was a layer of annoyance. The Lacy he had left behind two years ago had been cool, calm. And crazy about him.

Sam could privately admit that he'd half expected her to jump into his arms with a cry of joy when he came back. And the fact that she hadn't, stung. Not only that, he had thought he'd be dealing with cool dispassion from her. Instead, there had been temper. Fury. Which, he had to say, was arousing. He liked that flash of anger in her eyes. Liked the heat that spilled off her whenever they were together. And he knew Lacy liked it, too.

She could argue all she wanted, fight what lay simmering between them, but the truth was, she still felt it, whether she wanted to or not.

Those kisses proved him right on that score.

Now his skin felt too tight. There was an itch inside him—damned if he'd ignore it any longer. This all began and ended with Lacy, he told himself. When he left Snow Vista two years before, he'd been wrapped up in his own grief and fury. Losing his twin had sliced at Sam's soul to the point where even breathing had seemed an insurmountable task. He'd deliberately exiled himself from this place. From her.

He'd picked up Jack's dreams and carried them for his dead twin—believing that he owed it to his brother. But dreams were damned empty when they weren't your own. Now Sam was back. To stay? He didn't know. But while he was here, he and Lacy were going to straighten out a few things.

Behind him, the heat of the room swelled, while in front of him, the cold and the dark beckoned. And he knew that whatever was between him and Lacy, it was time they settled it. He reached back to snatch his jacket off a hook. He was shrugging it on as he stepped into the night and closed the door behind him.

It didn't take him long to cross the distance separating his cabin from hers. And in those few moments, Sam asked himself why the hell he was doing this. But the simple fact was, he had to see her again. Had to get beyond the wall she had erected between them.

Stars were out and a pale half-moon lit the path, though he didn't need it. He could have found his way to Lacy's place blindfolded. On her wide front porch, he looked through the windows and saw a fire in the hearth, a couple of lamps tossing golden puddles across a hardwood floor. And he saw Lacy, curled up in a chair, staring at the flames as flickering shadow and light dazzled over her.

Even now, his heart gave a hard lurch and his body went like stone—but then, passion had never been a problem between them. He knocked on the door and watched as she frowned, pushed to her feet and walked to it.

She opened the door and her features went stiff. "Go away."

"No."

Lacy huffed out a breath. "What do you want?"

"To talk."

"No, thank you." She tried to close the door, but he slapped one hand to it and held it open.

He stepped past her and walked into the main room, ignoring her sputter of outrage. "You should close that door before you freeze."

Glaring at him, she looked as though she might argue the point, even though all she wore was a flannel sleep shirt, scooped at the neck, high on her thighs. Her long, toned legs were bare and the color of fresh cream. Her feet were bare, too, and he noted the sinful red polish on the nails. Her blond hair was free of its braid, hanging in heavy waves around her shoulders, making him want nothing more than to fist his hands in that thick, soft mass again. But her blue eyes were narrowed and there was no welcome there.

Finally, though, the winter cold was enough to convince her to shut the door, sealing the two of them in together. Still, she didn't cross the room, but stayed at the door, her back braced against it, her arms folded across her chest. "You don't have the right to come here. I didn't invite you."

"Didn't used to need an invitation."

Her mouth worked as if she were biting back words struggling to escape. The flannel nightshirt she wore shouldn't have been sexy, but it really was. Everything about this woman got to him as no one else ever had. He had thought he could walk away from her, but the truth was, he'd taken her with him everywhere he went.

"What do you want?"

"You know the answer to that." He shrugged out of his jacket and tossed it on the back of the nearest chair.

"Don't get comfortable. You won't be here that long."

One dark eyebrow lifted. "You don't want me to go, Lacy, and we both know it."

Frowning, she stared at him. "Sometimes we want things that aren't good for us."

"Been reading Kristi's self-help books?"

A brief smile curved her mouth and was gone again in an instant.

The wind whistled under the eaves and sounded like a breathless moan. The fire in the hearth jumped and hissed as that wind passed over the chimney and the golden light in the room swayed as if it was dancing.

"You left once. Why can't you just stay away?" she whispered.

"Because I can't get you out of my head."

She looked at him. "Try harder."

Sam laughed shortly, shook his head and moved toward her. "Won't do any good. Been trying for two years."

Those memories, images of her, were so ingrained inside him, Sam had about convinced himself that the reality of her couldn't possibly be as good as he remembered. And maybe that's why he was here now. To prove to himself, one way or another, what exactly it was that burned between him and Lacy.

"Sam..." She sighed and shook her head, as if denying what he was saying, what the two of them were feeling.

"Damn it Lacy, I want you. Never stopped wanting you." He moved in close enough to touch her and then stopped. He took a breath, drawing her scent deep inside.

Silence crowded down around them, the only sound the hiss and crackle of the flames in the hearth. His heart pounding, Sam waited for what felt like an eternity, until she finally lifted her eyes to his and said simply, "Me, too."

In a blink, Sam reached for her and she came into his arms as if they'd never been apart. He fisted his hands in the back of her soft, flannel gown and held her tight, pressing her length against him until he felt her heart thundering in time with his own. Bending his head, he took her mouth in a kiss that was both liberation and surrender.

Fires leaped within, burning him from the inside out and it was still only a flicker of the heat he felt just holding her. His tongue tangled with hers in a desperate dance of need. She gave herself up to the moment, leaning into him, running her hands up and down his arms until the friction of his own shirt against his skin added a new layer of torture.

Lost in the blinding passion spinning out of control, Sam reached down for the hem of her gown and in one quick yank, pulled it over her head and off. Lacy's blond hair spilled across her bare shoulders and lay like silk over his hands. His first look at her in two long years hit him hard. She was even more beautiful than he'd remembered and he couldn't wait another second to get his hands on her. He tossed the nightgown to the chair beside him and then covered her breasts with his palms.

She sighed, letting her head fall back as a murmured groan of pleasure slid from her throat. His thumbs and fingers stroked and rubbed her hardened nipples and he watched those summer-blue eyes of hers roll back as sensations took her over.

Burying his own groan, Sam's gaze swept up and down her body briefly before he shifted his hold on her, catching her at the waist and lifting her up so he could taste her. First one breast, then the other, his mouth

moved over her sensitized skin, licking, nibbling, suck-
ling. The warm, tantalizing scent of her wrapped around
him, driving him mad with a hunger he had only known
with Lacy.

She clutched at his shoulders and lifted those long
legs of hers to wrap around his waist. Having her there,
in his arms, was so...*right*.

He cupped her bare bottom and held her steady as
she looked into his eyes, showing him the passion, the
desire that he knew was glittering in his own.

"Sam, Sam..." she asked, her voice breathless,
"what're we doing?"

"What we were *meant* to do," he murmured, dipping his head to nibble at the slender length of her neck.

She shivered and that tiny reaction reverberated inside him, setting off what felt like earthquake after-
shocks that rippled through his system. Who would have
guessed that as great as his memories of her had been,
they weren't even *close* to how good she felt in reality.

Her fingers threaded through his hair and she pulled
his head back to meet his gaze. "What're we waiting
for, then?"

"No more waiting at all," he ground out.

Sam squeezed and caressed her behind until she was
writhing against him and every twist of her hips hardened his body further until he felt as though he'd explode with one wrong move. *Not yet*, his brain screamed,
but his body was in charge now and rational or logical
or *slow* didn't come into it.

Two long years it had been since he'd touched her last
and now that he had her—naked, willing, wanting—he
couldn't wait any longer.

Lacy, it seemed, felt the same. She shook her long
hair back from her face, kissed him hard and deep, then

reached down to undo his fly. Buttons sprang free under her fingers and in a second, she was holding him, stroking him from base to tip and back again. Sam gritted his teeth, struggling for control and losing, since he felt as wild as a hormonal teenager.

Need was a living, breathing animal in the room, snapping its jaws, demanding release. Sam's brain blanked out, every thought whipping away in the surge of his reaction to her touch. With her fingertips smoothing over him, he couldn't think beyond breathing. That was all he needed anyway. Air—and Lacy.

Shifting his grip on her, he stroked the hot, damp core of her. She sucked in a breath and trembled, but she didn't release her hold on him. If anything, her grip tightened, her caresses became more determined, more demanding. As did his. He rubbed the small bud of sensation at her center and each time she quivered and moaned, it fed his need to touch her more deeply. More completely.

She twisted in his grasp; her heels dug into the small of his back. "Sam, if you don't take me right this minute, I might die."

"No dying allowed," he muttered, and fused his mouth to hers. Their tongues tangled together again, even more desperately this time.

He'd come here with the idea to either talk through the barriers standing between them or seduce her into a sexual haze. Now neither one was happening. This wasn't seduction. It was raw urgency. Sam took two long steps to the closest wall, braced her back against it and then broke the kiss so he could look into her eyes as he filled her in one long, hard stroke.

She gasped and he was forced to pause, willing himself to be still. She was so tight. So hot, it stole his breath and left him gasping. A moment passed, and then as if of one mind they moved together, Lacy taking him deep inside her and each of them groaning when he retreated only to slide back inside, even deeper.

Again and again, they moved frantically, the rhythm they set a punishing pace that left no margin for smooth, for slow, lazy loving. It was all passion and lust and a desperate craving for the release that rose within them, higher and higher as they chased it. Emotion, sensation poured through them both, and then were drowned in the immediate demands of bodies too long denied.

He felt the cold of the wall on the palms of his hands as he braced her there, pinned like a butterfly to a board. He felt her fingers, digging into his shoulders as she urged him higher, faster, deeper. He heard their breaths coming fast and sharp.

Sam reached between their laboring bodies and flicked his thumb across that tight, sensitive bud at the junction of her thighs. Instantly, she screamed out his name as she shuddered, splintering in his arms.

Her body tightened around his; those internal shivers driving him over the edge. When the first explosion took him, Sam groaned aloud and emptied himself into her.

Seconds, minutes…maybe *days* passed with neither of them willing to move. Frankly, Sam didn't think he could move even if he had to. His knees were weak and the only thing holding them both up at the moment was sheer willpower.

"Oh. Wow." Her voice was a whisper that sounded like a shout to him. "Sam. I think I might be blind."

He looked at her. "Open your eyes."

She did. "Right. Good. Wow."

"You said that already," he told her, hissing in a

breath as she moved on him and sent his still-willing body into overdrive.

Nodding, Lacy murmured, "It was two *Wows* worthy."

"Yeah," he agreed, slapping one hand to her butt to try to hold her still. "Gotta say it really was."

Breathing still strained, Lacy looked at him and said, "I should probably tell you to leave now."

"Probably," he agreed, even as he felt his body hardening inside her again.

She felt it, too, because she inhaled sharply and let that breath slide from her on a soft moan of pleasure. "But I'm not."

"Glad to hear it." Sam tightened his grip on her, swung her away from the wall and walked, their bodies still linked, to the hall. "Bedroom?"

"Yeah," she said, dipping her head for another taste of his mouth. "Bedroom."

It was a small cabin and Sam took a moment to be grateful for that. He laid her down on the bed they used to share and reluctantly drew out of her heat just long enough to strip out of his clothes. Then he was back on the bed, looming over her, sheathing himself inside her on a sigh of appreciation. His hips moved as he reclaimed her body in the most elemental way. She met his pace and rocked with him in a dance they'd always been good at. Their rhythms meshed, their breaths mingled and the sighs crashing in the quiet seemed to roll on forever.

Lifting her legs, she locked them at the small of his back and pulled him tighter, deeper. She groaned as he kissed first one hardened nipple then the other, sending a cascade of sensations pouring into her body. Again and again, he licked, tasted, nibbled, all the while his body rocked into her heat, taking her as she took him.

There was no hesitation. No question. There was only the moment and the moment was *now*. They'd been heading toward this night since Sam had arrived back on the mountain.

Her hands swept up and down his back, her short, neat nails scraping at his skin as she touched him, everywhere. Her scent rose up and enveloped him. Surrounded by her, in her, Sam pushed them both to the brink of oblivion, and when she cried out his name, she held him tight and took him over the edge with her.

Six

Lacy stared up at the ceiling and, just for a second or two, enjoyed the lovely, floaty feeling that filled her. It had been so long since she'd felt anything like this. For the past two years, she'd forced herself to forget just how good it had always been between her and Sam. She'd had to, to survive his absence. Had to put it out of her mind so that she could try to rebuild her life without him.

Now he was back.

And in her bed.

God, how could she be such an idiot? Those lovely sensations of completion and satisfaction emptied away like water going down a tub drain.

"We should talk."

A short, sharp laugh shot from her throat. "Oh, I so don't want to talk about this." She wanted to forget again. Fast.

He went up on one elbow, looked down at her, and Lacy steeled herself against the gleam in his grass-green eyes. If she wasn't careful, her oh-so-foolish heart would slide gleefully right into danger. Why did he have to come back?

Why did he ever leave?

His jaw tight, he stared into her eyes and asked, "You're still taking the Pill, right?"

She blinked at him. Not what she'd been expecting. Yet, now that he'd said it, a single, slender thread of panic began to unwind inside her. His words echoed over and over again in her mind, because now her stupidity had reached epic proportions. Sam Wyatt walked in her door and every brain cell she possessed just whipped away. Which explained why she hadn't thought of protection. Hadn't paid any attention. She really was an idiot.

"Since you just went white," he said wryly, "I'm guessing the answer is no."

"Well, now's a great time to ask," she muttered, wishing she could blame this situation on him, as well. But she was a grown-up, modern woman who took responsibility for her own body, thanks very much. So it was as much her fault as his that she was suddenly thinking she might be in really big trouble here.

"We didn't do much talking before."

"True." She sighed and stared at the ceiling again. Easier than meeting his eyes. Easier than looking at him while she was wondering if she might have just gotten pregnant by her ex-husband. At that thought, she slapped one hand over her eyes.

Unprotected sex. She had never once—even at seventeen when she'd given Sam her virginity at the top of the mountain under a full, summer moon—been that

reckless. Lacy was the careful one. The cautious one.
The one who looked at every step along a path before
she ever started down it. Now she couldn't even see
the path. Oh, this was a mistake on so many levels she
couldn't even count them all.

He pulled her hand aside and she looked at him.

"Now we have even more to talk about."

"No thanks." She didn't want to have a conversation
with him at all. And certainly not about the possibility
of an unplanned baby. *Oh, God.*

No way would fate do that to her, right? Hadn't it
screwed with her life enough?

"No thanks?" He repeated her words with a snort of
derision. "That's not gonna cover it. We just had sex.
Twice. With zero protection."

"Yeah, I was there."

"Damn it, Lacy—"

"Look," she cut him off neatly and tried to get him
off the subject, away from the thoughts that were already making her a little crazy. "It's the wrong time for
me. The odds are astronomical." Please let her be right
about this. "So don't worry about it, all right?"

He didn't like that. She could see the light in his eyes
and recognized it. Sam Wyatt never had been a man to
be told what to do and take it well.

"Yeah," he said flatly. "That's not gonna happen. I
want to know when you know."

"And I want a brand-new camera with a fifteen-zoom
lens. Looks like we're both going to be disappointed."

"Damn it, Lacy," he repeated. "You can't cut me out
of this. I'm here. I'm involved in this."

"For now." A part of her couldn't believe that she was
lying in bed with Sam, both of them naked and having
an argument about a possible pregnancy. That was the

sane part, she thought reasonably. The panicked portion of her was trying not to think about any of this.

Once he left the cabin she wouldn't be bringing up tonight with him at all. And she was going to use every part of her legendary focus to forget everything that had just happened—mainly out of self-protection. She couldn't think about being with him and *not* be with him. That was a recipe for even more craziness and more late-night crying sessions, so thanks, she'd pass.

When she didn't speak, he seemed to accept her silence as acquiescence, which worked for her—until he started talking again.

"I came over here tonight to talk to you," he said.

"Yeah," she said on a sigh, "that went well."

"Okay," he admitted, "maybe talking wasn't the only thing on my mind." He dropped one hand to her hip and slowly slid his palm up until he was cupping her breast, sending tingles of expectation and licks of heat sinking down into her bones.

Just not fair, she told herself sternly even as she felt that heat he engendered begin to spread. Not fair that the man who broke her heart could still have such an effect on her. Even when she *knew* it was a mistake to allow his hands on her, she couldn't bring herself to make him stop. And if she kept lying there, letting him touch her, it would start over again and where would that get her? Deeper into the hole she could already feel herself falling into.

Quickly, before she could talk herself out of doing the smart thing, she rolled out from under his hand and off the bed in one fluid motion. Just getting a little distance between them cleared her mind and soothed all those buzzing nerve endings.

He stared at her as she snatched up the robe she had

tossed over a chair only that morning. Slipping into the
soft terry fabric she tied it at the waist and only briefly
considered making a knot, just to make it harder to
slip off again. Once she was covered up, Lacy felt a bit
more in control. Tossing her hair back from her face,
she said, "I think you should go."

"I came to talk, remember? We haven't done that
yet."

"And we're not going to," she told him. "I don't feel
like talking and you don't live here anymore, so I want
you to go."

"As soon as we have this out." He settled on the bed,
carelessly naked, clearly in no hurry to get up and get
moving. "I've got a few things to say to you."

"Now you have things to say? *Now* you want to
share?" She laughed shortly and the sound of it was as
harsh as the scrape of it against her throat. Through the
miasma of emotions coursing through her, rage rose up
and buried everything else. "Two years ago, you left
without a word of explanation. Just came home from
the funeral, threw some clothes in your bag and went."

In a blink, she was back there. In this very cabin
two years ago when her world had come crashing down
around her.

The funeral had been hideous. Losing Jack to a
senseless accident after he'd survived cancer had cut
deeper than she would have thought possible. The Wyatt
family had closed ranks, of course, pulling into a tight
circle where pain shared had become pain more easily borne.

All of them but Sam. Even within that circle, he had
stood apart, forcing himself to be stoic. To be solitary.
He hadn't turned to Lacy once for comfort, for solace.

Instead, he'd handled all of the funeral arrangements himself, taken care of details to keep his parents from having to multiply their grief by dealing with the minutia of death. He'd given the eulogy and brought everyone to tears and laughter with memories of his twin.

But after everyone had gone home, after the ceremony had faded into stillness, she'd hoped he would finally turn to her.

He hadn't.

Instead he walked straight into their bedroom and pulled his travel bag out of the closet.

Stunned, shaken, Lacy could only watch as he grabbed shirts, rolled them up and stuffed them into the bag. Jeans were next, then underwear, socks and still she didn't speak. But as he zipped it closed and stood staring down at the bag, she asked, "Sam, what are you doing? Are we going somewhere?"

He looked at her then and his green eyes were drenched with a sorrow so deep it tore at her to see it. "Not *we*, Lacy. *Me*. I'm going. I have to—"

She swallowed hard against the knot in her throat. "You're leaving?"

"Yeah." He stripped out of his black suit, and quickly dressed in boots, jeans and a thermal shirt, then shrugged into his leather jacket

The whole time, she could only watch him. Her mind had gone entirely blank. It couldn't be happening. He had promised her long ago that he would never leave. That she would always be able to count on him. To trust him. So none of this made sense. She couldn't understand. Didn't believe he would do this.

"You're leaving me?"

He snapped her a look that said everything and nothing. "I have to go."

She couldn't breathe. Iron bands tightened around her chest, cutting off her air. It had to be a dream. A nightmare, because Sam wouldn't leave. He walked across the room then, his duffel swung over one shoulder, and she stepped back, allowing him to pass because she was too stunned to try to stop him.

He stopped at the front door for one last look at her. "Take care of yourself, Lacy." He left without another word and closed the door behind him quietly.

Alone in her cabin, Lacy sank to the floor, since her knees were suddenly water. She watched the door for a long time, waiting for it to open again, for him to come back, tell her he'd made a mistake. But he never did.

Now, thinking about that night, Lacy wanted to kick her former self for letting him stroll out of her life. For crying for him. For missing him. For hoping to God he'd just come home.

"I had to."

"Yeah," she said tightly, amazed that as angry as she was, there was still more anger bubbling inside her. "You said that then, too. You *had* to leave your wife, your family." Sarcasm came thick. "Wow, must have been rough on you. All on your own, free of your pesky wife and those irritating parents and sister. Wandering across Europe, dating royalty. Poor little you, how you must have suffered."

"Wasn't why I left," he ground out, and Lacy was pleased to see a matching anger begin to glint in his eyes. A good old-fashioned argument was at least honest.

"Just a great side benefit, then?"

"Lacy I couldn't explain then why I had to leave—"

"Couldn't?" she asked. "Or wouldn't?"

"I could hardly breathe, Lacy," he muttered, sitting up to shove both hands through his hair in irritation. "I needed space. It had nothing to do with you or the family."

Lacy jerked back as if he'd slapped her. "Really? That's how you see it? It had everything to do with us. You couldn't breathe because your family needed you? Poor baby. That's called *life*, Sam. Bad stuff happens. It's how we deal with it that decides who we are."

"And I didn't deal."

"No," she said flatly. "You didn't. You ran. *We* were the ones left behind to sweep up the pieces of our lives. Not you, Sam. You were gone."

His mouth worked as if he were trying to hold back words just itching to pour out. "I didn't run."

"That's what it looked like from the cheap seats."

Nodding, he could have been agreeing or trying to rein in his own temper. "You didn't say any of this at the time."

"How could I? You wouldn't *talk* to me," she countered. "You were in such a rush to get out of the cabin, you hardly saw me, Sam. So you can understand that the fact you want me to be all cooperative because *now* you want to talk, is just a little too much for me."

Scowling at her, he wondered aloud, "What happened to quiet, shy Lacy who never lost her temper?"

She flushed and hoped the room was dark enough to disguise it. "Her husband walked out on her and she grew a spine."

"However it happened, I like it."

"Hah!" Startled by the out-of-the-blue compliment when she was in no way interested in flattery from him, Lacy muttered, "I don't care."

He blew out a breath and said, "You think I wanted to go."

"I know you did." She could still feel his sense of eagerness to be gone. Out of the cabin. Away from her.

"Damn it, Lacy, Jack *died*."

"And we all lost him, Sam," she pointed out hotly. "You weren't the only one in pain."

He jumped off the bed and stood across from it, facing her. "He was my twin. My identical twin. Losing him was like losing a part of me."

Torn between empathy for the pain he so clearly still felt and fury that he would think she didn't understand, she blurted out, "Did you think I didn't know that? That your parents, your sister, were clueless as to what Jack's death cost you?" Her voice climbed on every word until she heard herself shouting and deliberately dialed it back. "We were here for you, Sam. You didn't see us."

"I couldn't." He shook his head, glanced around for his clothes, then reached down and snatched up his jeans. Tugging them on, he left them unbuttoned as he faced her again. "Hell, I was half out of my mind with grief and rage. I couldn't be around you."

"Ah," she said, nodding sagely as she silently congratulated herself for not throwing something at him. "So you left for *my* sake. How heroic."

"Damn it, you're not listening to me."

"No, I'm not. Not much fun being ignored, is it?" She gathered up her hair with trembling fingers and in a series of familiar moves, tamed the mass into a thick braid that frayed at the edges. "Why should I listen to you anyway?"

"Because I'm back now."

"For how long?"

He frowned again and shook his head. "I don't know the answer to that yet."

"So, just passing through." Wow, it was amazing how much that one statement hurt. And Lacy knew that if she allowed herself to get even more involved with him, when he left this time, the pain would be more than she could take. So she drew a cloak of disinterest around her and belted it as tightly as her robe. "Well, have a nice trip to…wherever."

The pain was as thick and rich as it had been two years ago. She'd gotten through it then, curling up in solitude, focusing on her job at the lodge and on her photography. The pictures she'd taken during that time were black-and-white and filled with shadows that seemed to envelop the landscape. She could look at them now and actually *feel* the misery she'd been living through. And damned if she would go back to that dark place in her life.

He took a breath and huffed it out again in a burst of frustration. "I'm not proud of what I did two years ago, Lacy. But I had to go, whether you believe that or not."

"I'm sure you believe it," she countered.

"And I'm—"

"Don't you dare say you're sorry." Her voice cracked into the room like a whip's snap.

"I won't. I did what I had to do at the time." His features were tight, his eyes shining with an emotion she couldn't read in the dim light. "Can't be sorry for it now."

Flabbergasted, Lacy stared at him and actually felt her jaw drop. "That's amazing. Really. You're *not* sorry, are you?"

Again, he pushed his hands through his hair and

looked suddenly as if he'd rather be anywhere but there.
"What good would it do?"

"Not an answer," she pointed out.

"All I can give you."

Cold. She was cold. And her thick terry-cloth robe
might as well have been satin for all the warmth it was
providing at the moment. For two years, she'd thought
about what it might be like if he ever came home. If he
ever deigned to return to the family he'd torn apart with
his absence. But somehow, she'd always imagined that
he'd come back contrite. Full of regret.

She should have known better. Sam Wyatt did what
he wanted when he wanted and explained himself to
no one. Heck, she'd known him most of her life, had
married him, and he'd still kept a part of himself locked
away where she couldn't touch it. He'd gone his own
way always and for a while, he'd taken her with him.
And she, Lacy thought with a flash of disgust, had been
so glad to be included, she'd never pushed for more—
that was her fault. His leaving? His fault.

"God," he said on a short laugh, "I can practically
see you thinking. Why don't you just say what you have
to and get it out?"

"Wow. You really have not changed one bit, have
you?"

"What's that supposed to mean?"

"You even want to be in charge of when I unload
on you."

"We both know you've got something to say, so say
it and get it done."

"You want it?" she asked, hands fisting helplessly at
her sides. "Fine. You walked out on all of us, Sam. You
walked away from a family who loved you. Needed you.
You walked away from *me*. You never said goodbye.

You just disappeared and then the next thing I know, divorce papers are arriving in the mail."

He blew out a breath.

"You didn't even warn me with a stinking phone call." Outrage fired in her chest and sizzled in her veins. "You vanished and Jack was dead and your family was shattered and you didn't care."

"Of course I cared," he snapped.

"If you cared, you wouldn't have left. Now you're back and you're what? A hero? The prodigal returned at last? Sorry you didn't get a parade."

"I didn't expect—"

She rolled right over him. "Two years. A few post-cards to let your parents know you were alive and that was it. What the hell were you thinking? How could you be so heartless to people who needed you?"

He scrubbed both hands over his face as if he could wipe away the impact of her words, but Lacy wasn't finished.

Her voice dropping to a heated whisper that was nearly lost beneath the moan of the icy wind outside, she said, "You broke my heart, Sam. You broke *me*." She slapped one hand to her chest and glared at him from across the room. "I trusted you. I believed you when you said it was forever. And then you left me."

Just like her mother had left, Lacy thought, her brain firing off scattershot images, memories that stole her breath and weakened her knees. When she was ten years old, Lacy's mother had walked away from the mountain, from her husband and daughter, and she had never once looked back. Never once gotten in touch. Not a phone call. Or a letter. Nothing. As if she'd slipped off the edge of the earth.

Lacy had spent the rest of her childhood hoping and

waiting for her mom to come home. But she never had, and though he'd stayed, Lacy's father had slowly, inexorably pulled away, too. Lacy could see now that he hadn't meant to. But his wife leaving had diminished him to the point where he couldn't remain the man he had once been. Her family had been shattered.

And when Sam convinced her to trust him, to build a life with him and then left, she'd been shattered again. She wouldn't allow that to happen a third time. Lacy was stronger now. She'd had to change to survive and there was no going back.

"You know what? That's it. I'm done. We have to work together, Sam," she said. "For however long you're here. But that's all. Work."

"Damn it, Lacy..." His features were shadowed, but somehow the green of his eyes seemed to shine in the darkness. After a second or two, he nodded. "Fine. We'll leave it there. For now."

She was grateful they had that much settled, at least. Because if he tried to apologize for ripping her heart out of her chest, she might have to hit him with something. Something heavy. Better that they just skate over it all. She'd had her say and it was time to leave her scars alone.

"And what about what just happened?" he asked, and she wondered why his voice had to sound like dark chocolate. "What if you're pregnant?"

That word sent a shiver that might have been panic— or longing—skating along her spine. "I won't be."

"If you are," he warned, "we're not done."

Another flush swept through her, heating up the embers that had just been stoked into an inferno. "We're already done, Sam. Whatever we had, died two years ago."

Her whisper resounded in the room and she could only hope he didn't read the lie behind the words.

Because she knew, that no matter what happened, what was between them would never really die.

Two days later, Sam was still thinking about that night with Lacy.

Now, standing in the cold wind, staring up at the clear blue sky dotted with massive white clouds, his brain was free to wander. And as always, it went straight to Lacy.

Everything she'd said to him kept replaying through his mind and her image was seared into his memory. He'd never forget how she'd looked, standing there in her robe, eyes glinting with fury, her mouth still full from his kisses. The old Lacy wouldn't have told him off—she'd have hugged her anger close and just looked…hurt.

What did it say about him that this new Lacy—full of fire and fury—intrigued him even more than the one he used to know?

Being with her again had hit him far harder than he had expected. The feel of her skin, the sound of her sighs, the brush of her lips on his. It was more than sexual, it was…*deeper* than that. She'd reclaimed that piece of his heart that he had excised so carefully two years before. And now he wasn't sure what to do about that.

Of course, he'd steered clear of the office for the past two days, giving himself the time and space to do some serious thinking. But so far, all he'd come up with was…he still wanted her.

Two years he'd denied himself what he most wanted— Lacy. Now she was within reach again and he wasn't about to deny himself any longer. She might think that what was between them had died…but if he had killed it, then he could resurrect it. He had to believe that, because the alternative was unacceptable.

He tossed a glance at the office window and considered going in to—what? Talk? No, he wasn't interested in more conversation that simply ended up being a circular argument. And what he *was* interested in couldn't be done in the office when anyone could walk in on them. So he determinedly pushed aside those thoughts and focused instead on work. On his plans.

Sam walked into the lodge and headed straight through the lobby for the elevator. He paid no attention to the people gathered in front of a blazing fire or the hum of conversations rising and falling. There were a few things he needed to go over with his father. One idea in particular had caught his imagination and he wanted to run it past his dad.

He found the older man in his favorite chair in the family great room. But for the murmuring of the TV, the house was quiet and Sam was grateful for the reprieve. He wasn't in the mood to face Kristi's antagonism or his mother's quiet reproach.

"Hey, Sam," his father said, giving a quick look around as if checking to make sure his wife wasn't around. "How about a beer?"

Sam grinned. His father had the look of a desperate man. "Mom okay with that?"

"No, she's not," he admitted with a grimace. "But since you got home, she's stocked the fridge. So while she's in town, we could take advantage."

He looked so damn hopeful, Sam didn't have the heart to shoot him down. "Sure, Dad. I'll risk it with you."

His father slapped his hands together, then gave them

a quick rub in anticipation. Pushing out of his chair, he led the way to the kitchen, his steps long and sure. It was good to see his father more himself. Bob Wyatt wasn't the kind of man to take to sitting in a recliner for long. The inactivity alone would kill him.

In the kitchen, Sam took a seat at the round oak table and waited while his dad pulled two bottles of beer out of the fridge. He handed one to Sam, kept the other for himself and sat down. Twisting off the top, Bob took a long drink, sighed in pleasure and gave his son a wide smile. "Your mother's so determined to have me eating tree bark and drinking healthy sludge, this beer's like a vacation."

"Yeah," Sam said, taking a sip of his own, "but if she comes in suddenly, you're on your own."

"Coward."

Sam grinned. "Absolutely."

With a good-natured shrug, Bob said, "Can't blame you. So, want to tell me why you're stopping by in the middle of the day?"

He couldn't very well admit to avoiding Lacy, so Sam went right to the point. "You know we've got a lot of plans in motion for the resort."

"Yeah." Bob took another sip and nodded. "I've got to say you've got some good ideas, Sam. I like your plan so far, though I'm a little concerned about just how much of your own money you're pumping into this place."

"Don't worry about that." Sam had enough money to last several lifetimes, and if he couldn't enjoy spending it, what was the point of accruing it?

"Well," his father said, "I'll keep worrying over it and you'll keep spending, so we all do what we can."

Sam grinned again. God, he hadn't even realized

how much he'd missed being able to sit down and talk to his dad. Just the simplicity of being in this kitchen again, sharing a beer with the man who had raised him, eased a lot of the still-jagged edges inside him.

"If you like the plans so far, you'll like this one, too." Sam cupped the beer bottle between his palms and took a second to get his thoughts in order. While he did, he glanced around the familiar kitchen.

Pale green walls, white cabinets and black granite countertops, this room had been the heart of the Wyatt family for years. Hell, he, Jack and Kristi had all sat around this table doing homework before the requisite family dinner. This room had witnessed arguments, laughter and tears. It was the gathering place where everyone came when they needed to be heard. To be loved.

"Sam?"

"Yeah. Sorry." He shook his head and gave a rueful smile. "Lots of memories here."

"Thick as honey," his father agreed. "More good than bad, though."

"True." Even when Jack was going through cancer treatment, the family would end up here, giving each other the strength to keep going. He could almost hear his brother's laughter and the pain of that memory etched itself onto his soul.

"You're not the only one who misses him, you know." His father's voice was soft, low.

"Sometimes," Sam admitted on a sigh, "I still expect him to walk into the room laughing, telling me it was all a big mistake."

"Being here makes it easier and harder all at the same time," his father said softly. "Because even if I can fool myself at times, when I see his chair at the table sitting empty, I have to acknowledge that's he's really gone."

Sam's gaze shot to that chair now.

"But the good memories are stronger than the pain and that's a comfort when you let it be."

"You think I don't want to be comforted?" Sam looked at his father.

"I think when Jack died you decided you weren't allowed to be happy."

Stunned, Sam didn't say anything.

"You take too much on yourself, Sam," Bob said. "You always did."

As he sipped his beer, Sam considered that and admitted silently that his father was right. About all of it. Maybe what had driven him from home wasn't only losing Jack and needing to see his twin's dreams realized—but the fact that he had believed, deep down, that with Jack gone, Sam didn't deserve to be happy. It was something to consider. Later.

Shaking his head, he said, "About this latest idea…"

Apparently accepting that Sam needed a change of subject, his father nodded. "What're you thinking?"

"I want to initiate a new beginner's ski run on the backside of the mountain," Sam said, jumping right in. "The slope's gentle, there're fewer trees and it's wide enough we could set it up to have two runs operating all the time."

"Yeah, there's a problem with that," Bob said, and took another drink of his beer.

The hesitation in his father's voice had Sam's internal radar lighting up. "What?"

"The thing is, that property doesn't belong to us anymore."

The radar was now blinking and shrieking inside him. "What're you talking about?"

"You know Lacy's family has lived on that slope for years…"

"Yeah…" Sam had the distinct feeling he wasn't going to like where this was going.

"Well, after you left, Lacy was in a bad way." Bob frowned as he said it and Sam knew his father was the master of understatement. Guilt pinged around inside him like a wildly ricocheting bullet. "So, your mother and I, we deeded the property to her. Felt like it was the least we could do to try to ease her hurt."

Sam muffled the groan building in his chest. His decision to leave was now coming back to bite him in so many different ways. Most especially with the woman he still wanted more than his next breath.

"So, if you're determined to build that beginner run, you're going to have to deal with Lacy."

Letting his head hit his chest, Sam realized that *dealing with Lacy* pretty much summed up his entire life at the moment. He thought about the look in her eyes when he left her cabin the other night. The misery stamped there despite what they'd just shared—hell, maybe *because* of that.

Leaving here was something he'd *had* to do. Coming back meant facing the consequences of that decision. It wasn't getting any easier.

"She never mentioned that you and mom gave her the land," Sam said.

"Any reason why she should?"

"No." Shaking his head, Sam took another pull on his beer. He wanted that land. How he was going to get it from Lacy, he didn't know yet. As things stood between them at the moment, he was sure that she would never sell him that slope. And maybe it'd be best to just forget about getting his hands on it. The land was Lacy's, and he ought to back off. But for now, there were other things he wanted to talk to his father about. "You know that photo of the lodge in spring? The one hanging over the fireplace here?"

"Yeah, what about it?"

"I'd like to use it on the new website I'm having designed so I'll need to talk to the photographer. I want to show the lodge in all the seasons with photos that rotate out, always changing. The one I'm talking about now, with Mom's tulips a riot of color and that splash of deep blue sky—the picture really shows the lodge in a great way."

"It's one of Lacy's."

Sam looked at his dad for a long moment, then actually laughed, unsurprised. "Of course it is. Just like I suppose the shot of the lodge in winter, with the Christmas tree in the front window is hers, too?"

His father nodded, a smile tugging at the corner of his mouth as he took a sip of his beer. "You got it. She's made a name for herself in the last year or so. We've had hotel guests buy the photos right off the walls." He shook his head, smiling to himself. "Lacy does us up some extra prints just so we can accommodate the tourists. She's been making some good money selling her photos through a gallery in Ogden, too."

"She never mentioned it."

And it was weird to realize that he was so out of touch with Lacy. There had been a time when they were so close, nothing between them was secret. Now there was an entire chunk of her life that he knew nothing about. His own damn fault and he knew it, but that didn't make it any easier to choke down.

His father nodded sagely. "Uh-huh. Again, any reason why she should have?"

"No." Blowing out a breath in frustration, Sam leaned back in his kitchen chair and studied his father. There was a sly expression on the older man's face that told Sam his father was enjoying this. "She doesn't owe me a thing. I get that. But damn it, we shared a lot of great times, too. Don't they mean something? Okay fine. I left. But I'm back now. That counts, too, doesn't it?"

"It does with me. Lacy may be harder to convince."

"I know."

"And Kristi."

"I know." Sam snorted. "And Mom."

Bob winced. "Your mother's damn happy to have you back, Sam."

"Yeah," he said, turning his head to look out the window at the pockets of deep blue sky visible between the pines. He'd felt it from his mom since he'd returned. The reluctance to be too excited to see him. The wary pleasure at having him home. "But she's also holding back, waiting for me to go again."

"And are you?"

Guilt reared up and gnawed at the edges of his heart. "I don't know yet. Wish I did. But I promised you I'd stay at least until these plans are complete and the way I'm adding things I might never be finished."

"All true," his father said. "You might ask yourself sometime why it is you keep thinking of more things to do. More things that will give you an excuse to stay here longer."

He hadn't thought of it like that but now that he was, Sam could see that maybe subconsciously he had been working toward coming home for good. Funny that he hadn't noticed that the more involved his plans became the further out he pushed the idea of leaving again.

"Anyway," his father said, "while you're doing all this thinking, you'll have to talk to Lacy about using her photos in the advertising you're planning."

"I will," he said.

"She's really good, isn't she?"

"She always was," Sam acknowledged and knew he was talking about much more than her talent for photography.

Seven

"You want to use my photos?"

Sam grinned at Lacy an hour later and told himself it was good to actually surprise her. He enjoyed how her eyes went wide and her mouth dropped open.

"I do. And not just on the website, I'd like to use them in print advertising, as well."

"Why—"

He tipped his head. "Don't pretend you don't know how good a photographer you are."

"I don't know how to respond to that without sounding conceited."

"Well, while you're quiet, here's something else to think about." He planted both palms on the edge of the desk and leaned in until he was eye to eye with her. "I'll want some of your photos made into postcards that we can sell in the lobby of the lodge."

"Postcards."

"Hey, some people actually enjoy *real* mail," he told

her and straightened up. "We can have a lawyer draw up terms—all nice and legal, but I'm thinking a seventy-thirty split, your favor, on the cards and any prints we sell. As for the advertising, we'll call that a royalty deal and you'll get a cut every time we use one of your photos."

She blinked at him and damned if he didn't enjoy having her off balance. "Royalty."

Sam leaned over, tipped her chin up with his fingers and bent to plant a hard, quick kiss on her mouth. While she was flustered from that, he straightened up and announced, "Why don't you think it over? I'm heading out to meet with the architect. Be back later."

He left her staring after him. His own heart was thundering in his chest and every square inch of his body was coiled tight as an overwound spring. Just being around her made him want everything he'd once walked away from.

Sam shrugged into his jacket as he left the hotel and headed out into a yard that boasted green splotches of grass where the snow was melting under a steady sun. He took a deep breath, glanced around at the people and realized that it had taken him two years of being away to discover that his place was *here*.

His life was here.

And he wanted Lacy in his life again. Smiling to himself, Sam decided he was going to romance the hell out of her until he got just what he wanted. That slope he needed for the lodge expansion was going to have to wait, he told himself as he headed for his car. Because if Lacy found out he wanted the property she owned, she would never believe he wanted her for herself.

Lacy's nose wrinkled at the rich, dark scent of the latte Kristi carried as the two of them walked along

Historic Twenty-Fifth Street in downtown Ogden. The street was narrow with cars parked in front of brick and stone buildings that had been standing for more than a hundred years. Twenty-Fifth Street had begun life as the welcome mat for train travelers, then it morphed into a wild blend of bars and brothels.

But in the 1950s, it had been reborn as a destination for shopping and dining, and today, it retained all of the old-world charm while it boasted eclectic shops and restaurants that drew tourists from all over. And depending on the time of year, Historic Twenty-Fifth hosted farmer's markets, art festivals, Pioneer Days, Witchstock and even a Christmas village.

Lacy loved it, and usually, strolling along the street and peeking into storefronts cheered her up. But today, she was forcing herself into this trip with Kristi.

"Since when do you say no to coffee?" her friend asked after another sip of her latte.

"Since my stomach's not so sure it approves of food anymore." She swallowed hard, took a deep breath and hoped the fresh air would settle her stomach.

"Well, that sucks," her friend said, shrugging deeper into her jacket as a cold wind shot down the street as if determined to remind everyone that winter wasn't over yet. "Something you ate?"

"Hopefully," Lacy murmured. She didn't want to think about other causes of her less than happy stomach. It had been two weeks since her night with Sam and she couldn't help but think that her sudden bouts of queasiness had more to do with a nine-month flu than anything else. Still, she didn't want to share any of this with Kristi yet, so more loudly, she said, "It's probably the cold pizza I had for dinner last night."

"That'd do it for me," Kristi acknowledged with a

grimace. "You do know how to use a microwave, right? Now that we've struggled out of the caves there is no need to settle for cold pepperoni."

"I'll make a note." They passed a gift store, its front window crowded with pretty pots of flowers, gardening gloves and a barbecue apron that proudly demanded Kiss The Cook, all lovely promises of spring. But the sky was overcast and the wind whistling down from Powder Mountain, looming over the end of the street, made the thought of spring seem like a fairy tale.

Unwell or not, it was good to be away from Snow Vista, wandering down Ogden's main street where she had absolutely zero chance of running into Sam. The man hadn't left the mountain since he got back. And for the past two weeks, she'd hardly spoken to him at all. After that wild bout of earth-shattering sex, Lacy had figured he'd be back wanting more—heaven knew she did. But he'd kept his distance and she knew she should be grateful. Instead, she was irritated.

"So you want to tell me what's going on between you and Sam these days?"

Kristi's question jolted Lacy and her steps faltered for a second. This woman had been her best friend for years. There was nothing they hadn't shared with each other, from first kisses to loss of virginity and beyond. Yet, Lacy just didn't feel comfortable talking about Sam right now. Especially with his little sister.

She gave a deliberate shrug. "Nothing. Why?"

"Please," Kristi said with a snort. "I'm not speaking to him, either, but *you're* not speaking to him really loudly."

"That doesn't even make sense." Lacy paused outside the cupcake shop to stare wistfully at a rainbow confetti cupcake. Normally, she would have gone in and bought herself one. Or a dozen. Today, though, it didn't seem like a good idea to feed her already-iffy stomach that much sugar. Just the pizza she'd eaten, she told herself. She'd be fine in a day or two.

"Sure it does. Mom says you were at the house a couple days ago, visiting Dad. And when Sam showed up you left so fast there were sparks coming up from your boot heels."

Lacy sighed. "Your mom's great but she exaggerates."

"I've seen those sparks, too, when you're in full retreat." Kristi gave her a friendly arm bump as they walked. "I know it's probably hardest on you, Sam being back and everything. But I thought you were over him. You *said* you were over him."

"I exaggerate, too," Lacy mumbled and stopped at the corner, waiting for a green light to cross the street. Her gaze swept along the street.

One of the things she liked best about Ogden was that it protected its history. Relished it. The buildings were updated to be safe, but the heart and soul of them remained to give the downtown area a sense of the past even as it embraced the future.

At the end of the street stood the Ogden train station. Restored to its beautiful Spanish Colonial Revival style, it boasted a gorgeous clock tower in the center of the building. Inside, she knew, were polished wood, high-beamed ceilings and wall murals done by the same artist who did the Ellis Island murals in the 1930s.

Today there was an arts-and-crafts fair going on inside, and she and Kristi were headed there to check out the booths and see how Lacy's photographs were selling.

"I knew you weren't over him," Kristi said with just a touch of a smug smile. "I told you. You still love him."

"No. I won't." Lacy stopped, took a breath. "I mean I don't." She wanted to mean it, even as she felt herself weakening. What kind of an idiot, after all, would she be to deliberately set herself up to get run over again? The light turned green and both women crossed the street.

"Any decent self-help book would tell you that what you just said has flags flying all over it." Still smug, Kristi gave Lacy a smile and took another drink of her latte. "You're trying so hard, but it's hopeless. You do love him—you just don't want to love him. Or forgive him. And I so get that." Shaking her head, Kristi added, "Tony keeps telling me that I've got to let it go. Accept that Sam did what he had to do just like we did. We all stayed and he had to go. Simple."

"Doesn't it just figure that a guy would defend another guy?"

"That's what I thought, too," Kristi admitted. "But in a way, he has a point."

Lacy snorted. "Hard to believe that Sam *had* to leave."

"Yeah," Kristi said on a sigh, and crossed the street, matching her strides to Lacy's. "That urge to bolt out of a hard situation was really more Jack than Sam. Jack never could stand any really deep emotional thing. If a woman cried around him, he'd vanish in a blink."

"I remember," Lacy said wistfully. Hadn't they all teased Jack about his inability to handle any relationship that looked deeper than a puddle?

"I love both of my brothers," Kristi told her, "but I always knew that Sam was the dependable one. Jack was fun—God, he was fun!" Her smile was wide for a split second, then faded. "But you never knew if he'd be home for dinner or if he'd be on his way to Austria for the skiing instead."

Kristi was right. Sam had always been the responsible one. The one you could count on, Lacy thought. Which had made his leaving all that much harder to understand. To accept. As for forgiving, how did you forgive someone you had trusted above everyone else for breaking their word and your heart along with it?

"I kind of hate to admit it, but Tony may be right," Kristi was saying. "I mean, I'm still mad at Sam, but when I see him with Dad, it makes it harder to stay mad, you know?"

"Yeah, I do." That was part of her problem, Lacy thought. She so wanted to keep her sense of righteous anger burning bright, but every time she saw Sam with his father, she softened a little. When she watched him out on the slopes just yesterday, helping a little boy figure out how to make a parallel turn. When she saw him standing in the wind, talking future plans with the contractor. All of these images were fresh and new and starting to whittle away at the fury she had once been sure would be with her forever.

"Dad's so pleased he's back. He's recovering from that heart attack scare faster I think, because Sam's over every day and the two of them are continuously going over all of the plans for Snow Vista." She took another gulp of coffee and Lacy envied it. "Mom's a little cooler, almost as if, like you, she's half expecting him to disappear again, but even she's happy about Sam being home. I can see it in her eyes and on the bathroom scale since she's still cooking the fatted calf for her prodigal nearly every night. Maybe," Kristi said thoughtfully, "it would be easier to forgive and be glad he was here if I knew he was staying."

Lacy's ears perked up. Here was something important. Had he decided to stay after all? And if he did, what would that mean for her? For *them*?

"He hasn't said anything to any of you?"

"No. Just sort of does his work, visits with the parents and avoids all mention of the future—outside of the plans he's got cooking for the resort." Kristi tossed her now-empty cup into a trash can. "So every day I wait to hear that he's gone. He left so fast the last time—" She broke off and winced. "Sorry."

"Nothing to be sorry about," Lacy said as they walked up to the entrance of the train station. "He did leave, and yeah, I'm not convinced he's staying, either."

And she didn't know if that made her life easier or harder. If he was going to leave again, she had to keep her distance for her own heart's sake. She couldn't let herself care again. And if he was staying…what? Could she love him? Could she ever really trust him not to leave her behind again?

What if she didn't have the flu? What if she had gotten pregnant that one night with him? What then? Did she tell him or keep it to herself?

Feeling as if her head might explode, Lacy pushed it all to one side and walked into the train station, deliberately closing her mind to thoughts of Sam for the rest of the day. Instantly, she was slapped with the noise of hundreds of people, talking, laughing, shouting. There were young moms with babies in strollers and toddlers firmly in hand. There were a few men looking as if they'd rather be anywhere else, and then there were the grandmas, traveling in packs as they wandered the crowded station.

Lacy and Kristi paid their entrance fee and joined the herd of people streaming down the narrow aisles. There were so many booths it was hard to see everything at once, which meant that she and Kristi would be making several trips around the cavernous room.

"Oh, I love this." Kristi had already stopped to pick up a hand-worked wooden salad bowl, sanded and polished to a warm honeyed gleam. While she dickered with the artisan, Lacy wandered on. She studied dry floral wreaths, hand-painted front-door hangers shouting WELCOME SPRING and then deliberately hurried past a booth packed with baby bibs, tiny T-shirts and beautifully handmade cradles.

She wouldn't think about it. Not until she had to. And if there was a small part of her that loved the chance that she might be pregnant, she wasn't going to indulge that tiny, wistful voice in the back of her mind.

Lacy dawdled over the jewelry exhibit and then the hand-tooled leather journals. She stopped at the Sweet and Salty booth and looked over the bags of snacks. Her stomach was still unhappy, so she bought a small bag of plain popcorn, hoping it would help. Nibbling as she went, her gaze swept over the area. There were paintings, blown-glass vases and wineglasses, kids' toys and outdoor furniture made by real craftsmen. But she moved through the crowd with her destination in mind. The local art gallery had a booth at the fair every year and that's where Lacy was headed. She sold her photographs through the gallery and she liked to keep track of what kind of photos sold best.

She loved her job at the lodge, enjoyed teaching kids how to ski, but taking photographs, capturing moments, was her real love. Lacy nibbled at the popcorn as she climbed the steps to the gallery's display. The owner was busy dealing with a customer, so Lacy busied herself, studying the shots that were displayed alongside beautiful oil paintings, watercolors and pastels.

Seeing her shots of the mountain, of sunrises and sunsets, of an iced-over lake, gave her the same thrill it always did. Here was her heart. Taking photographs, finding just the right way to tell a story in a picture—that was what fed her soul. And now, she reminded herself, Sam wanted to use her work to advertise the resort. She was flattered and touched and sliding down that slippery slope toward caring for him again.

The owner of the gallery, Heather Burke, handed Lacy's black-and-white study of a snow-laden pine tree to a well-dressed woman carrying a gorgeous blueberry-colored leather bag.

Pride rippled through Lacy. People valued her work. Not just Sam and those at the lodge, but strangers, people who looked at her prints and saw art or beauty or memories. And that was a gift, she thought. Knowing that others appreciated the glimpses of nature that she froze in time.

Lacy smiled at Heather as the woman approached, a look of satisfaction on her face. "I loved that picture."

"So did she," Heather said with a wink. "Enough to pay three hundred for it."

"Three hundred?" The amount was surprising, though Heather had always insisted that Lacy priced her shots too low. "Seriously?"

"Yes, seriously." Heather laughed delightedly. "And, I sold your shot of the little boy skating on the ice rink for two."

"Wow." Exciting, and even better, if she did turn out to be pregnant, at least she knew she wouldn't have to worry about making enough money to take care of her child.

"I told you people are willing to pay for beautiful things, Lacy. And," Heather added meaningfully, "now that spring and summer tourists are almost here, I'm going to need more of your photographs for the gallery. My stock's getting low and we don't want to miss any sales, right?"

"Right. I'll get you more by next week."

"Great." Heather gave her an absent pat on the arm and whispered, "I've got another live one I think. Talk to you later." Then she swept in on an older man studying the photo of a lone skier, whipping down Snow Vista's peak.

Lacy's heart gave a little lurch as it always did when she saw that shot. It was Sam, of course, taken a few years ago just before the season opened and the two of them had had the slopes to themselves. In the photo, the snow was pristine but for the twin slashes in Sam's wake. Trees were bent in the wind, snow drifting from heavy branches. She could almost hear his laughter, echoing in her memory. But, she thought as a stranger lifted the photo off its display board, that was then— this was now.

"I remember that day."

Sam's voice came from right behind her and Lacy was jolted out of her thoughts. She turned to look at him, but he was watching the photograph the older man carried.

"Jack was in Germany and it was just you and me on the slopes."

"I remember." She stared up at him and saw the dreaminess in his green eyes. Caught up in the past, she followed him down Memory Lane.

"Do you also remember how that day ended?" He ran one hand down the length of her arm, giving her a chill that was filled with the promise of heat.

"Of course I do."

As if she could ever forget. They'd made love in the ski-lift cabin as snow fell and wiped away the tracks they'd left on the mountain. She remembered feeling as though they were the only two people in the world, caught up in the still silence of the falling snow and the wonder of Sam loving her.

It had all been so easy back then. She loved Sam. Sam loved her. And the future had spread out in front of them with a shining glory. Then two years later, Jack was dead, Sam was gone and Lacy was alone.

Now he was watching her with warmth in his eyes and a half smile on his lips, and Lacy felt her heart take a tumble she wasn't prepared to accept. Love was so close she could almost touch it. Fear was there, too, though. So she pushed memories into the back of her mind.

"What are you doing at a craft fair?" she blurted out.

He shrugged. "Kristi told Tony where the two of you would be, so we decided to come down and meet up. Thought maybe we could join you for lunch."

Just the thought of lunch made her stomach churn enough that even her popped corn wasn't going to help. She swallowed hard and breathed deeply through her nose. Honestly, she was praying this was something simple. Like the plague.

"Hey." He took her arm in a firm grip. "Are you okay? You just went as pale as the snow in your pictures."

"I'm fine," she said, willing herself to believe it. "Just an upset stomach, I think."

He stared at her, his gaze delving into hers as if he could pry all her secrets loose. Lacy met his gaze, refusing to look away and give him even more reason to speculate. "You're sure that's the problem?"

He was thinking *baby*, just as she was. But since she didn't have the answer to his question, she sidestepped it. "I'm sure. Just not very hungry is all."

"Okay…" He didn't look convinced, but at least he was willing to stop staring at her as if she were a bomb about to explode. Glancing back at the prints being displayed in the booth, he said, "Your photography's changed as much as you have."

"What does that mean?"

He shifted his gaze back to her, then reached out and helped himself to some of her popcorn. "You've grown. So have your photos. There's more depth. More—" he looked directly into her eyes "—layers."

Lacy flushed a little under the praise and was more touched than she was comfortable admitting. Over the past two years, she *had* changed. She'd been forced to grow up, to realize that though she had loved Sam, she could survive without him. She could have a life she loved, was proud of, without him. And though the empty space in her heart had remained, she'd become someone she was proud of. Knowing that he saw, recognized and even liked those changes was disconcerting. To cover up the rush of mixed feelings, she asked, "Is that a backhanded compliment?"

"No," he said with a shake of his head. "Nothing backhanded about it. Just an observation that you're a hell of a woman."

He was looking at her as if he was really *seeing* her—all of her—and she read admiration in his eyes. That was a surprise, and damned if she didn't like it.

A little too much. He was getting to her in a big way. What she was beginning to feel for Sam Wyatt now was so much more than she'd once felt and that worried her. When he left before, she'd survived it, but she didn't know if she could do that again.

"Well, I should look for Kristi—"

"Oh, she left with Tony," Sam told her with a half smile that made him look so approachable, so like the Sam she used to know that it threw her for a second. The then and now blended together and became a wild mix of *throwing Lacy for a loop*. When his words finally clicked in, though, she said, "Wait. She left?"

"He offered to buy her a calzone at La Ferrovia."

"Ah." Lacy nodded, understanding why her best friend had ditched her for her boyfriend. "He does know her weak spots. But who can blame her? Those calzones are legendary."

"Yeah," he said, and started walking alongside her as she turned to move down the crowded aisle. "When I was in Italy, I tried to find one as good as their spinach-cheese calzone and couldn't do it."

"Italy, huh?" Her heart tugged a little, thinking about the time he was away from her. What he'd done, seen. And yes, fine, who he'd been with. She shouldn't care. He'd left her, after all. But it was hard to simply shut down your own feelings just because someone else had tossed them in your face.

"It was beautiful," he said, but he didn't look pleased with whatever memories were rising. "Jack always loved Italy."

"Did you?"

He took more of the popcorn and munched on it. "It was nice. Parts of it were amazing. But seeing something great when you're on your own isn't all that satisfying, as it turns out." He shrugged. "There's no one to turn to and say, *isn't that something*? Still, it was good to be there. See it the way Jack did. But I never did find a calzone as good as La Ferrovia's."

An answer that wasn't an answer, Lacy thought, and wondered why he was bothering to be so ambiguous. She would have thought that he'd love seeing the top skiing spots in Europe. The fact that he clearly hadn't, made her wonder. And she hated that she cared.

"But you're happy to make do now with my popcorn," she said.

"And the company," he added, dipping one hand into the bag again. "This stuff is great, by the way."

"Chelsea Haven makes it, sells it at all the craft fairs and at one of the shops on Twenty-Fifth." She took another handful and added, "I got plain today because, you know. Stomach trouble."

His eyebrows lifted, but she ignored it.

"She's got lots of great flavors, too. Nacho, spicy and—my personal favorite—churro."

He laughed a little. "You're a connoisseur of corn?"

"I try," she said with a shrug, and stopped at the next booth. Wooden shelves and a display table held colorful, carefully wrapped bars of handmade soaps. From bright blue to a cool green, the soaps were labeled with their scents and the list of organic ingredients. Lacy picked up two pale blue bars and held on to them until she could pay for all of her purchases at once at the exit.

Sam studied the display for a long moment before he picked up a square of green soap, sniffed and asked, "Who makes all of this stuff?"

"A small company in Logan. I love it."

She sniffed at the bar of soap, smiled, then held it up for him to take a whiff.

"It's you," he said, giving her a soft smile. "The scent that's always clinging to your skin." He thought about it a moment, then said, "Lilac."

"Good nose," she told him, and started walking again.

"Some things a man's not likely to forget." He bent his head to hers, lowered his voice and whispered, "Like the scent of the woman he's inside of. That kind of thing is imprinted onto your memory."

She quivered from head to toe and, judging by his smile, he approved of her reaction. Her body was tingling, her brain was just a little fuzzed out and breathing seemed like such a chore. When she looked into his eyes and saw the heat there, Lacy felt her heart take another tumble, and this time she didn't try to deny it. To stop it.

When it came to Sam, there was no stopping how her body, her soul, reacted. Her brain was something else, though. She could still give herself a poke and remind herself of the danger of taking another plunge with Sam Wyatt. And yet, despite the danger, she knew there was nothing else she'd rather do. Which meant she was in very big trouble.

Then he straightened, scanned the crowd surrounding them and muttered, "I feel sort of outnumbered around here. Can't be more than a handful of men in the whole building."

"Gonna leave?" she asked, shooting him a quick look.

He met her gaze squarely. "I'm not going anywhere."

And suddenly, she knew he was talking about more than just the craft fair.

Sam stayed with her for another hour as they cruised through a craft fair that normally he wouldn't have been caught dead in. But being with Lacy on neutral ground made up for the fact that he felt a little out of place in what was generally considered female territory.

But while they walked and Lacy shopped, his mind turned over ideas. He carried her purchases in a cloth bag she'd brought with her for that purpose, and together they stepped out of the train station. Sam paused to look up, to the end of Historic Twenty-Fifth and beyond to the snow-covered mountain range in the distance. Trees were budding, the air was warmer and the sun shone down, as if designed to highlight the place in a golden glow.

"I missed this," he said, more to himself than Lacy. "I don't think I even knew how *much* I missed it until I was home again." The wind kicked up as if reminding everyone that spring was around the corner but winter hadn't really left just yet.

"Are you?" she asked, and Sam turned his head to look down at her. That long, silky braid of blond hair fell across one shoulder and loosened tendrils flew around her face, catching on her eyelashes as she watched him. "Are you home?"

Reaching out, Sam gently stroked the hair from her face and tucked it behind her ear. He'd wondered this himself for days. He hadn't been able to give his father a direct answer because he was still too torn. Leave? Walk away from the memories this mountain held and spend the rest of his life running from his own past? Or stand and face it all, reclaim the life—and the woman— he'd left behind?

And wasn't it just perfect now to realize that the woman he wanted owned the property he wanted? If he tried romancing her now, she'd never believe he wanted her for herself. Seemed as though fate was really enjoying itself at his expense.

He'd have to find a way around it, Sam told himself. Because he was done trying to hide from the past. It was time to set it all right. Starting now.

"Yeah, Lacy. I'm home. For good this time."

Eight

"I want to open a gift shop," Sam said, and watched as surprise had Lacy goggling at him. He'd been doing a lot of thinking since the two of them had walked through the arts-and-crafts fair the day before. Though he hadn't been tempted into buying anything himself, Sam was astute enough to realize that other people were. He figured that tourists would be just as anxious to shop for items made by local artisans.

He smiled at Lacy's confusion, then said, "Yeah, I know. Not exactly what you'd expect me to say. But I can see possibilities in everything."

"Is that right?"

"You bet." He eased down to sit on the corner of the desk in her office. "I already talked to you about using the photos you have of the lodge…"

"Yes?"

He grinned at her, enjoying having knocked her a

little off balance, and said, "It struck me when we were at that craft and art fair. There's a hell of a lot of talented people in the area."

"Sure," she said, warily.

"That's why I'm thinking gift shop. Something separate from the lodge, but clearly connected, too. Maybe between the lodge and the new addition that's going up." He nodded as the image filled his mind and he could actually envision what it would look like. "I'd want to have some refrigerated snacks in there, too. For people who are hungry but don't really want a full meal. Like prepackaged sandwiches, drinks, fruit, that kind of stuff…"

"Okay, that's a good idea, but—"

"But more than a snack shop—I want to display local artists. Not just your stuff, which is great, but like the wood-carver at the fair, the glass artist I saw there. I'll still want your postcards and we can sell framed prints, too."

"I don't know what to say."

Shaking his head, he said, "Knowing you, that won't last long. But my point is, if we're expanding Snow Vista, we could bring a lot of the local artists along with us for the ride. I think the tourists would love it and it would give the artists another outlet beyond the fairs to sell their stuff."

"I'm sure they'd love that," she said slowly, cautiously.

That was fine. He could deal with her suspicion. She'd see soon enough that he meant what he was saying. "We'll have a lawyer draw up agreements, of course. Specific to each artisan and what they sell."

"Agreements."

He nodded. "I'm thinking a seventy-thirty split with everyone, same as you and I will have."

"That's amazing," she said, tipping her head to one side and looking up at him as if she'd never seen him before.

"Okay, I know what you're thinking," he said. "I've never really involved myself in anything beyond the lodge or skiing itself."

"Yeah…"

"Like I told you before. People change." He shrugged and mentally brushed off whatever else might be running through Lacy's mind. "Back to the financial aspect, I think what we'll offer is fair. And we'll do well by each other, the lodge and the artists." His gaze met hers. "I want a range of different products in this shop. I want to showcase local talent, Lacy. Everyone from the artists to the chefs, to the woman who makes the blackberry preserves we use at the restaurant."

"Beth Howell."

"Right." He grabbed a piece of paper off the desk and scribbled down the name. "You know her, right? Hell, you probably know all of the artists around here."

"Most, sure…"

"That's great—then as resort manager you can be point on this. Talk to them. See what they think. When it gets closer to opening time, we'll set down the deals in legalese."

She blinked at him. "You want me to take charge of this?"

"Is that a problem?" He smiled, knowing that he'd caught her off guard again.

"No," she said quickly with a shake of her head. "I'm just surprised is all."

"Why?" He came off the desk and stood in front

of her before leaning down, bracing his hands on the arms of her chair. "You know your photos are great. Why would you be surprised that I'd want to showcase them, help you sell them?"

She blew out a breath and fiddled nervously with the end of her blond braid. "I suppose, because of our past, I wonder why you're being so...nice."

"I want you, Lacy. That one night with you wasn't enough. Not by a long shot."

She sucked in air and a faint flush swept up her cheeks, letting him know she felt the fire still burning between them.

"I'm home to stay. That means we're going to be part of each other's lives again."

Shaking her head, she started to speak, but he cut her off. "It's more than that, though. I want to dig in, make the kind of changes that are going to put Snow Vista on the map. And mostly, I want to convince *you* that I'm here and I'm not leaving."

"Why is that so important to you? Why do you care what I think?" Her voice was whisper soft and still it tore at him.

"You don't trust me," he said, and saw the flash in her eyes that proved it. He hated that she was wary of him, but again, he could understand it. "I get that. But things are different now, Lacy. I told you I've seen how much you've changed. Well, I've changed, too." He reached out and captured her nervous fingers in his. "I'm not the same man I was when I left here two years ago."

"And is that a good thing?" she asked quietly. "Or a bad thing?"

Leave it to this new Lacy to lay it out there so bluntly.

His mouth quirked. "I guess you'll have to discover that for yourself."

"It shouldn't matter to you what I think," she said.

"Yes, it should," he argued, and briefly looked down at her fingers, caught in his. "You more than anyone. I had a lot of time to think while I was gone."

"Yeah," she said shortly. "Me, too."

He nodded, acknowledging what she said even as he mentally kicked himself for putting her through so much pain. He hadn't been able to see anything beyond his own misery two years ago. Yet now everything looked clear enough to see that he'd set this whole situation in motion. He had to dig his way out of the very mess he'd created.

"My point is, I took some long, hard looks at my life. Choices made. Decisions. I didn't like a lot of them. Didn't much care for where those decisions had taken me. So now I'm home and I'm going to live with whatever it was that brought me back here."

She took a breath when he rubbed his thumb across her knuckles and he felt the soft whoosh of heat simmering into life between them. Her summer-blue eyes narrowed in caution. He understood why she was looking at him as if expecting him to turn and bolt for the door. But he was done looking for escape. He was here to stay now and she had to get used to it.

"I understand your suspicion," he said, capturing her gaze with his and willing her to not look away. "But I'm home now, Lacy. I'm not leaving again and you're gonna have to find a way to deal." He leaned in closer. "I left two years ago—"

She took a breath. "You keep reminding me of that, and trust me, it's not necessary."

"The point is, those two years changed us both—but

nothing can change what's still between us and I'm not going to let you deny that fire."

She licked her lips, clearly uneasy, and that slight action shot a jolt of heat right to his groin.

"Sam—"

Oh, yeah. She felt it. She was just determined to fight it. Well hell, he'd always liked a challenge. "I'm going to *romance* you, Lacy."

"What? Why?" She pulled her fingers from his grasp, but he saw her rubbing her fingertips as if they were still buzzing with sensation.

"Because I want you," he said simply. He wasn't going to use the *L* word—not only because she wouldn't want to hear it, but because he didn't know if he could say it again. He'd had that love once before but it hadn't held him. He wasn't ready to try and fail again. Failure simply wasn't an option, to quote some old movie. So he was going to keep this simple.

Looking deeply into her eyes, he added, "It's not just what I want, Lacy. You want me, too."

She looked as if she wanted to argue, but she didn't, and Sam called that a win. At least she was admitting, if only to herself, that the burn between them was hotter than ever.

"You're really trying to keep me off balance, aren't you?" she asked.

He gave her a slow, wicked smile. "How'm I doing?"

"Too well."

"Glad to hear it." He stood up abruptly and announced, "I'm headed over to the architect's office. I want to talk to her about designing this gift shop."

"You've already got so much going on…"

"No point in wasting time, is there?" And he meant

both the building and what lay between them. He was sure she understood that, too.

"I suppose not."

"So, talk to a few of your friends," he said, heading for the door. "See if they'd be interested in being involved."

"I'm sure they will…"

"Good," Sam said, interrupting her as he opened the office door. "We can have dinner later and talk about everything."

He took one last look at her and was pleased to see she looked completely shaken. That's how he wanted her. A little unsteady, a little unsure. If he kept her dancing on that fine edge, she'd be less likely to pull back, to cling to her anger. Sam was determined that he would find a way back into her life. To have her in his. And he knew just the way to do it.

Back in the day, he hadn't given Lacy romance. They'd simply fallen into love and then into marriage, and it had all been so easy. Maybe, he thought as he stalked through the lobby and out the front door, that was why it had fallen apart. It was all so easy he hadn't truly appreciated what he'd had until he'd thrown it away.

He wasn't going to make that mistake again.

Two hours later, Lacy was at home, closed up in the bathroom, staring down at the counter and the three— count them, *three*—pregnancy tests.

She'd driven into Logan to buy them just so she wouldn't run into anyone she knew in the local drugstore. She'd bought three different kinds of early-response tests because she was feeling a little obsessive and didn't really trust results to just one single test. And for the first time in her life, she got straight A's on three separate tests.

Positive.

All three of them.

Lacy lifted her gaze to her own reflection in the bathroom mirror. She waited for a sense of panic to erupt inside her. Waited to see worry shining in her own eyes. But those emotions didn't come. Her mind raced and her heart galloped just to keep pace.

"Oh, my God. Really?" Her voice echoed in the quiet cabin. All alone, she took a moment to smile and watched herself as the smile became a grin. She was going to have a baby.

Instinctively, she dropped one hand to lay it gently against her abdomen as if comforting the child within. When she and Sam were together, she had daydreamed about building a family with him. About how she might tell him the happy news when she got pregnant.

"Times change," she muttered. "Now it's not *how* to tell him, but *if* to tell him."

She had to, though, didn't she? Sure she did. That was just one of the rules people lived by. They'd made a baby together and he had a right to know. "Oh, boy, not looking forward to that."

Funny, a couple of years ago, there would have been celebration, happiness. Now she was happy. But what about Sam? He said he wanted her, but that wasn't love. Lust burned bright but went to ash just as quickly. And love was no guarantee anyway. He had loved her two years ago, but he'd left anyway. She loved him now, but it wasn't enough.

"Oh, God." She stared into her own eyes and watched them widen with realization. Kristi was right. Lacy *did* still love Sam. But that love had changed, just as she had. It was bigger. More grown-up. Less naive. She knew there were problems. Knew she wasn't on steady ground, and it wasn't enough to wipe away what she felt. Especially when she didn't know if she *wanted* it wiped away. God, she really was a glutton for punishment. Just pitiful.

The baby added another layer to this whole situation. Yes, Sam had to know.

"But," she told the girl in the mirror, "none of the rules say *when* you have to tell him."

The problem was, she wanted him to be here right now. Wanted to turn into his arms and feel them come around her. She wanted to share this...magic with him and see him happy about it. She wanted him to love her.

Stepping away from the counter, she plopped down onto the closed toilet seat and just sat there in stunned silence. She was still in love with the man who had once shattered her heart. She might have buried her emotions and her pain for two long years, but she hadn't been able to completely cut him out of her heart. He had stayed there because he belonged there, Lacy thought. He always had.

But loving him was a one-way ticket to misery if he didn't love her back. And if she told him about the baby, he'd say and do all the right things—she knew him well enough to know that for certain. He'd want to get married again maybe. Raise their child together, and she would never really know if he would have chosen *her* without the baby. Would he have come not just back home, but back to *her*?

She couldn't live an entire life never knowing, never sure.

Slowly, she pushed to her feet, stared at the test kits, then swept all three of them into the trash can. Patting her abdomen, she said, "No offense, sweetie, but I need to know if your daddy would want me even if you weren't here. So let's keep this between us for a while, okay?"

"You all right?" Sam asked the next morning when he caught her staring off into space. "Still have an upset stomach?"

"What?" Lacy jolted a little. "Um, no. Feel much better." Not a lie at all, she told herself. Once she got past the first fifteen or twenty minutes of feeling like death, everything really lightened up. Of course, she really missed coffee. Herbal tea was just…disappointing.

"Okay." He gave her a wary look as if trying to decide if she was telling the truth or not. "You were acting a little off last night when I stopped by your place with dinner, too."

Because she had still been reeling with the shock of finding herself pregnant. She hadn't really expected him to show up, especially bringing calzones from La Ferrovia. And once he was in the cabin, she had assumed that he would make a move to get her back into bed. But he hadn't. Instead, they'd talked about old times, his new plans for the resort, everything in fact, except what was simmering between them.

For a couple of hours, they'd shared dinner, laughter and a history that was made up of a lifetime of knowing each other. And darn it, Lacy thought, she had been completely charmed and thrown off balance again. He'd said he was going to give her romance, and if last night was the beginning of that, he was off to a great start.

"Have you had a chance to talk to any of your friends about the gift shop?"

"Oh, I did get a couple of them on the phone and

they're very interested." Excited, actually. Thrilled to be asked and to have another venue to sell their wares.

"Good." He shoved both hands in his pockets and stared out the office window at the view. "I'm meeting with the architect in an hour. I want the plans drawn up as soon as possible."

"I don't think that'll be a problem," she said wryly.

He glanced at her. "Why's that?"

"Nobody says no to you for long, do they?"

Sam's mouth quirked. "That include you?"

She felt her balance dissolving beneath her feet. One smile from him, one whispered comment sent jagged shards of heat slicing through her. It just wasn't fair that he had so much ammunition to use against her.

Rather than let him see that he was getting to her, Lacy replied, "As I recall, I also said 'yes' a couple of weeks ago."

"Yeah," he said, gaze moving over her like a touch. "You did."

She squirmed in her chair, then forced herself to settle when she noticed him noticing.

"Don't get jumpy," he said, coming around the desk to lean over her.

"If you don't want me jumpy, you should back up a little."

That smile came again. "Seduction in the office isn't romance, so you're safe from me at the moment."

It could be, she thought wistfully. Lock the door, draw the blinds and—oh, yeah, the office could work. Oh, boy.

He kissed her light and quick, then straightened up. "I'm heading into Ogden to the meeting with the architect. If you need me, you've got my cell number."

"Yeah. I do." *If you need me.* She smothered a sigh. She did need him, but probably not in the way he meant.

"Okay then."

He was almost at the door when she remembered something she had to run by him. "I hired an extra chef to give Maria some help in the kitchen. He starts tomorrow."

"That works," he said, and gave her a long look. "You don't have to run this stuff by me, Lacy. You've done a hell of a job managing the resort for a long time now. I trust you."

Then he left and Lacy was alone with those three words repeating in her mind. *He trusted her.*

And she was keeping his child a secret from him. Was she wrong to wait? To see if maybe his idea to romance her had more to do with reigniting love rather than the flash and burn of desire?

How could she know? All she had to go on were her instincts and they were screaming at her to protect herself—because if he shattered her again, she might not be able to pick up all the pieces this time.

For the next few weeks, Sam concentrated on setting his plans into motion. As February became March and spring crept closer day by day, he was busier than ever. It felt good, digging back into Snow Vista, making a new place for himself here. And Lacy was a big part of that. They had dinner together nearly every night—he'd taken to showing up at the cabin bringing burgers or Italian or Chinese. They talked and planned, and though it was killing him not to, he hadn't tried to smooth her into bed again yet.

He was determined to give her the romance neither of them had had the first time around. And that included sending her flowers, both at work and at her house. The wariness in her eyes was fading and he was glad to see it go.

A roaring engine from one of the earth movers working on the restaurant site tore through his thoughts and brought him back to the moment. The construction team was digging out and leveling the ground for the foundation. As long as the sun kept shining and temperatures stayed above freezing, they'd be getting the lodge addition started by next week. The hard-core, hate-to-see-winter-end skiers were still flocking to the mountain, but for most of the tourists, the beginning of spring meant the end of looking for snow.

Which brought him back to the latest plan he'd already set in motion. Right now there was an engineer and a surveying crew laying out the best possible route for his just-like-Park-City forest ride. There would be rails for individual cars and the riders would be able to slow down if they didn't like the speed attached to careening down a mountain slope. The architects were busily drawing up plans and making the changes that the Wyatt family insisted on.

Sam smiled to himself, stuffed his hands into the pockets of his battered black leather jacket and turned his face into the wind. Here at the top of Snow Vista, the view was, in his opinion, the best in the world. Damned if he hadn't missed it.

He'd been all over the planet, stood on top of the Alps, skied amazing slopes in Germany, Italy and Austria, yet this was the view that for him couldn't be beaten. The pines were tall and straight in the wind, and the bare branches of the oaks and aspens chattered like old women gossiping. Soon, the trees would green up, the wildflowers would be back and the river through the canyon would run fresh and clear again.

His gaze swept across the heavily wooded slope that was unusable for skiing. The alpine ride he wanted installed would make great use of that piece of land. Like a roller coaster but without the crazy dips and climbs. It would be a slower, open-air ride through the trees, displaying the fantastic views available from the top of the mountain. Like Park City, Snow Vista could become known for summer as well as winter fun.

He could see it all. The lifts, the alpine coaster, the restaurant offering great food at reasonable prices. Hell, Sam told himself, as he turned to shift his view to the meadow, still blanketed in snow, with a gazebo and a few other additions, they could open the resort to weddings, corporate getaways…the possibilities were endless.

And he'd be here, to see it all. He waited for the urge to leave and when it didn't come, he smiled. It really was good to be back.

"I know the sun's out, but it's still too cold to be standing around outside."

Chuckling, Sam turned to face his sister.

"It's spring, Kristi," Sam said. "Enjoy the cool before the summer heat arrives."

She walked toward him, her hair pulled back from her face, a black jacket pulled over a red sweater and jeans. As she approached, her features were as cool as the wind sliding across the mountain. His little sister hadn't really said anything about his decision to stay and Sam knew that she and Lacy were the ones he'd have to work hardest to convince. He was pretty sure he had Lacy halfway there, but maybe now was his chance to get through to his sister.

"You haven't even been back a full month and you've

got the whole mountain running to catch up with your ideas."

Sam shrugged. "Now that I've decided to stay, there's no point in holding back." He looked away from Kristi and sent a sharp-eyed look at the men working the half-frozen ground. "I want the resort to be up and offering new things as quickly as possible."

"Hence the bonus money offered the crew if they get both foundations poured before April 1?"

Sam grinned. "Money's a great motivator."

"It is," she acknowledged. "And Dad's really happy with everything you're doing."

"I know." It felt good, knowing that his father was excited about the future. That meant he was thinking ahead, not about the past or about his own health issues. Sam was still stopping in at the lodge every day to go over the plans with his father. To keep the older man engaged in what was going on. To get his input and, hell—just to be with him. Sam had missed that connection with his parents over the past two years. Being here with them again was good for the soul— even with the ghost of Jack hanging over all of them, whether he was spoken of or not. But even with that, with the memories of sorrow clinging close, even with the complications nearly choking him, it was good to be on familiar ground again.

"What about you, Kristi?" His gaze shifted to her again. "How are you feeling about all of this? About me?"

She took a breath and let it out. "I like all of the plans," she said, lifting her eyes to meet his. "But the jury's still out on what I'm thinking of you."

Sam felt his good mood drift away and decided that now was the time to get a few things straightened out with his little sister. "How long are you going to make me pay?"

"How long have you got?" Kristi shrugged, but her eyes were clouded with emotion rather than anger.

"I can't keep saying I'm sorry." Apologizing had never come easy for Sam. Not even when he was a kid. Having to swallow the fact that he'd screwed up royally two years ago wasn't exactly a walk in the park. But he was doing it.

"I came back," he told her. "That has to count, too."

"Maybe it does, because I am glad you're back, Sam. Really." She shoved both hands into her jacket pockets and tossed a strand of hair out of her eyes with a single jerk of her head. "You being here is a good thing. But what you did two years ago affected all of us and that's not so easy to get past."

"Yeah, I know." He nodded grimly, accepting the burden of past decisions. "Lacy. Mom. Dad."

"*Me,*" she snapped out, and stepped up close enough to him that the toes of their boots collided. Tipping her head back, she glared up at him, her eyes suddenly alive with anger, and said, "You leaving taught me that trusting *anyone* was too risky. Did you know Tony's asked me to marry him twice now and twice I told him no?"

He inhaled sharply. "No, I didn't know that."

"Well, he did. And I said no because—" her voice broke off, she swallowed hard and pinned him with a hot look designed to singe his hair. "Because if *you* could leave Lacy, how could I possibly trust that Tony would stay with me? What's the point, right? I couldn't make myself believe, because you ripped the rug out from under me."

"Damn it, Kristi." Talk about feeling lower than he would have thought possible. Somehow in screwing over his own life, he'd managed to do the same for his baby sister. One more piece of guilt to add to the burden he already carried. Sam gritted his teeth and accepted it. Then he dropped both hands onto her shoulders and held on.

"You can't use me as an excuse for not trying. I messed things up pretty well, but they were *my* decisions." Bitter pill to choke down, but there it was. "You can't judge everyone else by what I did. Tony's a great guy and you know it. You're in charge of your own life, Kristi. Make it or break it on your own. Just like the rest of us."

"Easy to say when you're not the one left behind."

She had a point, though it cut at him to admit it. Damn, the repercussions of what he'd done two years ago just kept coming. It was like dropping a damn rock into a pond and watching the ripples spread and reach toward shore. But even as he acknowledged that, he tried to cut himself a break, too.

When Jack died, Sam hadn't been able to think. Hadn't been able to take a breath through his own pain, and he'd reacted to that. Escaping the memories, the people, who were all turning to him for answers he didn't have. The emptiness he'd felt at his brother's death had driven him beyond logic, beyond reason. Now, his decision to come home again meant he was forced to face the consequences of his actions. Acknowledging the pain he'd dealt others was hard to swallow.

He looked at Kristi and saw her in flashing images through his mind at every stage of her life. The baby his parents had brought home from the hospital. The tiny blonde girl chasing after him and Jack. The prom date Jack and he had tortured with promises of pain if he got out of line with their sister. The three siblings laughing together at the top of the mountain before hurtling down the slope in one of the many races they'd indulged in. Slowly, though, the memories faded and he was looking into her eyes, seeing the here and now, and love for her filled him.

Going with instinct, he pulled her, resisting, in for a hug, and rested his chin on top of her head. It only took a second or two for her to wrap her arms around his waist and hold on. "Damn it Sam, we needed you—I needed you—and you weren't here."

"I am now," he said, waiting until she looked up at him again. She was beautiful and sad, but no longer furious and he was silently grateful that the two of them had managed to cross a bridge to each other. "But, Kristi, don't let my mistakes make you miss something amazing. You love Tony, right?"

"Yes, but—"

"No." He cut her off with a shake of his head. "No buts. You've always been nuts about him and it's clear he loves you, too, or he wouldn't put up with all of those self-help books you're always quoting."

She snorted and dipped her head briefly. The smile was still curving her mouth when she looked up at him again.

Shaking his head, Sam said softly, "Don't use me as an excuse for playing it safe, Kristi. Nobody's perfect, kid. Sometimes, you have to take a chance to get something you want."

She scowled at him, then chewed at her bottom lip.

He smiled and planted a kiss on her forehead. "Trust Tony. Hell, Kristi, trust *yourself*."

"I'll try," she said, then added, "I'm so glad you're home."

"Me, too, kid. Me, too."

Nine

The talk with his sister was still resonating with him when Sam stopped at Lacy's cabin later that night. For hours, he'd heard Kristi's voice repeating in his mind as he came to grips with what he'd put everyone through two years ago. Realizing what he'd cost himself had brought him to the realization that he not only wanted but *needed* Lacy in his life again. Now he had to find a way to make that happen.

The occasional night with her wasn't enough. He wanted more. And Sam wasn't going to stop until he had it.

He brought pizza and that need to be with her. To just be in the same damn room with her. To be able to look into those eyes that had haunted him for too long and realize he had a second chance to make things right.

"Bringing a pizza is cheating," Lacy told him, settling back into the couch with a slice of that pizza on a stoneware plate.

He laughed. "How? Gotta eat. You always loved pizza."

"Please." She rolled her eyes and shook her head. "Everyone loves pizza."

"Not many people love it with pepperoni and pineapple."

She took a bite and gave a soft groan of pleasure that had his body tightening in response. "Peasants who don't know what's good," she said with a shrug.

Ordinarily he might enjoy bantering with her, but tonight, he couldn't seem to settle. Sam set his pizza aside and looked into the fire that burned cheerily in the hearth. The hiss and crackle of flames was a soothing sound, but it did nothing for the edginess he felt. He couldn't shake that conversation with Kristi.

"What's wrong?"

He looked at her, firelight dancing across her face, highlighting the gold of her hair lying loose across her shoulders. That same flickering light glittered in her eyes as she watched him. She wore jeans, a deep red sweater and a pair of striped socks, and still, she was the most beautiful woman he'd ever seen.

"Sam? What is it?"

He got to his feet, stalked to the fireplace and planted both hands on the mantel as he stared into the flames. "I talked to Kristi today."

"I know. She told me."

Of course she had. Women told each other everything—a fact that gave most men cold chills just to think about it. He turned to look at her. "Did she tell you that she's been putting her whole damn life on pause because of what I did two years ago?"

"Yeah, she did."

He pushed one hand through his hair, turned his back

on the fire and faced her dead on. His brain was racing; guilt raked his guts with sharpened claws. "I never realized, you know, how much my decisions two years ago affected everyone else."

Lacy set her pizza aside and folded her hands in her lap as she looked at him. "How could they not, Sam?"

Scrubbing the back of his neck, he blurted, "Yeah, I see that now. But back then, I couldn't see past my own pain. My own misery."

"You wouldn't let any of us help. You shut us all out, Sam."

"I know that," he said tightly. "I do. But I couldn't reach out to you, Lacy. Not when the guilt was eating me alive."

"Why should you feel guilty about what happened to Jack? I don't understand that at all."

He blew out a breath, swallowed hard and admitted, "When Jack first got sick—diagnosed with leukemia— that's when the guilt started."

"Sam, why? You didn't make him sick."

He choked out a sharp laugh. "No, I didn't. But I was healthy and that was enough. We were *identical twins*, Lacy. The same damn egg made us both. So why was he sick and I wasn't? Jack never said it, but I know he was thinking it because I was. Why him? Why not me?"

A soft sigh escaped her and he didn't know if it was sympathy or frustration.

Didn't matter now anyway. He was finally telling her exactly what had been going through his head back then, and he had to get it finished. But damn, it was harder than he would have thought. Shaking his head, he reached up to scrub one hand across the back of his neck and started talking again.

"I was with Jack through the whole thing, but I

couldn't share it. Couldn't take my half of it and make it easier on him." His hand fisted and he thumped it uselessly against his side as his mind took him back to the darkest days of his life. "I felt so damn helpless, Lacy. I couldn't *do* anything."

"You did do something, though, Sam," she reminded him. "You gave him bone marrow. You gave him a chance and it worked."

He snorted at the reminder of how high their hopes had been. Of the relief Sam had felt for finally being able to help his twin. To save his life. "For all the good it did in the end."

"I never knew you were feeling all of this." She stood up, walked to him and looked into his eyes. "Why didn't you talk to me about this then, Sam?"

He blew out a breath. Meeting her eyes was the hardest thing he'd ever done. Trying to explain the unexplainable was just as difficult. "How could I tell my wife that I felt guilty for being married? Happy? Alive?" He pushed both hands through his hair, then sucked in air like a drowning man hoping for a few more seconds of life before the sea dragged him down. "God, Lacy, you were loving me and Jack had no one."

"He had *all* of us," she countered.

"You know what I mean." He shook his head again. "He was *dying* right in front of me."

"Us."

She was right, he knew. Jack's loss was bigger than how it had affected Sam. He could remember his parents' agony and worry. The whispered prayers in the mint-green, soulless, hospital waiting room. He saw his father age and watched his mother hold back tears torn from her heart and still... "I couldn't feel that then," he admitted. "*Wouldn't* feel it. I was watching my twin die and I was so messed up I couldn't see a way out."

"But you finally found one…"

"Yeah," he said softly, looking into those eyes of hers, seeing the sorrow, the regret, and hating himself for causing it then and reawakening it now. "I don't know if you can understand what I did, Lacy. Hell, I don't even know if I do, now."

"Try me." She folded her arms across her chest and waited.

God, two years he'd been holding everything inside him. Letting it all out was like—he couldn't even think of the right metaphor. It was damned painful but it was long past time he told Lacy exactly what had happened then. Why he'd done what he'd done.

"After the bone-marrow transplant, after it worked and Jack was in remission, it was like…" He paused, looking for the right words, and was sure he wouldn't be able to find them. Not to explain what he had felt. Finally, he just started talking again and hoped for the best. "It was like fate had suddenly said, 'Okay, Sam. You can go ahead and be happy again. Your brother's alive. You saved him. So everything's good.'"

He could remember it so well, the nearly crippling relief, the laughter. Watching his brother recover, get strong again, believing that their world was righting itself.

Lacy reached out and gently laid one hand on his forearm. It felt like a damn lifeline to Sam, holding him to this place, this time, not letting him go too deeply into a past filled with misery. He covered her hand with his, needing that warmth she offered him as he finished.

Sam looked down at their joined hands and said softly, "Jack was full of plans, Lacy. He was well again, and after so long feeling like crap, he couldn't wait to get back out into the world."

"I remember," she said quietly.

The snap and hiss of the flames was the only sound in the room for a few seconds. "He showed me his 'list.' Not a bucket list, since he wasn't dying anymore. It was a dream list. A *life* list. His first stop was going to be Germany. Staying with some friends while he skied the slopes and reclaimed everything the cancer stole from him."

She didn't speak, just kept looking at him through eyes gleaming with the shine of tears she wouldn't allow to fall.

"He was well, damn it." Sam pulled away from her and scrubbed both hands over his face like a man trying to wake up from a nightmare. "Jack was happy again and on the road and then he *dies* in a damn car wreck on the freeway? It was crazy. Surreal."

"I know, Sam. I was with you. We all were."

"That's the thing, Lacy." His gaze caught hers again as he willed her to understand how it had been for him. "You were there but I couldn't have you. Couldn't *let* myself have you because Jack was dead and his dreams with him. I *saved* him and he died anyway. It was like fate was screwing with us just for the hell of it. None of it made sense. I couldn't bring him back. So I told myself I had to do the next best thing. I had to at least keep his dreams alive."

Seconds ticked past before Lacy stared up at him and said, "That's why you left? To pick up the list Jack left behind and make it happen?"

"He had all these plans. Big ones. And with him gone, those plans were all I had left of him. How could I let them die, too?"

"Sam—" She broke off, took a breath and said, "Did you really think fulfilling Jack's list was going to keep him with you?"

God, why did it sound stupid when she said it? It hadn't been at the time. But that's exactly what he'd thought. By living his twin's dreams, in essence, his twin's *life*, it would be as if Jack never died.

"It was important to me," he muttered thickly. "I had to keep him alive somehow."

"God, Sam…" She lifted one hand to cover her mouth and her beautiful eyes shone with tears.

"Keeping Jack with me meant distancing myself from the reality of his death. That's why I had to leave. I couldn't be here, facing the fact, every day, that he was gone."

God, he felt so stupid. So damn weak somehow for having to give up his own life because he'd been unable to accept his twin's death. He rubbed one hand across his mouth, then said, "I took Jack's dreams and lived them for him. For a while, I lost myself in ski slopes, strangers and enough alcohol to sink a ship." He snorted ruefully as memories of empty hotel rooms and staggering hangovers rose up to taunt him. "But drinking only made the pain more miserable and even skiing and being anonymous got old fast."

"You should have talked to me, Sam."

"And said what?" he asked, suddenly weary to his bones. His gaze locked on hers and everything in him wished that they were still what they had once been to each other. It rocked him a little to realize just how much he wanted her back. How much he still loved her. "What could I possibly have told you, Lacy? That I wasn't allowed to be happy because Jack was dead? You couldn't have understood."

"You're right," she said, nodding. "I wouldn't have. I'd have told you that *living* was the best way to honor Jack. Living your own dreams. Not his."

He sighed. She was right and he could see that now. He wouldn't have then. "My dreams didn't seem to matter to me once his were over."

"Did it help?" she asked quietly. "Leaving. Did it help?"

"For a while." His mouth quirked briefly. "But not for long. I couldn't find satisfaction in Jack's dreams because they weren't mine. But I owed it to him to try."

She reached up to cup his face in her palms and the soft warmth of her touch slid deep inside to ease away the last of the chill crouched in his heart. God, how had he lived for two years without her touch? Without the sound of her voice or the soft curve of her mouth? How had he been able to stay away from the one woman in the world who made his life worth living?

"Sam," she said quietly, "you don't owe Jack your life."

"I know," he said, covering her hands with his. It was too early to tell her he loved her. Why the hell should she believe him after what he'd done to their lives? Their marriage? No, he'd sneak up on her. Be a part of her world every day, slowly letting her see that he was here to stay and that he would never leave her again. "That's why I'm back, Lacy. To rebuild my life. And I want that life to include you."

"Sam…"

"Don't say anything yet, Lacy," he told her. "Just let me prove to you that I can be the man for you."

Her breath hitched and her eyes went shiny with emotion.

"Let's just take our time and discover each other again, okay?"

She nodded slowly, and in her eyes he read hope mingled with caution. Couldn't blame her for it, but he silently vowed that he'd wipe away her trepidation.

"You can trust me, Lacy. I swear it."

"I want to, Sam," she whispered, "for more reasons than you know…"

"Just give me a chance." When he pulled her close, bent his head and kissed her, she leaned into him, curving her body to his, silently letting him know that she was willing to try. And that was all he could hope for. For now.

Tenderness welled up between them and in the soft, flickering firelight, they came together as if it were the first time and the shining promise that was the future was almost in reach.

Lacy was still smiling the next morning.

She felt as though she and Sam had finally created a shaky bridge between the past and present. At long last, he'd told her what had driven him to leave, and though it still hurt, she could almost understand. As sad as they'd all been when Jack died, for Sam it had to have been even more devastating. Like losing a part of himself. And she could admit, too, that she hadn't been capable of being what he needed back then. She'd been too concerned with her own insecurities.

When Jack died, all she'd been able to think was *thank God it wasn't Sam*. She'd been too young and too untried—untested—to be able to see what Sam was going through, so how could she have helped him?

Now it was as if they were both getting a second chance to do things right. She laid one hand on her belly and whispered to the child sleeping within, "I think it's going to be all right, baby. Your daddy and I are going to make it happen. Build a future in spite of the past."

And just to prove to herself—and him—that she was willing to trust him, willing to believe, she had decided to tell him about the baby that night at dinner.

Whoa. Her stomach did a quick twist and spin at the thought. Nervous, yes, but it was the right thing to do. If they were going to work this out between them and have it stick this time, she had to be as honest as he had been the night before.

She gave the baby a gentle pat, then, smiling, she headed through the lobby. There were guests sprinkled around the great room, enjoying the fire, having a snack, chatting. She ignored them all, stepped outside and took a deep breath of the chill spring air. Tulips and daffodils were spearing up, trees were beginning to green.

It was as if the snow was melting along with the ice in her heart. Lacy felt lighter than she had in two years. And she was ready to let go of the past and rush to a future that was suddenly looking very bright.

"Lacy! Hey, Lacy!"

She turned and grinned at Kevin Hambleton as he jogged toward her. Kevin was young, working his first season at the lodge. He was helping out at the ski-rental shop, but had been angling for an instructor's position.

"Hi, Kevin," she said as he started walking with her toward the ski lift that would take her to the new construction site. Not only did she want to see how the building was coming along, she could admit to herself that she wanted to see Sam, too. And she knew that if he wasn't at the lodge, working in the office, he would be at the site, watching his plans come to life. "I'm just going up to check on the guys, see what progress they're making."

"It's great, isn't it?" His face practically shone with excitement. "A lot of things happening around here now that Sam's back."

"There are, with more to come," she said, thinking about the gift shop, the portico and the expansion to the lodge. Within a couple of years, Snow Vista would be a premier tourist destination.

"I know, I read that in the paper this morning."

"What?" She looked up at him. As far as she knew, the gift shop hadn't been announced.

"Yeah, there was this article, talking about all the changes and how Sam's going to put in a new beginner's run on the back side of the mountain and all…"

Lacy shook her head, frowned and tried to focus on what he was saying. But her heart was pounding and her brain was starting to short-circuit. "He's building a run on the backside?"

"Yeah, and I wanted to put my name in with you early, you know?" He grinned. "Get in on the ground floor. I really want to be an instructor and I figured starting out with the newbies would be a good idea, you know?"

"Right." Mind racing, Lacy heard Kevin's excited voice now as nothing more than a buzz of sound. The cold wind slapped at her, people around her shouted or laughed and went about their business. It was all she could do to put one foot in front of the other.

"With a new run going in, you'll need more instructors, so I just, you know, wanted to see if maybe you'd think about me first."

He was standing there, staring at her with a hopeful

grin on his face, the freckles across his cheeks bright splashes of gold.

The edges of her vision went dark until she was looking at Kevin as if through a telescope. She felt faint, her head was light and there was a ball of ice in the pit of her stomach. Through the clanging in her brain and the wild thumping of her heart, Lacy knew she had to say *something*.

"How did you hear about the new run?"

"Like I said," he told her, his eyes a little less excited now, "I saw it in the paper. Well, my mom did and she told me."

He was looking worried now, as if he'd done something wrong, so Lacy gave him a smile and a friendly pat on the shoulder to ease him. No reason to punish him just because *her* world was suddenly rocking wildly out of control. "Okay then, Kevin. I'll put your name down."

"Thanks!" Breath whooshed out of him in relief. "A lot, really. Thanks, Lacy."

When he ran off again, she watched him go, but her mind wasn't on Kevin any longer. It was fixed solely on Sam Wyatt. The lying bastard. God. She thought about the night before—as she had been doing all morning—only now she was looking at it through clearer eyes.

And heck, it wasn't just last night, it was the past few weeks. Romancing her. She nearly choked. He'd said he was going to romance her, but that wasn't what he'd been doing. This whole time, he'd been conducting a sort of chess match, with her as the pawn, to be moved wherever he wanted her. He'd spent weeks softening her up, until he could apply the coup de grâce last night. Then he rolled her up in sympathy, let her shed a few tears for him, for them, then he'd swept her into bed, where rational thinking was simply not an option.

"Oh, he was good," she murmured, gaze fixed on the top of the mountain where she knew he was, but not really seeing it. "He actually convinced me. He had me."

And wasn't that a lowering thing to admit? Lacy cringed internally as she remembered just how easily she'd fallen for charm and lies. Sam had slipped beneath her radar and gotten past every one of her defenses. He'd made her feel *sorry* for him. Made her forgive him for what he'd done to her two years ago. Made her *believe* again. Last night, he'd convinced her at last that maybe they had a chance of rebuilding their lives.

But he wasn't really interested in that at all. Or in *her*. She was a means to an end. All he wanted from her was the land his family had given her. For his plans. For his changes. He was sweeping her aside just as he had two years ago. And just like then, she hadn't noticed until she had tire tracks on her back.

Temper leaped into life and started pawing at her soul like a bull preparing to charge. Well, she wasn't the same Lacy now. She was tougher. Stronger. She'd had to be.

And this time, he wasn't going to get away with it.

She found him at the construction site, just where she'd expected him to be. Sam spent half his time up here, talking to the men, watching the progress of the new restaurant going up. And all the while, he was probably planning his takeover of her property, too.

The ride on the ski lift hadn't calmed or soothed Lacy as it usually did. Normally, the sprawling view spreading out beneath her, the sensation of skimming through the sky was enough to ease away every jagged edge inside her. But not today. The edges were too sharp. Cutting too deeply.

The rage she'd felt when Kevin first stopped her and spilled his news had grown until it was a bubbling froth rising up from the pit of her stomach to the base of her throat. Her hands shook with the fury and her eyes narrowed dangerously against the sun glinting off what was left of the snowpack. Shaking her head, she jumped off the lift when it reached the top and before she could even *try* to cool down, she followed the steady roar of men and machines to the site.

Sam stood there, hands in the pockets of his black leather jacket, wind tossing his dark hair into a tumble and his gaze fixed on the men hustling around what looked to her like the aftermath of a bombing. He couldn't have heard her approach over the crashing noise, but as she got closer, he somehow sensed her and turned to smile. That smile lasted a fraction of a second before draining away into a puzzled frown.

"Lacy?" His voice was pitched high enough to carry over the construction noise. "Everything okay?"

"*Nothing* is okay and you know it," she countered, sprinting toward him until she was close enough to stab her index finger against his chest. "How could you do that? You lied to me. You used my own pain against me. You played me, Sam. Again."

"What the hell are you talking about?"

Oh, he was a better actor than she'd given him credit for. The expression of stunned surprise might actually have been convincing if she didn't already know the truth. "You know damn well what I'm talking about so don't bother playing innocent."

God, she was so furious she could hardly draw a breath.

But the words clogging her throat didn't have any trouble leaping out at him. "Kevin told me what's really going on around here. I should have known. Should have guessed. Romancing me," she added snidely. "Flowers. Dinner."

If anything, the confusion on his face etched deeper until Lacy wanted to just smack him. She'd never been a violent person, but at the moment she sorely wished she was.

"Why don't you calm down," he was saying. "We'll go talk and you can tell me what's bothering you?"

"Don't you tell me to calm down!" She reached up and tugged at her own hair, flying loose in the wind. "I can't believe I fell for it. I was this close—" she held up her thumb and index finger just a whisker apart "—to trusting you again. I thought last night meant something—"

Now anger replaced confusion and his features went taut as his eyes narrowed. "Last night *did* mean something."

"Sure," she countered, through the pain, the humiliation of knowing it had all been an act. "It was the cherry on top of the sundae of lies you've been building for weeks. The grand finale of the Romance Lacy Plan. My God, I went for it all, didn't I? Your sadness, your grief." She huffed in a breath, disgusted with him, with herself, with everything. "I've got to give you credit— it really did the job on me. Then slip me into bed fast and make me remember how it used to be for us. Make me *want* it."

A couple of the machines went silent and the drop in the noise level was substantial, but she kept going. She was aware of nothing beyond the man staring at her as if she were speaking in tongues.

"You set this whole thing up, didn't you? Right from the beginning."

"Set *what* up?" He threw both hands in the air and let them fall to his sides again. "If you'll tell me what you're talking about maybe I could answer that."

"The backside of the mountain," she snapped. "*My* land. The land your folks deeded to me." Her breath was hitching, her voice catching. "You want it for a new beginner run. Kevin told me he saw it in the paper this morning. Your secret's out, Sam. I know the truth now, and I'm here to tell you it's not going to work."

"The *paper*?" he repeated, clearly astonished. "How the hell did—"

"Hah!" she shouted. "Didn't mean for the word to get out so soon, huh? Wanted a little more time to sucker me in even deeper?"

"That's not what I meant—never mind. Doesn't matter."

She gasped. "You son of a bitch, of *course* it matters. It's *all* that matters. You lied to me, Sam. You used me. And damn it, I let you." She was so stupid. How could she have been foolish enough to let him get into her heart again? How could she have, even for a moment, allowed herself to hope? To dream?

"Now just wait a damn minute," Sam blurted out. "I can explain all of this."

She took a step back and didn't even notice when the last of the construction machinery cut off and silence dropped on the mountain like a stone. "Oh, I bet you can. I bet you've got stories and explanations for any contingency."

"Just a minute here, Lacy…"

"How far were you willing to go, Sam, to get what you wanted from me? Marriage?"

"If you'll just shut up and listen for a second…"

"Don't you tell me to shut up! And for your information, I'm done listening to you." She backed up a step, lifted her chin and gave him the iciest glare she could manage. "You want the land? Well you're not going to get it. The one thing you want from me, you can't have."

He moved toward her. "That's not what I want from you."

"I don't believe you." She shook her head and her gaze fixed with his. "I know the truth now. I know the real reason you've been spending so much time with me, *reconnecting*."

"You don't know anything," he said, moving in closer. "I admit, I wanted a new beginner run on the backside, but—"

"There. Finally. *Truth*." She jerked her head back as if he'd slapped her. "Did it actually hurt to say it?"

"I'm not finished."

"Oh, yes," she told him, "you are. *We* are. Whatever there was between us is done."

"It'll never be done, Lacy." His voice was dark, deep and filled with determination. "You know that as well as I do."

"What I know, is that once I believed you when you said you would never leave me. You *knew* what that meant to me. Because my own mother left me. You promised you wouldn't. You swore to love me forever." Oh, God, this was so hard. She couldn't breathe now. There were iron bands around her chest, squeezing her lungs, fisting around her heart. "And then you left. You walked away. Broke your word *and* my heart. You don't get a second chance at that. Damned if I'll bleed for you again, Sam."

"You're upset," he said, his voice carrying the faintly

patient tone that people reserved for dealing with hysterics. "When you settle down a little, we can talk this out."

She laughed and it scored her throat even as it scraped the air. "I've said what I came to say to you—and I don't want to hear another word from you. Ever."

Lacy spun around and hurried to the ski lift for a ride back down the mountain.

Sam watched her go, his own heart pounding thunderously in his chest. Silence stretched out around him, and it was only then he noticed all the men had stopped working and were watching him. They'd probably heard every word. He turned his head and caught sight of Dennis Barclay.

"Seems you're in some deep trouble there, Sam," the man said.

Truer words, he thought, but didn't let Dennis know just how worried he was. He'd never seen Lacy in a tear like that before. Even when she was furious when he first got home, even when she had yelled at him about past sins, there'd been some control. Some sort of restraint. But today there had been nothing but sheer fury and bright pain. Pain he'd caused her. Again. That thought shamed him as well as infuriated him.

How the hell had that tidbit about the beginner run made it into the paper? He hadn't told anyone. Hadn't said a word.

"She'll cool off," Dennis said, offering hope.

"Yeah," Sam agreed, though a part of him wasn't so sure. The pain and fury he'd just witnessed wasn't something that would go away quickly. If ever. Had he screwed things up so badly this time that it really was over?

Misery blossomed in his chest and wrung his heart

until the pain of it nearly brought him to his knees. A life without Lacy?

Didn't bear thinking about.

Ten

Sam's instincts told him to go to Lacy right away. Follow her. Force her to listen to him so he could straighten all this out. But his instincts two years ago had been damned wrong, so he was hesitant to listen to them now—when it mattered so much.

He denied himself the urge to go to Lacy and instead went to the lodge and upstairs to the family quarters. He wasn't even sure why, but he felt as if he needed more than being alone with the black thoughts rampaging through his mind.

The great room was empty, so he followed his nose to the kitchen. The scent of spaghetti sauce drifted to him, and in spite of everything, his stomach growled in appreciation. Another thing he'd missed while he was gone was his mother's homemade sauce. Sam stopped in the doorway and watched her at the stove while his father sat at the round oak pedestal table, laying out a hand of solitaire.

"Sam!" His father spotted him first and his mother whirled around from the stove to smile in welcome. "Good to see you," his father said. "How's the work on the mountain going? Tell me all about it since your mother won't let me go up yet."

"Everything's fine," Sam said, and walked to the table to take a seat. The kitchen was bright, cheerful, with the sunlight pouring in through windows sparkling in the light.

"You don't look too happy about it," his mother said.

He glanced at her and forced a smile. "It's not that. It's…"

"Lacy," his mother finished for him.

"Well," Sam chuckled darkly, "good to know that your mother radar is still in good shape."

Connie Wyatt grinned at her son. "It wasn't that hard to guess, but I'll take the compliment, thanks."

"So, what's going on?" his father asked as Sam sat down opposite him.

He hardly knew where to start. But hell, he'd come here to talk, to get this all off his chest. He just had to lay it all out for them, so he took a breath and blurted out, "Apparently someone talked to a reporter. It was in the paper today about me wanting to build a beginner run on Lacy's property."

"Ouch." His father winced.

"And she found out," Connie said.

"Yeah." Sam drummed his fingers on the table. "She let me have it, too. I just can't figure out how the reporter heard about it. I mean, I changed my plans when I heard the land was Lacy's."

"That's probably my fault."

"Bob," his wife demanded, "what did you do?"

Grumbling, the older Wyatt glanced first at his son,

then his wife. "A reporter called here the other day," he said, with a rueful shake of his head. "Asking questions about all the changes happening around here. Got me talking about the different runs we have to offer, then she said something about how she was a novice skier and I told her we could teach her and that you had wanted to build a brand-new beginner run on the back of the mountain, but that the plans weren't set in stone so not to say anything…and I guess she did anyway."

Sam groaned. At least that explained how it had made the paper. And, it would be a lot simpler if he could just blame this latest mess on his father. But the reality was, if Sam had just been honest with Lacy from the jump, none of this would be happening.

"Don't worry about it, Dad. She was bound to hear about it sooner or later anyway."

"Yeah, but it would've been better to hear it from you," his father pointed out.

"That ship sailed when I didn't tell her." Sam slumped back in the chair and reached for the cup of coffee his mother set in front of him. Taking a long sip, he let the heat slide through him in a welcome wave.

"So what're you going to do about all of this?" his mother asked quietly.

He looked at her. Connie was standing with her back braced against the counter, her arms folded over her chest.

"That's the thing," Sam said honestly. His chest ached like a bad tooth and he suspected his heart wasn't going to be feeling better anytime soon. Not with the way things stood between him and Lacy. "I just don't know."

And that was the truth. With Lacy's words still echoing in his mind, the wounded glint in her eyes still fresh in his memory, Sam couldn't see clearly what he should do. He knew what he *wanted* to do. Go to her. Tell her he loved her. But damned if she'd believe that *now*. It had been easier—if more selfish—two years ago, when he hadn't considered how his decision to take off would affect anyone but himself. Now, though, there was too much to think about. Just one more rock on the treacherous road his life had become.

"I almost went after her—"

"Bad idea," his father said. "Never beard a lioness in her den when she's still itching to take a bite out of you. I speak from experience," he added with a sly glance at his wife.

"Very funny," Sam's mother quipped, then turned back to Sam. "And just how long do you think it's going to take for her to cool off?"

"A decade or two ought to do it," Sam mused, only half joking. He raked one hand through his hair and sighed. "Hell, me coming home has thrown everyone off their game. Maybe it'd be best for everyone if I just left again and—"

"Don't you even say that," his mother warned, her voice cold steel. "Samuel Bennett Wyatt, don't you even *think* about leaving here again."

Shocked at the vehemence in her tone, Sam could only look at her. "I really wasn't going to leave again. I was just thinking that maybe it would be easier on everyone if I—"

"If you what?" his mother finished for him. "Disappear again? Leave us wondering if you're alive or dead again? Walk away from your home? Your family? *Again?*"

Now it was his turn to wince. Damned if Sam didn't feel the way he had at thirteen when he'd faced down his mother after driving a snowmobile into the back of the lodge.

"Mom," he said, standing up.

"No," she interrupted, pushing off the counter as if she were leaping into battle. And maybe she was. Connie took three short steps until she was right in front of her son, tipping her head back to glare at him. "Ever since you got back, I've kept my peace. I didn't say all the things I was bursting to say to you because I didn't want to rock the boat. Well, brace yourself because here it comes."

"Uh-oh," his father whispered.

His mother's eyes were swimming with tears and fury, her shoulders were tense and her voice was sharp. "When you left right after Jack died, it was like I'd lost both of my sons. You might as well have been dead, too," she continued. "You walked away, left us grieving, worrying." Planting both hands at her hips, she continued, "Four postcards in two years, Sam. That's it. It was as if you'd disappeared as completely as Jack. As if you were as out of reach as he was."

No one could make a grown man feel quite as shameful and guilt-ridden as his mother. Sam looked down at her and knew he'd never be able to make it up to her for what he'd done. "I had to go, Mom."

"Maybe," she allowed tightly with a jerking nod. "Maybe you did, but you're back now, and if you leave again, you'll be no better than Jack was, always running away from life."

"What?" Staggered, Sam argued, "No, that's wrong. Jack was all about living life to the fullest. He grabbed every ounce of pleasure he could out of every single day."

She sighed heavily and Sam watched the anger drain

from her as she shook her head and reached up to cup his cheek in her palm. "Oh, honey. Jack was all about *experiences*, not living. The fastest cars. Best skis. Highest mountain. That's not *life*. That's indulgence."

He'd never really thought about his brother in those terms. It would have been disloyal, he guessed, but with his own mother pointing it out, it was impossible to argue.

"I loved Jack," she said, fisting her hand against her chest. "When he died, I lost a piece of my heart I'll never get back. But I'm not blind to my children's faults just because I love them to distraction." Connie gave him a wistful smile. "When it came to adventure, there was no one better than Jack. But he never had the courage to love one woman and build a life with her. To face the everyday crises that crop up, to pay bills, get a mortgage, take the kids to the dentist. *That's* life, Sam. A real life with all the ups, downs, tears and laughter that come with it. That kind of thing terrified him and he did everything he could to avoid it."

Sam thought about that and realized his mother was right. Jack had always gone for the one-night stand kind of woman. The kind who hated commitment as much as he did himself.

"You had that courage once, Sam. When you married Lacy and began to build a life together." She sighed a little and stared into his eyes. "You walked away from that, and I'm not going to say now whether that was right or wrong because it's done and can't be undone. My question is, do you still have that courage, Sam? Do you still want that life with Lacy?"

The question hung in the air between them and seemed to reverberate inside him, as well. He looked at his mother, then at his father. At the room around them and the memories etched into the very walls. His life was here. It was time he picked it up and claimed it once and for all. He did want that life that he'd once been foolish enough to throw away. He wanted another chance to build what his parents had built.

He wasn't Jack. Sam wanted permanent. He wanted the everyday with the one woman who would make each single day special. All he had to do was find the way to make Lacy listen. To make her understand that he damn well loved her, and she loved him, too.

"Yeah, Mom," he said softly, reaching out to pull his mother close. "I do."

She hugged him hard—no more wary caution from her—and for the first time since he'd come back to Snow Vista, he really felt as if he was home again.

"You're *pregnant*?"

"Yes, and don't tell your brother."

"Not a word," Kristi swore, fingers crossing her heart, then flying up into a salute of solidarity. "How far along are you? Never mind. Can't be far. He's only been home a month. It *is* Sam's, right?"

Lacy gave her an exasperated look.

"Right, right," Kristi said, using both hands to wipe away her words, "it's Sam's. The idiot."

"That about covers how I'm feeling about him right now."

Lacy had been ranting about Sam for the past hour, and when news of the baby had slipped out, she'd had to swear her friend to silence. But she couldn't regret sharing her big secret with her best friend. It had felt too good to tell *someone*.

Lacy was still so furious she could hardly see straight, but mostly at herself, for falling for Sam's stories again. Seriously. *If you're going to make mistakes*, she thought, *at least have the good sense to make some new ones along the way.* But how could she have avoided letting herself be sucked back in? She still loved him. Though she was going to find a way to get over it. Maybe *she* should start reading those self-help books that Kristi was so addicted to. What she needed was a book called *How to Wipe That Man Out of Your Life*.

"What're you going to do?"

Lacy dropped into the closest chair and stared at the fire in her hearth. "I'm going to have a baby and never speak to your brother again."

"Hmm…" Kristi leaned into her own chair. "I applaud the sentiment, but it's gonna be tough. What with you both living here and all."

"He won't stay," Lacy muttered. "Soon enough, he'll be gone again, chasing his dead brother's dreams."

"I used to think Jack was the dummy, but I'm sorry to say," Kristi mused, "turns out Sam's the lucky winner there."

Lacy cringed a little. "I'm sorry. I shouldn't be dumping all of this on you. He's your brother. You shouldn't be in the middle."

"Are you kidding? In matters like these, it's all about girls versus boys as far as I'm concerned."

She smiled. "You're a good friend, Kristi."

"I could be better if you'd let me go kick Sam."

"No." Anger was now riding hand in hand with misery, and the two were so tangled up inside her, Lacy could hardly breathe. But she did know enough to realize that giving Sam any more attention at all would be just what he wanted. So she was going to ignore him. Forever.

Oh, for heaven's sake, how would she ever be able to

pull that off? It wouldn't be long before she'd be show-ing and Sam would know about the baby and…

"Maybe I'm the one who should move."

"Don't you dare," Kristi countered in a flash. "What would I do here without you to talk to? Besides, you've got my niece or nephew in there—" she waved one hand at Lacy's tummy "—and I want to meet them."

"Yes, but—"

"Mostly, though," Kristi said smugly, "if you leave, you let Sam think you were too afraid to stay in your own home."

Oh, she didn't like the sound of that at all. Plus, the truth was, Lacy didn't want to move. She loved her cabin. She loved her job. She loved the mountain. She loved *Sam*, damn it.

"Can your head actually explode?" she wondered aloud.

"I hope not," Kristi said solemnly. "Now, why don't we go out for dinner or something? Get your mind off my idiot—er, brother."

Lacy smiled as she'd been meant to, but shook her head. "No thanks. I just want to stay home and bury my head under a pillow."

"Sounds like a plan." Kristi pushed up from the chair. "I'll leave you to it."

Lacy got up, too, and wrapped her friend in a tight hug. "Thanks. For everything."

"You bet. This'll work out, Lacy. You'll see." There was a knock at the door and Kristi asked, "Want me to get that and send whoever it is away?"

"God, yes. Thanks."

Kristi opened the door and Lacy heard Sam's voice say "I want to talk to her."

"Surprise," Kristi shot back, "she doesn't want to talk to you."

Lacy groaned and went to face Sam because she couldn't put siblings at war over her. It was too soon, was all she could think. It had only been a few hours since that horrible scene at the top of the mountain. She needed a day or two or a hundred before she was willing to speak to Sam again. Yet it seemed fate didn't care about what she needed.

"It's okay, Kristi, I'll handle it."

"You sure?" Her friend's eyes narrowed in concern.

"Yeah, I'm fine." Of course she wasn't, but she wouldn't give Sam the satisfaction of knowing just how off balance she was with him here. She would be calm. Cool. Controlled, damn it!

"Okay, I'll leave," Kristi announced with a glare at Sam. "But I won't be far. Idiot."

"Thanks," he said wryly, "that's nice."

"Be grateful Lacy made me promise not to kick you," she called back over her shoulder.

Lacy watched him give his sister a dirty look, then grit his teeth as he turned around to face the door. Sadly, she didn't have enough time to slam it shut before he slapped one palm to it and held it open.

He was still wearing the black jacket and jeans. His dark hair still looked windblown and completely touchable. His eyes were shadowed, his mouth grim, and in spite of everything, her heart leaped and her body hummed with a desire that would probably never end. Mind and heart were at war inside her, but for her own good, for the sake of her baby, she had to be strong.

Behind him, she saw the soft, dying streaks of sunlight spearing through the pines. The dark green stalks of soon-to-bloom daffodils popped up all over her yard and the last of the snow lay in dwindling, dirty mounds.

"Lacy, you had your say on the mountain," Sam told her, dragging her gaze to his. "At least hear me out now."

"Why should I?"

He looked at her for a few long seconds, then admitted, "I can't think of a single damn reason. Do it anyway."

Sam walked into the main room and took a moment to gather himself. He looked around at the familiar space, the comfortable furnishings, the hominess of it all and felt his heart ease. Funny, he'd spent most of his life thinking of the mountain as home. But it was this place. It was *Lacy*.

Wherever she was, that was his home. He only hoped she would take him back.

An invisible fist tightened around his heart and gave a vicious squeeze. Was she still so furious she wouldn't listen to him? Wouldn't let him fix this? What could have been panic scratched at his guts, but he shoved it down, ignored it. He wouldn't fail at this, the most important thing he'd ever done. He'd make her listen. Make her understand and then make her admit she loved him, damn it.

Lacy walked into the room behind him, but stopped three feet away. She crossed her arms over her chest, lifted her chin in what could only be a fighting stance and said, "Say what you came to say, then leave."

She'd been crying. Her lashes were still wet, her face was flushed and her mouth trembled even as she made an attempt to firm it. *Bastard*, he thought, bringing her to this, and if he could have punched himself in the face, he would have. But it wouldn't have solved anything.

"First," he said tightly, "let's get this off the table. Keep your land. I don't want it."

Her eyebrows lifted into twin blond arches. "That's not what the newspaper reported."

"They were wrong." He pushed one hand through his hair. "Okay, I admit that I did have the idea for building a new beginner run on the backside of the mountain."

Her mouth tightened further into a grim slash that didn't bode well for Sam. But he kept going, determined to say everything that needed to be said.

"But Dad told me they'd deeded the property to you, so I let that idea go."

"How magnanimous of you."

Scowling, he snapped, "Damn it, Lacy, I didn't know you owned the land. When I found out, I changed my plans."

"And I'm supposed to take your word for that?"

"Believe me or not, doesn't matter," he countered, and took a step toward her. She didn't move away and he didn't know if that was sheer stubbornness or a willingness to listen. He took it as the latter. "The only thing you need to believe is that I love you."

Her eyes flickered with emotion but he couldn't tell if that was good or bad, so he kept talking. "Took me two damn years to realize what I had. What I lost. But I know now, we belong together, Lacy."

She huffed out a breath and shook her head. Her hands tightened on her own arms until her knuckles whitened, but she didn't speak. Didn't order him to get out. That had to mean something.

"I know I hurt you when I left."

She snorted. "You crushed me."

He winced and kept talking. "I did and I'm sorry for it. But even when we were first married, things were shaky between us. You kept waiting for me to disappoint you. To walk away, like your mother did."

"I was right, wasn't I?" She whispered it, but he heard and ached for her.

"Yeah, I guess you were. But you know, you always looked at what your mother did—leaving—as what love was really all about. So you thought I'd do what she did. You never really believed that I'd stay. Admit that much at least."

She took a breath and said, "To ease your guilt? Why would I? I can tell you that I wanted to believe you, but if I had believed, completely, your leaving would have killed me."

Pain slammed into the center of his chest and he deserved it for putting both of them through this.

"But I trusted you, Sam," she said, adding to the misery he felt now. "And you broke my heart."

Sunset was streaking across the sky outside, but inside, where the light was dim, shadowy and still, he could see the hurting in her summer-blue eyes.

"I know and I'll always regret that, wish I could go back and change it." His voice dropped into a husky whisper that tore at his throat even as her words clawed at his heart. "But, Lacy, your mother wasn't an example of love. Your father was. He *stayed*. He stayed with you. Right here. He lived through the unhappiness and never let it affect how he treated his daughter. That's the kind of love I'm offering you now."

A couple of long seconds ticked past as she considered what he said.

"You're right about my father," she agreed. "I never

thought about it like that, but you're right. She left. He stayed. He was lonely. Sad. But he stayed. *You* didn't."

"No." He hated admitting to that. "But I'm back now. And I'm not going anywhere."

She shook her head again, unwilling to take him at his word, and he only had himself to blame for it.

"I'm here forever, Lacy," he told her, willing her to believe. To trust. "I want a life with you. Children with you. I want to grow old and crotchety on this mountain and watch our kids and grandkids running Snow Vista."

She swayed a little and Sam took that as hope and moved another step closer. "If I have to spend the next ten years romancing you to get you to believe me, then that's what I'll do," he vowed. "I'll bring you flowers every day, dinner every night. I'll kiss you, touch you, make promises to you and eventually, you'll believe in me again."

"Will I?"

"Yeah," he said softly, a smile curving his mouth. "Because you love me, Lacy. As much as I love you."

She took a fast, shallow breath and held it for a long moment.

Sam looked at her standing there, her long hair loose and soft, her features tight, unsure, her eyes damp with tears, and his heart swelled until he thought it might burst from his chest.

"Lacy, I hurt you. I know that and if I could change the past I would. But all I can do is promise you tomorrow and all the tomorrows afterward." Breathing ragged, he took another step toward her. "You know, last night, after we talked, after I told you everything, I realized something I never had before."

"What?"

One word only, but he took that as a good sign, too.

"It wasn't just losing Jack that drove me from here—though that was devastating. I was scared. See, I loved you so much more than my own twin, the thought of losing you was unimaginable."

"Sam…"

"No," he said quickly, "just hear me out. I couldn't stand the thought of maybe losing you, as well. Seems stupid now, to leave you because I was afraid of losing you."

"Yeah," she agreed wryly. "It does."

"But leaving didn't stop the fear," he told her. "I still thought about you. Worried about you. *Loved* you. Staying with you is the only thing that can stop that fear. I know that now. I want to be with you. Dream with you, for however long we live." He took a long breath, let it out and said, "I want to risk the pain to have the love."

Lacy's heart was galloping in her chest. Her mind was reeling. She looked up into his eyes and knew that he was right. About everything. At the start of their marriage, she had been waiting for Sam to let her down. She'd kept her guard up, prepared to be hurt. As much as she'd loved Sam, she'd never really gone all in. She'd held a part of herself back. Always cautious.

She *had* forgotten that her father had always been there for her. In her pain over the loss of her mother, she'd refused to see that love doesn't always leave. Sometimes it stayed. And it was something to count on. To trust in. *That* was the love she wanted to believe in. The kind that never left. The kind that lasted forever.

Yes, she thought, looking up at him, Sam had made mistakes, but so had she. If she had been stronger in her own right, more self-confident, she might have forced him to talk to her in those days after Jack's death. They might have worked this out together. But she'd been half expecting him to leave, so when he did, she'd let it happen instead of fighting for what she wanted.

Now she was willing to fight.

He was watching her through those beautiful green eyes of his and she knew that the next step was hers to take. It always had been. She had to forgive. Had to believe. And looking into his eyes, she knew she did.

Love wasn't perfect. No doubt in the future they'd both make mistakes. But they would both stay. Together.

"You're right," she said, and watched as some of the tension drained out of him. "About a lot of things. But mostly," she said, "you're right that risking the pain is the only way to have the joy I feel when I'm with you."

"Will you risk it?" he asked, gaze never leaving hers. "Will you marry me again, Lacy? Will you trust me to be there for you and to always love you? Will you have my children and build a family with me?"

There it was, she thought. Everything she wanted, shiny and bright and laid at her feet. All she had to do was reach out and take it.

She held her hand out for his, and when his fingers closed around hers, she felt the warmth of him slide down inside and ease away the cold. "Yes, Sam. I'll marry you. I'll believe in you. And I'll love you all my life."

He gave a tug and she flew into his arms. As he held her, he whispered, "Thank God. I love you, Lacy. Now, always, forever, I love you."

"I love you, too, Sam. I always have. Always will." She nestled her head on his chest and listened to the thundering beat of his heart.

His arms encircling her, he asked softly, "What do you say we start making babies right away?"

A slow, satisfied smile crossed her face as she leaned

back to look up at him. "You can cross that one off your to-do list, Sam."

"What do you—" Understanding dawned and his eyes widened even as his jaw dropped. "You mean... are you...already?"

She nodded, waiting for the pleasure to ease past the shock. It didn't take long. His grin spread across his face and lit his eyes with the kind of joy she had once dreamed of seeing. Reality was so much better.

"We're going to have a great life," he promised her as one hand dropped to tenderly cup her flat belly.

She laid her hand over his and said, "We've already started."

Then he kissed her and Lacy's world opened up into a bright, beautiful place.

Epilogue

Lacy had a private room in the maternity ward at McKay-Dee Hospital in Ogden. Outside, it was snowing, but inside, there was a celebration going on.

Sam looked down at his wife, cuddling their newborn son, and felt everything in him surge with happiness. Contentment. The past few months had been full and busy and *great*. The restaurant opened in the fall and was already packed daily. The gift shop was a huge hit not only with the tourists, but also with the local artisans, and the lodge addition was nearly ready to take in guests.

But best of all was the time spent with Lacy. Rediscovering just how good they were together. They were living at her cabin, though they'd added so many rooms to the place, it was barely recognizable now. There were four more bedrooms, a couple of baths and a country kitchen that Lacy rarely wanted to leave. They had plans to fill that cabin with kids and laughter, and they'd gotten their start today.

"You were amazing," he told her, bending down to kiss her forehead, the tip of her nose and then her lips.

Lacy smiled up at him. "Our son is amazing. Just look at him, Sam. Isn't he beautiful?"

"Just like his mom," Sam said, trailing the tip of one finger along his son's cheek. He never would have believed how deeply, how completely, you could love a person not even an hour old. He was a *father*. And a very lucky man.

"He's got your hair and my eyes. Isn't that incredible? His own little person but a part of both of us." She sighed happily and kissed her son's forehead.

"How are you feeling?" Worry colored his words, but he could be forgiven for that. Hadn't he just watched her work and struggle for eight hours to give birth? A harrowing experience he was in no hurry to repeat. "Tired? Hungry?"

She laughed a little at that, caught Sam's hand in hers and gave it a squeeze. "Okay, yeah, I could eat one of Maria's steak sandwiches and swallow it whole. But I feel *great*. I have so much energy, I could get up and ski Bear Run."

The fastest, most dangerous slope at Snow Vista. Shaking his head, he said, "Yeah. You can forget about that for a while."

Lacy grinned and shrugged. "I suppose, but I'm really not tired." Narrowing her gaze on him, she said, "But you're exhausted. You should go home and rest."

"I'm not going anywhere without you." Thankfully, the hospital provided cots for new fathers to sleep on in their wives' rooms. Though he'd have stayed, even if he'd had to sleep in the chair by her bed. He kissed her again, kissed the top of his son's head, and then straightened and threw a glance at the door. "The family's waiting to come in. You ready to face them?"

"Absolutely."

He walked over, waved in the crowd of Wyatts and moved to the head of Lacy's bed as everyone crowded around. His parents were beaming, his father clutching an impossibly bright purple teddy bear, his mother carrying a vase of sunshine-yellow roses. His sister, Kristi, was there, holding her husband Tony's hand. The two of them had finally married last May, and Kristi was already pregnant with their first child.

"He's gorgeous," Connie Wyatt exclaimed.

"Handsome boy," Bob agreed.

"What's his name?" Kristi asked, looking from Lacy to Sam.

He looked down at his beautiful wife and smiled when she said, "You tell them, Sam."

He dropped one hand to Lacy's shoulder, linking them, making them the unit they'd become. Sam looked at his family and said, "His name is Jackson William Wyatt. Named for Jack and for Lacy's dad."

Sam watched his mother's eyes well with tears and she didn't try to stop them as they spilled along her cheeks even as she gave them both a proud smile. "Jack would be pleased. We are, aren't we, honey?"

Bob Wyatt dropped one arm around his wife and pulled her in tight. "We are. It's a good thing you've done, you two."

Sam watched the family talk in excited whispers and half shouts. He saw Lacy hand baby Jack over to his mother and watched as she turned to Sam's father and the two of them cuddled and cooed at their first grandchild.

Life was good. Couldn't be better. All that was missing, he thought with a lingering touch of sorrow, was his brother. He wished that Jack could know somehow that they had survived his loss. Found happiness, in spite of missing him.

A flicker of movement caught Sam's eye and he turned his head, shooting a look at the corner of the room, where the watery winter sun painted a pillar of golden light.

Sam's breath caught.

Jack was there, in the light, a part of it. Heart thudding in his chest, Sam could only stare at his twin in disbelief. The buzz of conversation around him softened and drifted away as he and his twin stared at each other from across the room, across the chasm between life and death.

Jack nodded, as if he understood just what Sam was feeling. Then he gave his twin a slow, wide smile, just as he used to. And in moments, as Sam watched, Jack drifted away with the last of the light until the corner of the room was empty and dark again.

"Sam?" Lacy called his name, and still bemused by what he'd seen, he turned to her, a half smile curving his mouth. "Are you okay?"

He glanced back at the corner of the room. Had it happened? Or was it wishful thinking? Did it matter? Jack was a part of them, always would be. Maybe he'd just found a way to let Sam know that he was okay, too.

Turning back to Lacy, Sam let go of the last of his pain and welcomed the joy he was being offered.

"I'm more than okay," he assured her. "Everything's perfect."

Then he turned his back on the past and stepped into the future with his wife and son.

* * * * *

MILLS & BOON®

The Chatsfield
Collection!

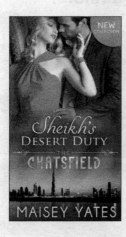

Style, spectacle, scandal…!

With the eight Chatsfield siblings happily married and settling down, it's time for a new generation of Chatsfields to shine, in this brand-new 8-book collection! The prospect of a merger with the Harrington family's boutique hotels will shape the future forever. But who will come out on top?

**Find out at
www.millsandboon.co.uk/TheChatsfield2**

MILLS & BOON®

Desire™

PASSIONATE AND DRAMATIC LOVE STORIES

A sneak peek at next month's titles...

In stores from 20th March 2015:

- **For His Brother's Wife** – Kathie DeNosky
  and **Twins on the Way** – Janice Maynard

- **From Ex to Eternity** – Kat Cantrell
  and **From Fake to Forever** – Kat Cantrell

- **The Cowgirl's Little Secret** – Silver James
  and **The Nanny Plan** – Sarah M. Anderson

Available at WHSmith, Tesco, Asda, Eason, Amazon and Apple

Just can't wait?
Buy our books online a month before they hit the shops!
visit www.millsandboon.co.uk

These books are also available in eBook format!

0315/51